The Ojanox

All Fall Down

Daemon Manx

Published by Last Waltz Publishing

5 Midland Ave, Pompton Plains, N.J. 07444

www.lastwaltzpublishing.com

Edited by Lisa Lee Tone

Original developmental edits by Ben Eads

Library of Congress Cataloging-in-Publication Data

Robert R. Chiossi, 1967-

The Ojanox Series / Daemon Manx

TXu 2-417-807 2024
ISBN 979-8-9909638-1-8

Book Cover by Christy Aldridge (Dark Poppy Designs)

Illustrations by Christy Aldridge and Don Noble

First edition September 2024

ALSO BY DAEMON MANX

PRAISE FOR THE OJANOX

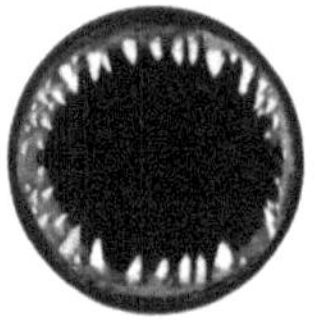

"In *The Ojanox*, Daemon Manx creates a community and cast of characters you feel like you know personally, like you've known them all your life. And when you lose one of those characters, you've lost one of your own. Manx makes you care and makes you hurt. *The Ojanox* is a masterclass on characterization." – Patrick C. Harrison III, Author of *Grandpappy* and *100% Match*

"*The Ojanox* harkens back to the horror boom of the '70s and '80s, in a very good way. Manx has a knack for creating characters you'll love (or hate) and putting them through the wringer. His dialogue is sharp and storytelling gripping and fas- paced. Now that I'm hooked, I need to read the rest!" – Duncan Ralston, Author of *Woom* and *Ghostland*

"Every so often, a writer reads a coming-of-age tale that they wish they had written themselves. That's how I felt with Daemon Manx's *The Ojanox* series. Exciting, genuinely nostalgic, and scarier than hell!" –Ronald Kelly, Author of *Fear, The Essential Sick Stuff,* and *Southern-Fried & Horrified*

"Daemon Manx has wrapped up a delicious candy treat that you won't be able to resist gobbling down, razor blades and all. *Scream in the Dark* will put you in the Halloween spirit no matter what time of year you read it. You'll be holding out your plastic jack-o-lanterns for more!" — Jeff Strand, author of *Twentieth Anniversary Screening*

"In Garrett Grove, the time for evil has arrived, Manx serves up scares like Halloween candy—the good kind, too … full-sized, nostalgic, and satisfying to the end."—Gaby Triana, author of *Moon Child;* editor of *Literally Dead: Tales of Halloween Hauntings*

"Daemon Manx has proven in a short time, he is the real deal. And he doesn't mess around. This is a must-read series, and one of the best books I've read this year." –Mike Ennenbach, author of *Cuckoo*

"If you are like me and love horror mixed with great storylines and twisted endings, you must read Daemon Manx. And when you are through, hug the pillow, hide under the covers, and repeat over again, it's only a novel … or is it???"—Jason Knight - ECW Original

"Written with beautifully descriptive scenes, *The Ojanox* places you directly into the quaint, small town of Garrett Grove during the Halloween season where everything is pleasant … until it isn't. An ancient, dark entity is accidently excavated and escapes into the world with chilling results. *The Ojanox* is a fresh, original, plot-driven page-turner that I couldn't put down. I highly recommend it and am looking forward to Part Two of this excellent series." – Jeani Rector, Editor of *The Horror Zine*

CONTENTS

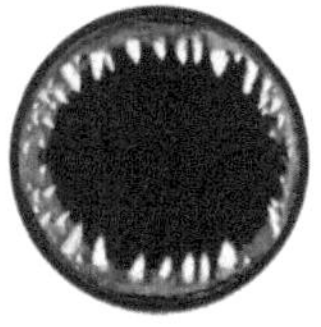

For Wendy and Dawn
Who helped bring this monster to life

FOREWORD

GAZING INTO THE ABYSS

The year is 1979. A small New York town prepares to welcome the fall season in all the expected ways: young children bicker and boast over Halloween costumes, secret lovers meet in clandestine corners, and a tortured soul plots wicked deeds. All the while, hidden just out of view, patient and hungry … an ancient evil lurks.

I know, I know. You've heard all this before. You've read the book, watched the film adaptation, and probably even caught the two-part podcast. If you're a fan of old-school horror, like I am, then you'll swear that you know how the plot will unfold. What the primeval horror is. Who will live, who will die, and even in what specific order said deaths will occur.

Hey, I get it. I thought so too.

But I was wrong, dead wrong. You'll probably be wrong too. And, let me tell you, rarely has it felt SO good to be incorrect. To be legitimately surprised. To revisit a hallowed era of storytelling in such a creative way.

Let's be honest: vintage horror is a difficult thing to effectively pull off in today's market. Try too hard and you alienate your target audience, skewing far afield from that elusive "feel". Half-ass it and you're derivative, lazy, or a hefty combination of both.

For anyone who is familiar with his talent, Daemon Manx has, quite unsurprisingly, accomplished something special with *The Ojanox*, making the familiar feel wholly unfamiliar. Pulling us back to the gritty world of late-70s to early-80s horror without stepping on any toes in the process. This is neither an homage nor an emulation. This is a book that could very well have been borne of that halcyon era, resting on some half-askew bookshelf this whole time, just waiting to be discovered. But, as much as *The Ojanox* is a glimpse across decades, it is also a gateway into Manx's mind–one can glean various details about the novelist through the terrors nestled within the typeface.

Much like there are no atheists in foxholes, there are no innocents amongst horror authors. We write from the darkest of depths, from places where light falters and even whispers carry great weight. Yes, the stories we create are ultimately meant to startle, to shiver, and to scare. To invoke those primal sensations of fear and dread. But there is so much more to it than that. We are also, through prose and plot, offering the world a glimpse of our vulnerable sides. Our hopes and fears. The hardships we have endured. Mistakes we've made, and the fallout that followed. From pen to page, our pain is made manifest. Some people suffer for their creations–horror authors put themselves through anguish for their art. And, during this process of composition, this literary baring of souls, we allow ourselves to examine our personal hauntings, be they self-induced or inflicted by others. To exorcise our own demons, keystroke by keystroke. True, we may never completely vanquish the darkness inside us. For many horror authors, those hurts are grafted to our very essence, as much a part of us as blood and bone, woven into the very fabric of who we have become. But, while those shadows may yet linger, we at least get the chance to look our fiends in the eye with an unflinching gaze.

Daemon has never been shy about his personal struggles, of which he has had plenty. I respect both his candor and his fearlessness in facing those dark years. Perhaps that deep well of experience is what gives his writing that extra bit of compelling oomph. Some of us have pint-sized imps on our shoulders, gently reminding us of past indiscretions, tempting us back with honeyed words. Manx has a thousand-pound gorilla clinging to his back, beating its chest and bellowing a mighty roar of misdeeds, yanking at the chains of the past with inhuman strength.

And that, dear reader is what you get with *The Ojanox*. A beast of both the literal and figurative sense. A peek at the demons without ... and those within. This is a massive story, years in the making, touching on a myriad of topics, many of which are just as pertinent today as they were in '79. From a word count perspective (it shouldn't matter, but we're novelists ... it matters) it is an imposing body of work, rivaling the hefty behemoths of the era, as is only fitting. From my first involvement with *The Ojanox*, I have always maintained that Daemon writes like Laymon, but with a more literary bent. This isn't a knock at all: Laymon penned some classics. He was great at concepts, with a knack for the perverse and deft skill at setting a scene. The only place I was occasionally left wanting was with the narrative voice itself. Daemon rectifies that shortcoming with the ease of raw ability, wrangling words in the best of ways. In all honesty, it wouldn't shock me in the slightest to see Manx and Laymon sharing space on bookstore shelves in the not-so-distant future. I am hard pressed to think of an indie author who deserves it more.

But don't take my word for it. See for yourself. Curl up in your favorite space, dim the lights, crack open *The Ojanox*, and step into the town of Garrett Grove. What you find just might surprise you.

Jack Wells

Author of *Jack of All Trades* and the *Monochrome Noir* series.

Trick or Treat

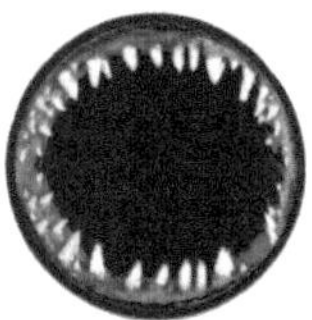

I hope you will indulge me just a little before diving into the book, as the origination of *The Ojanox* is almost as interesting as the story itself. I began the writing process during the spring of 2020 while I was serving my final year of incarceration in a halfway house in Newark, New Jersey. Yes, you read that right. I spent nearly a decade in state prison prior to that. The short story: I made some terrible mistakes because of addiction (rarely are addicts known for making good ones), and that landed me in a very dark place.

But that was only the beginning of my journey because prison is where I finally got clean (Eleven years and four months as I write this today) and it's where I turned my life around. But something else happened while I was serving my days behind the wall. I started writing again. Addiction had stolen everything I loved, and my creative muse was only one of the casualties. But as the fog lifted, my desire to create returned, and it was in a cold, lonely cell where I started to live once again.

By the time I reached the halfway house, years later, I had written dozens of short stories and novellas but had never tackled any larger projects. It was January of 2020, and I had just received permission to leave the halfway house for a few hours a day to attend college in person. I even got a couple months under my belt, and then Covid hit. The house was put under quarantine lockdown, and no one was allowed to leave. Unfortunately, the virus had already found its way into the building.

And that was life for the next seven months. We started out with almost three hundred men in the facility, and that number quickly diminished to less than a hundred. We all got sick during that time, some more than others, and many of the men were taken back to the prison system's medical facilities … never to return.

To pass the time, I started writing what I thought would be a short story, one that encapsulated the feeling and the mystery of Halloween the way I remembered it as a child. I sat down and wrote the first lines of what is now chapter one, and *The Ojanox* was born. Within a few days, I realized this was not going to be a short story. I had no idea just how massive it would be, but I was about to find out.

I owned a portable word processor called the Alpha Smart 3000, originally intended for my college classes. If you're not familiar, The AS3K is a battery-operated unit with a small screen that allows the user to see three lines of script at a time. There are eight files you can fill with text, but once they are filled, you must transfer the data to a Word doc and zip drive. I would fill the files every night, writing from 6p.m.–11p.m. non-stop. The next day I would use the house's library computer to transfer my work and ultimately free up space for another night of writing.

I should mention that I shared the room with ten other men who were anything but quiet. Who can blame them? We were all stir-crazy. While they were listening to music, playing poker, and screaming to one another in the confines of our 12 x 12 room, I would don my headphones, crank up the tunes, and write, write, write.

And yes, it was like that. I wrote in a fever; the words flowed as if they were coming from somewhere other than me. It was very stream of consciousness, but it was also methodical. During the day, I would map out the next ten scenes in outline, and that night, I would write. Oddly enough, not once did I experience even an ounce of writer's block.

On October 30, 2020, I typed the words *The End* and looked down at a massive file containing 520K words. I had finished the first draft in six months. Seven days later, I was released.

Now would come the hard part. The rewrite. Little did I know, I would be rewriting this beast for the next four years and editing out over 160K words, all for the betterment of the story, I assure you.

Now it's true that this story was created under some very adverse conditions. You could even say it is a byproduct of that suffering. But that's not why *The Ojanox* was written in such a short period of time. To be honest, I have been working on this story since I was ten years old myself. Like Troy Fischer, when I was in fourth grade, I had a Halloween party and built a haunted house in the garage. Yep, you guessed it, it was called Scream in the Dark. In *The Ojanox*, many of the settings, themes, and circumstances are inspired by my memories of Halloweens gone by and my own life experiences as well. However, this story isn't just a tribute to my own childhood but to childhood itself. If I have done this correctly, it is to pay respect to that initial sense of mystery we all felt when we heard our first ghost story, to that chilling fright when we saw our first horror movie.

Although the coming-of-age factor is just a small portion of this story, as *The Ojanox* is pure horror with its fair share of violence, I mention it because that's where it started for me ... when I was a child. My love for horror, that is.

If I got any of this right, I hope you are taken back, if only for a moment, to that innocent time in your life when you set out to grab a pillowcase full of candy on Halloween and returned home with all the peanut butter cups you were hoping for ... and more.

Daemon Manx

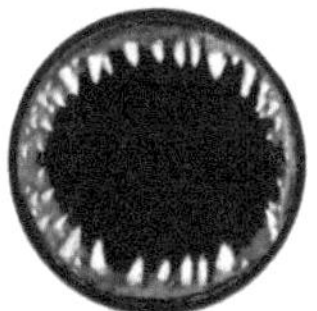

"Like a raven seizing a shrew. You fight to breathe as you struggle to escape its grip. But it's too late. You succumb to its gravity, paralyzed with fear, and may never know the beast by name ... for it has many names. And it's older than time itself." ~ Lois Fischer

CHAPTER 50

Wednesday

Sheriff Carl Primrose pulled his cruiser into the front lot of the courthouse and did a double take, finding almost every parking spot was filled. News of the meeting had spread faster than even he anticipated. His heart quickened, and he prayed for strength; the bomb he was about to drop would be a difficult pill for most to swallow. However, he had some backup. His deputies and close to a dozen men from the fire department had all witnessed something last night, something that couldn't be explained. Carl was sure the men's stories had already spread like wildfire and was hoping their testimonies would help with what he prepared to do. He figured Burt to be a wild card who might sway the crowd either way depending on how the old man represented himself. Which was fine because this morning, Carl was counting on Father Kieran and figured the validation from the respected priest would carry the most weight. He was hoping so, at least, and drove around to the back of the building and eased the cruiser into his reserved spot.

Yesterday had been the longest day of his life, eclipsing anything that had transpired in Vietnam. Carl had struggled to settle down as he lay in bed reliving the nightmare over and over. But exhaustion proved to be too much, and sleep came regardless. He woke up feeling only slightly better than had he not slept at all. The hot shower and strong coffee helped more than anything else.

Before leaving the house, he tried calling Burt, only to find that the phones were out, which most likely had something to do with the fire at the Texaco station. Severe winters and heavy storms made it a common occurrence in this part of the state, and the Grove's residents had gotten used to losing service several times a year. Carl had dismissed it, figuring he would send one of his men to the relay station once the meeting was over.

Carl sat in his cruiser waiting for either his confidence or his gut to tell him it was time to go inside. He hoped he might make it past the front doors before being bombarded by the deluge of questions but thought it unlikely. Turning off the ignition, he watched as a familiar sedan pulled into the lot and parked a few spots over. Carl couldn't help but stare when Burt Lively exited the vehicle, walked to the passenger side, and opened the door for Doris TenHove. The old man kissed the nurse square on the lips, then proceeded to squeeze her ass with both hands. Doris returned the gesture and pinched Burt's for good measure.

You old son of a bitch! Carl watched the couple with his mouth hung open. He didn't have to be a seasoned lawman to solve this mystery; Burt had finally gotten laid. *Good for you, old man. Good for you.* He waited for Burt and Doris to enter the building, then took a deep breath, collected himself, and followed them inside.

Carl was met by a throng of people, most of whom he knew on a first-name basis. But instead of an ambush incited by an angry mob, he was greeted with smiles and shouts of "Good morning, Sheriff." Word of his quick thinking and rapid deployment of additional recruits had spread, winning him the popular vote. He wondered how long their approval would last once they heard what he was about to say. *Let's see how much you like me in another hour. I'll be lucky if you don't try to hang me.*

He approached Burt, who stood close enough to Nurse TenHove to be standing on her shoes. "Sleep well, Burt?" He exchanged a smirk with his friend, then turned to Doris. "Good morning, Nurse TenHove. You're looking exceptionally chipper today."

Doris blushed and pretended to fix her hair. "Oh, Sheriff. You have no idea." She winked.

Carl took Burt's arm and pulled him to the side, noticing the purple bruise on his friend's throat. "How's the neck?"

"Looks worse than it feels." Burt lowered his voice. "Whatever happens, I got your back. If you need my help, just give a nod and I will bail you out."

Carl pictured Burt standing up and telling the crowd how Felix Castillo's body had walked out of the morgue on its own. And that's just how he would break the ice; after that, he would throw in a bunch of medical terminology like, "really weird crap" and "smelled like a turd." Carl figured he could do without the assistance.

"Thanks, Burt. I'll let you know if I find myself in over my head."

There were far more people in attendance than Carl anticipated. From his vantage point at the front of the room, he felt exposed and on display. His hands slicked with sweat and his throat tightened as he called to the spirit of Allen Primrose for guidance. Although his old man never dealt with anything like this, Carl was sure he would have known exactly what to do if he had. He wished he was half the man his father had been. *Shit, at the moment, I would settle for one quarter.*

He stood at the podium, flanked by Deputies Kovach and Rainey on his right, and Andrea Geary and Bob Jones to his left. Burt and Father Kieran sat in the front row next to Nurse TenHove, Ed Koloski, and Nick Gomes. The rest of the attendees consisted of firemen, medical workers, and retired deputies. Scanning the crowd, Carl searched for Tara and Ted but didn't see their faces anywhere. He was about to begin when Jessica Marceau entered the room and took one of the empty seats. From what he could tell, Jessica was the only member from the town council who had shown up. Not even Mayor Gilbert had made it, which was more than unfortunate. This was going to be hard enough, and Carl didn't want to have to do it more than once.

The sound of growing whispers and concerns started to escalate as the crowd grew restless. Carl rapped his knuckles against the solid oak of the podium, casting the room into an immediate hush. He cleared his throat and began to speak; even he was surprised how easily it all came out.

"Good morning and thank you for coming." He started by retelling the story of Felix Castillo and watched as every face in the crowd turned white. However, they continued to listen, and they didn't say a word. There were looks of disbelief, but the crowd appeared to be digesting everything he told them as if they already sensed something terrible was happening in Garrett Grove and had been waiting for someone to confirm it.

Carl explained what Drs. Malcolm and Ziegler discovered when the three children were brought to the medical center and shared the news of their tragic deaths to cries of shock and surprise.

Bob Jones and a dozen other firemen were able to confirm they had also seen the strange creatures, and Deputy Rainey offered his own account of what had happened the night at the morgue. Most everyone in town knew the Campbell, Negal, and Barnes families and were shocked to hear the horrific news. Then Carl spoke about the two explosions and explained how Dr. Malcolm was responsible for the one at the medical center. He told them how the man had been controlled by the same thing that attacked his deputy.

"I intended to contact the state police and alert them of our situation, but as you know, the phones are down. Our police band radios won't reach past the mountain, so I'm sending a deputy into Warren to notify them. We'll check out the lines at the relay station and see if we can get them up and running." Carl looked to Jessica Marceau. "I was hoping the mayor would be here. Have you seen him?"

"I stopped at Mayor Gilbert's house this morning, but there was no answer. He was expecting me. I am a bit concerned."

"Okay." Carl let out a heavy sigh. "We'll check that out as well. I know you all have a lot of questions and are probably thinking I've lost my mind. But I want you to know we are doing everything we can to keep you safe."

"Sheriff." Tim Colbert stood up. "You said Mr. Lively believes there may be a correlation between the children's infections and the foothill's woods. Did you ever complete the search of the area?"

Carl shot a quick glance at Burt in the front row. They hadn't gotten back to investigate the paths at the base of the mountain, but Burt had been certain if they were going to find anything, it would be in those woods. Then all hell broke loose. "We've been spread a bit thin over the past couple of days. But we plan on getting out there today."

"I've seen these creatures near the rectory," Father Kieran said. "I believe they are gathered somewhere on the mountain. Yesterday morning, I witnessed something peculiar. Packs of animals running from the woods, all clearly frightened. Not just the smaller ones but bear and mountain lions as well. Animals that don't typically scare easily were running for their lives." This was met by an eruption of concerned voices.

"I'm sorry, but do you hear yourselves?" Fireman Nick Gomes said. "This is insane, Sheriff. How do you expect us to believe any of it? There were two fires last night, and that was a bad day for Garrett Grove. But that's all it was, just a bad day. I haven't seen any monsters or strange creatures—because there's no such thing!" He sat down after saying his piece, which was enough to spread disbelief and agitate the crowd. The sound of voices struggling to be overheard quickly escalated into an uproar.

Bob Jones watched the crowd unravel thanks to the young fireman. The sheriff had dumped a lot on their plates, which was hard enough to digest. Bob stood up, shot Nick an evil eye, and raised his hands. "Ladies and gentlemen."

The crowd ignored him, their voices growing louder by the second. Bob was usually a soft-spoken man; however, he was big with a deep booming voice and could make sure he was heard when he wanted to be.

"Ladies and gentlemen," he said again, then raised his voice and bellowed at the top of his lungs: "SHUT THE FUCK UP!"

The crowd fell silent and stared at the giant at the front of the room.

"I saw what happened to Dr. Malcolm, and I've been trying to make sense out of it all night. Something changed the doc. It was awful. His entire body was altered. Whatever this infection is, you can best believe it's real and it's no fucking joke. Dr. Malcolm looked like some type of monster, there is no other way to describe it. Now you can sit there and argue that there is no such thing, but if you saw what I did, you wouldn't waste your time. Half of my men saw something just as horrible at the gas station. I don't like it, but I believe every word the sheriff said, and I would suggest you do as well."

The shocked faces stared back at him in silence. No one said a word, except for Nick Gomes, who stood up again.

"All right, that's fine. I didn't sign on for this, but I'll play along. I'd like to volunteer to take the trip to Warren. I can alert the state police, but I want a handwritten letter from you, Sheriff. Because they're not gonna believe one word of this."

"Good idea. Thank you." Carl looked down the line at his deputies. "Does anyone know where Tara is?"

They turned to each other and shook their heads.

"All right, folks. I don't have to emphasize the need to exercise caution. Most of the activity has occurred at night, but that doesn't mean taking unnecessary risks. I will brief my deputies after the meeting, and since Mr. Gomes has agreed to make the trip to Warren, the state police should be here in a few hours—until then, please stay indoors." He met the eyes of the crowd and prayed that his words sank in. It was insane he was even having this conversation, but sanity had taken a backseat when Felix Castillo got off the slab and walked out of the morgue Sunday morning.

"I'll take Koloski and head out to the relay station," Bob Jones said. "We'll see what's going on, whether the problem is up there or if something else got burnt from the fire. In the meantime, we can use the police band and the fire radios to stay in touch. They'll only reach so far but should make do till the phones are up and running."

"Great." Carl was glad Bob had been there. "I guess that's all for now, people. Thank you and stay safe." There was a dizzying number of individual questions, and Carl did his best to answer them all. Then the crowd started to thin, and he was allowed to exit the building. The sun was bright, and from his vantage point, it looked like just another autumn day.

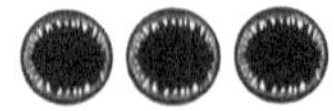

It had become a ritual for Don Fischer and Dr. Stephanie Thompson to meet at the trailer and enjoy a couple mugs of coffee before the sunrise.

"I don't think your wife likes me very much," Stephanie said.

Don couldn't help but laugh. "Well, I'd say, join the club. But that wouldn't be very nice of me, now would it?" He took a long sip from a mug that said *World's Greatest Geologist*.

Stephanie gave him a look of disapproval. "Oh, come on now, if it were that bad, you wouldn't be married. She seems nice. Maybe a little possessive, that's all. Troy's a real sweetheart. I think Janis may have a bit of a crush on him."

"Really? Did she say so?"

"Not in so many words. But a mother knows these things. I can tell by the way she looks at him and the way they joke around with each other. Seemed obvious to me."

"It's got to be tough moving around so much. What's going to happen when you're finished here?"

"Well, they'll send me where I'm needed. Possibly back to D.C. or who knows where."

Don hadn't noticed her aversion to the question and continued to probe.

"That's got to be hard on Janis. How does she adapt to changing schools so frequently? Has it ever become problematic?"

Stephanie stared into her coffee mug for a minute before answering him. "It's been difficult, of course. As soon as she makes friends, we end up having to move. She's taken it well so far, but I'm worried. Don't get me wrong, she's a resilient kid. Still, it kills me to put her through it. Up until now, I haven't had to worry about the whole boy thing, but she's started to notice them, and I'm pretty sure they've noticed her as well." She wasn't about to tell Don that her ten-year-old daughter had already started to develop breasts. He would figure that out when he met her. Troy had invited the girls to the house, and Don said he would be there to help chaperone.

"It sounds complicated." Don smiled.

"Everything about women is complicated. I don't know if you've noticed."

"Believe me, I've noticed. You seem to forget that I'm married. It's funny, actually. Troy has already come to some conclusions that have taken me years to figure out."

"Oh, and what conclusions might those be?" She tilted her head and met his stare.

"That trying to not look like a complete fool in front of women can be a full-time job. However, he seems to be doing a much better job than his old man."

"You don't come across foolish to me, and I'm a woman. At least I was the last time I checked. Don't be so hard on yourself; you're a brilliant geologist. How did you develop such a complex anyway? So, you didn't end up where you thought you would in life. Who does? I sure as hell didn't. But you got a beautiful son, and your wife is a real cutie too, even if she doesn't like me all that much."

"I don't think it has as much to do with you as it does with me. She's frustrated with the way things turned out and feels disappointed. I'm married to the job and am rarely at home. And when I am there, she's mad at me. She won't say it, but she only married me because I got her pregnant. She was in love with someone else. So, her life didn't turn out the way she was hoping either." He paused for a moment. "Why the hell am I telling you all this? I just met you, for crying out loud."

Stephanie wiped her eyes and swallowed back the giant lump in her throat. "That's some pretty honest shit right there. It's refreshing to hear a man talk like that. I hope Troy grows up to be just like his father. My ex screwed everything under the sun. I never heard an honest word out of the guy's mouth. Maybe your wife didn't get the man she thought she wanted, but she's lucky she got the one she did. You're a good man, Donald Fischer. Don't ever tell yourself otherwise."

For a moment, they stared at each other from across the trailer, allowing nothing but silence to resonate between them. It wasn't an uncomfortable silence. In fact, neither could remember the last time they had felt such a comfortable one.

"What's going on here?" he asked.

"Nothing," she said. "Nothing is going on here at all."

Neither spoke. They sipped coffee and sat in the quiet, enjoying each other's company. Gail was the first to knock on the trailer door and interrupt the moment. It was time to start another day, but they had had the chance to bond and enjoy a small reprieve, however fleeting it might have been.

Lois told Troy she was keeping him home from school, and he went ballistic, pouting that it wasn't fair and throwing in her face how she promised that his friends could come over. "I just want you home today, Troy. There's a lot going on right now, and I would feel better if you were here with me."

"But I have plans with Janis and Wendy, and you already said they could come over. You said so." She *had* said so. What made it worse was she had made that promise in front of Janis's mother and aunt. Lois was still trying to digest what Carl said. She hadn't left town as instructed, and there had been a huge fire. She tried to talk to Don last night, which was also a mistake, and she decided she would leave without him if that's what she had to do. The only thing that mattered was Troy's safety; Don could fend for himself like he always did. But committing herself to leaving proved to be more difficult than she imagined.

There was Alice and her family to think about. Billy was at Chilton, and Eric was still missing. She needed to talk to her sister, but the phones had been out since last night. And if they really were leaving, she still had to pack. It only made sense to keep Troy home from school. She wrestled with the same battle last night, comparing their situation to the citizens of Pompeii. Then the sky ignited. If that wasn't the biggest omen, she didn't know what was.

"I can't believe you're really gonna keep me home from school. This is so unfair." Troy started to cry.

Dammit, Troy, don't do this to me. She looked out the front window to see nothing out of the ordinary in any way. The sun was shining, and the world looked at peace. Then she thought about everything she needed to accomplish. Could she really get it all done with Troy underfoot? She hadn't told him about Billy and Eric and didn't plan to, at least not yet. She couldn't bring him to the medical center, and she still had to speak with Alice. Also, she wanted to talk to Carl and couldn't do that in front of him either. It was a no-win situation, and with a bright morning sun rising in what appeared to be an average autumn sky, Lois Fischer's world looked no different than it had on any other day. Concerns about the gas station fire and Carl's warnings of imminent danger didn't hold the same gravity they had just last night. Lois looked out the window one last time and reached for her purse.

"Fine, Troy! Get your books and let's go before you're late." She prayed it wasn't a decision she would live to regret.

After leaving the courthouse, Father Kieran returned to the rectory. The woods bordering the property were quiet. He listened to the wind rattle the fallen leaves and the branches of the indifferent oaks and maples. The lonesome howl it created didn't sound any different than it had before the creatures showed up. Almost as if they were no longer there, but Kieran knew better.

At one time in his life, Kieran believed his true calling was to serve beside his brothers in Vietnam. He hadn't been a fighter in the typical sense, but neither was David, and the bible was full of stories of unlikely heroes who prevailed over insurmountable obstacles and adversaries. However, Father Michael had had other plans and sent him to Garrett Grove to lead the parish at Our Lady of the Mountain. Which had been a true gift from the Lord. And now, Father Kieran was finally the priest and the man he knew he could be.

He'd been called upon last night to come to the aid of a member of the flock. Burt Lively had been attacked by one of the creatures from the woods. The coroner dropped his gun when the beast grabbed him by the throat. Kieran didn't have time to think. He saw the gun on the floor, picked it up, and fired.

It was a feeling he hadn't been prepared for. Kieran had never fired a gun in his life, certainly had never killed another living being. But the thing that grabbed Mr. Lively was not one of God's creatures; it was one of Satan's imps. Kieran had silenced its existence.

And it felt good.

Instead of being sent to war, he was chosen to lead the parishioners of Garrett Grove; however, war had found him regardless. He was never meant to serve in battle; his true calling was to lead his parish in the war against evil. He had simply misinterpreted the Lord's original message.

He opened the front doors of the church, dipped his hand into the holy water, and blessed himself. The first Mass of the week was today, Wednesday, at one o'clock, which was typically light in attendance. But with All Saints Day approaching and given the current situation in Garrett Grove, Father Kieran imagined there might be a slightly larger turnout. And he had a special sermon in mind for those who showed up.

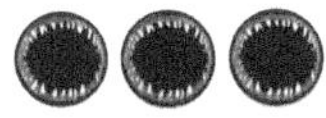

After the meeting, Carl addressed his deputies and those newly appointed in the briefing room. Burt and Nurse TenHove were invited to stick around along with Jessica Marceau.

"Okay, this is how it will probably go down. Mr. Gomes is on his way to Warren, and it shouldn't take him much longer than an hour to reach the state police barracks. Backup should be here no later than noon. I imagine they will assume the operation of the department. You will be taking orders directly from them. I am still your sheriff, but it's unlikely I will be in command. I'll be too busy answering questions and caught up in so much red tape and paperwork you probably won't see me till next Christmas. They're gonna have a hard time digesting what's going on here, but the evidence speaks for itself. Once they see what we have to show them, they won't have any choice but to believe." He rubbed his temples, cleared his throat, and continued.

"I want someone to go check on Tara, and I need someone to head over to the mayor's place. I don't think I need to emphasize 'extreme caution' but I'm going to anyway. Burt, I'm hoping you can figure something out at the lab. Now that Dr. Ziegler's gone, you are our best hope. Arrange to have the bodies transported to the morgue as soon as you can."

Then he turned to the others. "Nurse TenHove, I know you're understaffed. Miss Marks and Mr. Santos will accompany you. Also, I want everyone to take a radio before you leave. Check in with dispatch every hour. No exceptions; every hour. I'm going to take Tim and check out the woods behind the Boyle place. I don't know what we're looking for, but I'm pretty sure we'll know it when we see it. Any questions?"

There were a few but nothing Carl couldn't answer. He instructed Andrea to distribute the radios and gave them their assignments. "Remember, once the staties get here, they are in charge. Until then, be careful."

Carl figured that one o'clock was the latest he would be handing over command of the department. Never in his life did he imagine he would be happy to step down.

CHAPTER 51

Before leaving Garrett Grove, Nick Gomes stopped at Wilson's Diner to grab a quick cup of coffee for the long trek into Warren. He parked next to a green Maverick, the only other vehicle in the empty lot, and made his way to the front entrance. Nick took one step inside the establishment and froze, half in and half out of the doorway. He surveyed the empty diner, not sure what to make of it. The place was deserted; not a soul occupied a single seat. Dick Wilson stood behind the counter, instead of at his usual station at the grill, and offered Nick a defeated roll of the eyes.

"Morning, Dick. Kind of slow, huh?" It was more than just slow; the place looked like a morgue.

"You can say that again; only had a few customers all morning. Mandy and Roger didn't show up for work. I'm guessing folks got freaked out by the fire at the Texaco and are trying to steer clear from this side of town."

Nick doubted if the fire had anything to do with it and thought it more likely that word had already spread about the bullshit Sheriff Primrose was selling. The man had laid it on thick this morning, but Nick still wasn't buying any of it. However, he'd been outnumbered. The sheriff had somehow convinced the entire crowd that the sky was falling. Nick figured it was best to let them chase ghosts while he did something that would actually help. He volunteered to make the trip to the state police barracks in Warren for two reasons. The first was to deliver the letter Sheriff Primrose had given him, and the second was to file a report with a detailed account of what transpired at the morning meeting and the near panic the sheriff had incited. One thing was sure to happen when the staties showed up in Garrett Grove; Sheriff Carl Primrose would promptly be removed from office, and that would be the end of the madman's witch hunt.

"The phones are out," Dick said. "Must have gotten damaged in the fire. Maybe that has something to do with why it's so slow."

"Yeah, probably. Say, could I get a large light and sweet and a bacon, egg, and cheese on a roll?" Nick felt bad after seeing how empty the place was and decided on the sandwich as an afterthought.

"Coming right up." Dick headed to the grill and went to work.

No one entered as Nick waited for his order, and there wasn't much traffic on the road either, which was also bizarre. When his order was up, Nick paid and left Dick a decent tip, then got back on the road.

He sipped the coffee as he pulled onto Route 3 and headed out of town. His stomach grumbled at the aroma of the freshly cooked sandwich. He hadn't had time to eat before the meeting and underestimated how hungry he was. Resting the coffee between his legs, he rummaged through the bag to get at his breakfast, then peeled away the tin foil and tore into it. His tastebuds reacted to the savory bacon that he barely chewed, and Nick swallowed two bites with the diner still visible in his rearview.

With the Gables Bridge fast approaching, Nick set the sandwich down on the passenger's seat and readjusted the cup of coffee between his thighs to better focus on his driving. The two-lane bridge had been built long before Nick's parents were even born, and a simple patch job wasn't going to do the trick; it should have been torn down and replaced years ago. There wasn't a square inch of steel that wasn't covered in rust, and the concrete was in such a state of disrepair it needed repaving every other month. If one were to push their vehicle over twenty-five while traversing the bridge, they would regret it. The blanket of ruts and numerous potholes were known to throw out the alignment of most cars and had snapped more than its share of tie rods.

Nick eased his foot off the accelerator and put both hands on the wheel. He hated driving over the damn bridge, even in the daytime. There were always accidents, since it hadn't been designed for full two-lane passage; neither lane was standard size, which forced vehicles dangerously close to the guardrails and each other as they passed.

Noticing there weren't any vehicles approaching from the other side, he tapped the brakes as the front tires of his Oldsmobile touched the bridge. Nick held his breath; a superstitious ritual he did every time he crossed the river. Sweat slicked his brow, and his pulse quickened; he chanted off the possible sudden approach of an oversized straight job, a nightmare scenario that no one wanted to experience while crossing the Gables Bridge. Fortunately, no vehicles tried to cross as Nick neared the halfway point.

The sensation of scalding heat between his legs caused Nick to jump in his seat and scream. He'd been so focused and tense that he had squeezed the Styrofoam cup, spilling the coffee onto his crotch. Then he dumped even more of it by reacting. The coffee was boiling hot and felt like someone had turned a blowtorch on his nutsack.

"Jesus!" he shouted, grabbing the cup with one hand and the steering wheel in the other. He transferred the coffee to the dashboard and managed to recover. Nick looked up just in time to watch the section of the bridge in front of him disappear.

Concrete and steel erupted in a massive concussion that shook the bridge and his vehicle with it. A thirty-foot section of the structure vaporized before him; the debris rocketed into the air and assaulted his car like machine gun fire. A chasm appeared where the Gables Bridge had once been.

Nick had enough time to hit the brakes, but it wouldn't have mattered if he didn't. The car skidded for almost three seconds, then the front tires went over the edge and were followed by the back ones. The Oldsmobile flipped once in mid-air and crashed into the Lenape River upside down.

He managed to remain conscious, thanks to his fastened seat belt—which was most unfortunate. The frigid water rushed in through the open driver's side window and hit him like a cinder block. He choked on a mouthful of river as the car was swept away with the current. The cab flooded at a rapid pace; still Nick struggled to free himself. But it was too disorienting; he was upside down and the water was arctic cold.

Working at the seatbelt with numb fingers and panic surging through his nervous system, Nick fought to hold his breath. It grew darker as the car sank deeper beneath the surface. His lungs screamed for a single breath of air, just enough to buy him a few more seconds to loosen his harness. Then the world began to blur. He clawed at the seatbelt latch, tearing off several fingernails in his last-ditch scramble for life. Nick screamed again, and a rush of dark water filled his lungs. A second later, the world went black, and everything that Nick Gomes knew ceased to exist.

Bill "Buzzy" Delaney worked for DuCain as the company oiler. It was his job to maintain all the heavy equipment. From the backhoes to the front-end loaders, it was Buzzy's job to ensure that all the machinery remained functional. There were grease joints that needed to be lubed every morning, batteries to be charged, and fluids topped off. Hydraulics were most important and needed to be inspected daily; a broken or dry-rotted hydraulic line could ruin your day, especially if you were the son of a bitch standing under a load when it went. So Buzzy was there every morning, shortly after Don, inspecting and maintaining DuCain's bread and butter.

Don had just finished setting a load of safety gear near the cavern entrance when he heard Buzzy scream. He looked up to see the man running full tilt, ranting like a lunatic.

"Don, Don! They're fucked—they're all fucked!" Buzzy was out of breath by the time he reached him.

"What the hell is going on? What's fucked?" Don asked.

"Someone got into the pen last night and took an axe or something to the hydraulic lines." The pen was the gated-off area where all the heavy equipment was stored overnight. Sometimes kids got into the quarry and thought it a good idea to climb up into the loaders and backhoes. The pen prevented most vandals and usually deterred trespassers.

"What? What the hell are you talking about?" It sounded like he said someone had messed with a machine.

"Someone got into the pen last night. They cut the hydraulic lines, just sliced them to ribbons."

"Christ, what machine did they get? Don't tell me they got the CAT. It's brand new, for Christ's sake." Don felt his stomach lurch as he envisioned a rather heated conversation between him and old man DuCain. *How the hell am I going to explain this?*

"All of them! Every goddamn machine we got; they cut the hydraulic lines on every damn one. And it looks like they fucked with the electrical system on the big dogs."

Don heard a loud pop originate from somewhere deep inside his head, then all he saw was red. He tore off in the direction of the pen with Buzzy trailing behind him. His blood boiled, and he could feel his pulse throb in his temples like his heart had jumped into his throat. He arrived at the pen to find the chain used to lock the gate had been shattered and lay broken on the sand. The carnage was everywhere; hoses and wires littered the ground in a tangled mess of mechanical macaroni. It reminded Don of an episode of the *Twilight Zone* where a gremlin had sat on the wing of an airplane, ripping the guts of the engine apart and tearing the plane to shreds.

Don fought the overpowering urge to vomit. *Jesus Christ, there's no way a couple of kids could have done all of this.* He kicked a massive length of hydraulic line that had been extracted from the front-end loader. The hose hadn't just been cut—it had been ripped apart.

"Oh, for fuck's sake!" Don yelled, inspecting the engine block of the CAT. The oil pan was cracked down the center, allowing a dozen gallons of oil to cover the quarry floor. He ran from the CAT to the dozer to the Komatsu—all their oil pans had been smashed. It was a total loss, and none of the equipment would be operating for a long time. Don felt dizzy and was sure he was about to pass out. He bent over and grabbed his knees, taking in slow, deep breaths.

That's when he heard the explosion. Both he and Buzzy jumped; Don was sure the mountain would rain down on him at any moment.

CHAPTER 52

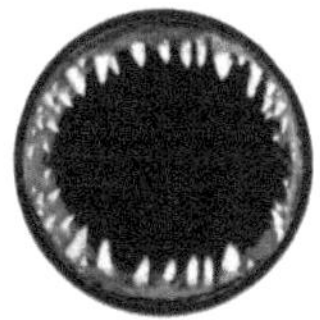

After having been involved in what he believed to be a vehicular homicide, Jared Neibolt resigned himself to an extended leave of absence from his delivery position for the Fink Bakery. Rick Edwards was given half of Jared's route, and the other half went to Fred Rafer. And although the number of deliveries had been divided equally, their locations had not. Rick had drawn the short straw and been assigned the stops in Garrett Grove, the most remote of the locations. The trek over Garrett Mountain was a treacherous ride to make for only two deliveries. Sunset Road was narrow, with blind corners and a steep incline that corkscrewed like a drunken sailor along the side of the mountain. This inconvenient addition to Rick's route added an extra two hours to his day, which was a royal pain in the ass.

Rick carefully navigated the difficult two-lane road as he approached the peak, the most dangerous part of the Pass over the mountain. The slow bend and the massive outcropping of rock on the left were only half of the problem. The real danger lay on the right, where the shoulder ceased to exist just a foot past the guard rail. From there, it was a three-hundred-foot drop straight down. If any unfortunate soul were to go over the edge, it was unlikely the body would ever be recovered.

The outcropping on the left constantly rained loose granite onto the road. It was bad in October, but during the winter, it was a death trap, and the road was often closed. Rick passed two signs as he navigated the dead man's curve. One said Welcome to Garrett Grove, the other said Danger Falling Rock. "Fuck Garrett Grove," he said as he crossed the town line.

One second, he was chugging along with a white-knuckled grip on the wheel, the next, it felt like the truck had been hit by a train. A thunderous roar came from somewhere above. Rick jumped in his seat as his ears popped from what he was sure had been a detonation. With his nerves screaming and his heart on fire, he struggled to keep both hands on the wheel, knowing the hell he would find if he lost control for even one second. Dust and smoke rained down on him, and the truck was pelted with small rocks and debris. Rick checked his side mirror and watched as thousands of pounds of rock and dirt fell from the mountain and buried the road.

His hands went slick against the wheel, and his stomach cramped. There was nowhere to pull over. Not sure what he should do, Rick continued to make his way into Garrett Grove until he saw a vehicle approaching from the opposite direction. He lowered his window and flagged the car down.

"Hey!" The driver was an old man who looked at Rick as if he were on drugs. "You don't want to go that way. There's been an avalanche or something; it looks like half the mountain came down. The road is blocked."

The man snarled at Rick, then drove off toward the disaster ahead of him.

"Well, fuck you too," Rick said, figuring the old bastard would find out soon enough. He pressed his foot to the gas, leaving the avalanche and the old man behind him, and made his way into town. He would stop at the sheriff's station and tell them what happened. Then he would make the rest of his deliveries and get the hell out of Dodge. *Now I got to drive over the damn Gables Bridge.* Rick hated that bridge almost as much as he hated Sunset Road, but not nearly as much as he hated Garrett Grove.

"Fuck Garrett Grove!" he repeated.

Lois and Troy were leaving the house when the first explosion echoed in the distance. They stood on the front steps looking at each other for a moment, then the second blast occurred. It was a bit early to start detonating at the quarry, and Lois was sure she hadn't even heard the warning signal. Usually, there were three short blasts from a whistle that was almost as loud as the explosions themselves. Also, Don had mentioned the discovery of the cave had halted quarry production; she assumed that meant blasting as well.

The other thing that seemed odd was the first detonation sounded as if it came from the opposite side of town. But noise tended to bounce around in the valley, and it was often difficult to pinpoint the exact location of the origin. The second blast, however, definitely sounded like it came from somewhere on the mountain.

"I didn't know Dad was blasting today." Troy looked up at his mother and smiled. He loved hearing the detonations in the distance and was more than a little enamored with the idea that his father blew things up for a living.

"He doesn't tell me anything either, kiddo," Lois said and immediately wished she'd responded differently. The last thing she wanted was to put Troy in the middle of her and Donald's problems. She looked down at him and rubbed his head. "He must have forgotten to mention it. Let's get going before we're late."

"Mom, can I call Rob after school? Maybe he's feeling better and can come over too." The way he looked at her made Lois want to cry right there. How was she ever going to tell him about his friend? She didn't even know where Rob was, and Carl had told her things about the boy and his family that were impossible to digest. Again, she prayed everything would be all right.

"Come on," she said. "Let's go, kiddo."

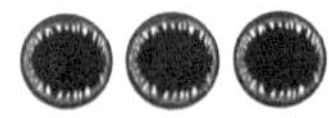

The communications relay looked as if it had been torn apart by a very intentional saboteur. The wires had been ripped from their terminals, and the housings were smashed. Bob Jones and Ed Koloski gawked at the mess in disbelief. Nothing about the damage could be mistaken for accidental, which clarified a grave implication. They both saw something last night and heard what the sheriff said at the meeting this morning. The damage to the relay station proved that whatever they were dealing with was intelligent.

Bob wondered if Carl understood just how cunning this thing was. If it had wanted to prevent them from being able to call for help, it had certainly done so. The phones would be out of service for a very long time. Bob thanked God that Nick Gomes was on his way to Warren to contact the state police. He had a feeling they were going to need all the help they could get.

"Is this thing intelligent?" Koloski asked.

"It looks that way."

"What the hell are we dealing with, Chief?"

"I haven't got a clue." Bob jumped and covered his head as a massive concussion shook the ground beneath their feet. "What in the name of God?"

Both men pivoted toward the tree line to see the debris cloud rise into the air. From their vantage point just off Route 3, it looked like they were less than a mile from the explosion. Neither knew for certain, but the Gables Bridge was the only structure in that direction. Bob felt ice water run through his veins and settle in his guts. Then it occurred to him: if what they were dealing with was intelligent enough to take out the phone, then wouldn't it also attempt to destroy their only escape routes? Bob ran to the truck with Koloski hot on his heels. He peeled out of the relay station parking lot, spitting up tiny pebbles as he turned onto Route 3. He sped off towards the Gables Bridge.

Lois dropped Troy off in front of the elementary school. He opened the car door, leaned over, and gave her a kiss like he did every morning. But today she hugged him and didn't let go for quite a long time.

"Mom," he whined. "Everyone's gonna see. Stop it."

"Everyone can see me hug my son." She eased her grip and looked him in the eye. "I want you to be careful, okay?"

"Yeah, Mom. Don't worry. I'll see you after school." He pulled away and exited the car.

"Troy," she yelled after him. "I love you."

"I love you too, Mom." He slammed the door, ran up the sidewalk, and entered the building.

Troy walked down the same hallway he had walked with his mother on his first day of school. He looked at the door to the kindergarten classroom. It had appeared gigantic and terrifying, but he had been so small back then. Now he was in fourth grade and there was nothing scary about it at all. He even had a girlfriend.

He approached the door to the kindergarten class, feeling older and important, and peered through the window. There was no one inside yet.

Even the classroom looked smaller. That had been a strange first day. The children had gone insane when their moms left. Troy thought he probably would have gone nuts too if it hadn't been for Rob Boyle. The boy had remained calm and mature while the rest of the children lost it.

Troy knew his mom was hiding something about Rob. Every time he mentioned his friend's name, she acted strange. *Maybe Rob is still sick and won't be able to come out on Halloween. Maybe that's why she's acting so strange.*

"What are you looking at?"

Troy jumped at the sound of Wendy's voice; he'd been staring into the window of the kindergarten classroom, lost in his daydream.

"Oh, I was just thinking about my first day of school." He checked the hallway to see if anyone was coming, then leaned in and kissed her on the lips. Wendy's eyes flew open wide in reaction to his sudden burst of confidence, but she didn't resist.

"Wow, what's got into you?"

He felt a little embarrassed but not enough. "I don't know. I thought I was supposed to kiss my girlfriend hello."

Wendy blushed; a sheepish grin spread across her face. "Oh, okay."

They walked down the hall and turned the corner to enter the fourth-grade classroom. Troy opened the door for her, and they both stopped short.

Almost half of the class was missing. Troy scanned the rows, taking note of who was there and who was not. Despite nearly every other chair being empty, Troy was happy to see Janis had made it to school. The girl's face beamed the moment he and Wendy entered the class, and she immediately waved them over to her desk.

"I brought some money so we could stop at the toy store on the way home." She pulled out a ten-dollar bill. Troy had never even held one before and had no idea his new friend was so rich.

"Where did you get all of that money?" He stared as she held the bill up for them to see.

"Do you think it's enough to get some magnets and wrist rockets?" she asked.

"Are you kidding?" Wendy said. "You could buy half the store with all that money. Put that back in your pocket before you lose it."

Janis crammed the bill into her jeans as if it were nothing more than a bubble gum wrapper.

"It's only ten bucks," she told them. "My dad sends me money all the time. Do you think we can get what we need on the way to Troy's house? Is there a toy store close by?"

"Yeah, Marco's Playmart is on the way. We can stop there and get what we need, then you can see the haunted house." Troy heard the door to the classroom open behind him. He turned around to see Miss Boriello, his old kindergarten teacher.

"Miss Boriello, what are you doing here?" he asked.

"It's nice to see you too, Troy." She smiled, then spoke up so the entire class could hear. "Miss Walsh won't be in today, so I am going to be your teacher. I hope that's all right with everyone." They had all had Miss Boriello for kindergarten and loved her. The only students who didn't know her were Janis, Wendy, and Yvonne Munoz, who had all moved to town later.

"Do you know how to teach fourth grade, Miss Boriello?" Troy asked, and Wendy punched him in the arm.

Miss Boriello smiled. "Well, if I have any problems, maybe you could help me out, okay?"

Troy liked the idea of that. It made him feel important, mature in yet another way. "Sure, no problem."

The children took their seats and waited for Miss Boriello to begin. Troy looked around again, alarmed by just how many of his classmates were absent. There were twenty-five students in the class, but today, only twelve had shown up. Troy didn't know how to figure out percentages, but he knew it wasn't good. He raised his eyes to Wendy, who had to be thinking the same thing. That this was a lot worse than a simple case of the flu.

Miss Boriello began taking attendance. She called out name after name and waited for a reply of "here" or "present," but most of her calls went unanswered. The teacher furrowed her brow as she scanned the class. It was obvious to Troy she was concerned by the number of absentees as well; still, she smiled and continued.

Janis poked him in the back and leaned close to whisper. "Where is everyone?" she asked. "You don't think we're too late, do you?"

Troy thought maybe. He had seen those things in the graveyard, and so far, the only people who believed him were Wendy and Janis. The deputy didn't listen to him and neither did his mother or father. That was the problem with being a kid; nobody listened, even when you were right. *This is bad.* Not only was half the class out sick but so was Miss Walsh. Troy wondered just how many people in town were home sick today. More so, he wondered how many people in Garrett Grove weren't even home at all.

Deputy Rainey was about to pull out of the municipal building parking lot when the Fink Bakery truck came to a screeching halt next to his cruiser. He'd heard the explosions and thought it odd that there'd been no warning signal from the quarry. He was about to take a trip up there to see who forgot to sound the alarm when the driver of the truck rolled down his window and yelled:

"Oh, Jesus Christ. It's a real fucking mess. You got to get up there before someone gets killed."

"Easy!" Deputy Rainey yelled back. "What the hell are you talking about?"

"There's been an avalanche on Sunset Road. I swear to God it looks like half the damn mountain came down."

"What? When was this?"

"About fifteen minutes ago. It happened right behind me. If I'd been just a few minutes later, I'd be dead right now. God, it's a mess."

Rainey turned on the cherries and picked up the radio. "This is Deputy Rainey en route to Sunset Road. There's been a report of an avalanche at the top of the Pass." He took off in the direction of the high school; from there, it was two miles up Sunset Road to the top of the Pass.

"This is Primrose. I'm on my way. ETA ten minutes."

"Roger that, Sheriff," the deputy said as he pulled out onto the turnpike and sped off.

"Sheriff, this is Andrea, do you want more backup? I could get Deputy Kovach to meet you both up there."

"Negative. I'll be in contact as soon as we have a look."

"10-4, Sheriff." Andrea's voice broke up as she signed off.

CHAPTER 53

Deputy Kovach had just pulled up to Tara's house and was about to report to Rainey's call when he heard the sheriff's transmission. *What the hell is that all about? An avalanche? That has to be a phony report.* Sure, Sunset Road was dangerous, and some loose rock fell from time to time, but there'd never been anything like an avalanche. He exited the cruiser, walked up the stone path to Tara's front porch, and stopped. The door had been left open. He unholstered his weapon and grabbed his handheld radio.

"This is Deputy Kovach. I'm at Tara's place. Someone left the door open, and she may need assistance."

"Kovach, this is the sheriff; I'm dispatching Deputy Colbert to your position. Do not enter the house until backup arrives. I repeat, do not enter the house until backup arrives."

"Copy, Sheriff." Kovach had no intention of disobeying the man and stood outside Tara's door, looking into the house. He peered in through the cracked open door and noticed there were footprints; something that resembled tar had been tracked throughout the house. The footprints led out the front door and continued along the walkway. *Whoever made these has already left.*

Kovach could hear the sirens in the distance and knew Colbert was on his way, but a gnawing sensation continued to eat at him. *Something's wrong; I can feel it.* As much as he didn't want to break protocol, Tara was a fellow deputy, not to mention a friend. Despite every rule he knew about waiting for backup and years of always doing the job exactly by the book, Deputy Kovach pushed the front door inward and entered the house.

"Deputy Jeffries!" he shouted. "Tara, it's Joel. Are you all right?" His call was answered with silence; the house was still.

Joel Kovach climbed the steps, following the dark footprints with his gun drawn. "Tara, are you there?" There was dead quiet. He turned the corner at the top of the stairs and entered the kitchen to find the floor covered in the same black fluid. Someone had walked through the mess, then left out the front door. It resembled tar or possibly oil. Then Kovach noticed a second set of prints, the owner of which had walked around the kitchen in circles, then exited to somewhere in the back of the house.

He followed the tracks down a hallway to where they ended at a closed door. The prints staining the carpet were smaller than the other set, and Kovach was almost positive they belonged to Tara. *Sweet Jesus.* He was certain something had happened to her. Kovach could hear the fast-approaching sirens and decided to proceed—he had already broken protocol. If Tara was injured and needed medical assistance, there wasn't any time to spare. He held his breath, turned the knob, and let the door swing inward—the room was empty. Black footprints led across the carpet to the bed sitting in the center of the room. There, they scuffed and smeared and disappeared; it looked as if Tara had walked into the room and crept underneath the bed.

"Tara, are you in here?" The only sound Kovach heard was the beating of his own heart, fast and loud inside his temples. He forced himself to suppress his jangled nerves and proceeded toward the bed. It reminded him of the scene at the Negal house, where he had lifted the mattress and found the little girl hiding underneath. A sense of déjà-vu washed over him.

Tara's bed was much bigger than Dawn Negal's, and there was no way he could overturn it. He knelt on one knee, removed the mag-light from his belt, and clicked it on. With his gun in one hand and the light in the other, he lifted the duvet and cast the beam into the darkness.

There was a flurry of motion, then white-hot pain. He screamed as it ripped into his soft flesh. It felt like he had stuck his arm inside a furnace; the sensation of a million fire ants tearing into his skin simultaneously set every nerve in his body screaming. Kovach buckled under the gargantuan pain. *Jesus Christ!* The single thought raced through his mind as he struggled to free himself. Finally, it released him. The deputy fell back and crashed into the dresser with his arm spouting a river of red. He looked down at the massive bite that had been taken out of him; his skin and muscle had been extracted. A heavy flow of arterial fluid pulsed in time to the beat of his frantic heart. Kovach's vision blurred, and pain flooded his entire world.

There was a deep gurgling sound as something emerged from under the bed. It clawed its way from out of the shadows and lifted its head. Insanity tipped Kovach over the edge. A maniacal laugh escaped his lips. The creature that lumbered before him was Tara Jeffries—only it wasn't Tara anymore. She still wore her uniform and still possessed distinct facial features, but that's where the similarities ended. Her body had grown; her muscles had doubled in size and ripped through the fabric of her clothing. She had been waiting for him, hiding under the bed.

Kovach tried to focus on a single rational thought but could only focus on the blinding pain. The room heaved and spun off its axis, making it impossible to see straight. He tried to raise his gun, attempted to aim his weapon, but was too dizzy and there was so much blood. It covered the floor and shot onto the bedspread in arcing spasms.

Tara crawled through the carnage and grabbed Kovach by the leg. Her skin was mottled and grey like a cadaver left in the hot sun. Puncture wounds covered her face and body, and dark tar ran from every wound; it oozed from her eyes and mouth as well.

The Tara-creature hissed as Kovach raised his gun and pulled the trigger. The bullet entered her shoulder. With the speed and accuracy of a jaguar, she lunged at him and tore into his belly with her bare hands. Tara buried her face into the deputy's guts and started to feed on him. Kovach tried to scream but only managed a weak gargle. He choked on his own blood and bile as the woman ripped him apart. He had disobeyed the sheriff and broken protocol; it was the last mistake he ever made.

Bob Jones and Ed Koloski stood on the Grove side of the Lenape River; neither had words to describe what lay before them. The Gables Bridge had been destroyed. Twisted metal dangled over the edge on either side, half submerged by the raging current. The structure had been old, the steel and concrete both brittle from age and decomposition, and the bridge had disintegrated as if it had been made of sand.

Both men had spent years working for the fire department and were familiar with the sound of an explosion. Even though the bridge was old, there had been plenty of life left in it. It hadn't collapsed on its own, it had been destroyed, but the question was by who, or more accurately ... by what?

Koloski turned to the chief. "This is bad; someone did this on purpose."

Bob didn't know how to respond. It was worse than bad; Garrett Grove was in deep shit. He prayed that Nick Gomes had made it out of town before the bridge had been destroyed. What worried Bob even more was that while he and Koloski were en route to the bridge, he could have sworn he had heard a second explosion. He hoped he was mistaken.

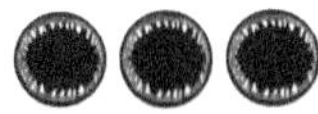

It looked as if half of the mountain had come down. Carl got out of his cruiser and stared at the debris. Giant boulders had fallen from the cliff face and destroyed the road. They not only blocked the passage but had hit the pavement with such force, the blacktop had buckled from the impact. Carl imagined it would take at least a week to clear the mess, even with a bucket loader on each side.

He looked up at the area where the rocks had come dislodged. *This was no accident. No way.* Someone had set off a charge. By the sound of it, there had been two separate detonations used to take down the cliff wall. One thing was certain; no one was getting out of town this way.

Carl knew he was in over his head. Whatever they were dealing with was smart enough to send Dr. Malcolm to destroy the MRI machine and now showed a tactical initiative by cutting off one of the town's only means of escape. *Damn! The bridge?* The realization resonated in his head like a bassoon. They had all heard two blasts; there had been a second detonation that hadn't come from the direction of the mountain. *Jesus Christ, not the bridge!*

Carl ran to the cruiser and opened the door; the radio crackled with static.

"Sheriff, come in, Sheriff."

"Go ahead." His gut churned sour.

"Sheriff, it's Bob Jones." Carl braced himself but knew it was futile. "Sheriff, the Gables Bridge has been destroyed. It looks like someone may have set charges underneath it. There's nothing left." Carl stared at the pile of dump-truck size boulders blocking Sunset Road. There was no way out of town.

Deputy Rainey pulled up behind the sheriff's cruiser with his lights flashing. Carl was sure the young officer had been listening to the transmission and waved him over just as Bob started speaking again.

"Someone sabotaged the communications relay as well. The phones won't be working any time soon."

Carl depressed the button and spoke into the mic. "Did Nick Gomes make it out of town before the bridge was destroyed?" He waited for a reply.

"I think so." Carl let out a sigh of relief. If Nick had made it out of town, then the state police would find their way into Garrett Grove one way or another. "Sheriff, I could have sworn I heard a second detonation. Any idea what that was?"

Carl had already kept information from his people, and Dr. Ziegler had paid the price because of it; he wasn't about to do it again. They had a right to know just how bad things were. "Someone set charges to the rock face above Sunset Road. The Pass is blocked; there's no way in or out of Garrett Grove." Carl could only imagine what was going through the minds of every deputy and dispatcher listening to the transmission. He had expected the state police to be stepping in and taking control of the situation sometime this morning; it looked like it was going to take much longer than that.

"Bob, are your men armed?"

"No, we turned in our weapons last night."

"I want you to return to the station and get them." He cleared his throat and nodded to Rainey. "This is Sheriff Primrose. I want *all* deputies and dispatchers to carry loaded sidearms at all times. I also want every member of the fire department issued a weapon. Andrea, coordinate with Chief Jones the distribution of guns to his men. Do you copy?"

"Copy that, Sheriff." Andrea's voice sounded shaken. Carl knew she had monitored the entire transmission and understood the gravity of the situation. The people of Garrett Grove were on their own until help arrived … if it ever did.

After attending the morning meeting, Burt Lively drove Doris TenHove to the medical center, where she had left her car the night before. He pulled into the employee's parking area and hit the brakes. The emptiness of the lot was glaring, with less than half the number of vehicles occupying their usual spots.

"Oh dear. Not again," Doris gasped. Yesterday, the place had been plagued with a rash of absenteeism, and if the state of the parking lot was any indication of what today held, they were in big trouble.

"This isn't good," Burt said. "I can't even stick around and help."

"It's okay," she said, grabbing her purse from the front seat. "I'll figure something out; I always do. But once Michelle and Joe finish dropping the bodies off, please send them back. I'm going to need them."

"I will, and if I get done early, I'll come right over." Burt put his hand on Doris's thigh and slid it up her skirt to within an inch of the goods. She placed her hand on top of his and stopped him, but not before allowing him to graze his target.

"Mind yourself, old man. I think we both know what this means," she said, referring to the empty parking lot. "Be careful, and don't do anything stupid ... Nothing more than usual, that is." She leaned over, kissed him firm on the lips, then slapped him across the face.

"I'll try to swing by around noon, if I can."

Doris exited the vehicle and walked to the employees' entrance. Burt focused on her backside the entire time.

The emergency room was empty except for Dr. Freedman, Nurse Burnes, and one candy striper—Doris wasn't sure but thought the girl's name might be Cindy. None of the beds were occupied, as last night's patients had all been discharged or admitted to the second floor. There had been no new emergency room patients, which was also strange; Doris figured there should have been at least one.

"Oh my. Where is everyone?" She had a feeling she didn't want to know the answer.

Doris walked to the front desk and picked up the phone. The internal lines were working, but there was still no way to call outside. *Doesn't hurt to try.* Only twelve hours ago, the center had looked like a MASH unit. There had been a heavy influx of injuries from the explosion in the imaging wing, and they'd been terribly short-staffed. Firemen, deputies, and paramedics had flooded the emergency room and bailed them out of what could have been a far greater disaster. Doris doubted the center could handle anything even remotely serious happening right now. She scanned the empty waiting area. *God help us.*

Dr. Freedman approached the desk with a cup of coffee in his hand.

"Nurse TenHove. Do you have any idea what's going on?" The man looked lost, as if he were waiting for someone to tell him what to do. He had no clue what was happening, and Doris thought it was probably better that way. She doubted if he would be able to handle it.

"I really couldn't say, Doctor," she replied. "I hear there's a flu bug going around."

Carl and Deputy Rainey set up barricades and Road Closed signs at the base of Sunset Road, two miles below the rockslide. There wasn't much more they could do. The detour sat at almost the exact spot where Felix Castillo had been hit by the bread truck. Carl looked over to the ditch where the man's body had landed, wishing he could go back to Sunday morning and do things over. Not that it would have made much difference.

The disappearance of the children and Dr. Malcolm was nothing he could have predicted or done anything about. But the Felix Castillo fiasco weighed heavy on his shoulders; it hadn't been all Burt's fault. They had the chance to nip it in the bud Sunday night, but Carl decided to bury the evidence and hide the fact they had lost the body. He and Burt had gone back to the morgue and gotten drunk when they should have continued searching the foothills. It could have made all the difference ... and that was on him.

Things were bad—really bad. The bridge was out, and so was the Sunset Pass. The phone lines had been destroyed, and the radios only reached so far. The damn mountain interfered with the signals, making sure no communications left the Grove. The Lenape called it Lonesome Mountain, and Carl thought they had nailed it with that one.

How many people have already been compromised? Which led him to the next question: *How many of those things are out there?* It was something he didn't want to think about, but he *had* to.

He needed answers fast, and with Dr. Ziegler gone, he was counting on Burt to figure something out. If there were as many of those things as he thought, they were going to need a plan.

Maybe there's a chance we could clear the road. If the guys at the quarry can get a bulldozer up here, they might be able to move some of the larger stones out of the way. Carl figured if he could still get people out of town, that would solve most of his problems.

He picked up his radio. "Sheriff Primrose to Deputy Kovach; come in, Deputy Kovach." He was met with silence. "Sheriff Primrose to Deputy Colbert." Tim didn't answer either. Carl's head started to throb again. "Andrea, this is Carl. Has Kovach or Colbert returned to base or contacted you yet?"

"Negative, Sheriff. I haven't heard from either one. They're still checking in on Tara."

"Deputy Rainy and I are en route to Tara's house. I want you to send Deputy Jenkins to the quarry. See if they can spare a front-end loader or a bulldozer and get it up to this mess on Sunset. Tell them Sheriff's orders."

"10-4, Sheriff." Andrea signed off.

CHAPTER 54

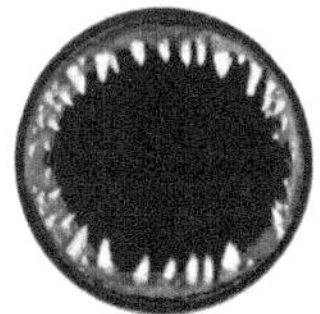

Deputy Colbert arrived at Tara's house to backup Deputy Kovach but was too late to do the man any good. He found the front door open, and when he called into the house, there was no answer. He followed the dark footprints up the stairs and into the kitchen, just as Kovach had. The same dark substance had been tracked all over the linoleum floor. It looked like motor oil that hadn't been changed in far too long. The goop had dried but not before someone had walked through it in circles, as if in a drunken stupor. The smaller of the two sets of prints led into the hallway and then to one of the bedrooms.

Colbert heard a faint noise coming from the room at the end of the hall. It almost sounded like something sloshing around, something wet. He unholstered his weapon and made his way in the direction of the strange noise. The closer he got to the bedroom, the louder it grew and the more pronounced it became—now he was sure it was a slurping sound. *What the hell is that?* He slowly approached the room.

The retired deputy poked his head through the doorway and froze, his mind unable to comprehend the scene spread out before him. The ocean of crimson and the haphazard arrangement of discarded organs sent Colbert's defenses into overdrive. Tara Jefferies had her face buried in Deputy Kovach's guts. She dug into the man's belly like one of those dead things in the movies. *She's fucking eating him like a zombie.* The woman was so intent on her meal that she hadn't noticed him standing in the doorway. She reached deep into Kovach's belly and pulled out a long strand of the man's intestines.

Kovach was dead—his face was stark white, and his uniform was saturated in blood. He still held his gun in one hand and flashlight in the other, and lay with his back against the dresser while the thing that had once been his coworker feasted on his insides.

Dear God, Sheriff Primrose was right. Colbert had listened to the man but hadn't quite believed him. Some of it—but not the part about the dead guy walking around killing people. But now ... *Jesus Christ! Carl was right.*

Colbert had retired over three years ago, but he still went to the range twice a week. "Hey!" he shouted into the room. The thing that had once been Tara Jefferies lifted her head and hissed at him. Colbert watched a piece of Kovach's intestine fall from the woman's mouth like a yo-yo bobbing at the end of a string. It stretched from its own weight and swung for a moment before coming loose and splatting onto the floor.

Tara opened her mouth and screamed; the noise penetrated Colbert's skull like a bullet. He didn't have time to think as the creature sprang to its feet and came at him. But having been trained by Allen Primrose, he didn't need to think and just reacted. He raised his weapon and fired. The bullet hit Tara in the front of her skull, peeling back the top inch of her hair and the bone beneath it. She looked at the deputy as if in shock, with eyes the color of midnight. He fired a second round, which hit its mark one inch below the first. Tara stopped moving and fell face first onto the floor. The same dark fluid oozed from her wounds like an overturned bottle of soy sauce. Deputy Colbert swallowed hard and thought he might be able to control the urge, then every muscle in his body contracted, and he vomited onto Tara's bedroom carpet. Wiping his chin, he ran out the front door, glad to be in the open air.

Jesus Christ, Carl. You were right.

Four corpses lay strapped to the freezer shelves in the morgue, all of which had stainless steel pans covering their faces. Burt hated to treat the body of Dr. Ziegler in such a way but believed the man would have understood. He wasn't about to take chances either way. *If it bothers you, Zig, you can let me know next time I see ya.* The way things were looking, Burt thought that might be sooner than later.

From his initial examination of the bodies, it looked as if two had been infected with the toxin and two had not. It was obvious in the case of Dr. Malcolm and the thing found at the Texaco fire. But Dr. Ziegler and the body of the gas station attendant appeared to be fine. If the attendant had been exposed, Burt was guessing the extreme heat from the blast had fried the man's brains to a cinder, incinerating the infection in the process.

To play it safe, Burt took tissue samples from all the cadavers and examined them under the microscope. The two from the fire had been seriously damaged, and he needed to cut deep into the flesh to extract the samples. And as suspected, he found signs of the infection in both Dr. Malcolm and the creature from the fire, but it was also present in the attendant as well. The only body that was clean was Dr. Ziegler's.

Burt removed the stainless steel basin from Ziegler's head. The man's throat and spinal cord had been crushed. His injuries were extensive and indicative of an aggressive attack. Which struck Burt as counterproductive. Infections didn't get stronger by killing their hosts. But this had been different; this had been a premeditated attack and carried out in a fit of rage.

"Looks like you pissed it off, Doc," Burt whispered. Ziegler had stopped Rainey from killing the sheriff and been operating the MRI machine that killed Abe Gorman.

Before Abe died, something had been extracted from his body. It appeared to be some type of gas or vapor and looked an awful lot like smoke. *Was that the physical presence of the infection itself?* It wasn't the most unbelievable thing he had seen this week.

Burt continued to examine the samples from the other bodies, comparing them to the ones taken from Castillo and Abe. In all cases, the infection appeared to have died along with the hosts.

His mind wandered to thoughts of Doris and their night together. Doris had been a very receptive lover; a childish grin found its way onto Burt's face as he relived the evening. He had taken a shower, and Doris had given him a fresh set of clothes belonging to her late husband. After being saturated in smoke, the hot water and new set of duds made Burt feel like a new man. And Doris had done a bit more afterwards to make him feel even better. At some point in the evening, he had transferred his belongings from his old coat into the new one and tossed it in the trash without realizing he no longer had Carl's gun.

Burt refocused the microscope, examining the tissue sample taken from Dr. Malcolm. Something about the cellular structure of the bacterium had struck him as familiar when he first inspected it the other night. But after scouring his old medical journals, he'd been unable to identify it. He wasn't any closer to figuring it out now and knew that Carl was counting on him. With a slick sweat breaking on his brow, Burt could feel the stress getting to him. He removed his jacket and placed it on the table.

He took his glasses from his shirt pocket, put them on, and looked into the lens once again. The red blood cells were compromised; the proteins had been denatured. And although the cellular damage indicated a bacterial toxin, there was something about it that wasn't exactly organic. Then, something happened. It was slow at first, hardly detectable at all. But … there was movement on the slide.

Burt squinted and rubbed his eyes, then he adjusted the magnification and looked again. It was gradual, but sure enough, there was cellular movement within the sample. Only these cells were dead. "What the hell?" he gasped.

He refocused the aperture again and watched the red blood cells migrate to the right side of the slide. *Why in that direction?* He removed the slide, turned it around, and replaced it under the lens to see if the cells would continue moving, only this time to the left. He looked into the lens and held his breath. The cells stopped moving for a moment, then resumed their previous course of direction, gravitating to the right once again.

What's going on?

Burt repeated the action, removing the slide and rotating it, and the exact same thing happened. The red blood cells stopped moving for a second, then reversed direction and began to migrate to the right. "It's like they're being pulled by something," he whispered.

There'd been no movement on the slide only a moment ago. *So, what changed?* Then he noticed it. He had taken off his jacket and set it on the table near the microscope—on the right side. But that didn't make sense. Burt picked up the jacket, moved it to the other side of the microscope, and looked through the lens. The red blood cells stopped for a quick second, then slowly began to migrate to the left.

"Son of a bitch!" he shouted. He had no idea what it meant, but he knew it had something to do with the jacket, or maybe …

Burt grabbed the jacket and started to remove the items from the pockets. He pulled out a handful of change, the small bottle of the teeth he had taken from the ashes, and his car keys. He thought that was it, then felt one last smaller item in the very bottom of the left pocket. He reached in and pulled out the tiny ladybug. He stared at the bright red design with the little black dots on its back and flipped it over. A round magnet sat in the center of the bug's body. "Jesus Christ," he gasped. "The MRI is one big fucking magnet!"

He held the magnet against the right side of the slide and looked into the lens. He watched as the cells gravitated to the right. He repeated the experiment, switching the magnet to the left side of the lens … The cells immediately changed direction and raced in that direction as well. The cells were being drawn by the magnet. *How is that possible?* Burt knew magnets worked on metal and polarized ores, that opposite poles attracted and like poles repelled, but he had never seen anything like this.

He jumped up from his seat and walked around the room to stretch his legs. "Okay," he said out loud. "It's a blood infection affected by magnetization. It attacks the red cells like a poison and has a bacterial signature." He paced the lab several times, then walked down the hall to the office. The book he had been looking at the other night still lay on his desk. He sat down and thumbed through the pages.

The desk and the chair he sat in shook for a quick second, causing Burt to pause; a half second later, he heard the explosion. It echoed in the distance, sounding as if it had happened somewhere on the south side of town. It was followed by a second detonation, louder and closer than the first, possibly originating from somewhere on the mountain. Then there were sirens. Burt swallowed back a sour pit that had formed in his throat. *What in the hell was that?*

It hit him in the leg, a quick pressure that was easily dismissed, then it happened again. Deputy Ted Lutchen slept in the chair next to the bed and woke when the strange sensation touched his leg a second time. He opened his eyes to see the eager face of the German Shepherd staring up at him. The dog whined, then slapped his paw onto the deputy's knee.

"I'll bet I know what that means."

Baxter cocked his head to the left and whined again. The girl in the bed rolled over and opened her eyes. She offered the deputy a confused look as she rubbed the sleep crumbs away. Then she saw her dog and smiled. Baxter looked at her and whined a third time.

"He needs to pee," Dawn said.

Ted yawned, stretched his back, then got up and grabbed the dog's leash. "Well, I guess we should take him out then."

Dawn jumped off the bed and helped him with the leash. Then Ted opened the door and the three stepped into the hallway. He checked to the left and right but didn't see anyone in either direction. There were no nurses working at the front desk and not so much as a janitor sweeping the floor. Ted held his breath and offered the child his most confident smile. They looked up at the sound of a squeaking door hinge to see a lone orderly emerge from one of the rooms. The man started when he saw the trio, as if he hadn't expected to see anyone himself, but Ted figured it had more to do with the presence of the dog.

"Good morning," Ted said. "Where is everyone?"

"I have no idea." The man appeared shaken and out of breath. "I've been wondering the same thing since I got here."

The orderly approached them, pushing a cartful of breakfast trays.

"Are you here by yourself?" Ted asked.

"No one showed up for work today. I mean some did, but more than half of the staff is out. And there's no way to get in touch with them, not with the phones out." The man's voice trembled as if he were on the verge of tears.

"You're taking care of the patients alone?"

"Elisabeth is here somewhere, but other than that, it's just me. And someone had to feed them."

"Okay, we'll help you. I'm Deputy Lutchen, and this is Dawn, and this guy who has to go potty is Baxter."

The man shook Ted's hand. "I'm Greg. Nice to meet you."

"Same here, Greg. We're going to take Baxter out, then we'll come back and give you a hand."

The sheriff's words echoed in Ted's head like a gong, and a picture of the men laid out in the freezer flashed before him. The events of yesterday felt like an impossible nightmare, but Ted knew it wouldn't help anyone to dwell on it. There were people who needed him, patients who had been left behind by a staff that hadn't shown up for work—or had been unable to. Ted didn't know which group to feel sorry for.

He and Dawn headed to the first floor and then outside to allow Baxter to relieve himself, only to find the rest of the facility was equally deserted. Although some staff had made it in, the absence of the ones who hadn't was more than noticeable.

While the pup chowed down, the trio ate at the nurses' station.

"How many patients are on this floor?" Ted asked.

"Eighteen to twenty."

"And on the other floors. Would you say about the same?"

"Yeah, sure. I mean give or take. Probably about the same." Greg gave Ted a puzzled look.

"So, about sixty patients. Is that what you think?" Ted watched Dawn as she ate from a single-serving-size bowl of Fruit Loops.

"Sounds about right."

"Are most of the patients mobile, or are they bedridden?" Ted continued. "I mean, do you think they could be moved if they had to be?"

"Why do you ask? What's going on?" Greg's voice wavered.

"I'm just wondering what you think. How many could be moved if you had to?"

"I don't know. I guess about three-quarters if we absolutely had to. But I don't know why you would, unless you know something I don't. Do you? Deputy, do you know something that I don't?"

Ted thought about what the man had said. About three quarters of the patients could be moved if they had to, approximately forty-five of them. Leaving roughly fifteen that were either bedridden or couldn't be moved for other reasons. That wasn't a very good ratio.

"No, I don't know anything that you don't. I was just wondering in case there was a problem like we had last night. Let's just hope that doesn't happen." Ted tried to look confident but was unsure if he pulled it off.

"Yeah," Greg said. "Let's hope not."

CHAPTER 55

Deputy Beau Jenkins pulled into the quarry and was intercepted by Don Fischer, who charged the cruiser waving his arms in the air with his face as red as salmon. Jenkins put the cruiser in park and rolled down the window a few inches.

"What seems to be the problem?" Beau asked, leaning back from the open window.

"Someone broke in here last night and destroyed all the machinery! Everything—the Komatsu, the Deere, even the CAT. We're talking hundreds of thousands of dollars in damage. You got to arrest these little bastards!" Don screamed at the older man who had just pulled up.

"Whoa, just slow down a second and start over. What are you talking about?"

Donald tried to regain his composure and took several deep breaths. Not wanting to look like a mental patient, he started over. "We keep all our equipment locked up in the pen. Look, it would be easier to just show you."

Jenkins exited the cruiser and allowed Don to lead him to the equipment pen. The damage was obvious as soon as they entered the storage area.

"Someone got into here last night. See the chain?" Don pointed to the broken links scattered around the gate. Jenkins examined them, then moved on to the equipment as Don continued. "They ripped the hydraulic lines out of the fittings. Do you have any idea how difficult that is? Those are under high pressure. And look at this; they cracked all the oil pans."

The deputy walked around the heavy machinery, examining the damage. The hydraulic lines had indeed been yanked from their fittings. They hadn't been cut or sliced. He bent down to look at the oil pan on one of the big machines. It hadn't just cracked; it had been smashed by something heavy and powerful.

"This wasn't a couple of kids messing around, Mr. Fischer. This is a whole lot more deliberate than something kids would do. This was some-one trying to make a point. Someone wanted to hit you where it hurts—the wallet."

"What are you talking about?"

"Do you have any enemies, Mr. Fischer? More importantly, does your boss have any enemies? Is there someone who might have something to gain by seeing the quarry shut down?"

"What? Of course I don't have any enemies. I'm a geologist, not Jimmy Hoffa, for Christ's sake."

"What about your boss, Mr. DuCain?"

"I have no idea. He's never here, stays at the corporate office in Virginia. Who would want to do something like this?" Some of the workers had gathered around to watch him lose his mind. Stephanie and Gail stood near the entrance of the cavern looking at him as well. He couldn't see their faces but imagined they were surprised to see this side of him.

"Did you and your men walk through the area this morning?" Jenkins asked.

Don looked at the sand around the equipment and realized what he had done. Both he and Buzzy had walked around the machines nearly a dozen times assessing the damage. "Oh Christ."

"Hmm-mmm." Jenkins studied the tracks, stepping around them to examine a bit closer. "I see three distinct sets of tracks. Judging by those boots you're wearing, I can see a lot of them belong to you. The other set of boot prints, I'm guessing belong to your man over there." He pointed to Buzzy, who stood just outside the pen. "Then there's another set; unfortunately, you men stepped on most of them."

Don knew he had done most of that himself.

"The guy who made those tracks was one big son of a bitch. That's at least a size thirteen boot, probably bigger, I'm guessing." The deputy pointed to one of the oversized tracks.

"So, it wasn't kids?"

"I don't think so, Mr. Fischer. I'd say the owner of these prints was definitely not a kid."

Don wondered if they had an enemy that he didn't know about, someone who wanted DuCain out of business. It didn't sound right; the quarry had been there for years and no other company had any vested interest in the mountain. None of it made any sense. "How did you even know to come here this morning, Deputy?" Don finally asked the obvious. "No one called; the phones are out."

"You heard the explosions a little while ago?"

Donald nodded.

"Well, there've been a couple situations in town. The Gables Bridge was destroyed and the other being a rockslide on Sunset Road; both look like they were done intentionally. I'm here because the sheriff wanted to get one of those machines up to the Pass to start clearing the road."

Don felt the blood drain from his face. Things were about to get worse. He could feel it.

"After seeing this, Mr. Fischer, I'm wondering if all your explosives are accounted for. Do you mind if we have a look?"

Don's lungs cramped like he had been kicked in the chest. *This isn't happening.* He wanted to scream and tear his hair out, but all he could do was look at the deputy and say, "Follow me."

He led Jenkins to the explosives shed, a miniature bunker set far away from the trailers behind two chain-link fences. The shed itself was constructed out of double cinderblock, reinforced by a steel interior. The doors were solid steel as well, with three padlocks, each one thicker than a man's finger.

All the locks had been broken and not cut as if done by a saw or pair of bolt cutters. They had been shattered, like they had been flash-frozen and then smashed. Don opened the door, expecting the shed to be empty. He was surprised to see it wasn't, but there was a hell of a lot of shit missing.

He grabbed the inventory sheet off the door and looked through it but could already see what was gone; it was his job to keep track of all of it. In total, six blasting caps along with fifteen sticks of dynamite, three rolls of primer cord, and two detonators had been removed from the shed. He went over the list with the deputy.

"Do you still think this was done by kids, Mr. Fischer?" The deputy studied the inventory sheet.

"What the hell should I do?" A serrated blade of tension stabbed Don in the center of his forehead as he struggled to form a cohesive thought.

"I would suggest you find a safer place to store the explosives that *haven't* been stolen from your job site. This shed isn't as safe as you think. I need to report this to the sheriff. I imagine he'll want to question you. I'm sure you understand."

The throbbing in his skull escalated. Don had never even spent a night in the drunk tank and couldn't imagine the trouble he might be facing. Someone had stolen explosives from his job and used them to blow up part of the mountain. *I am so fucked.*

"Why would someone do this, and why would they want to block the road?"

"I think I'll let the sheriff answer that, Mr. Fischer." The deputy walked to the cruiser and called the sheriff on the radio.

Sheriff Primrose and Deputy Rainey arrived at Tara's house moments before Beau Jenkins tried to contact him. Carl exited the vehicle, leaving the call unanswered, and raced across the front lawn to where Deputy Colbert stood on the walkway vomiting into the bushes. Both men approached him as he bent over and heaved one last time.

Colbert's face had gone grey; a thin layer of sweat slicked his brow. The man looked like he had aged ten years in the past hour.

"What the hell is it, Tim? What happened?" Carl watched his old partner attempt to regain control of his stomach. Tim dry-heaved, then straightened himself upright.

The men were alerted by the sound of shuffled footsteps coming from the foyer, just on the other side of the open door. Carl looked up in time to see Deputy Kovach emerge from the house. A scream rose in his throat but never left his lips.

Kovach's innards hung from a gaping wound in his abdomen. Carl moved to help the man, then recoiled in shock as the deputy's lips pulled back in a snarl. A thick oil-like substance coated the deputy's teeth and gums and had consumed his eyes as well. Kovach took an awkward step forward, and a splash of organs dumped out of him onto the front steps. His legs tangled in a coil of large intestines, the pink bands tightening around his ankles as he approached.

Tim Colbert attempted to retreat but tripped over a planter set along the walkway. He fell backward, landing hard on his ass, and looked up at Kovach. The beast glared at him through a lifeless black abyss and opened his mouth.

Carl froze, expecting a serpentine tongue like the one used by Felix Castillo to rocket from the deputy's mouth. But the only thing that came out was a tendril of dark smoke. It lifted from Kovach's open jaws and swirled before his face like a churning cloud. Then it shot like a viper at Colbert, who lay on the ground trying to right himself.

The smoke disappeared into Colbert's open mouth. The man recoiled, grabbing his throat, and rolled onto his back, gagging.

Carl and Rainey each took a step backward as Kovach turned toward them and opened his mouth even wider. Carl finally reacted and raised his gun. But before he could pull the trigger, the front of the man's face disappeared in a crimson wash. Deputy Rainey fired a second round into Kovach's chest, and the abomination toppled to the ground in a lifeless heap.

Colbert convulsed on the ground with dark threads rising from his nostrils in tiny wisps. The man opened his mouth, allowing even more of the strange substance to disperse into the air around him. Carl jumped as Deputy Rainey fired a round into the top of Colbert's head. The man fell back against the pavement and stopped moving; the cloud was carried away on the wind.

The concussion from Rainey's bullets ripped through Carl like a cardiac arrest. He'd jumped at the sound of the first one, his muscles clenching in his throat and shoulders. Then his stomach twisted as the smell of gunpowder fused with Kovach's innards in a putrefying waft. By the time the deputy fired a second time, Carl had been frozen with fear. The urge to vomit rose in his esophagus, forcing him to bite back and swallow hard. It had happened so fast and so sudden, that he just stood there. He had ordered his men not to hesitate, and Deputy Rainey followed his directions to the tee. He watched as the young officer reloaded his weapon.

"Are you all right, Sheriff?" Rainey asked.

"Yeah," he said, knowing that he wasn't … not even a little.

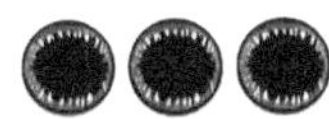

Lois stared across the empty floor of the medical center to the reception area where Doris TenHove stood. A mutual understanding exchanged between them in a flash—something terrible was happening, yet they were both still here. Lois imagined a similar look had been shared by the passengers on the *Titanic* after the last lifeboat had been lowered into the water. Some had missed the opportunity to abandon ship, while others had not taken the threat seriously. They all died the same in the end, regardless to which group they belonged.

Which group do you belong to, Nurse TenHove? Lois thought the woman was probably wondering the same thing about her. Lois knew she fit into both. She had heard the warning from Carl and even taken heed, at least for a moment. Then she let reason and rationale stop her from reacting. Lois looked at the nurse behind the desk and realized the woman probably didn't belong to either category. Nurse TenHove was here because she chose to be. She was here out of a sense of duty and commitment to the people entrusted in her care. She wasn't about to leave her patients behind, even if that meant going down with the ship.

Lois held her head up and approached the reception desk.

"Good morning, Mrs. Fischer," Doris said.

"I'm not so sure that it is, Nurse TenHove. Could we speak candidly? You know, one woman to another." Lois placed her purse on the counter and met Doris's stare.

"What would you like to talk about?" Doris laid her clipboard next to Lois's purse. "Would it have something to do with the meeting at the courthouse this morning?"

"I didn't know there was a meeting, but I spoke with the sheriff yesterday about some things that I'm having a difficult time accepting. You look like you might know what I'm talking about. Can you help me understand what's going on?"

"I take it you haven't seen anything to convince you?" Doris lowered her voice. "Dr. Malcolm came back last night."

Lois's spirit picked up for a brief second but was shattered just as quickly.

"Only it wasn't Dr. Malcolm anymore. Something had happened to him; he had changed. His face looked more like an ape's or something prehistoric. And he killed Dr. Ziegler."

Tears welled up in the corners of Lois's eyes as the concussion of her own heartbeat echoed in her head like a bass drum. The stark white light of the waiting area assaulted her, and the suffocating smell of alcohol and disinfectant suddenly made her sick. She gasped and tried to wrap her head around what the nurse had said. She had just seen Dr. Ziegler yesterday. *No, that can't be.*

"I'm sorry, Mrs. Fischer. Dr. Ziegler died trying to stop Dr. Malcolm. Don't worry, your family is upstairs and they're safe. Billy was moved to the second floor before the explosion happened."

"Explosion! What explosion?" Lois raised her voice in a dramatic contrast to the silence of the waiting area. "What are you talking about?"

Doris reached across the counter and took Lois's hands. "Dr. Malcolm set off an explosion in the imaging wing. There was an awful lot of damage, and there was a fire. We had quite a few injuries, but your family is safe." The nurse held Lois's hands tight and looked her in the eyes. "The sheriff had a meeting at the courthouse this morning for all deputies and emergency care workers. It's an infection … It's changing people, turning them into something awful. And it's highly contagious. Those who become infected can pass it on. There doesn't appear to be any cure, but Burt Lively is trying to find one." Doris TenHove leaned in closer and lowered her voice even more. "Mrs. Fischer, the infection appears to be intelligent. It made Dr. Malcolm set off the explosion."

Carl had already told her a great deal about the infection, which she had struggled to accept. He told her to take Troy and get out of town, and before that, Dr. Ziegler had suggested she do the same. Each time, Lois had convinced herself that neither man knew what they were talking about. She wondered how long she would accept what Nurse TenHove was saying before she found a way to talk herself out of it a third time.

"Carl, I mean the sheriff, told me all of this yesterday, but I just couldn't believe it."

"It's difficult to believe, Mrs. Fischer. Why weren't you at the meeting this morning? I mean, if the sheriff took his time to tell you all this, I would think he would want you there as well."

Lois had never felt more foolish in her life. It was obvious why she hadn't been told about the meeting: Carl hadn't expected her to still be in Garrett Grove.

"I don't suppose the sheriff made any preparations to have Billy transferred, did he?"

"No, I imagine with everything that happened yesterday, it was overlooked. I know this all sounds crazy, like something out of comic book, but you need to do everything you can to keep you family safe, Mrs. Fischer, trust me." The woman's words fell heavy and hit Lois like a brick.

She had let Troy go to school today. *How could I have been so stupid?* "What about you, Nurse TenHove; what are you going to do?"

The woman smiled, and it showed in her eyes; it was a genuine smile if Lois had ever seen one. "I am going to take care of my patients. That's what I am going to do. I was just considering how I would accomplish that, as short-staffed as we are. But I need to start doing something because I have a feeling we may be in for some trouble like we have never seen."

Lois could feel the seconds ticking away and sensed the lifeboats being lowered around them while she and Nurse TenHove spoke about the things they should be doing instead of actually doing any of it.

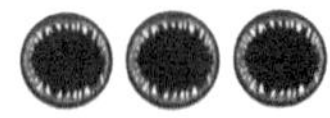

When Kovach emerged from the house, disemboweled and infected, all Carl could do was stare as the man lumbered toward them, dragging his organs like a toy wagon. He had been expecting the assault to come in the form of a serpentine tongue, like the one Castillo had developed, but that hadn't been the case. The real threat was the dark cloud that surfaced from the creature's mouth; it was the same stuff that had been extracted from Abe. *That's how this thing spreads.*

It had been lightning quick, and then the creature turned its sights on them. Rainey had already been ambushed once by this presence; he had raised his weapon and put Deputy Kovach down, then he fired on Colbert before the man had time to get up. All the while Carl watched, unable to move.

"Come in, Sheriff. This is Deputy Jenkins at the quarry." Beau had been trying to reach him for the past half hour.

Carl picked up his handheld. "Copy that. How are we looking?"

"Bad, Sheriff." Carl winced. "Someone broke in here last night or early this morning. Whoever it was made off with an awful lot of dynamite, some blasting caps, and a few other items. I'm guessing that's what was used on the bridge and the mountain."

Carl figured the explosives had come from the quarry; it was the only place in town with a readily available supply. "Beau, what's the chance of getting one of those machines up to Sunset Road? You told them what happened?"

"Unfortunately, whoever stole the explosives also sabotaged the machines. They ripped them apart, Sheriff. They're not going anywhere." Beau finished the transmission and was met with an extremely long interval of silence.

"Roger that." Carl turned to Deputy Rainey, removed his hat, and rubbed the bridge of his nose, just between his eyes. His headache had come back and begun to throb like a pulse. "David, let's get these bodies in the house before anyone sees them. They'll have to stay here till someone can come pick them up."

It was a horrible way to treat his own people, but Carl didn't have much of a choice. They were taxed to the limit. Burt didn't have the extra manpower, and now neither did he. The department had lost three deputies, and Carl was guessing that once they stepped inside the house, they would find the body of Tara Jefferies as well. That would bring the count to four, including Deputy Forsyth, who had to be considered compromised as well.

"Sheriff," Rainey said, scanning the neighborhood. "Where is everyone? With all the gunshots, someone should have gotten curious."

Carl looked toward the other houses on the block. The deputy was right; not a single neighbor had gotten curious and checked to see what was going on. If there was one thing people always did, it was put themselves in harm's way. Gunshots, car accident, fires—their natural reaction was to open their doors and see what the hell was going on. But not a single neighbor had so much as cracked a curtain. Carl had a bad feeling that if anyone was home behind those closed doors, they had a lot more to worry about than a few gunshots.

"Come on, David," he said. "Let's move these bodies."

Chapter 56

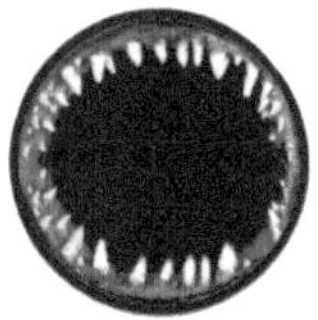

The original owners and staff of the Garrett Mountain Sanatorium had abandoned the facility decades ago, but the place didn't remain empty for long. Its new occupants, the multitude of woodland creatures who found their way in through the broken windows and breaches in the foundation, enjoyed the relative escape from the elements that the structure offered. But now, they, too, had vacated the premises. It was no longer hospitable for any living creature.

A necrotic puissance had invaded their home, festering like a cancer or a mold into every crevice of the old hospital. The animals could smell it. Unnatural and intrusive, a combination of ammonia and hot metal and something far worse—the odor of poison. Most animals recognized the smells of things that could kill them. The thing that had taken over the sanatorium smelled exactly like that, like something that would kill you.

But it wasn't just the stench that sent the tiny critters running for their lives, it was the malevolent awareness that tainted every square inch of the place. It occupied the complex like a hermit crab taking a new shell, the structure not only acting as its home but a living extension of the presence itself.

Garrett Mountain had been a place of suffering for decades, and the infestation that now gestated in the basement sensed that. Like a memory hanging in the air, an echo reverberating off the walls, repeating itself over and over, it had acted like a homing beacon and attracted the Entity like a moth to a flame.

The place was dark and cold and reminded the creature of the emptiness of its origin. The emptiness to which it would again return—after it destroyed every living creature on this rock.

Now the basement of the sanatorium resembled a mass grave. The bodies of the infected lay on the cold floor, side by side and on top of one another. The process had begun. Soon, its children would wake, and they would be ravenous.

Miss Boriello called an early recess since half the class was missing and the children who were present hadn't been paying attention to her lesson anyway. The kids were too preoccupied by the emptiness of the classroom. The trio of new friends retreated to their usual spot on the playground and began calculating how to spend Janis's ten dollars. To Wendy and Troy, the sight of the crisp bill was equivalent to being handed the keys to Fort Knox. But Janis was unfazed; cash was just another thing her father threw at her to compensate for his absence, like toys, jewelry, or *Star Wars* figures.

Wendy was also a child of divorced parents. She lived with her mother, who worked an excessive number of hours. But she was a happy child, for the most part, although she did get aggravated with Troy from time to time. And although Troy thought it was his fault, that wasn't the case.

Wendy's parents had gone through a messy divorce—was there any other kind? She hadn't seen much of her dad since he remarried, and he already had children with his new wife.

Her mother felt scorned by the man who left her for a much younger woman. But rather than keeping the marital problems to herself, she used her daughter as her personal counselor. Wendy was fed an endless diet of gripes focused on the shortcomings of her father and the entire male population. Men were immature and women were forced to tolerate their foolish antics—"so you better get used to it, Wendy." It was a miracle she turned out as adjusted as she had.

Wendy was a survivor and possibly the smartest kid in the class. It was easy for her to discern her mother's rantings for the slander that it was. However, it had tainted her opinion of boys ... just a little. Wendy knew women were superior to their male counterparts and it was only a matter of time before they took their rightful place in the hierarchy. She was a natural-born feminist—Gloria Steinem, eat your heart out. For the most part, she'd been disgusted by the foolishness of the boys at her previous school before moving to Garrett Grove. Then September came and she met Troy, who was different. And just like that, all the things her mother said didn't apply anymore. She'd found an exception to the rule, and that changed everything she thought she knew about boys. Her mother had been very wrong; boys weren't bad at all. In fact, Wendy thought she kind of liked them.

"Well, if nobody's gonna say anything, I guess I will," Wendy spoke up. "Half the class is missing. Every day, there's less and less. At this rate, how long will it be before one of *us* doesn't show up?"

The trio scanned the ever-shrinking population of students gathered on the playground. It wasn't only fourth graders who were missing, it was nearly half the students from every class. It was noticeable to all of them, especially Janis, who had watched the numbers decrease since arriving three days ago.

"Why aren't the adults doing anything?" Janis asked. "We can't be the only ones who notice."

Troy wondered if the grownups even knew something was going on. Adults were concerned about other things, like work and paying bills, and were so caught up in their day-to-day activities they probably hadn't even noticed.

"What does your mom think, Janis?" Troy figured if there was anyone in town who might know something, it would be Dr. Thompson. "I mean, she studies this stuff."

"She didn't say anything. She's been working a lot lately."

Troy nodded; his father had been doing the same thing.

"I don't think she knows anything's going on. It's not like she's friends with a lot of people in town." Janis blew a long blonde curl out of her eyes.

"Well, no one's going to listen to *us,*" Wendy said. "I mean, we're saying that whatever chased Troy through the graveyard is responsible for all the missing kids. That's what we're saying, right?" Janis and Troy nodded in agreement. "Do you think they're all dead?"

Troy allowed her words to resonate. He had been thinking an awful lot about it. "I think that if one of those things gets you, then you become one yourself." A wave of guilt washed over him; his entire body stiffened, and he braced himself for what he was about to say. "I don't think Rob had the flu. I think he ran into one of those things last week. When I found him in my garage after the party, he wasn't himself. H-he came after me like he wanted to bite me."

"What?" Wendy gasped. "Why didn't you say something before?"

"I dunno. I guess I was trying to forget. I was hoping it really was the flu. I told the sheriff; I think he believed me. Maybe he knows something's wrong."

"You should have said something about this right away," Wendy scolded, then her stern look softened into a smile. "It's okay. It must have been scary."

"Yeah," Janis said.

"So, what's the plan? Because if there are that many"—Troy looked around, trying to calculate how many children were missing—"how are we going to stop them?"

"Well, we don't know that *everyone* turned into those things. Maybe it just kills you and you don't change," Janis said, trying to be optimistic.

And although it was a horrible attempt, Troy thought she made a good point. They didn't really know anything, not for sure. Rob had acted strangely, and Troy had been chased by something he couldn't explain.

"I don't know," Wendy said. "To be safe, we should assume everybody did. That's what always happens in the movies. You know, werewolves, zombies, vampires."

"Yeah, but those things aren't real," Troy said.

"Well, up until a couple days ago, there was no such thing as an Ojanox either, but I'd say we have a big Ojanox problem."

Troy cringed every time Wendy said the name and wished his mom had come up with something that didn't sound so ridiculous.

"If there's that many, we won't be able to stop them, but at least we can protect ourselves when the time comes," Janis said. "We have to try to make some adults believe us. What about your mother, Troy? She made up that story and seemed nice."

"I don't know; she didn't even believe me when I told her something chased me."

"What about the sheriff?" Wendy asked.

Troy figured if there was anyone in town who had an idea what was going on and could help them, it was Sheriff Primrose.

"So where do we start, and how do we convince people?" Janis asked.

Troy shifted where he sat in the grass just beneath the tire swings and scanned the playground once again. Which gave him an idea. They weren't going to get a larger crowd than the one they had right now, and he thought with the girls beside him, the other children might just take him seriously.

He looked from Wendy to Janis and then back. A strange sensation swelled in his chest. It felt a bit like butterflies, making his stomach shaky and his nerves all aflutter, but there was something exhilarating about it as well. A surge of confidence rose within him, and a strange warmness spread across his face and rushed to the top of his head. Then before he could talk himself out of it, he climbed onto the large truck tire at the base of the monkey bars and shouted loud enough for all the children to hear.

"Hey, everyone!"

The kids turned and looked at him as if he were nuts, then quickly refocused on what they had been doing.

"Everyone, I got something important to say. I'm serious!" he yelled. "Don't you even care that all our friends are missing?" Which seemed to grab the attention of a few of them. Caroline Smith and Kelly Rainey approached him where he stood atop the large tire. They were joined by Scott Cole and Steve Lambert. Then slowly, other children began to take notice and gravitate toward him.

"Okay, dork. What the heck are you talking about?" one of the fifth-grade boys barked out.

"My name is Troy," he said. "And I saw something the other day in the graveyard." Wendy's jaw dropped as she watched him, and Janis wore a smile a mile wide. "I was chased by something Monday after school. There was more than one of them, and they were really fast. I didn't get a good look because I was running, but they weren't friendly."

Looks of doubt and disbelief suggested that most of the children thought he was playing with them. But Troy saw another look on more than just a few of the faces in the crowd. It was a look of understanding. Some of the kids had seen something too. "Maybe some of you have seen these things yourself. I don't think I am the only one. What I saw almost looked like giant dogs, but they were super-fast and moved kinda funny."

"I thought I was the only one," Caroline Smith said. "I heard something in the backyard last night and looked out my bedroom window. It looked like a monster; I thought I was dreaming."

There was a stirring as many of the children nodded their heads in agreement.

"My friend Rob got sick last week, and then he showed up in my garage in the middle of the night. He walked to my house in his bare feet. At first, I thought he was sleepwalking, but then he tried to grab me. I think he wanted to bite me."

"You mean like a vampire?" Ralph Walsh, one of the third graders, asked.

"Yeah, I think exactly like a vampire. And I think that's why our friends aren't in school. I think if you get bit by one of those things, then you turn into one." Troy raised his hands not even aware of what he was doing.

Janis leaned over and whispered in Wendy's ear. "He's a natural. Where did all of this come from?"

"I have no idea," Wendy answered without taking her eyes off Troy.

"Look around." Troy spread his hands out to emphasize the number of missing classmates. "Where is everyone? There's no way they're *all* sick. In fact, I don't think *anyone* is. I think they all ran into one of those things. That's what I think."

"My brother never came home last night," a young girl said.

"My mom said that my cousin is missing and the sheriff can't do any-thing about it yet," another boy shouted.

"Oh, give me a break!" Jerry Santos, one of the popular fifth-grade students, pushed through the crowd. "You all sound like a bunch of babies. Everyone has the flu, that's all."

"You're wrong, Jerry. I saw one too!" The cry came from one of Jerry's fifth-grade classmates. "Something happened to my neighbors—the whole family. They all disappeared, just like that."

"I'm not saying this because I want to scare you!" Troy raised his voice. "I'm telling you because I want you to be ready. I want you to convince your parents that something's wrong. If we all do that, then there's a chance we can stop these things."

"What can we do?" someone yelled.

"The first thing is to protect yourself. We aren't sure, but we think that magnets might hurt them. Especially if you were to use a sling shot and the magnet was sharp."

"How do you know all of this, huh?"

"Yeah, how do you know, Troy?"

The children were skeptical but at least they were still listening, which was a good thing.

"Yeah, big mouth, how do you know?" Jerry continued to heckle.

"Because his father is the geologist at the quarry, and Mr. Fischer dis-covered a cave made out of lodestone." Wendy jumped onto the tire and joined him. "It's really old and filled with weapons the Lenni Lenape used to fight these things centuries ago."

Troy stared in shock to see her standing by his side on top of the tire. He had never said those exact words, but she had decided to run with it anyway. "My dad said that the whole cave is made from lodestone and that's what the weapons are made from."

"Oh yeah, what the heck is a lodestone, dumbass?" Jerry asked.

"It's a natural magnet found in nature."

"Oh, come on. That's stupid!"

"It's true! My mother is an archeologist in charge of the cave." Janis grabbed onto the top of the tire and pulled herself up. They were quickly running out of room, but having the girls on either side filled Troy with even more confidence, and it appeared to help the other children take them seriously. "She works for the Museum of Natural History, and she's been studying these things for a long time. Everything that Troy and Wendy said is the truth."

"If you don't believe them, then you should look at these," Janis said, pulling something from her pocket. She held out a handful of teeth and began to show them to the children standing closest to the front.

Cries of excitement and awe spread as Janis stepped off the tire and maneuvered through the crowd with her strange collection of sharply pointed teeth.

"Oh my God, it's true," one of the younger girls cried, and was met with a flurry of agreement.

"They're so sharp!"

"You need to tell your parents that something bad is about to happen," Troy said. "Then you need to find whatever magnets you can and a slingshot or a wrist rocket. It won't be easy to hit them, they're really fast, but it's better than nothing. And don't go outside at night. They chased me just as it was getting dark, so they probably come out more at night. That's why we haven't seen too many of them."

Troy watched the faces in the crowd change from doubt to acceptance. They had done it; they had convinced them. Maybe not Jerry and a few of the other fifth graders, but if the rest of the kids told their parents, then maybe that was enough to get the grownups to see what was going on. His eyes followed Janis as she made her way back to the tire, and spotted Miss Boriello standing there. She stared back at him with her hands on her hips and looked upset.

"Troy Fischer, Wendy Sirocka, and Janis Thompson, come with me to the principal's office … now!" Miss Boriello stormed off towards the school.

Troy knew they were in trouble, but they had done it. They had begun to spread the word. It was a small group, just a bunch of kids in elementary school, but every movement had to start somewhere.

CHAPTER 57

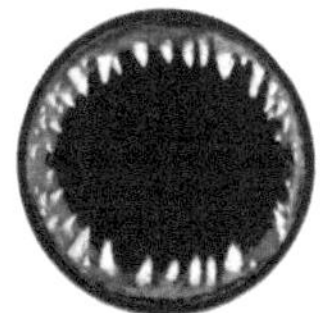

Deputy Rainey and the sheriff arrived at the mayor's house to find two cars in the driveway and received no answer after knocking on the front door for nearly five minutes.

"Thanks for covering my ass today," Carl told his deputy.

"It's my honor, Sheriff. Besides, it's the least I could do for almost killing you the other night."

"I'm trying to forget you did that." Carl jiggled the knob to find it locked. Then after pressing his shoulder against the door, he backed up and slammed his weight hard against the wood. The door flew inward. Deputy Rainey had his revolver drawn and at the ready.

"Mayor, it's Sheriff Primrose. If you're home, say something."

The men entered the hallway and spotted the blood trail. It painted the floor in large splatters and had dried dark brown, always dark brown. It traversed the staircase of the bi-level, leading both up and down, making it impossible to tell which direction the victim had traveled. If Carl had to guess, he would have said down.

The men navigated the staircase with their guns drawn, trying hard not to step in the gore-soaked treads. They entered onto the first floor to find a large family room. The blood was everywhere. It had poured out of its owner at an alarming rate, coating the tile and soaking into the carpets like a flood. It trailed to a back door smeared with bloody handprints.

Carl removed a handkerchief from his pocket and opened the back door. The trail that led outside into the backyard consisted entirely of the strange dark fluid. Carl imagined that whoever left the house had undergone a change similar to the one experienced by Felix Castillo.

"Sheriff, I don't think we're going to find the mayor."

Deputy Rainey had been right; neither Mayor Gilbert nor his wife were anywhere to be found. The blood trail began in the master bedroom, where an apparent struggle had taken place. Two separate blood stains on the bed indicated more than one victim, which confirmed what Carl imagined to be true, that the couple had been ambushed in the bedroom while they slept.

Only one of the neighbors had bothered to poke their head out to see what was going on. And when Carl and David knocked on the doors of the other seven houses on the block, no one answered. It was obvious to Carl that last night had been an unimaginable loss. While they had been busy fighting fires, more than half the town had slipped through their fingers. They had lost a major battle last night, the outcome of which tipped the scales drastically against them.

If there was any way to save the ones who were left, Carl knew he needed to get to them first. He had to keep them safe, and the only way to do that was to round up every last soul and get them some place secure. He was down men, and the plan he was considering would take an army. Still, Carl knew it was the only way.

What's the safest place in town? He needed something fortified and easy to protect, a place with only one or two entrances that could be guarded with an arsenal. Something like a vault or a bunker. *Son of a bitch!* It came to him in a flash; Carl knew exactly what he needed to do. They needed to get everyone into a bomb shelter, and he knew just the place. The high school basement was a shelter ... It was a goddamn fortress too!

The high school was built on solid bedrock, which had been blasted out to form the fallout shelter. The solid concrete and steel structure was stocked with K-rations and potable water and was originally designed for a percent of the town's population to ride out a nuclear winter if the commies decided to drop the big one. The fire department ran routine inspections and oversaw the job of keeping the place stocked. Most of the goods were old, but they didn't go bad; they were made for survival, not flavor.

Carl didn't want to estimate just how many of the town's citizens were missing and prayed there was enough room in the shelter. The real problem would be rounding everyone up and convincing them of the danger. Both he and Deputy Rainey needed to get back to the station and arm the rest of the fire department and anyone comfortable with a weapon. Then he needed to send out a message to every neighborhood in the Grove and get every living soul in that shelter before sundown. He knew if he failed, none of them would live to see another.

Burt didn't know what he was looking for. Something he had once come across in a medical text reminded him of what the children initially appeared to be suffering from. It wasn't a flu bug but a toxin with a biological signature that destroyed the cell proteins. There were clear characteristics of poisoning, but no toxin was capable of mutating the human body and taking over the host's mind. This sounded more like possession than poisoning.

And something in the blood was causing the cells to gravitate towards the magnet.

"I guess you've got too much iron in your blood, Dr. Malcolm," Burt mumbled to himself as he sat in his office thumbing through the medical journal. He laughed at his own joke, although there hadn't been anything all that funny or original about it. "Too much iron," he repeated.

He leaned back in his chair, took off his glasses, and rubbed the bridge of his nose, attempting to collect his thoughts. He wondered if maybe there was a bit more to that after all. The MRI had extracted something from Abe's body, and Burt had every reason to believe it was the infection itself. Also, the blood sample taken from Dr. Malcolm was attracted to the ladybug magnet. *What if the blood has been poisoned by something metallic?*

Then it clicked. Burt knew what he had been looking for in the medical text.

He flipped to the section where he believed he would find what he was looking for. He had already pored through the section on toxicity but had somehow missed it. Then, there it was, staring at him in black and white. *Mercury poisoning.* In severe cases, there was listed an array of symptoms almost identical to what the children had initially exhibited. High fever, bleeding of the gums, and the possibility of severe brain damage. Denaturalization of the cellular protein was also common in extreme cases. Of course, nothing as extreme as what happened to Felix Castillo, but Burt thought he was getting somewhere.

Heavy metals like mercury present in the blood would explain the magnetic attraction. In cases of mercury poisoning caused by ingesting seafood, it wasn't exactly the fish that ate the poison, it was a bacterial cycle. First the localized bacteria fed on the mercury contaminant, and then the fish fed on the bacteria. This went up the food chain until a human was infected from eating a bad piece of fish. Technically, a bacterium could absorb just about any substance and then infect a host. It was ubiquitous and resilient as hell. There were strains capable of surviving in arsenic, molten magma inside active volcanoes, and at the greatest depths of the oceans.

Burt had no idea where this bacterium had originated, but it was here now, and it was infecting the people of Garrett Grove. Science had always considered it to be a simple life-form, but what if it wasn't as simple as everyone thought? What if it was intelligent? This one was intelligent enough to control a human brain and make it do things against its will. Burt thought that sounded more than just intelligent, it sounded superior.

He got up from the desk and walked back to the lab with the book in his hand. "I just need to know how to stop you," he said out loud. "If the MRI killed you, then it's all in the strength of the magnet."

He returned to the microscope and looked through the lens again. He took the magnet from his pocket and placed it on the table next to the slide. The cells began to move once again.

"Maybe it just isn't strong enough," he said. "Maybe it has to be concentrated." Burt took the magnet and placed it directly against the slide. He looked through the lens to see if the proximity of the magnet altered the speed of movement.

Something did happen on the slide, only not what Burt expected. The red blood cells looked as if they were vibrating. They weren't traveling in one singular direction; they appeared torn between moving in many.

"Son of a bitch."

Then several of the cells started to separate. A cleavage line formed down the center, dividing them into two individual but very different cells on either side. *Dear God.* Burt watched as the magnet separated the infection from the human cell. The bacterial cell was like nothing he had ever seen before; it had attached itself to the blood cell and transformed it. The direct contact of the magnet removed the bacterium, leaving the red blood cell unfazed.

The strange regression occurred in one cell after another. The infected cell would begin to vibrate as if bombarded by sound waves, then the cleavage line would form, resulting in the separation of the parasite from the host.

"I got you, you bastard!" Burt shouted into the empty lab. He had successfully extracted the infection from the sample, just as the MRI had done to Abe Gorman. It had killed the man, and Burt was fairly certain the process would do the same to anyone else; he didn't put much hope in the possibility of anyone ever coming back from this. But he had found a way to stop it. That was if they could figure out how to subject the infected to a great enough magnetic force.

It wasn't Burt's field of study, but he had come up with a working theory. "Jesus Christ, Doc. You knew!" Burt realized Dr. Ziegler had been on to something. The man had dropped the ladybug magnet when the creature grabbed him. That had to be why he was holding it in the first place. "You knew, Doc, and the bastard killed you." Burt made the sign of the cross on himself and went back to work. Now more than ever, he wished the phones were working; he couldn't wait to tell Carl the news.

Bob Jones relayed the sheriff's orders to the rest of his men and was the first to arrive at the station with Ed Koloski. The requisition orders had been waiting for them along with a small arsenal of semi-automatic handguns, which Andrea had procured from the armory. Most of Bob's men were seasoned hunters and familiar with the operation of weapons. Bob doubted it would have mattered if they weren't; it sounded as if the sheriff was looking to outfit an army regardless. The men started to show up and were each met by both Bob and Andrea, who gave them the rundown as they were sworn in as official deputies of Garrett Grove.

Ed Koloski watched as the chief conducted a brief heart-to-heart with each of his fellow firefighters and did his best to convince himself this was really happening. Ed was a practical man, for the most part, who relied on logic and reason. At the moment, his best logic told him that seeing was believing. Still, some things were beyond understanding. Most of the men had witnessed something unexplainable last night, and now they were cut off from the rest of the world by something clearly intelligent.

The world held many mysteries about things that had yet to be explained. Natural occurrences like lightning and tornadoes had remained unexplainable for ages until someone finally identified their cause. Koloski believed what they were dealing with was just something humanity had yet to identify. He had a few theories and was leaning toward one that didn't sit well. Ed was under the impression that whatever had been found in the Texaco fire wasn't terrestrial. Or if it was, it was a life-form that hadn't been recorded in any of the science books. Logic told him it was something new, something far more advanced than any of them could comprehend.

"This is Sheriff Primrose to base." The sheriff's voice crackled over the dispatch speakers.

"Come in, Sheriff," Andrea answered.

"Did you equip the men from the fire department yet?"

"Almost done, Sheriff, just waiting for a few more guys to show up."

Koloski offered the chief a dubious glance. Five of their men were still unaccounted for. They had not responded when Bob sent out the call, and none of them had shown up to the meeting at the courthouse. Koloski was beginning to doubt if they would show up at all.

"Andrea, I want Bob Jones and Ed Koloski to meet me at the high school in half an hour."

She looked to the chief, who offered her a thumbs-up. "He said he will see you there."

"Also, I need Bob to leave two men at the station, then I want you to call Deputy Jenkins back to base. There are two cruisers with the keys in them at 12 Gray Street. Have Jenkins drive the men there to pick them up and bring them back to base; we are going to need them."

"That's Tara's address, Sheriff. What happened?" She held her breath and waited for his reply.

"I'm sorry, Andrea. Tara didn't make it." A pause as fatal as a stroke caused Andrea's heart to somersault in her chest. She froze at the microphone, waiting for the sheriff to continue. "We lost Deputies Kovach and Colbert as well ... I'm sorry."

"No—" She croaked, unable to move. *Not Joel.* The words echoed in her head. Andrea let out a noise that sounded like a feral animal caught in a trap, then she screamed at the top of her lungs. "No!"

Bob rushed behind the desk and scooped her into his giant arms as the dispatcher wailed like a lost child at the mall. Koloski watched and knew without a doubt that the five missing firemen were not going to make it to the station—ever.

CHAPTER 58

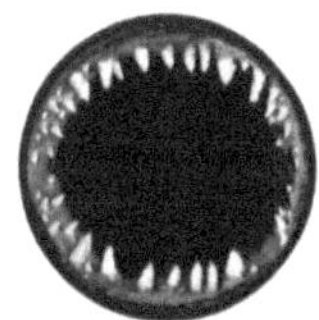

The stained glass windows at Our Lady of the Mountain depicted the Stations of the Cross. The large, ornate renditions of Christ's Passion sat on either side of the main room, refracting the morning sun in a polychromatic waltz of light. Father Kieran prepared for the noon Mass, stopping to pray at each station as he did. He blessed himself in front of the rendition of the Savior being comforted by Mary Magdalene.

Typically, the weekday Masses were light and reserved for the older members of the parish. Father Kieran didn't know who or how many might attend, since there was nothing typical about today. He finished his prayer, blessed himself, and approached the next station when he was startled by the sound of someone clearing their throat.

"Excuse me, Father?" the voice of a young woman echoed off the tall ceiling.

He turned to find a girl he had not seen in quite some time. Her parents were active members of the church, and she still attended Mass on the usual

Catholic holidays. However, it surprised Kieran to see her standing there, two hours before Mass.

"I didn't mean to interrupt you, Father. It's Allison, Allison Aigans." Dark circles hung beneath her deep bloodshot eyes; she had been crying.

"Of course, Allison. What's wrong, child?" Father Kieran blessed himself and walked to where she stood.

"I know I haven't been around much lately." She attempted to control her sobbing. "I'm scared, Father. My boyfriend is missing, and I know something terrible has happened to him." Allison looked around to the small cubicles on the back wall. "I was wondering if you had time for a confession?"

"Of course, right this way." Father Kieran led the girl to the confessionals and entered the one on the left-hand side. Allison stood outside, allowing the father a few moments before entering herself. She walked in and knelt at the tiny window.

"Bless me, Father, for I have sinned. It's been over a year since my last confession."

Father Kieran offered the sign of the cross. "In the name of the Father, and of the Son, and of the Holy Spirit, Amen."

Allison managed to control her tears and continued. "Father, I have taken the Lord's name in vain. I've disrespected my mother and father, and I have lied." She hesitated and took in a deep breath. "Father, I have fornicated with my boyfriend and have lusted in my heart. I've not been a very good Catholic and have been cruel to my sister."

"I see," he said. "Is there anything else you wish to confess?"

"Yes, Father." She took another deep breath and wiped her eyes with a tissue. "I think my boyfriend is dead."

Father Kieran straightened up in the confessional. "Oh. And why do you think that?"

"He's missing, Father. His parents went away and left him home alone. We were going to spend the week together."

"I see."

"Mick has been missing since Sunday. I went to his house, and he wasn't there. Also, his friends are missing as well. I think they went back up the mountain."

Father Kieran cleared his throat and listened intently as the girl continued.

"Saturday night, we all went to the old sanatorium. Do you know of it, Father?"

"Yes, I've heard stories. I believe it's quite dangerous up there."

"It is, Father, especially now. There's something up there, and I think it's evil. I think Mick went back there and he ran into it. Only this time, I don't think he was able to outrun it."

"You said it's evil. Did you see something, Allison?"

"We went there with Billy, and he had a flashlight."

Kieran nodded at the mention of the boy's name. He was beginning to get a clearer picture of what might have happened.

"We were about to go inside the building." Her voice tightened against the words. "Something ran across the front steps, only it didn't look like anything, really. It almost looked like smoke, or a cloud. It was very fast. Then it was behind us, chasing us, and we started to run. It flew over our heads like a bird or something. If it hadn't been for Mick, I think it would have killed us. You probably think I am crazy, but it's true, and I think it killed Mick and his friends."

"Bless you, my child." Kieran now knew how the mysterious boy had shown up on his doorstep. Billy Tobin was a warrior, much like King David. "I don't think you are crazy at all. I believe you."

"You do? I thought you might have me committed. I didn't know who to talk to, and there was no way I could tell my parents."

"Trust in the Lord, my child. You did the right thing. I have seen something similar, and you are correct, Allison; it is evil." He heard the girl's corduroy slacks swooshing as she moved in the confessional.

"What have you seen, Father?"

"I saw the same presence myself. It is evil, and it has begun to spread. I don't know what happened to your boyfriend, Mick, but the boy you spoke of, the one named Billy."

"Yes, Father." Allison raised her voice.

"Billy Tobin, I believe his name is. He showed up on my doorstep in bad shape." He listened as the girl gasped, and continued. "I tended to Billy and brought him to the medical center. He woke last night and is going to be fine. He is a fighter."

"Yes. He is, Father."

"So are you, my child," he told her.

"No, not me."

"Yes, you, Allison. You are the first to speak out against the evil that has come to the parish. You should be proud of yourself."

"I didn't know what to do, Father."

"I'd say you knew exactly what to do. You turned to the Lord. I believe James said it best: *If any of you lacks wisdom, let him ask God, who gives generously to all without reproach, and it will be given to him.*"

"Thank you, Father." Allison blessed herself.

"You are quite welcome, my child. Heavenly Father, Lord Jesus Christ, forgive this woman of her sins and give her the strength to stand against the evil that walks by night. Allison, I want you to say three Hail Marys and four Our Fathers, and I would like you to attend Mass at noon."

"Of course, Father."

"Allison, if the Lord called upon you to stand against evil, would you? Would you fight for the ones you love; would you fight for Mick?"

"Father." She had stopped crying. "I would do anything for the ones I love."

That was all Father Kieran had wanted to hear. Allison was the first. He prayed that more would follow in her footsteps. Simon Peter had been the first as well.

"You are absolved of your sins," he said. "Go forth, my child, and do the Lord's bidding. Stand against evil and spread the word of our savior Jesus Christ. In the name of the Father, and of the Son, and of the Holy Spirit, Amen."

"Amen. Thank you, Father." Allison left the confessional and walked up the aisle to a pew at the front of the church. She knelt and began her penance.

Father Kieran sat in the silence of the confessional for a moment, giving thanks to the Lord. He prayed for the protection of Allison and the rest of his flock and asked for guidance. *If it is your will, then surely you will deliver a sign; I trust in you, Heavenly Father.*

He left the confessional and stopped in his tracks. A line of people had formed at the back of the church. Father Kieran allowed a gasp to escape his lips. There were nearly twenty people gathered in the aisle. They had all shown up to receive confession. The Lord had delivered.

He looked at the faces of his parishioners; some he recognized and others he had never seen before. They all wore the same look. It told Kieran they had all seen something, something they couldn't explain. Something that could only be interpreted through the scriptures.

Stephanie watched the sheriff's cruiser leave the quarry from her vantage point at the entrance of the cave. She checked her watch to see it was nearly ten thirty. She couldn't imagine what was holding up Barry and Joe; they were always punctual, arriving at the dig site no later than seven a.m. every morning. She had heard the explosions earlier and hoped that nothing happened to them or anyone else. Last night, there had been that huge fire, and now this. Neither of the explosions sounded all that far away, and Stephanie figured they originated somewhere in town.

They had just started to work in the cave when Don was alerted to a problem on the job site. From what she overheard, it sounded like vandalism or something. Don had freaked out and sprinted to where the heavy machinery was kept. Stephanie watched with growing concern. Until now, she'd never seen him act like that. Then the sheriff's cruiser showed up, which looked like even more bad news. Don and the deputy walked around the machines for a few minutes and disappeared to the far end of the quarry. Whatever had happened, it wasn't good.

Then the deputy returned to his vehicle and left out the front entrance. She watched as Don stormed across the dust lot of the quarry, bounded up the steps of his trailer, and slammed the door behind him. It was obvious he was in distress, and she wanted to help.

"Gail, I'll be back in a few minutes. I got to check on something. Okay?" Stephanie made her way to the trailer.

She didn't bother to knock and walked into the supervisor's trailer to find Don standing in the middle of the room with his back to her. "Hey," she called. "Are you okay? What the heck was that all about?"

He stood there breathing heavy. The guy was pissed off; that much was obvious.

"It's nothing!" he barked.

Stephanie jumped back, shocked and caught off guard by his aggression. "Whoa, easy, cowboy. I just came to see if you were okay." Unsure how to respond, she walked up behind him and put her hand on his shoulder. "What's going on, Don?"

He spun around like a rattlesnake, reacting to the touch of her hand. His face was dark red, his fists were clenched, and his chest puffed out. The penetrating glare in his eyes frightened her, causing Stephanie to gasp. What happened next surprised her even more.

She felt the heat rise in her own face as it flushed like a fever; her breath hitched and became ragged. Donald stared at her, his features wild like some crazed animal. The moment seemed to stagnate as Stephanie watched his eyes glaring into her own for what felt like years. Then they lowered, focusing on her chest and proceeding to scan the rest of her in a most magnetic way. She had no idea she was doing the same until she caught herself watching his chest heave up and down like a prize fighter, then her eyes dropped even further. She felt herself go weak and reached for him.

Donald seized her by the shoulders and pulled her against him. Their mouths met and locked in a kiss that burned like the sun, their tongues intertwined and wrapped around one another's in a heated pulse. Then Donald lifted her off her feet. The next thing she knew, she was being carried across the room and lowered onto his desk.

Stephanie shoved his papers to the floor and pulled at his belt as he yanked her head back and kissed her deeper. Donald ran his hands down the sides of her body and grabbed at her breasts, squeezing them and pinching her nipples through her shirt. Stephanie moaned as he lifted the garment over her head and threw it to the floor.

She unbuckled his belt, unzipped his pants, and plunged her hand inside. It was hot against her flesh; it felt as if he were on fire. Burning, longing, and hard. She squeezed him. A gasp of pleasure escaped his mouth and echoed in the back of her throat as he kissed her deeper and stronger.

Donald dug his thumbs into the sides of her shorts and ripped them off in one motion. They caught on her boots but only for a second, then she was pulling him closer. She grabbed him and guided him into her. She tensed and offered a brief moment of resistance as he pushed himself into the warmth between her legs. Then she welcomed it, and he easily slid deep inside of her. Within seconds, they were in perfect synchronicity, working as one. Donald pushed and Stephanie arched her hips, counter to counter, movement to movement.

She cried out as he increased the pace and pulled her by the hair. Breathing into one another, their hearts beating in time. Their sighs and moans heightened, becoming louder and more urgent. Donald groaned, and Stephanie screamed, and just when the passion felt as if it were too much to bear, it happened. She clawed her fingers into his chest and felt the waves of his orgasm pulsate against that of her own.

Stephanie fell onto her back panting as Donald lowered himself and rested against her. He kissed her neck as their breaths slowed and steadied and their nerves recovered from the overload. She ran her fingers through his hair and pulled him closer. His warmth inside her was like nothing she had ever felt. She wrapped her legs around him, drawing him in even further, and started to cry. She didn't know if they were tears of joy or of sorrow. *What have I done?* She could barely ask herself. She pushed the thought out of her mind, refusing to go there. *Not yet.* For now, all she wanted was to feel his heart beating against her chest and to lay connected as one. Even if it was for just a minute more, she would take it. It was a perfect moment. She figured there would be plenty of time later to hate herself for what she had done.

Bob Jones and Ed Koloski met the sheriff and his deputy at the back entrance of the high school gym. The first thing the chief noticed when he stepped out and shook Carl's hand was how empty the parking lot was for a school day. Usually, there wasn't an available spot to be found, but now, as he turned three-sixty, scanning the area, it wasn't half full. The designated parking spaces of several of the staff sat vacant as well: Vice Principal Anderson was absent along with more than a few other teachers, including Mr. Gunderson, Miss Shane, and Mr. Rizlo.

The starkness of the grounds was unsettling, making the football field and track area look more like a deserted ghost town than a place where gym classes were usually held throughout the day.

"Christ, Carl. It's worse than we thought," Bob said.

"I got a feeling we don't know the half of it," Carl replied. "And we need to make sure it doesn't get any worse. When's the last time you and your men were down in the shelter?"

Bob knew what he was getting at and immediately loved the idea. "Me personally, about six months. But I send an inspection crew down four times a year to give it a once over, change batteries, and restock the water supply."

"I'd like to take a look. Can't remember the last time I was down there, probably during the flood."

Bob tried the large steel door facing the lot, half expecting it to be locked up tight, but it opened easily, allowing the men access to the gym. The place was emptier than the parking lot. The sound of their shoes echoed off the high ceiling as they squeaked across the polished wood floor. It was sinister how empty the place was. *Someone should be here.* Even if it was just a random student or a solitary gym teacher.

The men crossed the basketball courts to the far corner of the gym, where three doors stood. The ones on either side were vented on the bottom and labeled boys and girls locker room. The smell of perspiration and teen angst wafted from the slotted opening in the doors like discarded dreams. The door in the middle was of a different design, solid and sturdy and labeled Fire Dept Only. Bob retrieved a set of keys from his coat pocket, thumbed through them until he found the one he was looking for, and slid it into the lock. The thundering click of a bank vault being breached bounced off the back walls of the gym.

The door creaked on its hinges as Bob swung it open. It was heavy and thick and hadn't been oiled in some time. A mixture of mold, mildew, and dust rushed at them from the darkness. Bob reached for the wall and turned on the light, revealing a long concrete staircase that descended deep into the basement.

The chief led the rest of the men downward. The twenty or so stairs stretched out as if they went on forever, until finally, they arrived at the bottom, where Bob used the same key to open a second door.

The room was almost the size of the gym, just a bit smaller. The ceiling was high, and the main area was long and wide, with several doors situated on the side wall that led to the storage area, kitchen, bathrooms, and the air handler. Carl surveyed the room, estimating how many people could fit inside. He exhaled and cursed under his breath.

"What's the occupancy, Bob?"

"Well, it's designed to hold about a thousand, but I think if you crammed them in, you could bump that up to about twelve or thirteen hundred."

"That's it?" Carl asked.

Bob knew exactly what he was thinking, that there were a hell of a lot more people in town than that. Even if they already lost as many as he feared. That would leave a lot of people left out in the cold.

"What other shelters are there?" Carl continued to scan the room.

"Well, a few people have their own, but I wouldn't count on many opening their doors to the public. Folks can get a little funny when it comes to survival. It's kinda like asking them to give up their guns; you just don't do it. Know what I mean?"

"I do," Carl said.

Garrett Grove was a mountain community, and damn near everyone hunted. Owning a gun was like owning a set of snow tires—it was just smart.

"The basement at the medical center could do in a pinch. That could house a couple hundred more, I suppose," Bob said.

"Can you think of anyplace else?"

"Honestly, that's about it. There are a few other places that have basements, but nothing solid like a bunker or a shelter. If you're planning what I think you are, then you're looking for something strong. Not somewhere with more weaknesses than strengths."

"Exactly." Carl walked into the center of the large structure, taking in its defenses and features. Two-foot-thick columns sat staggered throughout the main area; the entire place had been fabricated out of poured concrete and reinforced structural steel. There were only two passages in or out. The first was the way the men had come in, through the gym entrance and down the stairs. The other was a back exit located in one of the smaller rooms. The air handler and filtration system area had an access hatch with a twenty-foot ladder leading to a janitorial closet located near the gym.

"I'm sure your men have checked the supplies recently, but I'd feel a whole lot better if you rechecked everything. Then we have a lot of work to do. I want everyone we can fit in either the center's basement or down here by five o'clock tonight. We're going to split our men between the two, and we're going to ride this thing out. I'm not willing to bet the lives of everyone in town that Mr. Gomes made it out before the bridge went down. At this point, we have to consider the possibility that the state police never got our message and they're not coming." Carl took his hat off and ran his hand through his hair. "It's a hell of a job to make sure that everyone gets the message. Some won't be easily convinced. But we need to make sure they understand just how serious this is. If they choose not to listen, they need to know they are on their own and we won't to be able to help them later."

The other men listened, a mixture of shock and awe on each of their faces as Carl laid out the particulars of his plan. It was a daunting task he was proposing, and they were already undermanned. Most of the heavy lifting would fall on the fire department, and Bob had a few ideas on how to get the most bang for the buck. He shared the information with the sheriff as Rainey and Koloski inspected the shelter's supplies and the integrity of the escape routes.

Carl needed to get back to the station, but first he had to stop at Chilton and check out the basement. There were a lot of patients who needed to be evacuated to the lower level, and that was going to take time and manpower. Two commodities they had little of.

CHAPTER 59

The three children stood in front of Principal Grace's desk, nervous and fidgeting like the James gang waiting to be sentenced. The two girls and the boy stared at the floor in a vain attempt to divert attention from their accusers. Miss Boriello glared at the little instigators with her arms folded and a scowl on her face. Both she and the principal scanned the children for any sign of weakness, but they had so far held their ground. The girls kept their emotions concealed with an innocent look that would have fooled even a hanging judge. Troy, however, allowed his eyes to dart from the left to the right as if he were trying to locate the nearest escape route. Principal Grace zeroed in on him; she had found the weak link. "Troy Fischer," she asserted. "Would you mind telling me just what you thought you were doing out there?"

Troy jumped and was sure his eyes doubled in size when she called on him. He had tried his best not to be noticed and prayed she would seek her answers from either Janis or Wendy. Sweat rolled down the back of his neck as he struggled to swallow, only to find his mouth too dry to perform the task. He had no idea what to say as he stood between his comrades, and looked to them for guidance. Wendy shot him a quick glance that resembled nothing like support. If he had to guess what she was thinking, it was close to, "*Say something, you idiot!*"

"I um," he said, looking to his cohorts one last time. It was no use, even Janis turned away when he peered in her direction. Troy knew he was on his own; the women had sold him out. His father had warned him this would happen one day, only he hadn't thought it would be so soon. There was only one thing left to do, and he figured that maybe this was the opportunity he'd been looking for. However, with the older women staring at him and the younger ones acting like they couldn't remember his name, he felt less than optimistic about the outcome.

"I was trying to explain to the rest of the school why so many students are out sick," he said.

"Is that so, Mr. Fischer? And what exactly did you tell everyone?" Principal Grace squinted down at him over her glasses, making him feel even smaller than he already did.

"I-um-told them-um." His ears began to ring, causing him to feel even more light-headed. *Why is it so hot in here? I think I'm gonna pass out.* "I told them what happened to Rob. He was really sick and showed up at my house Saturday night in his pajamas and bare feet."

Principal Grace's eyes opened a bit wider as she leaned back in her chair. Miss Boriello, who had her arms crossed up until that point, appeared to relax a little, and her face softened some.

"He didn't recognize me," Troy continued. "It was like he was sleepwalking. Then he came after me like he wanted to bite me."

"Bite you! Troy Fischer, your friend didn't try to bite you." The principal continued to stare at him with the eyes of a skeptic, but the look on Miss

Boriello's face was different. And despite the principal's initial reaction, she was still listening; they both were.

"Then he woke up and recognized me. He didn't know where he was, and he started shaking and fell down. My mom took him to Chilton, and then later she said he was getting better. But the other day I tried to call Rob's house, and nobody answered. I don't think he ever got better … not at all." Troy struggled to control himself and fought the tears. He didn't want to appear weak in front of all the women, but it was a battle he couldn't win. The more he thought about Rob, the worse he felt. The lump grew thicker in his throat, making it impossible to swallow, and a slow tremor started to crawl up his legs. He felt the first tear well up and overflow; it ran down his cheek and fell to the floor.

Wendy saw what was happening and so did Janis. The girls offered their support, each in their own way. Wendy took Troy's hand and squeezed it, while Janis put hers on his back and comforted him.

The grown-ups watched the emotional event unfold. The sight of the girls offering their compassionate support was moving and caused Miss Boriello to wipe the tears that had begun to mist over her own eyes. Principal Grace contained herself a bit better but appeared affected by the display as well.

"I'm sorry to hear about Robert. I know you have been friends for a long time. Troy, if you ever need to talk to anyone, that's what I am here for. You can always come see me."

He managed to stop the rest of the tears from falling, which was difficult with Wendy and Janis touching him. Their attention made him feel like crying even more. "Yes, ma'am, I know." He wanted to tell her everything he told the kids on the playground but couldn't push the words out of his mouth.

"Okay then." Principal Grace leaned over her desk. "The next time the three of you wish to address the student body, I want to hear about it first. It looked like you were inciting a riot out there." The three nodded their heads in agreement, although none of them knew what she was talking about. Whatever it was didn't sound good. "Mr. Fischer, might I suggest you consider running for class president. We are going to have an election in November, and I think with these two young ladies as your campaign managers, you would probably win by a landslide."

The principal smiled, and the children knew they had been spared. Troy had been certain they were in deep. He wasn't sure what had happened, but it felt like it went well.

"You three better go back to class," she said, and they walked out of her office, leaving the two women behind. The adults waited until the children entered the classroom before they started speaking.

"Jill," the principal said, "I didn't want to push him; he was clearly upset. What else did Troy have to say out there on the playground?"

Miss Boriello poked her head out the door to be sure the children weren't in earshot. "He was speaking about all the absenteeism and said he didn't believe there was a flu going around. He said something chased him through the graveyard the other day and they needed to be careful because there was something in Garrett Grove. He wanted the other children to warn their parents." Jill Boriello told her boss everything she had overheard before making her presence known on the playground. She explained how Troy delivered his message like George Patton preparing his men for battle. Initially, she had been upset with the boy, but after seeing his reaction in the office, she realized there was more to it. It hadn't been a joke, and he wasn't trying to scare the other children; Troy was scared himself. He believed every word he said, which was why he had been so effective.

Grace Austin looked up at the woman and took off her glasses. "What do you think about what's going on here, Jill? I've never known Sharon Walsh to not show up to work. There's no way for her to call with the phones out, but it's still so unlike her. Also, Karen Doremus didn't come in either. I had to combine two classes into one because I didn't have a substitute to fill her place. Where is everyone? Nearly half of the students are missing today. It just doesn't make any sense. Do you have any idea what's going on?"

"I don't know any more than you, but something strange is happening in Garrett Grove. I help my next-door neighbor, she's older and has a hard time with certain things. I bring in her papers and help with the groceries since she doesn't have any children of her own. Well, I picked up her newspaper this morning and let myself in through the front door. I called out, but there was no answer, which I thought was strange because she has no way of leaving the house on her own. She wasn't in the kitchen or her bedroom; she wasn't anywhere in the house. She was gone, Grace, and it looked like there had been a struggle. Her refrigerator door was left open; the milk had been spilt on the floor and left there." She started to choke on the words, finding it difficult to hold her composure. "There was something else on the floor. It looked like tar or ink. It was black, and it smelled horrible."

"Dear Lord, what did you do?"

"That's where it gets even stranger. I stopped by the sheriff's office to tell them about Mrs. Martin, and there was a big meeting going on in the courthouse. I didn't feel comfortable walking in there, so I stopped one of the deputies on his way in. I think his name is Kovach, and he said they would check into it. But he was in an awful rush, and I could tell by the way he was acting that whatever was going on in that courthouse was important."

"Do you think I should consider closing the school? It's not like we could get in touch with the sheriff if something were to happen. I thought the phones would be back on by now. It's beginning to feel a bit tense. These children are my responsibility, and their parents count on us to keep them safe. Is there more going on than either of us know about?"

"I don't know, Grace. I just don't know."

CHAPTER 60

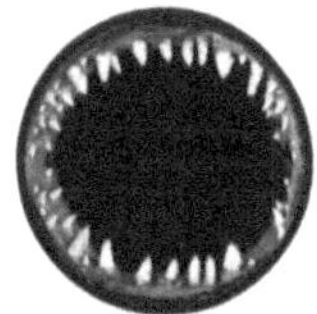

Lois took the stairs instead of using the elevator. After considering the recent fire that had taken place in the medical center, she wasn't about to risk getting stuck with the million things she needed to accomplish before picking up Troy at two forty-five. She had to convey the magnitude of the situation to her sister and brother-in-law, and prayed she wouldn't sound like a lunatic when she did. With her mind focused a bit more on what needed to be done rather than on where she was going, she rounded the landing and almost ran into the massive German Shepherd. The dog looked at her for a tense moment, then started to pant and wag its tail. Lois was startled by the sudden appearance of the animal and froze in her tracks. It was more the presence of the animal in such a place that struck her rather than the formidable size of the pup. She smiled, unsure how the dog would respond, and searched for a proper greeting. "Who's a good dog?" she believed would work.

And it had, as the dog sat down and raised his paw for Lois to shake. She took it and scratched the pup between the ears. "You are a good boy, aren't you?" Now that the dog was sitting, she could see he was in fact a boy, a big boy by the looks of it. "What are you doing here?"

"Baxter, come back here," the voice of a young girl called from one flight up. It was followed by the sound of fast approaching footsteps, then a sheriff's officer and a small child appeared.

"There you are," the girl said. "Bad dog, don't run away like that."

"I'm sorry about that. Oh-hello, Mrs. Fischer." Deputy Lutchen stood before her with a leash in his hand.

"Lois is fine," she said. "Nice to see you, Deputy Lutchen. And who is this?" Lois smiled at the girl.

"Dawn," she said, rocking back and forth and hiding behind the deputy's leg. The girl wore a pair of pajamas with fuzzy slippers. Her hair was wet as if she had just washed it, and she was carrying a doll that looked like it had also doubled as the dog's chew toy at one time.

"It's nice to meet you, Dawn." She turned to Ted. "What brings you here, Deputy?"

"Well, um, Lois. It's a long story, but we came here yesterday for the doc to check out my friend. Then we got stuck here last night. I'm sure you heard what happened." Dawn pressed against his leg and wrapped her arms around it.

"Nurse TenHove told me." Lois didn't want to say too much in front of the child and could tell the deputy was thinking the same thing. "My nephew was admitted yesterday, and I'm on my way to see him. My sister and brother-in-law are here with him."

"I think I saw them; the Tobins, right?"

"Yeah, that's them. I was hoping Billy would be released. I'd like to take a little trip with the family, you know, sooner than later." Lois watched the deputy's facial features deflate and knew he was about to say something she didn't want to hear.

"Mrs. Fischer." Lois held her breath and waited for him to drop the bomb. "There's been a situation—actually, a couple." He leaned closer so he could whisper without Dawn hearing. "The Gables Bridge is out of service as well as Sunset Road. We can't leave town."

Lois scanned his eyes to see if he was exaggerating. "What are you talking about?" Then she remembered the explosions she had heard early this morning. One of the blasts sounded like it came from the south side of town by Route 3, and the other one sounded as if it had originated from the mountain. *Dear God!* She suddenly knew why there had never been a warning siren. The explosions hadn't happened at the quarry—DuCain always sounded the horn before they blasted; it was the law. Visions of Pompeii and of lifeboats flooded into her head.

How could I have been so stupid? She had not only ignored the warning signs but she had also missed the lifeboats; she was a member of both groups. And now she had jeopardized Troy's safety as well.

"Mrs. Fischer, I didn't believe your son the other day. I should have."

Sirens sounded in her ears as the urgency to cry out welled up within her throat. Her hands shook, and her bottom lip had begun to tremble. "I need to see my sister," Lois said as she pushed past the dog, the deputy, and the little girl. "Excuse me, please." She covered her face and bounded up the stairs, trying to hide her hysterics.

"Nice to meet you, Mrs. Fischer," the child said as the woman ran past them.

Lois heard the innocent voice and burst into tears as she ascended the next flight and exploded onto the second floor. The door slammed shut, depositing her in an empty hallway. Lois doubled over and clutched her knees as the tears tore through her like an avalanche. She struggled to control her breath and fight it. Finally, she succumbed to emotion and wailed. *How could I have been so stupid? How could I have been so stupid?*

Ted had heard the frantic transmissions concerning the bridge and the Sunset Pass on his walkie-talkie. Things were unraveling at an alarming rate. An hour later, he heard the reports about Tara, Kovach, and Deputy Colbert. He could only stare at the radio as the sheriff broke the news to Andrea. He and Joel Kovach were working together when they found young Dawn hiding underneath her bed. And now the man was dead? That just couldn't be. Tara and Colbert? It wasn't possible. A thousand thoughts flooded his brain as he sat in silence, radio in hand and the world gone insane. He needed to be out there helping his fellow officers, but Dawn needed him too. With everything that was happening, there was no way she could survive on her own, although she had done a better job of it than most already. Still, she was Ted's responsibility, and he damn sure wasn't about to let her out of his sight.

Shortly after Ted heard the grim news, the sheriff asked him to check out the basement and said he would be arriving soon as well. So after Dawn had washed up and gotten a fresh pair of clothes, they headed down the stairs with Baxter leading the way and Drowsy, Dawn's favorite doll, tucked underneath her arm.

They opened the door to the basement, and Baxter was the first to enter. Ted and Dawn followed the pooch into the dark, musty chamber.

"It smells funny down here." Dawn wrinkled her nose at the damp odor.

Ted surveyed the room, which was big but not enormous by any means. He had been expecting the basement's footprint to be reflective of how large the medical center was. Which it wasn't; in fact, compared to the rest of the building, the basement was rather small. The foundation had been dug out only large enough to allow for the boilers, furnaces, and mechanical equipment. A network of pipes ran across the ceiling in every direction, along with the venting and filtration ducts. The pipes were painted an array of colors, and many of them were labeled for their various usage. There were hot-and-cold-water lines along with oxygen and nitrous lines as well. Several were labeled caustic, but Ted couldn't imagine what was inside them. Still, with all the equipment in the basement, there was room for quite a few people, which was what he had been thinking when he spoke to Greg the orderly this morning. Then the sheriff called and asked him to take a look. *Great minds.*

"I don't like it down here, Ted." Dawn nuzzled up against his leg and scanned the room. "It smells funny."

"Of course it smells funny." Ted looked down at her and smiled. "That's what leprechauns smell like. I bet there's a couple of 'em down here."

Dawn's stare doubled in size as she scoped out the room. "I don't see any leprechauns."

"That's because they're hiding. If you saw them, they would have to give you some of their gold." He struggled to keep a straight face.

Dawn let go of his leg and took a few steps into the room. A moment later, she was exploring with Baxter at her side.

"Not too far." He was happy to see a bit of her confidence return as she looked back and offered a quick nod, her head already filled with thoughts of leprechaun's gold.

There was a loud thud from the door behind them being thrown open. Baxter barked twice when Carl and Nurse TenHove entered the basement.

"How's our patient doing this morning?" Carl asked.

"Much better. I was worried with all the commotion going on last night. But I think she's more resilient than any of us. I can't even imagine after everything." Ted spoke low enough so that Dawn couldn't hear, even though she and the dog had already moved off to the middle of the basement floor.

Nurse TenHove shook her head with a scowl fixed to her face. "I see that dog is still here, Deputy." She peered at him over her glasses, then cracked a smile. "But I suppose it's okay, as long as you keep an eye on him."

Carl took several steps into the large area and removed his hat, surveying the room as he spun around on his bootheels. "Nurse TenHove." He turned to her. "How many patients do you have, and what will it take to get all of them down here before this evening?"

She stared at him with her mouth open as if he had asked her to construct an ark out of toothpicks, then the look of gobsmacked frustration was replaced as she began to ponder the question.

"Sixty-three, to be exact," she said. "But there are a few problems with that, Sheriff. First, nearly half of my staff didn't show up today. If I had enough orderlies and nurses, we could move the portable cots and supplies, which is the hardest part. The service elevator runs all the way down; the bay is in the back of the room." Doris took an exasperated breath and pointed to its location. "Transporting the patients is easy enough, except for the ones on the third floor. Many can't be moved. Some are on life support, and others are in critical condition or recovering from surgery. Without trained personnel, I wouldn't risk it. Then there's the elderly, and some are in traction. I'd say I have about twenty patients that I wouldn't try to move."

"Would you still make that recommendation if their lives depended on it?" Carl stood before Doris and stared into her eyes, allowing the gravity of the situation to register.

"I understand what you're asking, Sheriff. And yes, from a triage aspect, there are at least fifteen patients that I wouldn't even try to move." Doris bit down and wiped her eyes. She understood full well what this meant.

"Some might not even survive the trip in the elevator and will have to be left on the third floor. I will remain with them."

"We'll cross that bridge when we get there. Right now, you need to show me where you keep those extra cots, and I want you to start taking inventory of any medications and first aid equipment you'll need down here as well. Also, we're going to need medical supplies for the high school. There's going to be about twelve hundred there, and I want to be prepared for anything."

"I don't have the manpower to do half of this," she emphasized.

"I'll take care of that." Carl replaced his hat and nodded to his deputy. "Ted and Dawn will assist you with the medication, and I'll get you some help. I take it there's still some staff available; we're going to need all hands on deck to pull this off. I'm hoping there are a few doctors here as well?"

"I know Dr. Freedman and Dr. Halasz are around. The intercom system is working, so I can make an announcement if you need me to."

"I'm going to need a doctor at the high school along with first aid supplies ... just in case."

"How long do you plan to keep everyone down here, Sheriff?" Ted asked.

Carl inspected the area once again, noticing the girl and her dog, who had ventured to the far end of the basement. "As long as it takes or until help arrives. We can't be certain the outside world is aware of our situation. I doubt our messenger made it to Warren. By my estimate, and I pray to God I'm wrong, I believe we've lost somewhere between a third to one half of the town overnight. If we don't have everyone locked away safely in either this basement or the shelter, I don't think any of us will see the morning. For the most part, these things have been attacking at night, but that changed today. The ones we saw went down quick and didn't appear as strong as the ones we ran into the other night. I'm only guessing, but

I'm inclined to believe they are stronger at night. We've got just about six hours before sunset, then the shit is really going to hit the fan."

Ted and Doris understood the gravity of the situation and nodded in agreement. There was little time left to accomplish an impossible amount of work. If they managed to execute what the sheriff asked and they got most of the people into the shelters, there would still be losses. But when it came to triage, a calculated percent of casualties was acceptable, provided you could save the majority.

Andrea Geary sat at the dispatch station unable to wrap her head around the moment. What the sheriff had said just wasn't possible; she refused to believe it. Joel had gone to Tara's house to check on her whereabouts. She had told him goodbye just an hour ago and could still smell his Old Spice on her clothes. The clock that hung above her station thundered with every passing punctuation of the second hand. It hammered inside her, threatening to rip her from her delicate hold on reality. *You can't be dead.* Somehow, the sheriff had gotten it wrong.

She and Joel Kovach had been seeing each other for three months now and had done a good job of keeping a lid on it. They'd worked together for five years without Andrea ever suspecting he had feelings for her in that regard. Joel was as straight and by the book as they came, certainly not the type to date a coworker. But they had been talking a bit more lately, and then, out of the clear blue, he asked her to the movies.

Andrea couldn't have been more shocked and had probably insulted the poor guy by how surprised she acted. But she agreed, and they had a nice night out together. Joel Kovach was a gentleman who opened the car door for her and was always ready with a match for her cigarette. They'd gone out a few times after that, and Andrea believed she had feelings for him. But it had been over two months and she was still waiting for him to make a move. *Maybe he doesn't like me that much?* Joel had never gone any further than touching her breast through her shirt when they kissed. And Andrea had started to think that nothing would ever come of it.

That was until about two weeks ago, when Joel shocked the shit out of her. They had gotten together at her place, and Andrea made his favorite, roast beef with green beans and mashed potatoes. They shared a few glasses of red wine with dinner and had gotten a little drunk in the process.

Apparently, alcohol was the universal primer and all the confidence Joel needed. Before they could make it to the bedroom, Joel had Andrea half naked on the kitchen table with her legs in the air. From there, they proceeded to the couch, and then onto the floor. They finally made it to the bedroom with Andrea's clothes littered throughout the house like a trail of breadcrumbs. Joel had gone at her with an urgency to make up for lost time. They finished several hours later, bathed in sweat, exhausted, sore, and punch-drunk. Joel had literally fucked her brains out.

They had gone out again last Friday for an encore performance. Andrea had never experienced anything like that with another man and was beginning to think she might be falling for him. Joel gave her the eye at work when no one was looking, asked her to sneak off to the back room for a little foreplay and dirty talk. She even offered to give him a good tongue-lashing in the literal sense one day, but Joel was far too "by the book" to try such a thing at work. But Andrea figured he might *come* around.

This coming Friday was the night before Halloween, and neither were scheduled to work. They'd been looking forward to devouring each other like a couple of teenagers. Andrea couldn't believe any of it was real; she was damn near forty years old and having the best fucking sex of her life. She had never been so happy.

As far as Andrea knew, Sheriff Primrose didn't have a clue they were seeing each other. Which wasn't an excuse for how he treated her; the bastard had been so cold. He had delivered the news of their coworkers' deaths as if it were just another traffic accident. The room suddenly felt much smaller, and the ringing in Andrea's ears and the booming of the clock on the wall had become deafening. *You can't be dead; you just can't be.* She hadn't even kissed him goodbye.

Andrea struggled to pull herself together, but images of Joel's face appeared on every surface she stared at. Then Deputy Rainey entered the station and approached her. He wrapped his arms around her and said something that was lost in the din. Andrea stood up to accept his comfort and again allowed the tears to overflow their banks.

"I know," Rainey said. "I loved him too."

"Y-you know?" she asked between sobs. "Was it obvious?"

"Not at all." He held her a bit tighter. "I just saw the way he looked at you. He really loved you."

"Do you think so?"

"I know so. I'm a cop; it's my job to know these things."

"We were trying to be so careful." Andrea let out a strangled cry.

"No one has any idea. I'm sure of it." Rainey lowered his voice. "Are you gonna be okay, Andrea? Things are going to get crazy, and I think we're in for a fight. If you can't do it, just say so; we can get Jenkins to cover for you."

Andrea stepped back and wiped at her eyes. She took a heavy breath to steady herself, then straightened her shirt and walked back to the dispatch station. "Thank you, David, but I will be fine. I am a sheriff's deputy, and I am trained to work under pressure. Now, what needs to be handled first, and what exactly are we looking at?"

Rainey smiled and nodded his head. "Bob Jones is getting the fire department together. Half the men are going to the medical center and the other half to the high school. As soon as Jenkins and the other guys get back, we're going to start canvassing the neighborhoods. We need to let everyone in town know exactly what they have to do. It's going to be a big clusterfuck if we don't execute it to the letter. I hope your driving skills are up to snuff; as soon as we're ready, we'll be leaving the station."

"All right," Andrea said. "Let's do this."

Chris Fredricks was the first of Bob's men to arrive at the high school. The chief watched the boy, who had just turned nineteen and still lived with his parents, pull into the back parking lot in his Ford pickup. He was followed by another man in a similar-style vehicle, then another and yet another. Bob smiled as he watched the parade. If there was one thing you could count on, it was a fireman. Garrett Grove was a volunteer unit. These guys didn't do it for a paycheck, they ran into burning houses because they wanted to help people, and Bob trusted every last one of them. He counted at least ten heads so far, and the chatter on the radio told him that the other team had started to arrive at the medical center as well. He still hadn't heard from Deputy Rainey but wasn't worried a bit about the men assigned to his detail. *With any luck, we just might pull this off.*

Stephanie lay with her legs wrapped tightly around Don's waist and her fingers in his hair. She prayed that the moment wouldn't pass, that reality could wait just a bit longer to resume. Their breaths worked in tandem, and their pulses had synched. Stephanie could feel his heartbeat inside her and refused to let go. She couldn't remember ever feeling so completely fulfilled.

Don eased back and looked into her eyes. He pressed his lips against hers and kissed her; it was long, and slow, and bittersweet. Then she relaxed her grip and let him go.

He helped her off the desk and hugged her. "I had no idea it could be like that," he whispered in her ear.

Stephanie backed away and picked her clothes up off the floor. She offered a thin smile but didn't reply. She barely knew what she was thinking, let alone what to say, which even she found ironic.

"I've never—" he started.

"I know." She shrugged her shoulders and fumbled with her shirt. "You don't have to say anything. I was there too."

A smile as wide as the Ganges spread across his face. "What the hell was that?"

She approached him and kissed his cheek. "Amazing, that's what."

"Yeah, and then some. I sure as hell don't remember it being—"

She pressed her finger against his lips. "You talk too much. We don't need to fill the silence with words that won't change anything. It was perfect … Let's just leave it at that. It can't go anywhere." *Christ! I just fucked a married man!* She buttoned her shorts and kicked on her boots as the tears started to fall, then she rushed past him toward the door. Donald grabbed her by the arm and spun her around before she could leave.

"There's nothing left of my marriage … not that there ever was. We only got married to raise Troy. You said it yourself; life doesn't always turn out the way you expect it. Well, I sure as hell didn't expect this, but it happened, and I'm not letting you walk out that door."

She stood with her mouth open and her brain spinning a mile a minute. *What the hell is happening? I'm not stealing another woman's husband!* After what Brian had done to her, how could she entertain it ... even for a minute? But no man had ever made her feel like that before. It had been raw and animalistic, and so impossibly perfect. *Christ, what a horrible bitch I must be. Who does this?*

Donald took a step closer, and Stephanie's heart screamed; she put her hands against his chest and pushed him away. "We both need to calm down and think clearly. We have a lot of work to do, and if I stay in this trailer a minute longer, we both know what will happen. So, I'm walking out this door and going back to work. Meet me and Gail in the cave when you've got yourself together. We'll talk about this later."

Donald put his hand under her chin and lifted her head. She allowed him to kiss her, and then she walked out of the trailer and closed the door behind her.

CHAPTER 61

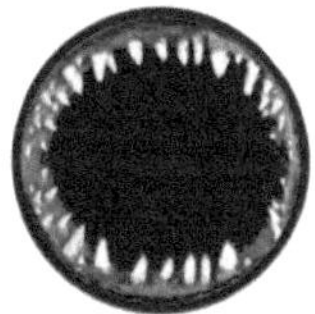

Lois struggled to control her sobs, her breath raking in her chest, heavy and fast like a diesel engine. Her hands trembled, and the hair on her arms bristled as if in tune to the static emptiness of the medical center. The acrid tang of disinfectant fused with the underlying stench of bedpans. Lois winced and forced herself to focus. She couldn't afford to lose it now; there were others who needed her. But as she emerged into the stark fluorescent light of the second-floor hallway, her grip on sanity slipped even more.

She searched to the left and right, expecting to find a doctor or even an orderly making their rounds. But there was no one. The long span of polished tile stretched out before her like a deserted runway. The drone of a nearby vending machine was the only sound, a jarring contrast that Lois could feel resonating in her teeth. Hunched over with her hands still on her knees, she focused on the small square of flooring and exhaled. The sudden squeaking of rubber soles on tile startled her. Lois looked up to see a young nurse exit one of the rooms. The girl plodded toward the reception area with her eyes glued in front of her and hadn't seen Lois doubled over in the hallway. The nurse moved fast, as if she had too many tasks to accomplish and no idea where to begin. Lois could see the girl was struggling as well, but somehow, she had managed to pull herself together and focus on the job. A wave of guilt washed over Lois as she watched the young girl. With all the strength she could muster, she straightened her back, wiped her cheeks, and approached the desk where the nurse stood, separating medications into tiny plastic cups.

"Excuse me."

The girl jumped, spilling several of the pills onto the counter.

"Oh." Her hands shook as she scrambled to gather them. "I'm sorry. I didn't see you there."

"I didn't mean to startle you. I was looking for my nephew; his name is Billy Tobin." Lois watched the girl fumble with the medication and could tell from the glazed look in the nurse's eyes that she was on the verge of tears. Pushing her own fear and anxiety to the side, Lois reached over the desk and took her hand.

"Here," she said. "Let me help you with that." Lois walked around the counter.

"I'm sorry," the nurse said in a voice as frail as a shiver. Then the tears started; the girl broke down and threw her arms around her.

Lois felt the child's sobs convulsing and radiating throughout their embrace. She hugged her back and forced herself to stay strong. "I thought I was going to be the only one who cried today."

The nurse chuckled between a series of tears, then stepped back and attempted to regain a fraction of her composure. "I'm sorry. That's so unprofessional of me."

Lois noticed the girl's name tag: Carole. "I don't think so." Lois pulled a tissue from her purse and handed to her.

"Hardly anyone came to work today." She struggled to control her breathing as she spoke. "At first, I thought—well, to tell you the truth, I don't know what I thought. But people have been talking, and some of the stories are starting to make sense after everything that's happened in the past twenty-four hours."

Lois searched for some words of reassurance, though she'd been struggling herself.

"Carole, right?" The girl nodded. "My name's Lois. I know exactly how you feel. I can't even count how many times I've cried today. You should have seen me a few minutes ago." Lois brushed a piece of hair from the girl's eyes. "But you know what? You came to work, and you stuck around because you know people are counting on you." Carole nodded in understanding. "I know your patients are glad you're here. And I also know we're going to get through this."

"Thank you." Carole wiped her cheek and picked up the medicine bottle. "Do you think you could stay and help me for a few minutes, just until I get the morning meds out? I never had to do it by myself before." Her giant eyes pleaded as she fought to hold it together.

"Of course. I'd be happy to. And when we're done, I want to introduce you to my nephew Billy."

A shadow crossed the girl's face. "I was a senior when Billy was a sophomore. I don't know if you've heard about Billy's girlfriend, Debbie—Debbie Horne?" Lois shook her head; she had never met the girl. "Debbie was in a car accident yesterday ... She didn't make it. I don't think Billy knows yet." Carole's voice trembled as she delivered the news.

Dear God. How much more? A black cloud had settled over Garrett Grove. The extent of grief that plagued the town in such a short period of time was impossible to comprehend. Lois tried to recall when it all started.

Saturday night, just five days ago? It had all started when Rob showed up in her garage dressed in only his pajamas.

"We're not going to say anything about that to Billy. He's been through enough already, and I don't want to upset him any more."

Carole nodded and looked up when a woman's voice broke over the intercom system. *"Attention all staff. There is a mandatory meeting in the cafeteria in fifteen minutes. Please be advised, in fifteen minutes, there will be a mandatory meeting for all staff. Thank you."*

"That can't be good," Carole said. "Lois, will you come with me, please?"

Lois checked her watch and smiled. "Of course." There was still time before she had to pick Troy up at school. Together, the women finished filling the tiny plastic cups and distributed the medication to the patients on the second floor. Then they checked in on Billy to find him sitting up eating his breakfast, which was the best news Lois had received all day. She hugged Alice and Will and promised she would be back soon.

She had been mistaken.

It took longer to distribute the medication than either woman anticipated, and Carole and Lois arrived several minutes late to the meeting. They entered through the double doors of the cafeteria and were bowled over by the crowd. The place was packed and not just with medical staff but a good number of the town's volunteer firemen. Head Nurse TenHove stood at the front of the room, flanked by Deputy Lutchen, the little girl named Dawn, and her dog. Lois scanned the room, overwhelmed by the sea of faces, most of whom she knew. It was a stark contrast to how empty the rest of the building was.

Lois and Carole started to push their way through the crowd when the doors burst open behind them. Lois spun around to find herself face-to-face with Carl.

She could read it in the expression on his face: *God Dammit, Lois. What the hell are you still doing here?*

He shook his head, then pushed his way to the front of the room. "I need to talk to you," he whispered to her.

Lois felt as if she had betrayed the man yet again and by doing so had also put her family in harm's way. She studied how weary he looked. Fresh crops of grey hair were visible at his temples, and his face was ashen and hard, as if he had aged years since yesterday.

He stood in front of the room and removed his hat. "We are officially under a state of emergency," he addressed the crowd and was bombarded by a flurry of comments and questions. He raised his hands and continued. "As you can see, a lot of people are missing. And if we don't work together, things will get a whole lot worse."

"What's going on, Sheriff? Where is everybody?" Dr. Freedman shouted.

"There's been an outbreak, Doctor. It started over the weekend and has continued to spread. We don't fully understand it, and that's why we need to get everyone to safety. This infection killed Dr. Malcolm and Dr. Ziegler. It appears to manifest in the body and control the host. A lot of people have already been infected, and we need to protect ourselves. This thing has killed four of my deputies already."

"How are we going to protect ourselves if it's killing cops?" a young man shouted.

"We're moving everyone into the shelters, and that's why I need you. The patients can't fend for themselves, so with the help of the fire department, we plan to move everyone into the basement. We're going to ride this out till help arrives."

"Why isn't help here already?"

He held his hands up again. "I'm afraid we're on our own. Both the Gables Bridge and the Sunset Pass have been destroyed."

"What?"

"What do mean destroyed?" Dr. Freedman shouted.

"Someone broke into the quarry and stole some explosives. They sabotaged the bridge and the Pass."

The room erupted in a flurry of voices louder than before. Most of which were cries of concern rather than screams of unacceptance. They had all seen something, had all heard the strange shrieks or witnessed their neighbors disappearing one by one over the past few days.

"No one may be coming for a little while. So I need to get everyone into the shelters, and I need your help. But time is of the essence, we have until about five o'clock. We need to be locked up tight before it gets dark. So listen to the firemen and work with them. Nurse TenHove is in charge; if you can't find either her or myself, speak to Deputy Lutchen." Carl pointed to Ted, who had given his hat to the little girl holding his hand.

Lois scanned the faces in the crowd, noticing how the combined looks of loss and despair were replaced by a sense of urgency. Carl had given them something to do and, with it, instilled a sense of purpose. Lois smiled as the crowd began to rush to their assigned tasks.

Nurse TenHove coordinated the allocation of work with the help of Deputy Lutchen and Derek Fisk from the fire department. For the most part, everyone had taken the sheriff's message seriously. However, there were two men who did not agree with Carl's all-for-one mentality and took it upon themselves to leave after the meeting ended.

Both Mark Walsh and Theo Spellman worked in the janitorial department. They had witnessed what happened in the imaging wing last night and figured they were better off on their own. Mark left out the back door, hopped into his van, and headed home to ride out the storm with his elderly mother. Theo simply walked out the front and never punched his timecard. He drove home to be with his pregnant wife, Nancy, and loaded his shotgun. He had his own family to care for and wasn't about to play hero for four bucks an hour. He damn sure wasn't about to die in some dusty basement. Neither man ever returned to work, or anywhere else for that matter.

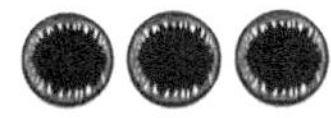

Carl took Lois by the arm and led her down the hall until he found an empty room, then urged her inside.

"Goddammit, Lois. I told you to leave. What are you still doing here?"

"It isn't that easy. The phones were out, and I couldn't get in touch with Alice. Billy is upstairs, and Eric is still missing. Then Troy gave me a hard time about missing school. I swear I must be the only mother whose child wants to go to school." Her voice trembled as she told him. "I can't explain, but the more I knew, the more reasons I found to talk myself out of it. It was all just so impossible I didn't know what to think."

He started to pace the floor. "Did you think I was making it up? Have I ever given you a reason not to take me seriously?" He rubbed his temples and squinted as if in pain.

"No."

"Then why now, of all times, would you choose not to listen? Christ, you should be miles away from here. I can't guarantee I can keep you safe."

"That's not what you told everyone in there."

"No, but if I said they might die tonight, I'd have a damn panic on my hands."

"You don't think you can protect them? Don't you think the shelters will work?"

"Honestly … I don't know. I hope so, but we have no idea what the hell we're dealing with. It's nothing anyone has ever seen, and it's superior in every way. Why didn't you leave, Lois?" Carl took his radio off his hip and handed it to her. "Do you still have the gun I gave you?"

She nodded and pulled it out of her purse, then she took the radio from his hand.

"Hold on to this in case we get separated. Just press the button and talk right here." He pointed to the microphone. "I have another, and I'll hear you."

"Thank you." She watched it tremble in her unsteady hands.

Carl checked his watch. "We still have time. You said Troy is at school. At two thirty, I'll take you there myself, we'll pick up Troy, and then I want you both in the shelter at the high school, no questions."

"Why not here with my sister and her family?"

Carl opened his mouth to speak, then stopped and looked away. Lois knew he was hiding something but didn't press further. "We'll figure it all out later," he said. "In the meantime, I need your help. There are a lot of patients that need to be relocated to the basement, and there's more work than people to do it. Maybe you could talk Alice and Will into pitching in too."

She studied his eyes, which looked even older than they had a minute ago. Deep crow's feet crawled from the corners as if he hadn't slept in weeks. Lois deposited the radio in her purse and took out her cigarettes. She lit one, then offered the pack to Carl, who accepted.

"I'm sorry I didn't listen—again. How are you going to get everyone into the shelters?"

He took a long drag and exhaled. "I don't think I will. Some—but not everyone. A good number will think they'd be better off on their own, and I can't force them. But I have an idea that should convince most."

Lois studied the lines in his face, allowing her heart to tear apart more than she thought it possibly could. She had put him through so much, and he was still going out of his way to help. Her marrying Donald had destroyed him, and then he had gone off to fight, which affected him even more. The war had changed Carl. It wasn't something everyone could pick up on, but she had and was sure that Burt had as well. He carried something back with him after leaving Vietnam, a burden he shared with no one. It was written on his face like the deep lines he now wore.

"Are you okay?" He had been talking to her.

"What?"

"There's a lot to do. I asked you if you were up to this."

"Yeah, I'm all right," she lied.

Carl held the door open for her, and they left the room empty once again. The smoke from their cigarettes was the only proof that they had ever been there at all.

When Lois walked into the room, Alice seized her into a bear hug and refused to let go. Billy, who had been sitting in a chair earlier, was now on his feet attempting to stretch his legs.

"Aunt Lois, how are you?"

"Never mind me, what about you? Are you sure you should be standing?"

"It's okay," he said. "I'm torn up a bit, but it's good to walk some. My head bothers me more than my legs. I still don't remember too much."

"Well, don't overdo it just yet," she said as Nurse Carole entered the room, causing Billy's disposition to brighten.

"I'm here to check on my patient."

Lois had asked the girl to show up and occupy Billy so she could speak to Will and Alice.

"If you wouldn't mind excusing us for a few minutes." Carole smiled while the rest of the family retreated to the hallway.

Lois told them about Carl's plans to get everyone into the shelters. Alice and Will had been through so much with the boys in the past few days, and the news didn't strike them nearly as absurd as Lois thought it might. There was some doubt, and Will jokingly asked if she'd been drinking, but they were rather easy to convince. The empty halls of the center and the fire the night before had primed them for just about anything. Also, they'd been served breakfast by a Sheriff's Deputy, a little girl in her pajamas, and a German Shepherd. They already knew something serious was going on.

Will and Alice agreed to help in any way they could. They always liked Carl and knew he cared about the people in town, even Billy, who had been one royal pain in his ass.

Stephanie and Gail were standing before one of the murals when Don entered the secondary chamber of the cave. He nodded and looked around for the other men. "Where are Barry and Joe? Don't tell me they're still not here?"

"Never showed up," Gail replied and snapped several photos in quick succession.

Stephanie caught his eye as he approached, and smiled. He offered one in return, then they both looked away.

The mural they examined the previous day was the most intriguing piece of work Don had witnessed so far. It was an accurate depiction of Earth's position in the solar system. The fact that it had been painted over five hundred years ago was mind-boggling.

The painting they now focused on was also of the planet, only in this one, the strange cloud had encompassed the earth, making the sphere look as if it were enveloped in fog. It was dirty and dark and looked toxic. The previous murals showed the cloud in the cosmos as a massive singularity, but this depicted it as part of Earth's atmosphere. Don had no idea what any of it meant but still found them fascinating. After all, it'd been a very long time since human eyes had gazed upon any of this.

Gail snapped away, with the flash of her camera making the place look more like a disco or one of the rooms in Troy's haunted house.

Stephanie moved on to the next mural and brushed against Don when she passed. "Oh, excuse me," she whispered, and continued.

The fourth mural wasn't a view of the planet, or even from space—it was a depiction of life on Earth. Reptiles and other lizard-like creatures had been drawn on the walls and colored with vibrant inks. The creatures appeared prehistoric, or at least some of them did. One looked similar to a small dinosaur that Don had seen in *National Geographic Magazine*. The paintings also held a striking similarity to the ones at the entrance of the cavern. The dark smoke, present in the picture of the woman and the holy man, was also visible in these and covered the reptiles in a most intrusive way. It surrounded their heads and invaded the beasts through their eyes and nostrils.

"Is that the same stuff surrounding the earth in this mural?" Don compared the two.

"It looks that way, doesn't it?" Stephanie nodded. "What do you make of it?"

"Well." Don thought about it for a moment. "Here it looks like a cloud or some type of pollution. It isn't painted in a flattering way. The Lenape didn't like it. But they didn't have pollution back then, did they? And here the animals are breathing it in, just like the murals in the front of the cave." Don stepped closer to the wall to get a better look. "Look at this. The snake and the lizard have those same black eyes, just like the man and woman in the other murals—just like it!" Don felt he could almost remember what it all reminded him of; it was on the tip of his memory.

"Pretty good, Mr. Fischer." Stephanie nodded in agreement. "Very perceptive, I'm impressed."

Don realized Stephanie knew exactly what she was looking at and had long before she arrived on his job site. She was hiding something. He hadn't been certain of it before, but their dynamic had changed, and now, he was positive.

CHAPTER 62

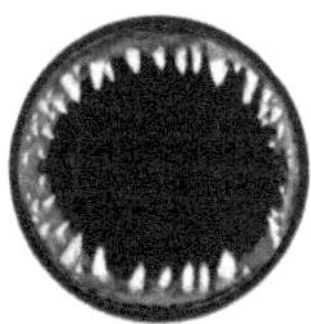

Bob Jones walked through the hallway of the high school, feeling like a giant as he passed the lockers and classrooms. He had gone to Garrett High, but the place felt a whole lot bigger back then. Of course, he had been smaller himself, but there was more to it than that. It wasn't just a matter of comparative perception; everything appeared larger to children. Bob figured it had more to do with the larger worldview shared by adults that made the places of one's childhood appear smaller. It happened after you went out on your own and had taken in all the experiences that eluded childhood. The good as well as the bad.

The world had happened to Bob after graduating from Garrett High. Prior to his senior year, the furthest he had ever been outside of town was his cousin's house in Pennsylvania. He had had one girlfriend, Sally Simpson, who he believed he would marry one day. And back then, he had even wanted to be an architect.

The country hadn't gotten involved in Vietnam yet, and although some of his friends had tried to convince him to join the Army, that hadn't interested Bob. He planned to attend college after high school; however, life had other plans. Bob's father suffered a stroke and become unable to work. And that had been the end of Bob's college plans, along with any dream of ever becoming an architect. He got a job in a print shop to help with the bills and found himself working an average of sixty hours a week.

He and Sally broke up the same year his father had the stroke, never to be married, not that Bob would have had much time for it. Which was no consolation, and it had hurt like a bitch. A few months later, Sally met a man named Earl Hillman and married the guy in a flash. Earl lived in Warren on a large piece of land his grandfather had left him. It was set far enough back into the woods and away from the neighbors so none of them could hear Sally scream on the nights when Earl came home drunk and proceeded to beat the tar out of her. The beatings went on for a few months, with each consecutive injury worse than the previous. Sally was treated for a concussion one week; the next, she was getting her arm set in a cast. And even though the couple lived in Warren, news traveled fast. Sally still came into town to visit her parents, who became increasingly concerned for her safety.

Bob had heard the stories about Sally and ran into her at the store one day. She wore a large pair of sunglasses, but the bruises under her eyes were visible. He offered to intervene, and Sally told him to mind his own business. And there was nothing more Bob could offer to do; it wasn't like she was his girlfriend anymore, despite how he still felt about her.

The following week, Sally showed up to see Dr. Malcolm with three broken ribs and a fractured pelvis. She was in rough shape, and Malcolm wanted to admit her on the spot, but Sally had refused, settling for a compression wrap and a prescription of codeine.

Bob decided he would approach Sally one more time and try to talk some sense into her. But she stopped showing up in Garrett Grove altogether. As the weeks passed without a word from Sally, her parents became more and more alarmed. Then Earl stopped answering their phone calls and had become even more elusive than usual.

Sally's folks finally notified the state police in Warren, who sent a patrol out to Earl's place to talk to the couple. The man was drunk when the officers arrived, and Sally was nowhere to be found. Earl became defensive, took a swing at one of the cops, was handcuffed and tossed into the back of the car. It was obvious to the troopers that the man was hiding something. They decided to take a tour of the property and found a freshly turned piece of soil the size of a grave.

Earl had killed Sally with a hunting knife and then buried her face down under nine inches of dirt. He hadn't even taken the time to properly hide her body. He had shown her no more respect in death than he had while she was alive. The troopers then removed Earl from the vehicle and stomped the living shit out of him. They broke his jaw, collarbone, and his left arm, which was proceeded by his court-appointed lawyer accomplishing the impossible. The case was overturned because the defendant's rights had been violated by the two officers. The charges were dropped by the state, and Earl Hillman had been free to go.

Life didn't change all that much for Earl. He still frequented the bars most days and began to boast about how he beat the case and showed those bastard cops just who they were messing with. The only thing that was different: he no longer had a live-in punching bag to come home to.

That was around the time Bob Jones took up drinking. He had suddenly found a reason to visit the bars himself, at least the ones that Earl Hillman preferred. He had been frequenting a dive called Sneaky Pete's, just enough to not look out of place but not often enough to be noticed.

"I'll take a Bud, and give my friend here another," Bob told the bartender one Saturday afternoon.

Earl looked up and raised his glass. "Thank you, friend."

The bartender poured Earl another shot of Wild Turkey and set a Bud long neck in front of Bob, who took a long sip and lit up a smoke.

"Want one?" He offered a cigarette to Earl, who accepted. "I see you 'round here some. Name's Brady, Cal Brady." Bob held out his hand.

"Earl. Nice to meet ya. From town?" he slurred.

"Na," Bob said. "Parker Plains, out by the rubber mill, been working there for the past two years. You know how hard it is to get the smell of burnt rubber out of your clothes?"

"Can't say that I do." Earl lifted his shot and sucked it back. "Woo, that'll put hair on yer nutsack. Know whatta mean, Cal?"

Bob laughed and took another sip of his beer. "Sure do. Bartender, another one for my friend here."

The bartender poured the drink and gave Bob a look that suggested, *Be careful of the company you keep*. Bob returned an understanding nod.

"Thanks, man." Earl turned from his refill. "Excuse me, gotta drain the old lizard," he said as he got up and made the drunken shuffle to the men's room.

Bob smiled and waited until the door closed behind the man, then took a calculated look around the bar to make sure he wasn't being watched. He removed a small piece of tinfoil from his cigarette pack, unfolded it, and emptied the powdery contents into Earl's whiskey. Giving the drink a quick stir with his finger, he crumpled the foil into a ball and waited. It hadn't been easy to find what he was looking for, but his longtime friend Peter Gillick had just gotten a job at Chilton Medical. Peter had been a good friend of Sally's as well and didn't want to know the details. "This will do the trick, trust me," Pete assured him when he handed Bob the packet of pills.

Earl returned to his place at the bar, downed his shot and several more after, and thirty minutes later was slurring his words with his head bobbing up and down like a yo-yo. The bartender, now pissed, came over to evict the man, who apparently made it a habit to get shit-faced and obnoxious. Bob laid a fifty on the counter and leaned toward the barkeep. "Please excuse my friend. I think he's had a little too much to drink."

The man took the crisp bill, slid it into his front pocket, and gave Bob another look that suggested, *I didn't see a fucking thing.*

Bob scooped up Earl, walked him outside, and deposited him into the front seat of his pickup.

The man didn't wake up once during the two hours it took to drive to the Queensland Pine Barrens. He finally started to stir when Bob pulled off the road and turned onto the wooded path.

The Pine Barrens were an expansive stretch of acreage that served as a game preserve and national forest. It was easy to get lost in such a massive piece of wilderness, but Bob knew where he was going and had mapped out the trails weeks prior. They were less than a mile from the spot he had picked out when Earl raised his head and opened his eyes.

"Wha the faah?" Earl slurred, then noticed the duct tape that bound his hands and feet. He struggled to move, but Bob had wrapped the seatbelt around him to secure him in place. Earl scowled at the man driving the truck, and a shock of recognition smacked his face.

"You, wha? Why ya do this?" He was still drunk and sedated from the Rohypnol.

"You like that, Earl? Keep struggling; won't do you a damn bit of good," Bob said.

"Lemme go, ya fuck!"

"Ha-ha," Bob laughed and punched Earl in the mouth. The guy's head snapped hard to the right; his lips split open and began to bleed. Bob thought he had possibly killed him right there and felt a surge of disappointment when Earl's head dropped to his chest and stopped moving. A second later, the guy started to snore, and a huge smile spread out across Bob's face.

Earl Hillman woke up an hour after Bob had parked the truck and carried him into the woods. He found himself seated on the forest floor, propped against a large pine with his arms drawn and duct-taped behind his back. Struggling to lift his head, he looked up to find Bob standing over him. After several moments of futile struggling, he stopped resisting and faced his captor.

"Why?" he asked. "What I do to you?"

Bob punched him in the face again, knocking out two teeth in the process. "It's not what you did to me," Bob hissed and knelt in front of the man. "It's what you did to Sally."

A look of disgust slicked Earl's features. He spit a bloody clot onto the ground and snarled. "Fuck that bitch and fuck you too!"

Bob nodded and reached into the knapsack set between his feet. He pulled out several large Tupperware containers filled with a dark liquid.

"What the hell is that? Lemme go, prick!" Earl screamed. "Help ... help me!"

"Yes," Bob agreed. "Help—help us!" He yelled even louder than Earl. "Scream all you want, asshole. You're five miles deep in the woods, and no one can hear you. But don't worry, you're gonna get plenty of practice. In fact, I think before this is over, you'll be damn tired of screaming." Bob opened one of the containers and threw the contents onto Earl. The dark liquid splashed him in the face and coated his clothes.

"Hey, what the hell is that?"

"That, my friend, is chicken blood." Bob took another container and stepped back to one of the many dens that littered the woods around them. Bob emptied half the container's contents onto one of the mounds of grasses and fallen limbs. Then he poured out a trail leading to the pine where Earl was tied. A muffled grunt broke the silence and was answered by another from nearby. "Oh-no. Do you hear that, Earl?" Bob fished out a third container and splashed the contents onto Earl's clothes and the ground where he sat.

"What the fuck is that?" Earl screamed.

"That, my friend, is a mama boar, and she sounds vewy hungwy, wabbit." Bob removed a hunting knife from its sheath and approached Earl.

"Get away from me!"

"Shut the fuck up, scumbag!" Bob barked, bringing the knife down into Earl's thigh. The man bellowed as Bob twisted the blade. He ripped it out of the man's flesh, leaving a wound six inches long and two inches deep. A scarlet river flowed from the gash and mixed with chicken blood on the ground. "With any luck, you'll bleed to death before they tear you apart. But honestly, you don't look that lucky to me."

The grunts grew louder as the scent of blood was detected by the local residents. The excitement of their rooting was picked up like a telegraph signal from the neighboring burrows. Bob had checked out the area a week earlier and found no less than forty individual dens in a fifty-yard radius. And if there was one thing wild boar couldn't resist, it was the scent of blood. That shit drove them nuts.

He removed the last plastic container from the knapsack and stood in front of Earl. He held it over the man's head and poured it slowly on top of him. It soaked his hair, covered his face, and dripped down the front of his clothes. "This is for Sally," he said as he turned, picked up his bag, and headed back to the truck.

Earl screamed until his vocal cords crackled like a paper fire. Bob continued walking, never turning back once to look at the man. Before he made it halfway to the truck, the timbre and velocity of Earl's cries amped into a tantric frenzy. The shrill that now pierced the night was the hysterical bleats of a man in agony. It should have been difficult to listen to—one would think—but Bob wanted to remember every minute of it. It took less time than Bob anticipated for the boar to take care of old Earl. All in all, the man had been consumed in just under fifty minutes.

Bob sat in the truck and waited, allowing several hours to pass so the animals could finish off the last of the scraps and head back home to sleep off their dinner. He returned later to see what was left of the man who had murdered his high school sweetheart—there wasn't enough to fill a waste basket. Bob scattered the remains near the various burrows and cleaned up what he could. He hadn't been able to save Sally, but one thing was for certain: Earl Hillman would never hurt another soul.

Bob Senior passed away later that year and was buried in the graveyard behind the Lutheran church, just a short distance from the plot where Carl's father would find his ultimate rest. Many of Bob's friends were sent to war only to return to the same piece of earth soon after. Bob had missed the draft, but the weight he carried after that day in the barrens was as heavy as any burden he would have taken home from Vietnam.

Bob had listened to the man die as a testament to Sally; it was the least he could do for her. And the moment had seared into his brain like a branding iron. The sound of Earl's gut-wrenching cries had begun to haunt him. At first in his dreams. Bob could hear Earl Hillman scream for mercy. He could see the man bound to the tree, covered in chicken blood. The bastard had deserved to die, and Bob believed he could carry the weight. But it would be years before Bob Jones could sleep through the night, and he would never erase the soundtrack that played on an endless loop when he closed his eyes. He told himself he had done the right thing and Earl had received far more mercy than he deserved. The bastard didn't get any less than he had given Sally.

Much had changed in the world since Bob last walked the halls of the high school, but nothing quite as much as Bob himself. He'd lived through things he never could have fathomed as a boy. He had grown, and he had gained the perspective of a man who carried a tremendous weight—and to carry that weight, one needed large shoulders. As Bob Jones navigated the narrow hallways, he was aware of the size of his shoulders and the tremendous weight they supported. Years ago, when he went to school here, Bob hadn't carried any of it. But that was a long time ago, and he was a different man now.

He turned down the main hall and entered the administration office, where a grey-haired woman stood behind the counter.

"Bob Jones, what brings you here? We aren't scheduled for another fire drill till next month." The woman looked at him through a pair of thick glasses.

"Miss Tailor, you're looking as attractive as ever," he told the woman, who was old enough to be his mother.

"Oh, you fresh thing. What can I do ya for, Bob?"

"I was wondering if Mr. Garish was in. I'd like to speak to him if I could."

"He's here, but he's in one of those moods. We had a number of staff absentees, and with the phones out, I had no way of finding substitutes. Oddly enough, even more students didn't show up as well. Is there something going on that I should know about?" She leaned over the counter and waited for the juicy gossip.

"There is, and we're asking the entire town to meet at the gym by five o'clock tonight. We need everyone in the shelter before sundown. I don't have time to give you all the details now because I really need to speak to Mr. Garish and then get the shelter ready. But believe me, ma'am, you want to take this seriously—as if your life depended on it."

"Oh, my dear," she said. "What should I do about classes?"

"I'm going to talk to the principal about that. I'm sure we'll have an answer for you in a few minutes. Just promise me, no matter what happens, that you will be in that shelter tonight. Okay?"

"Who am I to argue with the fire chief?" She forced a nervous smile and nodded to the principal's office.

Bob felt he had conveyed the urgency and was almost certain Miss Tailor would be in the shelter before the sun went down. He prayed they would be as successful with the rest of the town's citizens.

He walked around the counter and knocked on the solid oak door. There was brief commotion as if something had fallen or been moved in a hurry, followed by the startled voice of the principal saying, "Come in."

"Hello, Mr. Garish."

The principal looked disheveled and worn, as if he had been up all night. His shirt was opened at the collar, his tie was undone, and dark circles spread out around his eyes. He jumped up and shook Bob's hand.

"Mr. Jones, what brings you here this morning?" The man popped two Alka-Seltzer into a glass of water and watched the tablets fizzle.

"I'm sure you've noticed the number of students and faculty that didn't show up today."

The principal tilted back the glass of fizz and drank it down. "Ha, yes, I've noticed, believe me I've noticed. My secretary, Julie, never made it in.

I um, well, I hope she's okay. We had plans for lunch, and she never misses lunch. I hope her husband didn't—what I mean is, I hope she's all right." The man began to root through a stack of papers, unable to find what he was looking for.

"Mr. Garish, the sheriff has given me orders to take control of your gym and the shelter as well. I'm going to need you to make an announcement at one o'clock for all students and their families to report to the gym between four and five o'clock." Bob spoke with just enough authority to make his point.

"Oh my, that sounds serious. I knew something happened when I heard the explosions this morning. Was it methane? Is it poisonous gas?" The man continued to move the papers around his desk in an erratic fashion.

"No, sir, there's been an outbreak. The explosions you heard were detonations set off at the Gables Bridge and on Sunset Road. I'm afraid there's no way in or out of town. It's very important that you notify the entire staff as well as the students."

"Oh yes. Do you think Julie is all right? Maybe she's on her way here?"

"I don't know, sir. But you and everyone else in this school need to be in that shelter by five at the latest. It might be a good idea for you to dismiss the students early so they have time to go home and talk to their parents." Bob studied the frantic movements of the principal as he searched his desk. The guy was already out of his mind, and the shit hadn't fully hit the fan.

"Yes, yes, that's a good idea. I should probably stop by Julie's house and make sure she's all right. Oh—I don't know—maybe that's not such a good idea. Perhaps you could? She lives on Woodland Place."

"I'll see what I can do." Bob was struck with a horrible premonition and hoped to God that the rest of the town hadn't already lost it like Mr. Garish. "I'll coordinate the closing of the school with Miss Tailor. She'll know what to tell the students and faculty."

"Oh, that would be perfect. Thank you, Mr. Jones." Principal Melvin Garish continued to look for God-knows-what.

Bob turned and left his office without saying another word. It was obvious the guy was banging his secretary and had his priorities jacked up. He probably hadn't been wrapped too tight to begin with and possessed zero coping skills. Bob doubted the guy would even make it till sundown at the rate he was going. More than likely, he would end up getting shot by Julie's husband.

Bob proceeded to convey the gravity of the situation to Miss Tailor, and the woman handled it much better than her boss. He gave her explicit instructions about what to say when she made her announcement. It was all he could do since he didn't have the time to visit each classroom himself. Bob hoped the younger people in town were dealing with the situation better than the principal. Lord knew they couldn't be doing any worse.

CHAPTER 63

Don coordinated with Mark Gold to have the remaining explosives relocated to a secondary safe site. A surprising number of DuCain employees had not shown up for some reason, and for the first time that morning, Don had a moment to evaluate his situation.

It was the worst case of vandalism he had ever seen, and it had happened on his watch. He couldn't imagine the trouble he was looking at with the company's explosives being stolen and then used in an act of terrorism. He was sure that charges would be brought up. *Can I go to jail for this?* At the very least, old man DuCain would see him swing from the tallest tree.

Then he thought about what had happened in the trailer with Stephanie, but the vision was replaced by an image of Lois and Troy. *Christ!* He had fucked up on so many levels and in such a short period of time. It had been amazing with Stephanie, like nothing he had ever experienced. *But was it worth fucking up your life?* The truth was he didn't know. Which was probably the wrong head doing the talking. He forced himself to get a grip and made his way toward the secondary chamber, where Stephanie and Gail stopped to examine something they had found near one of the murals.

Propped against the far wall were what appeared to be several cylinders carved out of either wood or cane. Stephanie inspected the tubular objects with her flashlight, being careful not to disturb them. They were approximately three feet long, no more than an inch and a half wide, with a small hole bored into each one near its base. The women were intently focused on the objects and neglected to see the mural that adorned the wall above them. But Don saw it and started to fit the pieces together.

"What do you think these were used for?" Gail asked.

"They almost look like water vessels or some type of storage unit," Stephanie said as she examined them.

"No, that's not what they are," Don said.

Stephanie looked up at him. "What makes you say that?"

He turned his flashlight onto the mural above them. The beam revealed exactly what the tubes had been used for, which had nothing to do with transporting water. The cylinders were weapons, and by the look of it, effective ones at that.

The scene on the cavern wall depicted a battle where many of the black-eyed creatures assembled against the Lenape. Some of the tribe members had been pinned down and consumed by the smoke-like substance, while others battled their attackers. Several of the beasts possessed clear human features, others looked like animals, and there were some that appeared to be a cross between the two, with both human and distinct reptilian features, all with the same horrific black eyes.

The tribe members that fought the beasts carried the same cane cylinders the women had found, and were using them like slings to hurl projectiles at their enemies. It was obvious to Don what the small hole in the side of the tubes was for. That was where the musket balls were inserted. From what the mural suggested, the weapons appeared effective, as many of the creatures had dropped and others were crying out in pain.

Stephanie looked from the mural to the tubes with a smirk of satisfaction on her face.

"This is the proof we've been looking for. You have no idea how important a find this is." She wiped at her cheek. "I wish my father was here to see this."

"This is just mythology we're looking at, right?" Donald asked; he studied the faces of the women who stood before him, not sure he wanted an answer.

"I don't think so," Stephanie said, examining the mural. "I think this is their story. This was how the Lenape disappeared. And this was how they fought them off." She motioned toward the cylinders.

"What exactly do you mean, fought them off? Who was them?"

"There has been a lot of stories and many different names for these creatures. The Lenape called it the Dark One—Matantu. The Mayans referred to it as Ah Puch. There are countless names for this Entity; it's been called everything from Apopis to Tezcatlipoca."

Don was pretty sure he had just had sex with the crazy girl from the museum and wondered how long it would be until she started making stuffed animals from locks of his hair. "Come on. Are you seriously saying the Lenape tribe went to war against the Devil?"

"Not in the biblical sense, of course not. And don't look at me like you think I'm nuts. My father spent his life studying the disappearances of countless civilizations, and nearly all of them recorded depictions of creatures like this. You said it yourself; it had to take the Lenape a long time to turn lodestone into perfect-sized musket balls. And they must have done it for a good reason."

"So, you're implying that these creatures are responsible for the disappearance of countless civilizations from different countries—hell different continents—and from different periods in Earth's history ... seriously?" Don looked around the floor of the cave, noticing just how many of the spherical stones littered the place.

"It makes for a compelling reason to believe in a force like a Devil, doesn't it?"

"You said Entity, but all I see are a bunch of animals and humans fighting against each other. Maybe the Lenape painted their enemies as beasts because of the ferocity of their attackers? It's impossible that the same creatures could have been in all those countless places at different times in history."

"It is possible. My father believed that the Entity called Matantu, also called Apopis, and even Satan, is an ancient life-form that has been here since the beginning. Look at this," she said, returning to the murals they had examined yesterday. "This shows two possible Entities." She pointed out the two different-colored clouds in the painting. "Now just hear me out because I can see you want to argue with me."

Don remained quiet and listened.

"In too many cultures for it to be considered coincidental, the story of creation is similar to this. Two opposing forces in the universe before there was anything else. One represented by the depiction of light, while the other 'Entity' a juxtaposition of dark."

"You're talking about matter and anti-matter." Don preferred to speak scientifically.

"Perhaps," Stephanie agreed, "or creation and destruction. Or maybe simply good and evil, who knows?" She shrugged. "It's been speculated by countless civilizations that when the two came together, the universe was created. Look here." She pointed to the mural that Don believed was the Big Bang.

"And the collective unconscious is how different civilizations were able to come to similar creation stories," Gail added.

"Thank you, Gail." Stephanie glowed as if her own child had just won the spelling bee. "And you can see in the next mural the way the darkness enveloped the earth. It looks as if it may have gotten trapped, possibly in our atmosphere." She moved further down the row of paintings. "If you look at the next three murals as a linear succession, you can see a timeline. I've seen similar depictions in Mayan cave drawings as well as on vessel pottery from the Indus River Valley."

Don stepped back so he could see all three paintings at once. The first one showed the ether-like substance entering the reptilian creatures, which could have been a scene from the Jurassic or Cretaceous era. The second scene could easily have taken place millions of years after the previous. The dark substance had moved on to primitive primates that Don thought resembled Australopithecus. He knew little about the evolution of the human race but was familiar with the discovery of the fossils in Ethiopia in '74, suspected to be early humans. The ape-like creatures depicted in this mural looked an awful lot like the primates that dated back about four million years ago. They certainly didn't look as evolved as the Homo erectus, which hadn't come along for another three million years after that.

"Is that an Australopithecus?" he finally asked.

"Don't you just love this guy?" Stephanie said to Gail, who only smiled, pointed her camera at Don, and took his picture.

The flash of the bulb caught him by surprise and temporarily blinded him. "Please don't do that," he said.

"Sorry." Gail turned around and snapped a few more shots of the mural.

"I think that's exactly what it's supposed to represent, or at least some early descendant of ours."

"How would the Lenape have knowledge of any of this? These are all fairly new discoveries we're talking about." Don looked at the women, who both wore *I-told-you-so* smirks on their faces. "You're gonna say collective unconscious, I guess." Both women nodded.

The next mural showed the substance affecting what was clearly Homo sapiens. The humans were members of the Lenape tribe.

"It's obvious this is a depiction of the progression of time, from prehistoric creatures to early humans, all the way to the time of the Lenape."

Don couldn't argue; it appeared that way to him as well. He was nearly positive that the one drawing was the very same primates that had been discovered in Ethiopia.

Stephanie used her flashlight to illuminate the next mural, since the floodlights were casting too many shadows into the furthest reaches of the cave. Don trained his light on the wall as well and was taken aback by what he saw. A momentary hush fell over the group as the mural was revealed in full light. Stephanie broke the silence and gasped at the scene painted before them.

The Lenape had immortalized several of their children on the cavern wall, all of whom possessed the same characteristic pitch-black eyes and mouthful of the horrible, pointed teeth.

"That might explain the small skeletons near the entrance," Don whispered.

Stephanie nodded in agreement and lowered her head. "The depiction of children is another commonality that's been recorded in other cultures. There is something about them that plays a significant role of importance to this Entity."

The totality of Stephanie's words hit Don like a bread truck. "You keep saying Entity, and I think you're implying consciousness. But are these murals suggesting that whatever the Lenape and these other cultures encountered turned them into creatures, like zombies or vampires or something?"

"All myths originate from some factual experience. The legend of the zombie originated in the Caribbean and speaks of people returning from the grave and walking the earth. It looks as if our holy man here did just that. At least that's what the mural implies. The legend of Dracula is based on the very real, Vladimir the Impaler, the Prince of Romania who was known to drink the blood of his enemies. Bram Stoker took a bit of the myth and threw his own spin on the story with other legends he had heard of. But the question is did Stoker come up with the story as an original idea, or was it derived from a greater place, collective unconscious?" Stephanie beamed as she hit her stride and continued. "Stoker assigned some very real qualities to the creature we all came to know as the vampire. For one, he gave his creature sharp fangs that were used to puncture the flesh of its victims. Also, the creature was limited to darkness. I don't know if you noticed what all these murals have in common, but take a closer look."

It didn't take long for Don to figure out what she was talking about; he was surprised he hadn't noticed it sooner. Not one of the murals was set during the day; the absence of sunlight was apparent. In fact, in most of the paintings, either the moon or stars were depicted in the background. "They all take place at night. None of them during the day."

"Don't get me wrong. I'm not saying that whatever attacked the Lenape tribe, or the inhabitants of Cahokia was a zombie or a vampire, but there is a good possibility it was the Entity that inspired the myth. In fact, my father believed that this Entity was responsible for our myths about most modern monsters. What if this presence is responsible for the belief in Satan and evil itself?

"And the Lenape killed Satan by throwing rocks at him?" Don said.

"A vampire can be killed with a wooden stake through the heart and by sunlight," Gail added.

"Don't forget the silver bullet," Don ribbed.

"That's a werewolf, not a vampire," Gail corrected him.

Don nodded as if he should have known that. He reexamined the mural of the battle scene where the Lenape fought the creatures. "So, lodestones are like wooden stakes to these things; that's what you're getting at, right?"

"Well, it looks as if that's what the Lenape used to fight them. And some of those stones are embedded into the remains we found at the front of the cave. I'm no physician, but if I had to guess a cause of death."

"So, a peaceful people come across something they've never seen before and figure out how to defeat it with magnetite?" Don shook his head.

"I never said they defeated it. If anything, it was the other way around. The Lenape in this area vanished," Stephanie said. "None of the cultures that recorded these creatures survived. This is only the latest of a string of singularities that correlate the presence of a terrestrial anomaly that science has yet to categorize."

"That is up until now." Gail smiled at her boss. "With all this, you're looking at a Nobel Prize, Doc."

"That's nice, but you know they don't issue a Nobel Prize for archeology." Stephanie grimaced.

"Well, maybe they'll make an exception this time. After all, we're talking about the discovery of the century. At the very least, they'll name it after you. How does The Thompson-Habilis sound?" Gail laughed.

"Actually, it's not my discovery," Stephanie said. "It's yours, Don. How would you like a new life-form named after you … 'The Fischer'?" She gave him a wink and flashed a quick smile.

"I don't know if I like the idea of a creature that resembles Count Dracula running around with my name." Don averted his eyes from her gaze for fear of Gail catching him. "If the Lenape got wiped out, then who created all these murals? I mean if they were all dead, someone had to be left to paint them."

"That's a good question." Stephanie picked up one of the lodestone balls and held it in her open palm. "Since the cave was sealed when you found it, I'm guessing whoever painted them never made it out. I wouldn't be surprised if some of these bones belong to our artist."

It was a morbid thought, but Don was inclined to agree. The cave had been buried under a ton of bedrock and concealed from his equipment by the massive deposit of magnetite. He hadn't even known it was there. "So, what happened to the original creature? I mean, you're saying that smokey substance was the original creature and it's been wiping out civilizations for damn near all of history. So, what happens? Does it hibernate, or does it go away for a few hundred years? What's your take on that?"

Stephanie shrugged her shoulders. "That's the million-dollar question. If I knew that, I'd be on the cover of *National Geographic*, not sandwiched between articles about the rainforest and the Gypsy Moth caterpillar."

"Well, maybe the Lenape killed it after all. You know, kind of the way Rocky Balboa and Apollo Creed knocked each other out at the end." It was an analogy Don could wrap his head around and helped add a little levity to all the doom and gloom of the moment.

"It's possible, except the Lenape weren't the first to use the lodestone. We found similar weapons at Cahokia and quite a few sites in Asia."

"So, you think this is really the same Entity in all those places. Why not individual entities instead of the same one?"

"Well, it's been my father's hypothesis, and I agree for several reasons. I guess the major one being that every original depiction of the Entity, where it existed in space, shows it as a singularity. Like a single-celled organism, an amoeba, only a lot more dangerous." Stephanie took a rubber band and pulled her hair back into a ponytail. A thin sweat broke across her forehead. She continued. "The museum has a skull they keep tucked away from the public. It isn't clear what species the skull belongs to. While it has clear primate features, there are reptilian qualities as well. But we're almost positive it started out as human. The mouth is filled with these horrible teeth, for the most part. But the back jaw contains human molars."

"How do you know they're human?" he asked.

"Because some of them have fillings. Some early dentist drilled out the cavities and filled the molars with gold. I don't know what type of creature it ended up as, but it started out life as a human; that much we are sure of."

"And you're positive it isn't a hoax?"

"Pretty elaborate hoax to make an entire civilization disappear."

The three of them sat in the silence of the cave for a moment as the gravity of what Stephanie said echoed off the walls like a cry for help. Finally, it was Gail who broke the silence. "I'm glad that whatever did this is long gone."

Stephanie looked at her assistant for a long moment, then nodded her head in agreement. "Yeah, me too," she replied.

CHAPTER 64

At 11:05 a.m. on Wednesday, October 28, Jessica Marceau became the mayor of Garrett Grove. Deputy David Rainey swore her in under the authority of Sheriff Carl Primrose. Jessica won the election without even submitting her bid for candidacy. She sat at the desk of former Mayor Gilbert staring at the papers in front of her. Not only had Mayor Gilbert gone missing but so had the Deputy Mayor and three members of the town council.

"I can't believe I am doing this. I've been the mayor for seven minutes, and I'm already Joseph Stalin." She proceeded to sign the orders.

"You're no Stalin. You're going to save this town," Rainey said.

"I don't like this one bit. What the sheriff is proposing is nothing short of what Russia did to the Ukraine in '32."

"We're doing this so we can take care of the people. Things are going to get crazy, and the sheriff is trying to gather as many resources as he can. He knows what he's doing."

"Well, that makes one of us because I'm flying blind here." She signed the last paper and put the pen down. "Tell me again that I'm doing the right thing, Deputy."

"You did the right thing, Mayor Marceau," Deputy Rainey told her as he picked up the papers and walked to the door. "And if you don't mind my saying, Joseph Stalin could never pull off that dress."

She laughed despite how horrible she felt. "Deputy Rainey," she called to him as he prepared to leave. "If we're both still here next week, you can take me out to dinner. I like Italian. That's an executive order, by the way." She forced herself to smile.

The Deputy stopped and gave her a look of surprise. "Yes, ma'am," he said, and walked out of the office.

Twenty minutes after Deputy Rainey left the mayor's office, he entered the A&P food store on Route 3, flanked by seven burley firemen. Usually, such a sight would raise an eyebrow or two; however, there weren't enough customers to notice, or employees. But Günter Bentley, the store manager, noticed the men and greeted them at the door.

"Ist der sumsing I can help you vit today, Deputy?" Günter had been born in West Berlin before the wall was built. Fortunately, he lived on the prosperous side and had been spared the communist presence that many of his cousins endured in the east. Raised under the watchful eye of his Uncle Sam, Günter had always dreamt of visiting America. He loved all things American, from cheeseburgers to baseball to Mickey Mouse. But what Günter loved most about America had nothing to do with the food or the pastimes. It was something every man his age could agree on no matter what country they were born in. The single greatest thing about America was Marilyn Monroe. Günter Bentley moved to the states in 1967 and married a girl who looked nothing like Norma Jean Baker. And although Hazel was no movie star, she was attractive, knew how to cook a mean cheeseburger, and was one hundred percent red-blooded all-American girl, which Günter found incredibly sexy. They had three children, and Günter became the manager of the supermarket. It wasn't exactly a Cinderella story, but for Günter, it was the American dream, and he was happy. He tried to lose the German accent, but old habits died hard. And even though he looked German and sounded German, his heart was as Yankee Doodle as they came.

Deputy Rainey smiled and greeted the man when he approached. "Hi, Günter. How are you today?"

"I am goot, zank you. And yourself?" Günter studied the men.

"Not so good, I'm afraid. I have a court order signed by the mayor." He handed him the paper. "I'm going to be requisitioning quite a bit of food. But I assure you, you will be reimbursed every dime." The firemen carried lists and orders of their own and hustled past the deputy and the manager.

"Vait! Dis must be sum mistake. I must clear dis vit my boss." Günter checked the paperwork.

"Whatever you got to do, Günter. We're not going to clean you out, but we are going to take a lot of the non-perishables. I'm sorry, but this is an emergency. There's nothing I can do about it." Deputy Rainey took Günter by the arm and led him far enough away so that the girls at the registers couldn't hear him. "Günter, I want you and your family at the high school by five o'clock. Close the store early and be there—no matter what. This is serious, I mean it. If you love your family, and I know that you do, make surc you are at the school by five. Only bring what you can carry and any medicine the children might need."

Günter's face went slack. He grew up a mile from communist Germany and took warnings seriously. "Mein Gott!" His native tongue resurfaced. "Vas ist das?"

"Life and death, Herr Bentley, life and death."

Deputy Rainey's words resonated like a detonation. Günter Bentley stepped to the side and allowed the men to collect everything they intended. He did his best to inventory the items, assisted by Claire Rizvi, one of the few cashiers that showed up to work that morning. The deputy and the men didn't clean the place out entirely, but they had come damn close. A half hour later, the firemen loaded the bags into their trucks and left. Günter watched as they pulled away, wondering if what he was feeling was anything compared to how his countrymen felt at the end of the war when the Russians arrived to liberate Berlin.

Harrison's Army and Navy had been around since 1955, serving Garrett Grove's avid hunters and fishermen for all their seasonal necessities. One could renew their game license, pick up a dozen night crawlers, and purchase a new pair of wranglers in one convenient trip. Tyler Harrison inherited the family business in '75 after his father Herman passed away at the ripe old age of fifty-seven. Herman Harrison had been a hunting enthusiast who not only held the record for the largest small mouth to ever come out of King Lake, at a whopping six pounds seven ounces, but was the only hunter to come off the mountain with a full 14-pointer. Both the rack and the bass were displayed proudly on the wall behind the register at the store on Route 3. There wasn't a gun Herman wasn't comfortable with, and he knew more knots than any fisherman in town. He'd been hunting since he was old enough to carry a shotgun and claimed to have never had a misfire in all his years in the woods. Strangely enough, Herman had never been stung by a wasp in all his years as a hunter either, that was until the fall of '75.

Herman set out in the early morning hours at the very start of buck season with the intention of beating his own 14-point record. The south face of Garrett Mountain had experienced a bout of Indian summer, and there were still a lot of chiggers and no-see-ums, and the little bastards had started to feast on Herman in the early morning sun. He never liked to use bug spray because the deer could smell the chemical from over a mile away. And any time he did, he always came home empty-handed.

Still, if he had squirted just a dab or two that Saturday, he might not have been so preoccupied when the buggers started swarming around his head. The black flies were especially bad that year and descended on Herman like sailors on a prostitute. They first attacked the back of his neck and then went to work on his face. Herman swatted at them, then set his shotgun down in a fit of rage. He was more than a little pissed off but not nearly as much as the hive of wood wasps he turned up with the butt of his gun. They were far more aggressive than the black flies and stung Herman repeatedly. He tore off running as soon as the first one hit him in the neck, and it took nearly a quarter of a mile at a full sprint to ditch the last of the wasps. It was then that Herman found it difficult to breathe and could feel his throat swelling up. He had no idea he was allergic to wasp stings, wood wasps especially. Having been lucky, or unlucky, to make it to fifty-seven without ever being stung, how could he?

He was found by a couple of hikers later that afternoon. By the time Herman was brought back into town, he was a dark shade of purple and his entire body had swelled so much it took Burt Lively an hour and a half to cut the man's boots off.

His son, Tyler, didn't inherit the outdoor gene from his old man and had no interest in killing Bambi's mother, or father for that matter. He reluctantly took over the family business at his mother's insistence but felt no love for the vocation. Tyler hated the outdoors almost as much as he hated mornings. He preferred going to sleep at five a.m. as opposed to waking up at that time. He'd been a fan of the disco era, and although the movement was coming to an end, that didn't mean the party was over.

The seventies had been a coke-fueled blur for Tyler and his friends, who spent their weekends at the clubs in Millville, the nearest city within a hundred-mile radius of the Grove. And although it wasn't mandatory to do cocaine while disco dancing, the two went hand in hand. It helped some men to be more outgoing, and for others, it acted as an aphrodisiac. For Tyler, it had done both and allowed him to feel less self-conscious. It also helped him to feel comfortable around other men who were interested in the same things he was—which was other men. Garrett Grove wasn't exactly the place where Tyler could openly display his sexuality. It would be decades before this little redneck burb would be ready for that.

Millville, on the other hand, was a bit less judgmental. Tyler had always had feelings for boys but kept them hidden for fear of what Herman would have done to him. As far as Tyler knew, there weren't any other men in town who shared the same tastes as he—although he would have been surprised to learn how many truly did. So Tyler kept his feelings concealed from his bigoted father throughout the week, but on Friday and Saturday nights, he was the dancing queen at the disco inferno.

Lately, he'd been seeing a guy from Millville named Carmine, who was far more comfortable in his own sexuality. Carmine had been interested in showing Tyler the ropes and promised to be gentle with him the first time. There had been nothing gentle about it—which was just fine for Tyler because, as it turned out, that was just how he liked it. The cocaine heightened the experience, fueling the men's appetites as well as the duration of the act. It had been a rollercoaster ride for several months when Tyler realized he might have real feelings for Carmine. He'd recently been thinking of expressing the idea of an exclusive relationship to his friend. Monogamy was uncommon within their circle, and Tyler didn't know if Carmine was ready for such a suggestion. Part of the magic of the lifestyle was the mystery of not knowing who you might end up with at the end of the night.

It had been weighing on his mind lately and was what he'd been thinking about when Deputy Beau Jenkins walked into the store with several firemen at his side. Tyler recognized one of them, Richard Marek, a guy he had gone to school with. Richard was a volunteer fireman and was in great shape. Tyler stared at Richard as he entered the store and received a surprising gaze in return. He had given him *the look*. Tyler wondered if maybe he wasn't quite as ready for a monogamous relationship as he thought.

"Hello, gentlemen, how can I help you?" Tyler asked as Beau approached the counter.

"Good morning, Mr. Harrison. How's business today?" Beau smiled, removed a manila envelope from under his arm, opened it, and pulled out several sheets of paper.

"Ughh," Tyler grunted. "How does it look? The only thing I've sold all morning is a dozen night crawlers."

"Well, I have some good news for you then." Beau handed him the papers, and Tyler began to read them. "The mayor has given me orders to requisition a few items from your establishment. You are to send the bill to the town treasurer, and you will be reimbursed for everything. Of course, the mayor is hoping for our usual discount."

Tyler finished reading the documents and looked past Beau towards Richard. "Well, I suppose I could let you take a few things. Lord knows I could sure use the sales to boost business. What are you men looking for?" He couldn't help smiling at Richard as he asked the question. The months with Carmine had helped build his confidence.

"Well, today's your lucky day, my friend," Beau replied with the smoothness of a used car salesman. "We need all the weapons and ammunition, and a large amount of the camping supplies."

Tyler's jaw dropped. "You're shitting me, right?"

"'Fraid not, sir. It's all here in black and white. I assure you, you will be paid in full as soon as checks are cut next quarter."

Herman would have fought the deputy tooth and nail and never allowed that much inventory to walk out the store at a discounted price, even if he had to sit on it for a year to get full retail. But Tyler wasn't his old man, and to him, it sounded too good to be true. Business had been slow lately, and today there had only been one customer before the men arrived. Tyler's lips parted, and a huge smile spread across his face.

"Help yourselves to whatever you need, Deputy. I'll unlock the cases for you."

The firemen fanned out and began to collect the items. Richard approached the counter and leaned over to speak to Tyler.

"You're going to want to be at either the medical center or the high school by five tonight. Something major is happening in town, and if you value your safety, you will be there." Tyler watched the young fireman's eyes check him up and down. "I'll be at the high school; I sure hope I see you there." Richard nodded and joined the other men at the back of the store.

Tyler watched as he walked away, thinking that today had certainly been a day for surprises. "I wouldn't miss it for the world," he said to himself.

There were other businesses that received visits from Garrett Grove's newly appointed deputies that afternoon. Ed Koloski headed a crew of men who proceeded to liberate every walkie-talkie and battery from the Radio Shack on Route 3. Frederick Nathan, the acting manager and only employee who had shown up for work, was unconvinced the signature on the paperwork was legitimate and asked the men to kindly leave the store.

When firemen Eric Collins and Kevin Grish began to remove items from the shelves, Frederick intervened and attempted to stop the men. He grabbed the radios from Kevin's hands and tried to prevent the man from taking any more. Kevin, who had been up half the night fighting the fire at the Texaco, was not in the mood. He dropped the rest of what he was holding and hit Frederick with a right cross that sent the manager toppling into a display of Atari game systems.

The cases flew in every direction as the man crashed into them, landing hard on his backside. The firemen continued to rifle through the store, collecting the items they had been tasked to collect.

Koloski extended his hand to help the man from the floor, but Frederick ignored the gesture. "You'll be hearing from my lawyer," he barked at the fireman.

"If we're lucky," Koloski replied. "I hope we'll be around that long."

A similar confrontation took place between fireman Kurt Hamilton and Howard Bell, the owner of Bell's Hardware. It hadn't been as physical as the incident at the Radio Shack, but it still sat like a bad oyster in Koloski's gut. His men were fatigued, on edge, and some had displayed a sense of entitlement. The mayor had given them permission to be bullies, and Koloski didn't like the talk he was hearing. Things were beginning to fall apart, and it wouldn't take much to push the men over the edge. They were volunteers, not seasoned vets, and they damn sure weren't law enforcement. But now they held documents that said they didn't have to be polite, and some of the guys were a bit rough around the edges to begin with. Koloski wondered what it would take to turn some of them into an angry mob. He didn't think it would take a whole hell of a lot.

The operation at the medical center went smoother than most of the supply runs, due to the presence of Sheriff Primrose and Deputy Lutchen. Cots were moved six at a time on the freight elevator, from the second floor to the basement, while Nurse TenHove worked with Lois, Will, and Alice in the pharmacy, separating medications and supplies into two equal stockpiles. There was still the matter of transporting patients, but at the rate they were going, Carl figured the task would be completed no later than three o'clock. At that point, Dr. Freedman and several of the staff would be sent to the high school

It was nearly twelve, and soon the entire town's population would receive their own call to action. Carl prayed they would follow directions. His men were already spread thin, and there was no way to round up people individually. *At least things are going smooth here*, he said to himself as he made his way to the pharmacy. A sudden shout of profanities erupted from somewhere down the hall.

Carl rounded a corner and arrived at the first-floor freight elevator to find a nurse and two firemen yelling at someone inside.

"What's going on?" Carl shouted.

Fireman Grady Martin turned to him with a look of exasperation "It's stuck between floors. I've got two men in there."

"Is it a breaker or something we can reset?" he asked.

"Dee Riker went to check it out." Grady and the other fireman worked at the doors and managed to pry them open, but the elevator was stuck below the first floor, closer to the basement.

"Can you go through the top to get them out? Isn't there a hatch?" the nurse asked.

"Yeah, in the movies, there's always a hatch; in real life, there isn't," Grady said.

The nurse looked at him as if she had just been told there was no such thing as Santa Claus. Then another fireman bounded around corner, sweating and out of breath.

"It's fried," he panted. "The circuit board is completely fried. It must have been damaged last night during the fire."

"Are you serious?" Grady shouted.

"Yeah, man, that was the last trip," Dee answered.

Carl felt his stomach turn and could swear he smelled the sizzling circuits even though they were on another floor. It had been going too well. He quickly reassessed the situation and didn't like their chances. There was no way that they could get all the patients and equipment into the basement by way of the stairs, not by five o'clock. *Christ, this is bad.*

"How many cots have been moved already?" Carl asked.

"I think about thirty," Grady answered.

"It will have to do." Carl wiped his brow. "Everything else is taking the stairs. We're going to have to start moving patients sooner than expected. Anyone who is bedridden or can't make the trip will have to ride it out on the floors."

The nurse glared at him with a mixture of hatred and disbelief in her eyes. "You can't just leave the patients unprotected."

"I didn't say they'd be unprotected; I said they'd be riding it out on the floors. My men and I will stay and protect them."

"I'll help you, Sheriff," Grady said.

"Thank you. Now let's get these men out of the elevator and get to work. Our job just got a hell of a lot harder."

Carl checked his watch; it was just twelve, and they still hadn't started to move patients yet. He prayed that the sensation in his gut was the stale donut he had eaten but knew better. Trouble was coming, and they weren't ready for it. *God, I hope they're doing better at the high school.*

CHAPTER 65

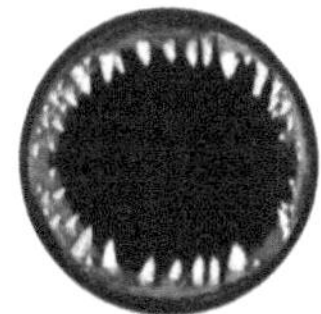

Father Kieran listened to more confessions that Wednesday morning than he had the entire month of October. He'd asked the Lord for a sign, and his prayers were answered. The men, women, and children arrived to confess their sins and ask for forgiveness, and Father Kieran offered them absolution. Then he presented each with a similar penance.

"Would you stand against the powers of evil and fight in the name of the Lord?"

Their replies had all been the same. "Yes, Father. I will."

Kieran then suggested they go back to their homes, collect their firearms, and return in time for Mass. Many of the congregation had already experienced a loss, whether it was a family member or a neighbor. Garrett Grove had undergone a change in the past few days, and everyone noticed it. It had been rapid and impossible to dismiss, like waking up one morning to find your nose missing. Now the congregation was ready to take action.

A young girl named Diane Nathan had recently discovered she was pregnant. She had lost her boyfriend in the fire at the Texaco station and was struggling with something horrible she saw on her street this morning. Two sheriff's officers had fired on their fellow deputies as Diane watched from her bedroom window, and one of the men had already been on the ground. The other had suffered a terrible stomach wound before being shot in the head. The officers moved the bodies into the house and then left. None of it made sense; the world had gone insane. First, she had heard the news about Chris and felt as if she could die herself; now men were being gunned down right outside her front door.

"The Lord works in mysterious ways, but I am afraid that Satan's works are even more mysterious. What you saw today was the work of a fallen angel. I'm terribly sorry about your friend Chris. He is with Jesus and is watching over you. He brought you here today."

"Yes, Father. I know," she said.

"The child that you carry is a blessing from the Lord, and that child needs his mother's protection. Will you do what's necessary to protect the child?"

"I will, Father." She looked to the man for direction.

"Then there is work that must be done. You may have to fight, but be not afraid; I will stand beside you. Trust in the Lord and your sins shall be forgiven. Go now and prepare for the Mass." Father Kieran listened to their confessions and delivered the same message to each of them. Then he told the ever-growing line at the back of the church that he would be more than happy to listen to the rest of their confessions after Mass. He retreated to the sacristy and prepared as the congregation took their seats. The usual organist had not shown up for the Mass, which weighed heavy on Kieran as he dressed in his chambers. Then as if on a breeze, the opening notes of "Blessed Assurance" lifted upon the air and greeted him behind the door. Kieran poked his head out to find Allison Aigans seated at the organ with the sheet music in front of her.

"Praise God." He made the sign of the cross on his forehead.

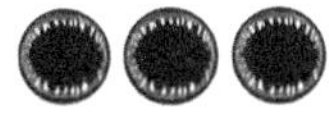

Troy sat beneath the monkey bars with Janis on one side and Wendy on the other. What happened in the principal's office had gotten him thinking about Rob and the possibility that he might never see him again. He had the perfect opportunity to tell Principal Grace and Miss Boriello what he told the kids on the playground. Instead, he told them about Rob and started to cry. Troy felt he had messed up big-time.

The wind picked up, sending a gusting chill across the playground. Troy turned to Wendy, who opened her lunch box, pulled out a bag of Chips Ahoy, and handed them to him.

"Here," she said. "I know how much you like them."

Then Janis placed a salami sandwich in front of him. "You can have my sandwich, if you want."

"I'm sorry about Rob," Wendy told him.

"It might just be the flu," Janis added. "We should stop by his house after school."

"I don't think he's home. I really don't." Troy struggled not to cry again but wasn't sure he would be successful. He zipped his coat as the wind picked up, sending an even icier chill in their direction.

A growing shadow inched its way across the playground, and the change in light was noticeable. Janis looked up at the darkening clouds as they began to block the sun. "Looks like it's gonna rain," she said, and Troy stiffened. "What's wrong?" she asked.

Troy watched the dark clouds stretch across the sky. The first one passed before the sun and moved on, but in the distance, there were more that followed. Also, the wind had increased, a clear sign it was going to rain.

He had been staring at the sky, not saying a word, when Janis finally raised her voice. "Hey, Troy, what's going on?"

"No," he hissed. "The other day when those things chased me, it had just started to rain. The sky got dark, and then when the storm came, so did they."

The girls now wore the same look as he. "What should we do?" Wendy asked. "We're not ready yet."

They looked at him as if he might hold the answers. Troy froze between the gazes of his friends as his mind went blank. He tried to think quickly, not his strong suit. It was all he could do to concentrate as the sky grew darker and the clouds drew near. If he was right, that was all the camouflage the creatures needed.

The bell rang, calling the children back into the building, and woke Troy from his unproductive trance. Racking his brain hadn't done him any good, but the sound of that annoying bell had. His eyes flew open wide, and suddenly, Troy knew exactly what to do.

He pulled both girls close and spoke low so not to be overheard. They nodded in agreement as he explained his plan. Then they closed their lunch boxes and waited while the other children assembled at the back doors. They followed the crowd at a snail's pace, making sure they were at the very back of the line. As the three friends stepped into the building, Troy turned to them and mouthed the word—*Now!*

The supply parties arrived at the back lot of the high school, where Bob and his men busied themselves separating the goods into two stockpiles. The mission had been a success, with Deputy Jenkins and his men delivering enough weapons and ammunitions to lay siege on a third-world nation.

An array of handguns, shotguns, and rifles were laid out in the beds of two full-size pickups. Deputy Rainey's men appeared to have cleaned out the A&P, and Koloski's group had done equally as well at the hardware store and Radio Shack. The men were all issued a weapon as well as extra ammunition and a radio.

Bob wanted to make sure the supplies were stowed away in both locations before they initiated phase two of the sheriff's plan. He spoke into the radio: "Come in, Sheriff. This is Bob over at the high school."

Carl heard the chief's voice break over the radio and left his position in the stairwell to get better reception near the front entrance.

"Yeah, Bob. How are you making out over there?" Carl stepped out the front door, feeling the sweat on his skin chill to the cool air.

"We're just about set over here. Shopping went as expected, with only a few incidents. I'm about to send over your share of the goods."

"Any chance you can spare a couple more men, Bob? The freight elevator shit the bed, and we're carrying everything down the stairs." Carl winced at the pain between his eyes. A dull thud of pressure caused them to water. Startled, he spun about as a discarded newspaper, kicked up by a sudden wind, rattled across the blacktop.

"Oh Christ, that's not good!" Bob exclaimed. "I'll send who I can, but I'm about to call my man at the station and give him the go ahead. We're running out of time, Carl."

"I know. Don't take anyone off the roundup crew. We need all those men out in the field." A dark shadow crept across the parking lot, covering the area where Carl stood. He looked up as the first heavy cloud passed in front of the sun. The throbbing in his head beat like a broken finger in response to the sudden change in air pressure.

"Disregard that request. I want all available men to begin the round up as soon as possible. I'll make do with who I have here. I think we got less time than we thought."

"What are you talking about? It's still early enough."

"Have you noticed the sky? I think we're in for some weather. I don't like how dark those clouds look in the distance."

From where Bob Jones stood, the skies were as clear as a bell, but he was facing the east, and typically, most storm fronts hit Garrett Grove from the west. He walked out to the middle of the parking lot, where he could get a better look over the top of the school. As soon he got a few feet away from the building, he felt the temperature drop as the breeze hit him. He peered toward the west and saw what the sheriff was talking about. Thick, dark clouds had begun to gather in the western sky and were rapidly approaching Garrett Mountain.

"I think you're right, Carl. I'll make the call. Ed Koloski and Chris Fredricks are on their way now, and you can put them to work if you need them. Stay in touch and keep me posted on your progress."

"10-4." Carl replaced the radio to his hip and made his way back to the building. The newspaper that had been blown across the parking lot cartwheeled through the air and snagged in the bushes next to the front door. He noticed the headlines on the page: REAGAN LEADS IN THE POLLS. He read the line as he entered the building. "Jesus Christ, it really is the end of the world," he said as the door closed behind him.

Allison played the intro to "How Great Thou Art," and the congregation rose on cue. Father Kieran made his slow progression up the aisle with two parishioners acting as altar boys since none of the usual ones had shown up. Diane Nathan and Josh Wilson were each assigned to read one of the scriptures before the Gospel. Father Kieran knelt at the altar, blessed himself, then opened the good book to the first page marker.

"In the name of the Father, and of the Son, and of the Holy Spirit, Amen."

The entire room answered him with a thunderous "Amen" that even surprised Father Kieran.

He continued, "Lord, have mercy. Christ, have mercy. Lord, have mercy." The congregation repeated every line. Father Kieran delivered the Homily and recited the Apostle's Creed, then instructed the parish to be seated. "Let us pray." He bowed his head, and they all followed. "Heavenly Father, for the sick and the suffering, Lord, hear our prayer. For our dearly departed brothers and sisters, Lord, hear our prayer. For Pope Paul, Francis our Bishop, and all of the Angels and Saints, Lord, hear our prayer."

He gazed upon the congregation and smiled. "Brothers and sisters, we find ourselves in a crisis. I look out among you today, and I see the children of the Lord. Some of you I have known for many years, and some I have just met. And I say, Praise be to God, for His flock is great. When I was a younger priest, I faced a crisis of my own. I questioned my place in this world, as the war in Vietnam had begun. I sought counsel from a senior member of the church, my mentor, Father Michael. And I prayed to the Lord for an answer to the problems that plagued me. The Lord worked through Father Michael, and I was sent here to Garrett Grove to lead the congregation. I trusted in God, and He showed me the way. Today, you have come with a crisis of your own. For some, it is a crisis of grief; for others, a crisis of guidance, possibly even a crisis of faith. Well, I say God Bless you all. Your crisis is a sign of your commitment. For those who have no faith have no crisis. Everyone sitting before you today sought solace in the House of the Lord, and that is a sign of strength. Blessed are the meek, for they shall inherit the Earth. And blessed are those who stand against the powers of evil and come in the name of the Lord."

Father Kieran blessed himself and took a seat behind the altar. The congregation began to take notice of one another and looked around the church to see the faces of the brothers and sisters who had also heard the call. Dick Wilson had closed the diner early and sat next to Frank Palumbo, the owner of the Texaco station. Both men were struggling to make sense out of a world that had changed overnight. Dick had watched his employees and customers disappear one by one, and Frank had literally witnessed his livelihood go up in flames. A man by the name of Rick Edwards, who drove for the Fink Bakery, decided to stop by the church after finding himself unable to leave town. He'd nearly been killed this morning by an avalanche on Sunset Road, which got him wondering about the last time he'd been to church; he figured a confession was in order. Bill Hamilton, the fire inspector, sat next to Amy Sterling, who worked part-time at Wilson's when Mandy wasn't there.

Julie and Luke Evans held hands as they listened to the sermon from the third row. They had been going through a difficult time in their marriage, and today, Luke convinced his wife to play hooky from her job at the high school. They woke last night to the sound of someone screaming in the street outside their home. It had been a terrifying animal-like scream, and after turning on the porch light and finding no one outside, they got to talking. The couple stayed up all night and made love in the early morning light. Julie cooked breakfast, and they had even taken a shower together, which was something they hadn't done in years. Julie didn't tell Luke she'd been sleeping with Principal Garish and decided that she would go to confession to help her cope with the burden. Father Kieran offered her a penance for her sins.

In the back row sat a man whose face was terribly scarred. Jim Reilly had simply been in the wrong place at the wrong time and had the unfortunate experience of ending up on the radar of the class bully. The thug had thrown a cherry bomb into the boys' room toilet moments before Jim entered the stall. The shrapnel from the explosion left him disfigured for life. He received a settlement from the school, but it couldn't buy him a new face. Jim found himself in a crisis of faith in the months and years that followed the accident but had finally found the Lord and been a loyal member of the church ever since; he never missed a Wednesday afternoon Mass. He believed he had a great deal to be thankful for; at least he hadn't been sitting on the toilet when it exploded.

Jim, who used to be called Jimmy, watched as the young girl approached the podium, just to the left of the altar. Diane Nathan stood before the congregation with trembling hands, cleared her throat, and began to speak.

"Today's reading is a Letter from Paul to the Corinthians. *And when I came to you brothers, I did not come proclaiming the testimony of God with lofty speech or wisdom. For I decided to know nothing among you except Jesus Christ and Him crucified. And I was with you in weakness and in fear and in much trembling, and my speech and my message were not in plausible words of wisdom, but in demonstration of the Spirit, and of the power, so that your faith might not rest in the wisdom of men, but in the power of God. This is the word of the Lord.*"

"Thanks be to God," the congregation responded as Diane blessed herself and returned to her seat. Father Kieran offered the girl a look of approval.

Josh Wilson read from the Book of Revelation for the second reading and did an equally impressive job. Father Kieran waited for the boy to be seated before he approached the altar to deliver the Gospel. He listened to the sound of the wind as it picked up outside the church and paused for a moment before continuing. The rustle of leaves being blown against the front doors broke the silence. It echoed throughout the large church, off the vaulted ceiling, and against the stained glass windows.

"Before we continue, I believe the Lord has given us a sign. If there is anything in your vehicles you would like to bring inside, whether it be food, clothing, or weapons, I believe that now is the time to collect those items. We will continue with the Mass when everyone has returned."

Almost every man in the church stood up and walked out the front door to their vehicles. Many of the women joined them as well. They had all come with the same goal in mind. They were looking for guidance, and there wasn't a soul in the place that hadn't lost something along the way. Whether it had been within the past couple days or years ago in a high school bathroom, they had all lost something, and they were prepared to fight for what they still had left.

The parishioners returned to the church carrying duffle bags filled with food and clothing. Some brought sleeping bags, portable lanterns, and flashlights. Father Kieran watched as the shotgun cases began to stack up against the back wall of the church near the confessionals. His heart swelled as he witnessed the flock parade into the church; they had come prepared to go to war. He always knew he had been chosen to lead during a time of conflict. And even though he had been spared from serving in Vietnam, he had been chosen after all. He returned to the altar after the last man took his seat. Looking out at the congregation, a sense of elation consumed him. It was warm, and overpowering, and spread out to his arms and legs. Kieran wiped his eyes and held out his hands.

"Thanks be to God," he said.

CHAPTER 66

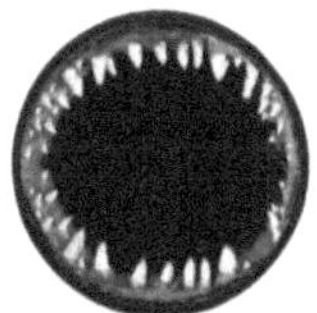

They followed the crowd at a snail's pace, making sure they were at the very back of the line. As the three friends stepped into the building, Troy turned to them and mouthed the word—*Now!*

Janis held the door from closing as Troy reached for the fire alarm, grabbed the handle, and pulled. At first, nothing happened. His heart floundered in his chest. It was the only plan he could think of, and he was sure it'd been a good one. He looked at Wendy, who shrugged her shoulders; neither knew what to do next. Then the thunderous sound of a dozen bells bleating at once filled the air.

Wendy's eyes lit up, and a huge smile crossed her face. She and Troy spun around, exited the building, and descended the stairs as Janis allowed the heavy door to slam behind them. Inside, the pandemonium had already begun. None of the staff had been prepared for the unscheduled fire drill. On top of that, the children never knew what to do or where to go, even when there were adults who knew what was happening.

The three children ran across the playground to the back part of the lot that bordered the ball field. Wendy was the first to hit the small four-foot fence and scaled it like a gazelle. Janis followed with an equal amount of grace. Troy was so excited he almost tripped before he even made it there but managed to right himself and bound over the small obstacle, although not quite as gracefully as the girls had.

They tore across the pitcher's mound and into the outfield before anyone emerged from the school. Janis proved to be the fastest and made it to the railroad tracks ten steps before the others. Troy and Wendy caught up to her and burst onto the dusty tracks laughing and ecstatic. It had worked like a charm, and it had been Troy's idea.

"Let's go before anyone knows we're missing." Wendy urged them down the tracks in the direction of Marco's Playmart.

"Oh my God, that was amazing," Janis cried. "I thought my heart was gonna explode." She punched Troy in the arm and gave him a look of approval.

Wendy leaned next to him and kissed him on the cheek. "That was pretty smart."

Troy beamed and felt as if he had finally done something right after being uncertain for so long. It was a feeling he thought he could get used to.

They ran down the tracks, congratulating each other on the amazing job they had done, when a strong gust of wind kicked up some loose dust, blowing the fine particles into the air. Troy looked toward the threatening sky; the clouds appeared to gain speed as they passed across the sun like horses on a carousel. He shivered and zipped his jacket even more, noticing it had gotten much colder since they'd left school. *Rain's almost here.* They needed to hurry if they were going to pull this off. Troy prayed that Mrs. Marco wouldn't question him about why he and the girls weren't in school. If he was lucky, someone else would be working at the register instead of her.

It was only two blocks from the school to the toy store, and they arrived at the back of the store in no time, out of breath and elated from their victory. They stopped for a few seconds and attempted to collect themselves in preparation for the second phase of the mission.

Troy had the hardest time settling down and found it impossible to wipe the smile from his face. Wendy looked at him and shook her head.

"You're gonna get us busted looking like that," she said.

He stared back at her as if he'd been injured. "Looking like what?"

"Come on, Troy," Janis said. "You look like you just pulled the fire alarm at the school. You can't go in there like that; we'll definitely get caught."

"She's right." Wendy nodded. "You're staying here. Me and Janis will go in and get what we need while you keep a lookout. And try not to get noticed by anyone."

Before he could argue, both girls had flung their lunch boxes at him and disappeared around the side of the building.

He felt a bit foolish standing there holding three lunch boxes, but that still didn't prevent him from grinning like an idiot. He looked around the building and tried to play it cool, doubting he was doing a very good job of it. Hopefully, no one would come along and see him standing there, acting as guilty as a dog with its head in the toilet.

He stood next to a dumpster filled with cardboard. He and Rob had liberated a stockpile of the stuff from the trash bin to build the Scream in the Dark haunted house in his dad's garage. Which felt like a very long time ago. Troy tried to remember the day he and Rob had gone over the details of the maze.

The whole plan had come quickly to the two boys as they sat on the playground during lunch recess. It had been late September when they first got to designing what would be the highlight of the party. Troy was going to lead the kids through the maze to where Rob would be hiding in the coffin.

"I bet Tommy throws up this year," Rob said as he sat on the grass with his notebook opened to a rough sketch of the maze drawn onto one of the pages.

"Yeah, he almost did last year, and that wasn't even scary. This is going to be so much better." Troy leaned over to look at what his friend had drawn.

"Everybody is going to walk in here." Rob pointed to the entrance. "What should we do first?"

"We need to start off with a big scare. That's what always happens in the movies."

"You mean like someone jumps out or chases them?"

"It should be pitch-black so they can't see anything. And they should be trapped. And then BAMM!" Troy screamed at Rob and startled him, causing the boy to scribble across the page with his pencil.

"Quit it, jerk!" he yelled. "That's not funny."

Rob tried not to smile but couldn't help himself, and then both boys burst out laughing. It had been pretty funny, after all.

"I want to do something in the first room that will make them scream," Troy said, trying to regain himself.

Rob put his pencil under his chin and started to think about what Troy had just said. "That's it!" Rob shouted.

"What, what's it?"

"We can call the haunted house Scream in the Dark."

"Oh my God! That's awesome. Scream in the Dark," he repeated, loving the way it sounded. "Now we just have to *make* them scream in the dark."

"We will. Don't look now, but I think someone's staring at you." He nodded to the girl on the swings across the playground.

Troy looked up and saw her sitting by herself. "You mean Wendy? I don't think she's staring at me. I don't think she even knows who I am."

"Are you kidding me? She's been staring at you the whole time. Tell you the truth, I think she's been looking at you since she moved here last month." Rob went back to doodling on his pad.

"Don't be stupid; she's just a girl. What would she be looking at us for?"

"My dad says that one day I'm gonna wake up and I'm gonna want to be friends with girls. I don't know why, but maybe Wendy wants to be friends with boys. My mom says that girls are more mature." Rob had been blessed with a wealth of knowledge for a fourth-grade boy and was always sharing his pearls of wisdom.

"I don't believe that, and the only people who say that are girls," Troy said.

"Well, my dad agreed with my mom when she said it."

"Yeah, my dad agrees with my mom a lot too, but I know he doesn't really feel that way. I think he does it just so she won't yell at him." Troy looked over at Wendy and caught her staring at them. *Oh my God! She is staring at us.*

"I think you should ask her." Rob elbowed him.

"Ask her what?"

"Duh." Rob made a face. "Ask her to come to the party, you dork."

Wendy averted her eyes when Troy looked up again. He had never said all that much to her. She was nice enough and all, but she was still a girl, and they didn't have that much in common. "Oh, come on, I'd feel stupid. Besides, I don't think she would want to come anyway."

"You'll never know if you don't ask. But I bet she says yes." Rob gave Troy a look of confidence that said, *go for it*. "Unless, you're chicken … Is that what it is?"

Troy felt heat rise within him. Now he *had* to ask. It was a no-win situation either way. If he did ask, she would say no, and he would feel like a total jerk. But if he didn't, then he would be a chicken, and that was even worse. He looked at his friend and considered pulling his hair out.

"That's okay if you're chicken," Rob said. "I'm sure there are a lot of chickens in the fourth grade. I mean … I don't know any, but I'm sure there are a whole bunch."

"Fine!" Troy shouted, then grabbed Rob's pencil and broke it in two pieces. He stood up and threw the pencil back to his friend. "Here's your stupid pencil, jerk face."

Troy walked across the playground to where the girl sat on the swings with her feet dangling a few inches from the ground. She looked down as he approached and started to rock back and forth. He stopped in front of her, lost his nerve, and stared at the top of her head for a moment. Her hair was dark and shiny, and Troy thought it looked incredibly soft. He had no idea why a thought like that had popped into his head, but for some reason, it had.

Then Wendy looked up at him, and for the first time, Troy noticed just how big her eyes were. They reminded him of Bambi's eyes in the Disney movie. He had never noticed, but she had long eyelashes too. He suddenly felt self-conscious and forgot why he had come over in the first place.

"What?" she snapped.

"What?" he repeated and realized he had been staring.

"What are you looking at?" she asked.

This was getting more awkward by the second. "I'm sorry. I wanted to see if you might ... um. Well, I mean if you don't want to ... that's ... um." He looked back at Rob and wanted to kill him. This was his fault, and now he was stuck looking like an idiot. Rob nodded to him and smiled, which helped him regain a little of his composure.

"I don't understand, Troy," she said.

Hearing Wendy say his name struck him like a hammer. That had been the first time she had ever said it, and he suddenly felt much better.

"I was wondering if you would like to come to my Halloween party. It's a costume party, and I'm building a haunted house." Troy let out a sigh of relief. At least he didn't have to worry about being called a chicken.

"Oh." Wendy acted surprised by the question. Then she looked back at the ground and began to rock again. "I have to ask my mom."

"Sure." Troy knew what that meant. He bowed his head and turned around to walk away.

"Hey, Troy," she called him back. "I'm sure she'll say yes. Is it okay if I dress as Princess Leia?"

He looked back with his mouth hung open. Had she actually said what he thought? "Yeah, that would be awesome. I love *Star Wars*. It's, like, the greatest movie of all time."

"Well, you're really going to like my costume then. I can't wait to see the haunted house. I hope it's scary."

"Oh, you can count on that. It's gonna be awesome."

"Thanks for asking me."

"Okay," he said. A warm rush spread across Troy's face as he turned back, almost breaking into a sprint to return to his friend's side. He sat down and didn't say a word.

"Told you," Rob said.

"Shut up." Troy wiped the sweat from his forehead.

"You owe me a new pencil, you big dork." Rob threw the broken pieces at him, causing a fresh fit of laughter.

Troy had no idea how Rob had known, but he had. There was something about Wendy that was different than the other girls in class. She was cool, and she even liked *Star Wars*; that was unbelievable.

"Now all we need to do is figure out the haunted house and we're all set. If this isn't scary, we're both gonna look stupid." Rob was right. They couldn't call it Scream in the Dark if it wasn't scary. That would be a big letdown for everyone.

Troy picked up the broken pencil pieces and played with them for a moment, trying to think what might scare everyone. He held them up in front of his eyes and looked at his friend, giving Rob the appearance as if he were behind bars, like in a jail cell. He thought about that for a second. *A jail cell! What if ... that's it!*

"I got it!" he shouted. Troy leaned over and explained his idea for the first room and how scary it would be if they could pull it off. Rob snatched the sharpened half of the pencil from his friend and began to sketch out the bars of a cage. Troy showed him where it should be hidden in the wall so the kids couldn't see it until the strobe light went on ... when the monsters were inches from their faces. It was brilliant. Their friends really were going to scream in the dark.

"Hey dork!" Wendy shouted.

Troy looked up to see the girls had returned.

"I thought I told you not to look guilty. Jeez, you're still grinning like a weirdo. Let's go before someone sees you like that."

It didn't bother Troy that Wendy thought he looked like a fool. He had forgotten all about that day on the playground and how he and Rob had planned out the haunted house room by room. That was the day he asked Wendy to go to the party, and he thought it was the day that he realized he liked her.

Janis held up a bag full of items.

"Did you get everything?" Troy asked.

Janis shook the bag and grinned. "We sure did, and then some. I didn't know you could buy so much with ten dollars."

Wendy started walking towards the train tracks and called back, "Come on, we can talk on the way. Look at the sky."

Troy noticed that the storm was nearly on top of them. He hurried to join her, juggling the lunch boxes as he ran, and Janis followed.

The sky had grown even darker. Heavy clouds with deep purple bellies loomed overhead and appeared ready to dump. The wind had also picked up, causing the temperature to drop. The children hustled to get to Troy's house, which was only a few blocks away, when the first flash of lightning cracked across the sky. About ten seconds later, it was followed by a slow rumble that reminded Troy of the bowling alley. The storm was coming, and they had little time left to get to his house.

"We need to hurry; let's go." Wendy started to run, and Troy and Janis took off after her.

Another bolt lit up the sky like a light saber. Troy was reminded of the day in the graveyard and the creatures that chased him. He kept his eyes focused on the path in front of him, not wanting to look to the left or right for fear of seeing the horrible beasts. He told himself, *As long as I don't look, they won't be there.* He prayed that was true.

CHAPTER 67

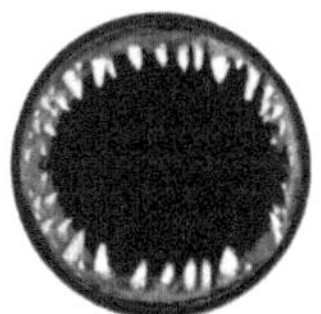

Deputy Jenkins and fireman Drew Halberg waited in the office of the fire station, staring at the radio. Soon they would get the go ahead to start the second phase of the operation. In all his years on the force, Beau had never experienced anything close to the nightmare the past twenty-four hours had been. First the Texaco station had gone up like a Roman candle, then the explosion at the medical center, and now his friends were dying. Tara was dead, Kovach was dead, even Tim Colbert, who had been Beau's partner for more years than he could remember.

Beau, Tim, and Allen Primrose had been the lifeblood of the department back in the day, long before Vietnam and the kids had started smoking grass. In his day, teenagers were content to swipe a little booze from their parents' liquor cabinets. That was all you needed to have a good time or get into a girl's pants; everyone knew liquor was quicker. He missed the days when all it took was a couple shots to put lead in the old pencil and grease the wheels. It had been longer than Beau could remember since his one-eyed trouser trout had even moved. It was a sick joke what happened to men his age, when the mind was still willing but the body was no longer able.

Years ago, it had been difficult to keep the damn thing from popping out of his pants every time a pretty skirt walked by. The sucker used to stand at attention and watch him shave every morning; now all it did was hang there and watch him tie his shoes. And it didn't appear interested in that either.

If anyone ever wants to make a million bucks, all they have to do is invent a pill that gives old guys boners.

"Chief Jones to base. Come in, Drew." The radio crackled to life.

Both men stared at it for a moment, then the young fireman leaned in. "Go ahead, Chief."

"Hit it, son. That's a go for Operation Air Raid."

"Roger that, Chief." Drew turned to Beau, who sat at the control desk.

"Well, here goes nothing," Beau said as he hit the control panel.

The siren screamed to life, erupting from the speakers attached to the exterior of the building and the ones positioned throughout the town. The growing timbre of the wail increased in volume and ceased to rest. It had been set to run continuously, which was a much different signal than the three short blasts for a brush or house fire. There was no mistaking what this signal meant as it grew louder without pause; it was the air raid warning, alerting everyone to report to the shelter.

Beau doubted if many would take it seriously, since it was '79 not '59. Most would just think the siren was broken. But they had been instructed to keep it running no matter what, which was sure to get folks' attention.

Then the bay doors opened, and Gabriel Ford pulled out of the station in the ladder truck, laying on the air horn as he did. He drove past the municipal building and headed onto the turnpike, followed by Tank Ferguson in the pump truck, also laying on the horn.

Three sheriff's cruisers took off from behind the station with their cherries flashing and sirens screaming. David Rainey was followed by Glenn Gillick and Mike Turino; the men had been given their own individual routes and neighborhoods to canvass. The first part of the job was to get the sirens going; the second was to canvass the neighborhoods and deliver the message.

Beau examined the exasperated look on Drew's face. The poor kid couldn't be any older than twenty-one and still had years to go before his pecker gave out on him. But sure enough, one day it would. Beau swore to himself that if he survived this nightmare, he would get right to work on that boner pill. Now that was a million-dollar idea.

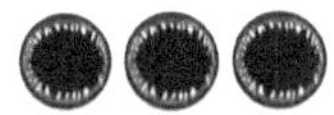

Carl worked transporting medical equipment into the basement. The supplies had arrived, and the weapons were in the process of being distributed. He ascended the landing into the lobby and heard the initial scream of the fire whistle. It wouldn't be long before one of his men showed up at the elementary school, which meant he and Lois needed to get moving. He wanted her and Troy in that high school shelter long before the storm hit. She had questioned why he didn't want her staying at the medical center with Alice and Will, and he had avoided answering. The truth was he didn't hold much faith in the center's ability to weather an attack; the high school was the only structure he felt somewhat confident about.

He froze as a flash of bright blue lit up the front entrance of the building. It was followed by a slow rumble of thunder that set his hackles standing. The storm had moved much quicker than he anticipated. Men ran both in and out of the building, carrying boxes and weapons in a desperate attempt to beat the rain. Nurse TenHove worked with Alice and Lois, transporting medications to the basement, when the lightning struck.

Lois and Carl looked at each other and exchanged an understood message; it was time. She set the box down and turned to her sister. "I have to go get Troy. Will you be okay till I get back?"

"I'll be fine," Alice said and hugged her. "Will is here and so is Billy, but hurry back."

"I will." Lois kissed Alice on the cheek and released her as a loud clap of thunder rocked the building like an avalanche.

"Nurse TenHove, it's time to get the patients into the basement. I'll be back as soon as I can," Carl instructed her as Deputy Lutchen and the little girl emerged into the lobby with the Shepherd at their heels. "Ted, keep them safe till I get back. The storm is about to hit, and we don't have much time." He had to shout to be heard over the siren.

He and Lois exited the main entrance and were bombarded by the blare of a fire whistle screaming as if it were in pain. A sharp crack of lightning spread across the sky like the crooked fingers of an arthritic man. It was followed by a concussion of thunder that felt as if it were on top of them. They entered the cruiser, and Carl turned over the ignition as the first fat drops of rain smacked against the windshield, loud as popcorn.

"Don't worry." He hit the gas and sped out of the parking lot. "One of my men is at the school making sure everything goes as planned."

Lois nodded, but a look of dread washed across her face. Another set of fat raindrops hit the windshield, and the sky grew even darker. It was going to be one hell of a storm.

Burt needed to share his discovery with Carl and had told Nurse TenHove he would do his best to be there by noon. It was already past twelve, and his stomach had started to do the Hokey Pokey. He now knew the bacterium carried a metallic signature, but it was still unclear what exact type of metal had caused the poisoning. If he had to guess, he was leaning toward a combination of several, with iron and mercury being the likely suspects. Still, there was something about the cellular composition that was entirely foreign, and he was willing to bet that if a chemist had a good look with a photon microscope, they would find at least one unidentifiable metal. It was only a hunch, but Burt was usually good when it came to his hunches.

The infection was vulnerable to magnetization, which meant if a powerful enough magnet were focused on any of the creatures, then it should be sufficient to kill it. Unfortunately, it would also kill the host; and from what they had seen so far, it appeared impossible to survive the infection. The fact that Malcolm had been sent to destroy the MRI machine proved he was on the right track. But there wasn't a powerful enough magnetic current that could be used on command or was transportable. Whatever they were dealing with was one clever son of a bitch.

He snatched his coat from the table, shut off the lights, and opened the back door of the lab. A blast of cold air slapped him across the face as soon as he stepped outside. Burt made his way to his sedan, feeling good about the progress he had made. Carl would be pleased, and he hoped to run into him soon. He fumbled with his keys for a moment as the first bolt of lightning lit up the sky. The wind picked up slightly, and the temperature felt as if it had dropped in a matter of seconds. It was going to rain; with any luck, he would be at Chilton before it started. It wasn't far, and it looked like they were in for a real boomer.

At first, it sounded like someone had crept up behind him and screamed. Then he recognized the familiar blare of the fire whistle. It grew louder and bolder, and Burt anticipated the ebb and flow of the siren's typical rhythm. But there was no pause of the steady horn as it reached full timbre, cutting through the air like a jet engine.

"Jesus H. Christ. What the hell is going on?" He turned toward the direction of the whistle. The siren continued, uninterrupted and steady. Burt had been around during the Cuban Missile Crisis and knew exactly what a steady siren meant. It was the universal signal for an air raid. *But that's not possible*. He wondered if the switchboard at the station had fried. Then he heard the horns from the trucks in the distance. Something was going on, and it sure as hell didn't sound good.

A hard drop of rain fell from the sky and landed against his face. It was followed by another that hit the ground in front of him. The droplets were so big and fat he heard them as they smacked against the pavement. Burt looked up and saw how dark and threatening the sky had become. The storm was moving fast, and the sudden cloud cover held the potential for disaster. If these things were predisposed to darkness, the storm was going to put the people of Garrett Grove at a huge disadvantage.

The din of police sirens mixed with the wail of the fire whistle, but Burt heard something else in the background. It was the sound of voices shouting over bullhorns; it was impossible for Burt to decipher a damn thing they were saying.

He jumped into his sedan dand sped out of the parking lot toward the medical center. Even with the windows rolled up, it was impossible to hear himself think. Burt dug his hand into his jacket pocket, looking to find the gun Carl had given him. Which was no longer there, not that it had done him a damn bit of good. He hoped it would be useful to Father Kieran; at least *he* had figured out what to do with it.

"Brothers and Sisters, A demon-oppressed man who was blind and mute was brought to Jesus, and he healed him so that the man spoke and saw. And all of the people were amazed and said, "Can this be the son of David?" But the Pharisees heard it and said, "It is only by Beelzebub, the prince of darkness, that this man casts out demons. Knowing their thoughts, Jesus said unto them, "No city or house divided against itself will stand. If Satan casts out Satan, he is divided against himself. How will his kingdom stand? If I cast out demons by Beelzebub, by whom do your sons cast them out? But if it is by the Spirit of God that I cast out demons, then the Kingdom of God has come upon you. How can someone enter a strong man's house and plunder his goods, unless he first binds the strong man. Whoever is not with me is against me, and whoever does not gather with me scatters."

"This is the word of the Lord."

A loud clap of thunder echoed in the distance as Father Kieran finished delivering the Gospel. The congregation took notice of the dramatic accent and interpreted it as a sign. Father Kieran was sure it was and welcomed it. "Brothers and Sisters, the time has come for you to gather with me. For we are a house undivided, and we are strong in the Holy Spirit. It is not by chance you all chose to be in the house of the Lord on today of all days. I feel the time for action is near, and I would like to bless everyone as you receive the Sacrament of the Eucharist. But we must hurry." Another concussion of thunder rattled the stained glass windows in their frames. "Forgive me if I rush this a bit, but I don't think we have much time. Please line up."

Father Kieran took the vessel containing the Eucharist from the altar and held it up. "On the night he was betrayed, he took bread, gave it to his disciples, and said, 'Take this, all of you, and eat from it; this is my body. Do this in remembrance of me.'"

The line quickly gathered, and Father Kieran blessed every man, woman, and child that approached the altar. He administered the Sacrament and was almost finished when the fire whistle began to sound. The siren increased in volume, ceasing to stop.

Father Kieran stood before them and spoke loud enough so they all could hear. "Brothers and Sisters, the time has come to stand. Stand in the name of the Lord." He reached beneath his robe into his waistband and removed the handgun. "I could use some twenty-five caliber bullets if anyone has a few they could spare."

The congregation erupted with an inspired roar of approval as the sirens were joined by the sounds of fire trucks in the distance. Another flash of lightning illuminated the images depicted in the stained glass windows and was followed by a loud rumble. No less than seven men approached Father Kieran and offered him ammunition for his weapon. He thanked them all with the same reply: "God bless you."

The fire alarm came as a shock to the staff at the elementary school. No one had scheduled a fire drill, and they were having a difficult time getting the children lined up on the playground. It would have been an impossible task for those who had made it to work if attendance hadn't been so light. Miss Davis, Miss Boriello, and Principal Grace worked like sheepdogs to round up the kids; it was looking like one of the little pranksters had pulled the alarm near the back entrance.

It was hard to get an accurate head count, but it looked like everyone was present. Principal Grace gave the go ahead for the children to return to their classrooms. With the sky growing darker by the second and the threat of rain looming in the distance, they all knew they'd be lucky to get everyone back inside before the storm hit.

Then the fire whistle started to howl. The children turned toward the station, which was less than two blocks away.

"What now?" Miss Boriello shouted as two fire trucks sped past the school blaring their horns.

The children, excited by the sight of the trucks, began to stray from their neatly formed lines and made their way closer to the street to get a better look. The siren grew louder and louder and refused to stop. It was something Jill Boriello never imagined she would hear in her lifetime: the single continuous blast of the air raid siren. *That's not possible. Maybe it's broken.* She watched as three police cruisers screamed past the school with their sirens blaring and their lights flashing.

One of the cruisers pulled up to the front of the school and that set the rest of the children in motion. They broke into two groups, with half of them heading toward the sheriff's vehicle and the other half meandering toward the back fence to get a better look at the fire house.

Jill Boriello screamed to be heard over the blare of the sirens and horns but was unable to raise the children's attention. She looked across the playground to Principal Grace, who had also lost control. Jill cupped her hands on the sides of her mouth and shouted once again, then felt something strain in the back of her throat. It was no use; things were falling apart, and she knew she needed to act.

From where she stood on the steps, Jill could see things unraveling fast. She turned back toward the door and looked inside, hoping to find anything that might help. The area was empty except for a few extra desks and the bin where the phys. ed. equipment was kept. It wasn't much, just a few balls and a large parachute. Then she saw it. Jill spun on her heels and ran into the school.

A second later, she stormed out the back door with a bright orange flag and something in her mouth. She started to wave the flag as if it were the last lap of the Daytona 500, then Jill bit down on the object between her lips and blew into it as hard as she could. The professional referee's whistle cut through the roar of the sirens like a scalpel, demanding the attention of every student on the playground. They turned on cue, as if they had all been caught cheating on a math test. Then she took the whistle out of her mouth and screamed. "Get inside NOW!" She waved the flag towards the open door, and every single child made their way back into the building with their tails tucked between their legs. Not one remained behind to watch the policeman get out of his car and enter the building.

Principal Grace watched the kindergarten teacher take matters into her own hands. "I have got to get that woman a raise," she said to herself.

After the last child entered the building, the rain started, followed by a violent bolt of lightning that sizzled out of the west. They had gotten the children back into the building ... just in time. Principal Grace followed the last student inside and met the deputy in the hallway. They walked to her office and closed the door behind them.

CHAPTER 68

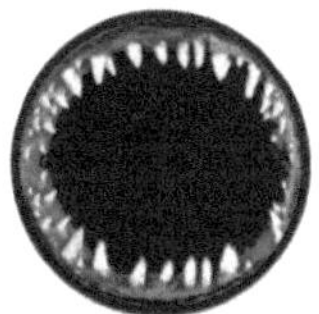

Troy and the girls arrived at his house before the rain started, with the thunder and lightning following them the entire way. He led his friends around the back to a flowerpot beside the door. He bent down and retrieved a key from underneath, then let them inside as a loud clap of thunder exploded overhead, causing all of them to jump.

They entered the first-floor rec room where Donald Fisher kept a large drawing board, an array of blueprints, and a couple small toolboxes. Janis poured the contents of her shopping bag onto the drawing board to show Troy what she and Wendy had bought.

Troy noticed the three wrist rockets were not the cheap, flimsy kind. These were the ones the big kids used to break bottles. He picked one up and examined it.

"Radical," he said, checking out the feel of it in his hand.

There were also several boxes of magnets that Wendy and Janis began to open and dump out onto the table. They were heavy and thick and looked like they would do the job—provided they could fashion the magnets into sharp enough projectiles.

Troy opened one of his dad's toolboxes, rooted around until he found what he was looking for, and produced a large pair of tin snips. "This should do it," he said and grabbed one of the large magnets. He positioned it between the blades of the snips and pressed down on the handles as hard as he could. Nothing happened. He tried again using all his strength and pushed even harder this time.

"Jeez, that's tougher than I thought." A bead of sweat fell from his forehead to the floor as he struggled to work the tool.

"Maybe you're doing it wrong," Wendy said.

"Ughhh." He bore down harder onto the magnet, feeling he might get it this time. The snips scratched into the magnet's surface, but the object remained intact.

Wendy dug into the toolbox and stood up with a hammer and chisel in her hand and a great smile on her face. She handed the tools to Troy. "Here, maybe these'll work."

Troy figured they couldn't do any worse than the tin snips. He took the tools and examined them, thinking maybe she was right. Troy laid the magnet on the hard tile floor, then rested the chisel against it. He raised the hammer, struck the top of the chisel. The magnet shattered into two pieces that shot like a couple of pinballs across the floor.

"Whoa!" he shouted as the pieces scattered.

"Yeah!" Janis and Wendy screamed in unison, then proceeded to collect the fragments.

Using the hammer and chisel, Troy cracked magnet after magnet, and the girls ran around collecting the sharp pieces. Together, they manufactured a stockpile of shrapnel and nearly depleted their supply of intact magnets.

"Let's try a couple out to make sure they work," Troy said to the girls, who nodded in agreement. Each child grabbed a wrist rocket and pocketed a handful of the shards.

He led them into the backyard where two large chestnut trees stood. Spiny cones littered the ground, and a family of squirrels were busy cracking them open and extracting the nuts. The animals looked up for a moment when the children exited the house, then went right back to work. Thunder continued to rumble in the distance, and the sky had gotten darker since they'd gone inside to manufacture their weapons.

"We better hurry up," Troy said, looking up at the sky.

"Okay, just a couple practice shots and we'll go." Janis placed a magnet into the pouch of the wrist rocket and pulled back on the rubber tubing. She aimed at the trunk of the closest chestnut tree and let go of the pouch.

The magnet whistled through the air and connected with the tree, making a wet *Thwack* as it buried itself into the bark.

"No way!" Troy shouted. "That works even better than I thought it would."

Thwack

Wendy sent a magnet flying into the tree, landing a few inches above the one Janis had let loose.

"So cool," Troy said and loaded his own projectile into the pouch of his wrist rocket. He pulled back on the tubing, surprised to find just how difficult it was, and grimaced. *Darn, how the heck did a couple girls do it?*

He finally managed to pull the bands back as far as he could and aimed the magnet at the trunk of the tree. He let go of the pouch, and the bands released. The magnet flew up and over his head and the rubber tubing snapped hard against his fingers.

"Ouch!" he yelled and shook his hand to knock the sting out of it.

Both girls smiled at his ineffective attempt to work the wrist rocket, and Wendy even let out a small chuckle. Troy felt the heat rise in his face. Embarrassed by his inadequacy but still determined, he loaded another magnet into the pouch, pulled back even harder, and aimed at the trunk of the chestnut tree. He wasn't sure what he had done wrong the first time but thought it might have been the way he released the magnet. He hadn't been that sure of himself and fumbled at the last minute. *That's why.*

He focused on the target and took a deep breath. Then he released the pouch, and the projectile sizzled away from him like a bottle rocket.

The magnet buried itself into the trunk of the tree with a hearty *Thwack*, landing even closer to where Janis's magnet had hit. Troy pumped his fists in a victory celebration.

"Hooray!" Wendy gave him the thumbs-up, and Janis showed him a toothy grin as a sign of approval. The squirrels weren't pleased with what they were up to and had taken to the trees to escape from the commotion.

A low rumble of thunder cascaded over the mountain, lasting for almost a full five seconds. As it faded, it was replaced by another sound that was very different and much higher pitched. The children looked at each other when the fire whistle started to blow and grew in intensity.

At first Troy thought it had something to do with the alarm he had pulled at the school. He stood there frozen with the siren screaming. But there was something different about the whistle, the way it continued to bellow out in one long, monotonous drone. It sounded as if it were broken or something.

Troy eyed the girls as a sharp flash of blue lit his face like the strobe of a camera. Lightning zigzagged across the sky, followed by a tremendous single clap of thunder that made all of them jump.

Other sirens joined in, accompanied by the deep bass blast of the horns from the fire trucks. Seconds later, there were voices barking out announcements over loudspeakers.

Oh no, they're coming. He turned to find both Janis and Wendy wore the same look of terror on their faces. He prayed the girls were ready but in truth was more worried how he would react.

It sounded like the world was coming to an end with all the sirens and horns blasting out in competition with one another. He tried to listen to what the voices were saying, but it was impossible to make out over the noise.

Troy didn't know what horror was headed their way, even though he had already encountered the strange creatures. He prayed he was wrong about the whole thing and the three of them would be able to laugh about it tomorrow. But as the noise continued to assault their ears and the sky turned black, he doubted they would.

As if the universe were listening to what was going on in his head, the rain started to fall. Just a drop or two at first, then a second later, the heavens opened and a torrent fell in a ceaseless downpour. It only took a moment to soak the children thoroughly. And although they weren't far from the back door, it was impossible to see the house from where they stood.

Troy ran to the girls, who huddled together, shielding themselves from the wind and rain. He grabbed his friends and urged them in the direction of the house but was halted when a shriek cut through the storm like a heart attack. The children tensed in horror as the color drained from their faces. There was a second shriek, more mournful than the first and sounding much closer.

Troy took both girls by the hand and forced himself to act, sloshing through the wet grass towards the back door. The heavy rain made it difficult to see as it hammered against his face and stung his skin. Janis and Wendy cried out, disoriented from the sudden downpour, but Troy continued to push onward. It was like being stuck in a dream; no matter how hard he tried to gain ground, it was impossible to move forward. Troy felt as if he were walking on a peanut butter sandwich as his feet sank into the over-saturated ground. Biting down, he leaned into the rain and pulled the girls along.

He saw it. Running along the right side of the house. It was one of those things, not exactly what he had seen in the graveyard but close enough. This one was bigger and didn't appear as quick, but it was difficult to tell with the rain in his eyes. The creature screeched like a wild cat caught in a trap as it skirted the fence on the side of his property. Then it spotted them and took off with a determination and speed that Troy remembered all too well.

"Run!" Troy yelled with his heart exploding in his chest. He watched the beast's accelerated approach and knew they would never reach the back door in time.

CHAPTER 69

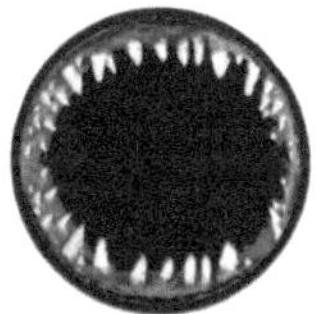

The ladder truck navigated its way through the Village with its lights flashing and sirens wailing. The residents who were still alive to hear the commotion looked out to see the big red spectacle with its newly mounted equipment fixed to the roof and the ladder itself. Gabriel Ford, who sat behind the wheel, grabbed the microphone and delivered the message. His booming voice exploded through the dozen external speakers attached to the truck.

"Citizens of Garrett Grove, this is an emergency. I repeat, this is an emergency. Report to the air raid shelter at the high school immediately. This is not a drill. Bring only what you can carry on your person and any medication you require. All citizens, report to the high school immediately." Gabriel continued to repeat the message as he maneuvered the vehicle at a snail's pace through the community.

The town's siren had been howling for a good fifteen minutes, and now it was up to the fire department to deliver the message and get people moving. But as Gabriel was leaving the Village and turning onto Winding Way, the skies erupted, complicating matters. The rain came down in a torrent of heavy droplets, making it almost impossible to see out the windshield, even with the wipers set on high. He white-knuckled the steering wheel with one hand as he gripped the microphone with the other.

"I repeat, this is an emergency. If you have children at the elementary or junior high school, you do *not* need to pick them up. They are already being transported to the high school. All citizens of Garrett Grove, this is not a drill."

Lynn Donovan poked her head out the front door as the fire truck rolled past and delivered its message. *Dear God, what's going on?* She looked down at the frightened beagle hiding behind a stack of boxes. "That doesn't sound very good at all, Peanuts. I think we better do what they say. If Janis is already there, she'll be looking for us."

Lynn ran to the kitchen to grab her car keys and the leash; she fixed it to Peanut's collar and urged the pooch along. "Come on, sweetie. Let's go." But the dog wasn't having it and parked itself in the hallway. Lynn pulled and begged the beagle to move. Finally, she got so frustrated, she scooped the dog in her arms and carried it outside into the rain. They were both soaked by the time they reached the car. Lynn plopped Peanuts into the passenger seat, pulled out of the drive, and made her way to the high school.

Deputy David Rainey arrived at the school moments before the rain started. He ushered Principal Grace into her office, closed the door behind them, and delivered the sheriff's message. The look of dumbfounded bewilderment on her face suggested she had either not heard him the first time or found the news impossible to digest.

"What—?" she asked. "Taking the children—I don't understand."

Rainey raised his voice and spoke in a deliberate, authoritative tone. "Miss Austin, in fifteen minutes, you and your entire staff, along with every child in the building, are going to line up and walk out the front door. You'll be transported to the high school, where you will remain in the shelter until the threat has passed. I don't have time to explain this a third time, so I need you to work with me and help get the children to safety."

Grace's hands began to tremble; the deputy's message appeared to register and hit home. However, she remained seated like a deer frozen in the headlights.

"We need to move—now, Miss Austin!"

Which got her on her feet and moving. She followed the deputy into the hallway and looked out the main entrance. Three school buses sat at the front curb idling, and a second police cruiser had pulled up behind them. Two people exited the vehicle and ran toward the building.

"We need to do this now!" Rainey urged as she led him into the third-grade class. They delivered their announcement to the stunned children and an even more surprised Miss Davis, and then made their way to the next room. They entered the fourth-grade class, but before Principal Grace could speak, she was ambushed by a frantic Miss Boriello. The woman was on the verge of tears.

"I can't find them anywhere. They must have snuck off during the fire drill."

"Wait a second," Grace said, trying to calm her. "Who are you talking about? Who can't you find?"

"Troy Fischer, Wendy Sirocka, and Janis Thompson. I looked everywhere."

Principal Grace suppressed a squeal and bit her lip. It was the same children who had made a scene on the playground, the ones who had warned the other students that something was wrong. "Jesus Christ," she said. "The little shits were right."

The door behind them was thrown open as Sheriff Primrose and Lois Fischer burst into the room. Lois scanned the class and started shouting. "Where is he? Where is Troy?" Her voice trembled as she spoke.

Principal Grace ushered Lois and Carl into the hallway. "Mrs. Fischer, someone pulled the fire alarm; we believe that Troy and the girls snuck out during the commotion."

"You don't know where my son is!?" Lois screamed. "Just what kind of a place are you running here?"

"We think he left with Wendy Sirocka and Janis Thompson. They couldn't be gone any more than a half hour at most."

Lois balled her fists and cursed under her breath. "He's been hanging out with girls for less than a week and he's already lost his damn mind!"

"We'll find them," Carl said, attempting to pacify the situation. "There's only a few places they could be." He took Lois by the arm and urged her down the hallway. "Get them moving, David," he called to Deputy Rainey as he hurried Lois out the front door and into the rain.

Minutes later, Principal Grace and the rest of the staff led a parade of children out the front doors of Garrett elementary and onto the buses sitting at the curb. She counted heads as they took their seats, allowing the number of those who were missing to sink in. Nearly half were absent. She couldn't bear to imagine where they might be or what had kept them home … if that's even where they were.

Burt entered through the emergency room doors of the medical center and did a double take. When he left the place earlier, it had looked like a ghost town, but now it held all the intention of a termite mound. Firemen and orderlies ran to the left and right carrying boxes of supplies, while nurses escorted patients followed by candy stripers holding IV bags. Doris wasn't behind the desk and was nowhere to be seen. Burt followed the conga line of activity all the way to the main entrance, only to find the area even more congested. Finally, he spotted Doris directing patients down a stairwell. Her eyes fixed on him, standing there with his jaw open, and she rushed to his side.

"You're a sight, old man." She kissed him.

"What the hell is going on here?" he asked as men passed them on either side.

Doris wiped her eyes and swallowed. "Where have you been, under a rock? The Gables Bridge and Sunset Pass were destroyed this morning. The sheriff doesn't think help is coming and has ordered everyone into the shelters both here and at the high school. There isn't much time, and I need your help—again." She leaned in and whispered in his ear: "Do this for me and I'll do something that will really curl your toes."

Burt was about to offer a witty reply when Ed Koloski burst through the lobby's double doors pushing a cart loaded to the hilt with heavy fire power and ammunition. Burt eyed the stockpile, and his hand once again searched his empty pocket for Carl's gun, which still wasn't there. "If you would excuse me a second, dear. This won't take but a minute." He intercepted Koloski and approached the array of weaponry with a grin on his face.

"See anything you like, Mr. Lively?" Koloski said.

"As a matter of fact, I do." Burt picked up a nickel-plated 9 mm Beretta from the cart and tested the feel of the weapon in his hand. The brown leather grip was comfortable, and it had a good balance to it. "I think this will do nicely, thank you."

"Excellent choice." He handed Burt a box of cartridges and then reached for a second. "Just in case you don't hit anything with the first fifty rounds."

Burt smiled. He liked the guy—a snarky bastard, much like himself.

"Um, excuse me, boys." Nurse TenHove joined the men at the cart.

"I don't suppose you have anything for my lady friend?" Burt asked.

Ed reacted as if he'd been insulted and then cracked another wide grin. "I have just the thing." He rifled through the selection and came up with a snub-nosed .25.

Doris soured her face and then pointed to a chrome .357 magnum with an eight-inch barrel that looked a lot like the gun Dirty Harry carried. "What about that one?"

"The customer is always right," Ed said and handed her the weapon. "And might I say, it matches your eyes perfectly." He handed her a box of ammunition, then pulled out a small duffle bag for her and Burt to stow their gear. "Thanks for shopping," he replied, then proceeded to push the cart to the entrance of the stairwell. His progress was halted when Deputy Lutchen stepped in front of him.

Andrea Geary peered into the rearview mirror of the bus, scanning the faces of the children as she pulled into the parking lot of the high school. It had been a short ten-minute drive, and thanks to Miss Davis, the kids remained well behaved for the most part, though it was obvious they were shaken up. The second and third bus pulled in directly behind them; the operation had gone off without a hitch. A cluster of concerned parents waited for their children near the back of the building, where Bob Jones and several of his men stood, directing everyone into the shelter. Andrea opened the door, and Bob stepped in out of the rain.

"Okay, everyone. We're going to have a little campout, so if your parents aren't here yet, don't worry, they will be soon. No pushing, nice and easy, right this way." He spoke loud enough to be heard over the sirens and with just enough authority.

None of the children made a peep as the large fireman instructed them, not even Jerry Santos, known heckler and class clown. The boy walked toward the front of the bus with his head lowered and exited in an orderly fashion.

"Jerry, Jerry!" His mother ran up and hugged her son hard enough to strangle him.

The boy and his mom were ushered through the back doors and shown into the shelter. Other parents were there to meet the buses as well and ran to their children as if they had been separated for years. However, there was a large number who hadn't arrived yet.

Andrea watched the children as they stepped off the bus and scanned the crowd. One little girl stood in the rain with her bottom lip quivering and the worst case of puppy dog eyes Andrea had ever seen. The child's mommy and daddy didn't run up to great her, and Andrea had a feeling they weren't going to. It was all happening so fast.

She leapt from her seat behind the wheel and charged out of the bus into the rain. Andrea rushed to the little girl's side and knelt before her.

"Hi, sweetie. My name's Andrea. I am going to take care of you until your parents get here. Is that okay?"

The child looked up, unable to speak. Tears ran from the corners of her eyes and disappeared in the rain. She nodded her head and allowed Andrea to take her by the hand. Several other children who also hadn't found their parents saw what Andrea had done and flocked to her side like a raft of ducklings. Miss Davis joined the group with a waddling of her own, and together, the women led the children into the shelter.

Fireman Anthony Leone drove the second bus, accompanied by Principal Grace and most of the youngest students, who had been crying the entire trip. By the time he entered the lot, Anthony had had his fill of children. He thought that rather than spend the night locked in a basement with a hundred screaming kids, he just might be better off on his own. He saw first-hand the thing that had burned up in the Texaco fire, and it was scary as hell. But the idea of stepping into that shelter with all those kids sounded a whole lot scarier. He had a .38 tucked in his waistband and was thinking of a quiet place where he could ride this thing out alone.

The little ones exited the bus kicking and screaming, and there wasn't a thing Principal Grace or Bob Jones could do to pacify them. Some of their parents had shown up, but the majority had not. And it was going to be a real clusterfuck if they didn't get there soon. Anthony hoped the chief knew how to handle that but doubted if he did.

The last bus pulled up to the school with a mixture of third and fourth graders and Miss Boriello holding the reins. Brandon Canfield, who was only a few years out of high school himself, sat behind the wheel. He stopped at the back of the gym and opened the door to the elements. The rain hammered sideways in torrential sheets and forced its way into the bus.

"Okay, everyone. We're going to get a little wet, but if we move quickly, it won't be too bad," Miss Boriello announced, then began to lead the children off. She turned back to Brandon and offered a quick smile.

Cars continued to pull into the lot, directed by firemen dressed in bright yellow slickers. The skies grew darker by the second, and the storm strengthened. Bob Jones looked up as another flash of lightning lit up the sky. He shouted something to one of his men, but his words were stifled by the storm.

Ted scanned the rifle selection, picked up a bolt action 30-06, and examined the scope. He slung it over his shoulder and removed a Mossberg 12-gauge as well. Then, without saying a word, he grabbed one of the duffel bags and proceeded to fill it with several boxes of shotgun shells, three boxes of 30-06 cartridges, one hundred .40 cal. bullets, and a semi-automatic handgun. Dawn crept up next to him, taking her usual spot at his side. She tilted the oversized deputy hat back on her head to get a better look at what he was doing.

Ted grabbed a walkie-talkie off the cart and handed it to her. "Here, this is for you."

Dawn smiled and accepted the gift, then stepped back to be with her dog.

The front doors burst open, allowing the blare of sirens and horns to flood the lobby; Chris Fredericks entered pushing another cart of weapons.

"How are we looking with the patients, Nurse TenHove?" Ted shouted to be heard over the weather and alarms.

"There are only a few more that can be moved. The rest have to stay on the third floor."

"Okay then." Ted turned to the firemen. "Ed, you're with Nurse Ten-Hove and myself on the third floor, and Chris, you're in the basement." The young firemen nodded in agreement, then Ted turned to Burt, who wrapped his arm around Doris's waist.

"Wherever she goes, I go," the coroner said, pulling Doris close.

That makes four. Ted knew he still had one small problem. He looked down at Dawn and exhaled. *What am I going to do with you?* He needed to get her tucked away safely in the basement but figured the only way she'd leave his side was kicking and screaming. He opened his mouth to speak, not sure what he would say, when a familiar face came into view.

Ted reached out and took Nurse Carole by the arm; the girl's eyes lit up when she saw him.

"Carole, I really need your help." Ted bent down to look Dawn in the eyes. "Honey, I want you to stay in the basement with Carole. She'll watch over you, and help you look for leprechaun gold. Okay?"

Dawn shook her head and bit her bottom lip. Her eyes grew wide and watered over, then she reached out and latched onto Ted, burying her head in the crook of his shoulder like a tick in the carpet. *This isn't going to work.* A dozen worst-case scenarios raced through his head at the thought of forcing Dawn to stay in the basement; none of them ended well.

"Okay, she's with us," he said, looking up at Nurse TenHove, who scowled for a moment, then let her own face soften.

"I'll come too," Carole said, straightening the hat on Dawn's head.

"Well, Deputy. That's about the last of them," Doris called over the dizzying commotion as several straggling patients were directed into the basement.

"All right, get these guns downstairs and distributed!" Ted yelled to Chris Fredericks, then he turned to Ed. "Koloski, find yourself a weapon and grab as much ammo as you can carry. We're headed to the third floor—now."

A bucket brigade of men formed on the staircase, making quick work of transporting the remainder of supplies and weapons into the basement. Koloski filled several bags, handing one to Carole and slinging another over his shoulder. Then ...

The sky exploded.

Lightning lit up the entire front of the building, causing the lights to flicker for a moment. Outside, the rain fell in monsoon proportions, and the sky was so dark it looked like night had already descended.

A sudden scream ripped through the air, loud enough to have come from inside the building. It overpowered the shrill of the sirens and echoed off the stark walls of the medical center. Ted stopped moving and looked at the members of his party. *Dear God, this is it.*

"Lock it up!" Ted shouted. He had hoped Sheriff Primrose would make it back before they needed to seal the doors, but there was no time. The sheriff was on his own. The patients that could be moved were in the basement, and a handful of residents had arrived seeking shelter. Not many, though; Ted prayed they had gone to the high school instead.

A pair of firemen ran to the front doors, wrapped a thick chain around the handles, and padlocked them shut. The other exits had been secured as well, and that was all they could do. The real protection relied on their firepower and the strength of the shelter door.

The third floor was a different story. It wasn't safe, and there was no way to fortify it. Ted figured it was up to luck and God—hopefully, one of them was on their side. He urged his group into the stairway, with Nurse TenHove and Burt in the lead, and Dawn, Carole, and Baxter following behind. Ted hurried them along with Koloski bringing up the rear, leaving the rest of the firemen finishing their transport in the lobby.

"Don't take too long with that!" he called back and made his way up the stairs. Ted's heart pounded like a greyhound with a case of pre-race jitters. Blood and adrenaline rushed to his head, making him feel almost intoxicated. He tried to steady his breathing as he took the stairs two at a time, but it was no use.

A second shriek ripped through the building, followed by the deafening roar of destruction. There was a violent crash, the electric shatter of breaking glass, and, a half second later, the sound of the building being ripped apart from the ground up.

"Faster!" Ted screamed and forced his party up the stairs. They reached the landing and rounded the turn when the door to the second floor burst open. A blur of movement flew out at them. It was on Burt and Doris in flash. Ted didn't have time to raise his gun and could only watch the ambush unfold in front of him.

Firemen Glenn Gillick and Mike Turino had volunteered to drive the police cruisers and were each given a specific neighborhood to canvass. The vehicles were outfitted with external bullhorns that Deputy Rainey and Andrea had removed from the storage locker. The men set out just before the rain started, delivering the same message as those in the trucks. Glenn steered the cruiser with one hand and operated the microphone with the other.

"Attention citizens of Garrett Grove, this is not a drill. Report to the shelter at the high school immediately, bring whatever medications you require. The children from the elementary and junior high schools are already en route. You are ordered by the sheriff's department to report to the high school immediately."

Glenn couldn't tell if the message was making a difference. There were few cars on the road and even fewer people had opened their front doors to see what was going on. As far as he could tell, Operation Round Up was a wash out. Still, he had a job to do and would continue until told otherwise. He headed toward the north end of town, making a left turn on Foothills Drive. It was near impossible to see through the windshield, even with the wipers set to high, and Glenn didn't notice the man until the last second. He slammed on the brakes as the figure darted in front of the vehicle. The back tires locked up, and the cruiser skidded, then fishtailed to the left.

The cruiser came to an abrupt halt, throwing Glenn hard against the steering wheel. He looked out the window, then checked the rearview, ready to give the prick a piece of his mind. But the road was empty, the guy had disappeared. "What the f—" he hissed into the cab, scanning the street again for the lunatic who had jumped in front of him. Still, there was no one. Glen shook his head and took his foot off the brake. "Fucking jerkoff."

It smashed into the driver's side with the power of a train. Glenn's head snapped hard to the right as the tires lifted from the impact. *Jesus Christ!* He checked his mirrors again, expecting to find the car that had hit him, but there was nothing. The heavy rain beat down on the deserted road.

The dark blur moved across the front of the cruiser and came at him in a flash. Glenn hit the accelerator; his foot pressed firmly to the floor as the tires screamed for traction. But he reacted a full second too late. It slammed into the car a second time and lifted the driver's side into the air. Before he could react, Glenn found himself upside down, and he hadn't been wearing his seatbelt. His head smacked against the roof of the cab, and his vision clouded. The world before him warped into a liquid wave of shadows. The windshield cracked into a million tiny spiderwebs, and the driver's side glass imploded.

There was a flurry of movement outside, both in front of and behind him. Then the howling started, carnal and urgent like a pack of wolverines had surrounded the vehicle. Glenn struggled to move, but his concussed brain wouldn't have it. They were on him in a frenzy, clawing their way into the car, grabbing his arms and legs, dragging him out into the street.

The rain fell hard into his eyes, making it impossible to see his attackers. But he felt them, a thousand individual teeth sinking into his flesh. It invaded him like a disease, filling his sinuses and ceasing his breath. Glenn was probed like a lab rat as it took everything he had been and consumed what it needed. And just like that, the pain was gone.

Darkness came early to the small town of Garrett Grove. The storm descended from the heavens, and the brood was awakened. It spoke to them in an urgent voice and commanded them to feed. Many of its children had already turned; others were well on their way. There was work to be done. A battle to be waged. An entire world waiting to be devoured.

CHAPTER 70

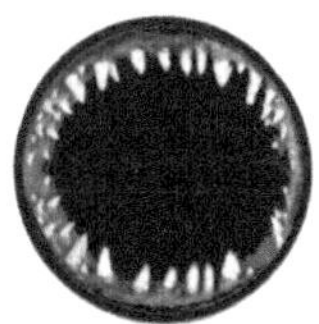

Troy diverted to the left, dragging the girls behind him. He yanked their arms so hard he was sure he would pull one from the socket. Still, he forced his legs to move like never before and led them through the backyard to the side door of the garage—the very door he and his cousins used to ambush his friends the night of the party, just a few days ago. *Is it still open?* He remembered his mom had asked him to lock it, but so much had happened since then.

The sirens continued to scream, and the deluge was unending, but above the roar was the sound of the beast that pursued them. Troy could hear it closing in as they approached the garage door. They were almost there. With just a few more steps to go, Troy felt his arm jerk and was suddenly pulled backward by the unseen force. He turned in time to see Janis's feet slip out from under her. She skated across the lawn for a moment, frozen in position, then came down hard on her backside. She splashed onto the wet grass and almost took him with her. Troy rushed to her side. Then he saw it—headed fast in their direction—almost on top of them. His throat tightened until it was almost impossible to breathe; panic rose in his chest and forced the blood to his face. He struggled to lift Janis from the ground, but his palms were slick from rain, and her hand slipped in his grasp.

It ran towards them in an almost apish way, on all fours, in bounding strides that were difficult to follow. Horns or possibly tusks protruded from the sides of the creature's face and the top of its head. It appeared hairless, but it was impossible to tell in the rain and from the speed at which it moved. The clearest feature was the beast's mouth, a massive opening filled with hundreds of those horrible pointed teeth. Troy knew it was over; there wasn't enough time to help Janis to her feet and make it to the garage. *No!* A scream entered his throat and silenced the noise. He sprang to action, and the world warped into slow-motion, as if it were playing out frame by frame.

He grabbed both her hands, planted his feet, and pulled the girl with all his strength. Janis shot into the air like a Jack-in-the-box, nearly knocking him down in the process. As he took her in his arms, he looked over her shoulder; the beast was now less than ten feet away. It lowered its head and bore down on them, preparing to make its final attack. There wasn't time to turn. Troy knew there was no chance they would make it to the garage.

Then there was movement, fast and reactive, just from the corner of his sight. The creature erupted with an oppressive scream. Then it fell to the ground, twisting and writhing like an uncoiled spring, clawing at its body as if it were on fire. Troy heard the snap of the elastic bands as Wendy released her second projectile. The magnet penetrated the ape-thing's side, causing the beast to shriek even louder. What looked like smoke began to pour from its open wounds. A steady stream of black lifted into the air and was absorbed by the rain. At least it looked like that to Troy, who was transfixed by the spectacle. The creature flopped around like a fish out of water and then stopped moving.

It worked. It actually worked! Troy turned to Wendy, who held her wrist rocket in the ready position. Her chest heaved in and out, and a wicked grin spread out like a rash across her face. But the moment of celebration was squashed when two more creatures blasted from the side of the house.

The children spun on their heels and slammed against the garage door. *Please be open, please be open,* Troy prayed as he fumbled with the knob. It slipped within his grip, and his heart stopped; his vision reduced to a series of pulsing lights. He grasped it again and twisted. The door opened, and they poured into the darkness of the garage. Slamming it hard behind them, Troy engaged the lock and pulled the girls away.

The entire building shook as the creatures slammed against the outside wall. The three children stood in the graveyard room, dripping and breathless, with a coffin set on the floor to their right and several headstones propped up behind them. Troy looked for something strong to wedge against the door, but everything had been made of cardboard. There wasn't anything sturdy that would stop the beasts for long.

"Follow me!" he shouted to the girls, who both looked close to tears. He led them through a doorway, then grabbed the piece of drywall Billy had used Saturday night. He leaned it against the wall behind them, knowing it wouldn't do much. Still, it was better than nothing, and he thought it might buy them a few extra seconds.

The garage shook again as the creatures threw themselves against the exterior like battering rams.

Troy ducked and urged the girls through a small trapdoor concealed at the base of the wall to their left. He led them into the inner workings of the haunted house, where all the secrets were kept, a place that only he knew everything about. Even Rob hadn't been around to see all the finishing touches he had made to the hidden passage. He navigated the girls down the tight corridor, past the board used to move the tangle of rat hoses and the pulleys that controlled the dayglow spiders. He moved them through the darkness until they couldn't proceed any further. They had come to the end of the passage—the dead end. Now they were trapped.

The pounding of the rain against the roof sounded like marbles being dropped from the sky. It rattled their nerves to the point of hysterics and jarred their senses. In a deafening roar, the side door crashed inward, and hell followed. A scream like a cross between a leopard and an eagle cut through the garage like a bandsaw. Troy pulled Wendy and Janis close; trying to be as quiet as possible, he spoke to them. It was so loud inside the small area he was unsure if they had heard a word he said. A second beast howled like a wolf caught in a bear trap. Troy fumbled in his pockets as the monsters ripped the graveyard room apart at the seams. There was no way to know if the creatures would follow the laid-out maze of the haunted house or just tear the place to shreds to get to them. He ran his foot along the floor, searching in the dark until it brushed against what he was looking for. There were too many things that could go wrong, especially if the girls hadn't heard him.

Something shrieked as it entered the rat room and fought with the hoses spread out across the floor. They were getting closer—much closer. Saturday night, Wendy had taken his hand and kissed him, just on the other side of the wall where they now hid. It felt like so long ago. Now they were crammed in the tight passage, fighting for their lives. *I hope this works,* Troy pleaded as Wendy's hand brushed against his.

CHAPTER 71

Principal Melvin Garish was more than a little distracted when Chief Jones visited him earlier. His preoccupation with his secretary, Julie Evans, was acute. For some reason, today of all days, the girl had decided to stay home from work. Melvin had listened as the chief relayed his instructions concerning early dismissal, but with thoughts of Julie eclipsing much of the message. Fortunately, Mrs. Tailor had also listened and carried out the chief's instructions to the letter. The announcement was delivered over the school's PA system for the faculty and students to hear. Everyone was to report back to the shelter no later than five o'clock. Melvin even stayed and listened to the announcement himself, then he exited the school and drove to Julie's house to see if her husband's car was in the driveway.

For the past month and a half, Mel had been giving Julie a little extracurricular physical education on their lunch breaks while Mr. Evans was at work. Sometimes, she would let him have her in the parking lot of the school in Mel's Chevy van. The fact that Julie was married thrilled Mel to no end. She'd been his secretary for years and had approached him about a raise. Mel informed her it would be a lot easier to fit it into the budget if she allowed him to fit it into her first. Julie had taken the proposal in stride and then took him up on the offer. And it had been amazing. Julie told him she and her husband, Luke, had been having problems for a long time and he hadn't touched her in over six months. Also, Mr. Evans had never been a fan of oral—giving or receiving. "What guy doesn't love a blowjob?" she had said. Apparently, the guy she had married. Fortunately for Mel, not only was he a fan of receiving, but he was a giver as well. Which Julie seemed to appreciate—at least for a while.

Then one day out of the blue, she told him it was over, which only made Mel want her more. He enjoyed the cat and mouse games she played and knew if he pressed hard enough, she would acquiesce to his advances. It was like a drug for Mel, and Julie was his fix. She was all he could think about. But it had started to affect his performance at work and even interfered with his sleep.

Mel noticed Julie had become more aloof than usual, fending off his plays with greater success than she had in the past. When she didn't show up for work today, he had been frantic. It was Wednesday, after all, and they always snuck off to her house on Wednesday for a little hanky-panky. He had been so desperate to see her at one point he even attempted to call her at home. However, the phones were still out.

Mel pulled his van to the curb across the street from the Evans' residence. He noticed Julie's car in the driveway and was pleased to see the absence of her husband's. "You little minx," he whispered, convincing himself this was all part of the game she'd been playing and she was probably expecting him. He imagined her waiting in the living room, naked on all fours. Mel felt the excitement growing just thinking about his secretary like that and shifted in the driver's seat to adjust his tightening pants.

There was only one light on in the house and, from what he could tell, no movement at any of the windows. Figuring it was time to make his move, he opened the door and stepped into the rain. The heavy wind snatched the umbrella from his grip and sent it careening down the street. He raised his collar as a brilliant blue flash of light sizzled across the sky, but was drenched before he made it two steps.

Mel sloshed up the walkway to Julie's front door with the constant blare of the fire whistle droning like a broken record. He looked around one last time, convinced himself he was doing the right thing, and climbed the steps of the porch. He reached for the doorbell and held his breath, then pressed his finger against it. The chime was barely audible over the whistle, so Mel pressed the button three more times. He waited, craning his neck to look through the small window. Then, a wash of movement, just out of the corner of his eye, darted across the yard and disappeared behind the house.

Mel bolted around, alerted by the motion, but saw nothing. *Probably a branch or garbage can tossed in the wind.* He turned back to ring the bell once more, and it happened. The figure smashed into him with the force of a head-on collision and knocked him into the screen door, shattering the storm windows and the frame as well.

Mel felt the wind rush out of his lungs as he fell onto his back. He looked up and was blinded by a deluge of overflowing water cascading down from the gutters. *What's happening?* He struggled to focus, squinted against the downpour, and was met by the creature's stare. *Fuuuck!* Something inside Mel's head fried like an overloaded fuse. The vision before him was impossible to comprehend.

The creature positioned itself on the center of his chest and sized him up through eight individual orbital sockets. Four eyes situated on either side of its skull stared down at him. Coarse black hairs as thick as fettuccini protruded from a face with a bulbous forehead and a beak-like nose. Antennae jutted from the top of the creature's head, probing and searching the air in front of Mel's face.

He struggled to push the beast off him, his hands grabbing at the coarse hairs covering its body. Mel screamed as all six of the monster's legs dug into him with their pointed mandibles. They punctured his flesh and pinned him to the wooden porch like a calendar tacked to a wall.

Then the creature erupted, vomiting a thick green sludge that covered his face. It flowed into his mouth and his eyes, a concoction as foul as death. Mel gagged as the vile snot landed on his tongue. It tingled and twinged, and then it started to burn. A noxious odor filled his sinuses; he howled as the feel of a hundred soldering irons pressed against his flesh. The smell of fat, hair, and vomit rendered in a deep fryer was all-consuming as the substance went to work on him like an acid. A prehistoric acidic compound, to be precise. One that had gone extinct over two million years ago.

Mel's face putrefied, congealing into something that looked an awful lot like cherry Jello. He tried to scream but was unable, his voice box melted along with his flesh. Instead, he gurgled and struggled to look up at the nightmarish creature. An agonizing second later, his eyes popped like tiny water balloons. Then the monstrosity spread its jaws and slurped up Melvin Garish's face like a spoonful of Campbell's cream of mushroom soup.

The ladder truck crawled through the neighborhood where only days before, a small girl hid beneath her bed as her brother attacked their parents. Brian Miller had called the police about the constant howling of his neighbor's dog, claiming to be concerned that something may have happened. In truth, Brian had been trying to sleep and the damn dog wouldn't shut the fuck up. He had just gotten home from a back-breaking night shift at Faber Chemical, taken a hot shower, and climbed into bed when the hound started going at it.

He had never been all that chummy with the Negal family, thought their son, Tommy, was a snot-nosed brat, and imagined, in a couple years, the little girl would be blasting her boom box and roller skating in front of his house with her friends. No doubt when Brian was trying to sleep. It hadn't occurred to him that something had really happened to the family; he simply thought they had left the dog unattended. He expected as much from Tommy; the kid didn't have his head screwed on tight.

He watched the truck pass with its lights flashing and siren blaring. The town's whistle was already loud enough to wake the dead, and now someone was screaming over a loudspeaker.

"Attention, this is not a drill. Report to the shelter at the high school immediately. This is an emergency. Bring only what you can carry and any medication you require. Children from the elementary and junior high schools are already en route. All citizens are ordered by the sheriff's department to report to the shelter at the high school. This is not a drill."

"Shut the fuck up!" Brian screamed as the truck made its way down the street. "The only emergency will be my foot in your ass if you don't quit that damn racket."

He slammed the door, attempting to shut the noise outside, but it was impossible. He walked to the kitchen, popped two Anacin into his mouth, and swallowed them dry. There was no use in fooling himself, he wouldn't be getting any sleep today. Brian rubbed his temples with the sound of a thousand clowns on a carousel bouncing against the inside of his skull like a ball bearing.

The thing that entered the world as Tommy Negal returned to the street where it once lived as if in answer to a call from its previous life. But the reality of it was far different. The boy had changed so much that his own mother wouldn't have recognized him—if she were still alive. Tommy had shed almost half of his body mass and morphed into something quite reptilian. The sides of the creature's neck flared into a pair of transparent leathery membranes. His lower jaw protruded, while the top appeared to have sunken in, swallowing his nose completely. The clothes he wore had fallen away, ripped to shreds from the dagger-like spines that grew from his back and torso. Webbed fingers that tapered into talons clung to the tree outside, and a pair of prehistoric eyes spotted the man in the house. With the speed of a rattler, a long black tongue shot from the creature's mouth, snatched a squirrel from its nest, and sucked it in. It crunched down on the tasty appetizer, then set its hunger on something a bit more satisfying.

Brian was reaching for a bottle of gin from the cabinet above the sink when the back door imploded, sending shards of glass and splinters flying inward. He spun around with the bottle in hand, prepared to fight off the intruder, but didn't have time to think as the projectile shot at him and seized his fist.

He stared as the massive tongue latched on to his hand, then his bladder let loose. The thing was no more than three feet tall and looked like it had crawled out of the Stone Age. It was mostly green with toxic red splotches and had several lethal rows of quills protruding from its body. The teeth that lined the rim of the beast's mouth looked like broken glass.

The abomination tilted its head back and allowed its great tongue to retract, taking Brian's arm with it. He was pulled only slightly off balance as the appendage was ripped from his shoulder socket. A fountain of arterial blood spouted from the ragged wound and pooled onto the floor, evacuating Brian's body fast and freely. It didn't hurt half as much as Brian imagined having his arm ripped off would. He swayed on his feet and began to lose consciousness.

The monster descended on him; its talons chewed into the porcelain tile floor as it raced toward him. There wasn't time to scream. As he fell to the floor, the massive tongue shot out again and seized him by the throat. Thankfully, it happened just as fast as the arm. The creature retracted its powerful tongue and snapped Brian's head off at the shoulders. The last vision he registered as he landed in the beast's mouth was several rows of razor-sharp teeth closing down on him. The sirens had finally ceased, and the world was quiet again, at least it was for Brian.

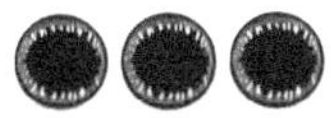

Lynn Donovan turned right onto Village Road with her heart racing to the drone of the sirens and adrenaline coursing through her veins like a hallucinogen. She fought the urgency to disregard the speed limit as the vehicle's windshield wipers carried out their own struggle against the never-ending rain. Both were losing the battle. Peanuts, who lay in the passenger's seat, whined and looked up at her, distraught as only a beagle in a thunderstorm could be.

"It's okay, girl. We'll be there in a minute."

Lynn approached the green light at the intersection of Jackson and brought the car to a slow crawl. A cross between instinct and zero visibility cautioned her to check both ways before inching forward onto the main drag. The blare of a horn, louder than the sirens and almost on top of them, caused her to slam on the brakes. Peanuts tumbled off the seat and onto the floor with a yelp as a station wagon sliced through the red light, missing them by less than a foot. Lynn watched the derelict vehicle scream down the road and was prepared to pull out a second time when four large animals tore through the intersection in pursuit. It was difficult to focus on them due to the heavy rain and the speed at which they moved, but Lynn thought they resembled oversized dogs. One of them jumped through the intersection dragging its arms like a gorilla.

Lynn turned in the opposite direction with a bit less respect for the speed limit, her tires spinning out on the wet surface until they finally gripped the pavement. The car fishtailed as Lynn banked onto Elm Street; she noticed the smoke right away. A house had caught fire and been consumed by the blaze. Flames erupted from every window on the first and second floors, and the roof had started to collapse. Then she saw it—stoic like a pillar on the front lawn, staring at the inferno. It had to be over seven feet tall and looked like it had been dredged out of a swamp. Although Lynn sailed past it doing fifty, she was certain she had seen gills lining the sides of the beast's neck. And she was positive she had seen scales covering its body like plates of armor. Lynn had a feeling her bladder had let go but was too terrified to check.

She blasted through the next intersection and stole a glimpse in the rearview. The enormous beast had followed her and was approaching fast. *What the fuck?* Hoping to coax just a bit more out of the screaming engine, Lynn pressed her foot to the floor. With the high school just two blocks away, she gripped the wheel with both hands and prayed. But it was almost on top of her, and she knew there was no way she would make it.

She steered to the right, and her back tires lost traction. They caught a second later as the vehicle turned onto Mandeville and approached the school. She checked the mirror again to find her pursuer just a few strides behind. Now she could see the long tentacles the thing used to propel itself and the suction cups that lined its appendages. Madness threatened to invade, but Lynn fought to maintain her wits. The front of the high school loomed into view ... Lynn's heart sank. Bright yellow creatures swarmed the lot and occupied the area. They were slimy and smooth and looked like they had been dragged from the depths themselves. There was nowhere to go.

She was about to drive past the parking lot when one of the yellow creatures began flapping its arms to get her attention. Lynn stared at the strange sight and was filled with a wash of recognition. It wasn't a creature, but it had been difficult to tell in the storm. Men in bright yellow raincoats waved her down and directed her passage. She sailed past the first man and was nearly thrown from her seat when the explosion rocked the car. It had been loud enough to pop her ears and to start Peanuts barking.

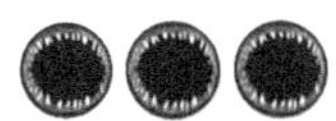

Firemen John Sampson and Eric Collins were stationed at the front entrance when the Pinto approached with the monstrosity nearly on top of it. Neither man could believe what they were seeing even though they'd been told to expect the unexpected. John waved the car in, then unslung the 12-gauge from his shoulder.

It came at him fast and looked like it had fallen out of some unlucky fisherman's net. He followed it in his sights and fired the first shot. The creature shrieked but didn't slow, not even a little, as pink ooze sloshed from a grapefruit-size wound in its side.

"Fuck, it has to be a head shot," John cursed under his breath. He exhaled and fired, this time taking out a chunk of the squid-beast's shoulder. A huge chunk of blubber fell, and more of the pink goo spurted out onto the wet pavement.

The monster entered the parking lot and came at him; John slammed another shell into the chamber and fired, this time missing his mark completely. He took a frantic step backward and pulled the pump. A thunderous concussion detonated from inches away. The beast's head exploded as the 30-06 slug from Eric Collin's Remington connected dead center. The repulsive heap fell to the pavement before the men's feet; it even smelled like it had been pulled out of the sea.

Lynn Donovan slammed on the brakes, bringing her Pinto to a halt at the back entrance of the gym. Bob Jones and Brandon Canfield rushed to her aid and helped her and the pup from the vehicle. "M—mmm—hel." She tried to speak but was incapable.

"Jesus Christ," Bob Jones said, arriving at the car from the side of the building. It hadn't been the first abomination the men had encountered, and far too many of the town's citizens had not been as lucky as Lynn Donovan. "Men, we can't stay out here much longer. We're going to have to chain the doors soon."

Eric Collins stepped back from the body of the creature. "What about Sheriff Primrose? He's still out there."

"I'm well aware of that," Bob said, lifting his radio from his hip. "Jones to Primrose. Dammit, Carl. Come in!"

Teresa Sirocka had been dealt a raw deal and was pissed about it. Her ex had left her for a younger chippy who was already pumping out little rug rats of their own. The deadbeat barely saw Wendy as it was, and now he had a one-year-old and another on the way. Since the divorce, Teresa hadn't had time to breathe, let alone go on dates herself. Not that she was interested. Being a single mom was demanding; she worked most days, and keeping up with Wendy was a full-time job—the girl was too damn smart. But her daughter was a good kid, far ahead of the curve, and unfortunately for Teresa, Wendy had already noticed boys.

Teresa had tried to fill her daughter's head with notions and cautionary warnings about the male members of the species—they were not to be trusted. And it appeared to sink in for a while. Then Wendy attended a Halloween party last Saturday, and when Teresa arrived to pick her up, she saw her daughter kissing a boy on the front steps ... All was lost. That was how it started. First, it's sneaking kisses at a boy's Halloween party, next she'd be having sex in his basement after school. It was just a matter of time before Wendy found herself married to a cute boy who was sticking it to some chippy half his age. She'd end up a single mother with no time for herself, standing in front of the television ironing a mountain of laundry.

Days of our Lives provided the much-needed background noise while Teresa worked the iron and thought about her daughter. She knew she'd been projecting her own issues onto her, but she had every right to be concerned; Wendy was her only child, after all.

Teresa was startled by the sudden eruption of sirens and horns in the distance. The town's fire whistle blew and refused to cease, growing in both timbre and duration. Then the distorted blare of voices echoed a message from not far away. She stopped what she was doing and ran to the stairs to listen closer. The man mentioned something about reporting to the shelter and then said something about the elementary school. Teresa panicked. Wendy was there and would be frantic and lost without her. She grabbed her keys and ran to her car without listening to the rest of the message or even turning off the iron. A second later, Teresa was tearing through the Village, driving too fast to be safe, and missed her turn on Jackson Ave. She quickly hung a U-turn and headed to the elementary school to pick up Wendy.

When she left the house, the skies were only dark, but before she had driven a mile, they were pouring down rain. Teresa turned the wipers on high, but even that wasn't enough to slap away the deluge. She took a right at Bell's Hardware and brought the station wagon to a full stop. Something was going on in front of the building. It almost looked like a pack of monkeys were attempting to break into the store, jumping and clawing at the windows and front door. Then Teresa noticed they weren't exactly monkeys, at least none she had ever seen in *National Geographic*. They were far too large, and something about their movements was all wrong. She watched, breathless and frozen, as one of the creatures turned to her and screamed. The shrill voice pierced her ears, sending a rash of gooseflesh down her arms and the length of her spine. The mouth on the creature was massive, far too big to belong to anything of this world, and housed a forest of jagged teeth.

Teresa threw the car in reverse and punched it, bouncing over the curb as she misjudged the turn. Several of the creatures took notice and abandoned their attack on the hardware store, suddenly moving her way. They bounded after her, hopping like apes with murderous intent as she fled.

Teresa pressed the pedal to the floor as she approached the light on Jackson Ave. She scanned the rearview to see her pursuers were nearly upon her. Knowing they would overtake her if she stopped or even slowed, she laid on the horn and blasted through the red light without looking, almost smashing into a Pinto at the intersection. Fortunately, the other driver stopped in time as Teresa sailed past with the strange primates in pursuit.

Unable to process what was happening and preoccupied by the sight of the beasts in the mirror, Teresa struggled to maintain control of the vehicle and outrun the monsters. She came upon the turn for the elementary school but continued straight for fear of leading the creatures to her daughter. Not knowing that Wendy and the other children had already left, Teresa did what she thought was best. She beelined down the Turnpike toward the east end of town. It wasn't that far of a stretch, and at the speed she was moving, it didn't take long for her to reach the end of the line.

She crashed through the old wooden fence at the entrance of the King Lake Recreational Center just as the first beast caught up to the vehicle and seized the bumper. It pulled itself onto the back and leered at Teresa through the large back window of the station wagon. It was primitive and evil and looked more like a gargoyle than any monkey. It was joined by another that looked similar but not identical, except for the mouth and all those horrible teeth.

Teresa pressed her foot to the floor, and the car chewed up the short distance across the dirt parking lot of the rec center. King Lake loomed before her in all its enormity. Formed by glaciers several million years ago, it was nearly as deep as it was wide, and far too big to see the opposite shoreline. The rain diminished her visibility, making it impossible to judge how far she was from the bank. She steered the car toward the massive body of water. The vehicle shook with a lurch as a third beast landed on the roof.

With the steering wheel gripped tightly in her hand, Teresa prayed that she hadn't messed her daughter up too much. She knew she had filled

Wendy's head with burdens no child should have to carry. She had dumped all her baggage into her daughter's knapsack and sent her off to school with a head full of nonsense. In truth, Teresa had done the best she could with the cards she was dealt.

"I'm sorry, Wendy. I love you," she said as the wagon hit the elevated bank of King Lake and was propelled twenty feet over the water. It came down hard, like it had hit a concrete wall, scattering the beasts on impact. Teresa's head smacked against the roof of the car, knocking her unconscious. She was spared the intrusion from a creature that never should have found its way to Earth to begin with.

The frigid water filled the car and sucked it to the bottom of the lake. Teresa Sirocka was one of the lucky ones who died that day in Garrett Grove. Burt Lively had been incorrect—sometimes there *was* dignity in death.

CHAPTER 72

The medical supplies were divided into two large stockpiles, one for the high school and another for the shelter in the medical center's basement. A third smaller allocation was stashed away at the nurses' station on the third floor, where the immobile patients remained. Dr. James Freedman and Michelle Marks loaded their share of the medication and equipment into the ambulance and sped off to join the group at the school. Michelle turned on the lights and sirens and pulled out of the parking lot. It was only a half a mile to the school, but the rain was relentless; she kept it well below the speed limit. Dr. Freedman sat in the passenger's seat, bouncing his legs up and down like he needed to use the bathroom.

"I don't see why they had to send us," he whined. "They could have sent Dr. Halasz."

"Maybe they needed someone qualified enough to deal with whatever might happen." Michelle believed the best way to deal with doctors like Freedman was to pander to their egos—even though she knew it had been a random decision on Nurse TenHove's part and qualifications had nothing to do with it.

"Yes, that's probably it," he said, then took to tapping the dashboard with his hand.

Michelle looked over at him and gritted her teeth, anxious to get to the high school before Freedman drove her batshit crazy; she pushed the gas a bit harder.

Michelle worked the day shift with Joe Santos. They were a good team; Joe knew his stuff. They had reported to the scene of the accident on Route 3 yesterday morning to find that none of the occupants of the vehicles had been wearing their seatbelts. Although the drivers and passengers of both cars had survived their initial injuries, it had been obvious to Michelle that not all of them would make it and came as no surprise when one of the high school girls and the old woman passed away late last night. It was sad, but it was part of the job and something you needed to know how to deal with or you had no business working in the field. Michelle found that almost impossible at first; she had lacked the much-needed ability to detach. She started out wide-eyed, compassionate, and looking to save the world. Joe recognized his coworker's naivety and had a heart-to-heart with her that first week.

"I get it, you became a paramedic because you want to help people. You're looking to save them all. But here's the thing." He pulled the ambulance over and looked her in the eyes. "You can try, but you never will. And if you can't accept that, you are in the wrong line of work."

Michelle smiled and thanked him but thought Joe was just another jaded prick. She believed she could handle anything and she would be the exception to the rule. She *was* going to save them—all of them. Joe was detached; he no longer cared. *How can you save anyone if you don't care?*

In the spring of '77, Michelle received her wake-up call. The King Dam had overflowed after heavy rains and an early thaw, flooding the south end of town and the low-lying communities along Route 202. She and Joe were dispatched to help the fire department rescue citizens stranded by the frigid rising waters. The biggest problem they were dealing with was hypothermia, as many had already been in the water for nearly an hour.

The fire department used boats to extract people from their homes and submerged vehicles, then began to deliver them to the paramedics on the banks. But their limited numbers were overwhelmed quickly as victims were passed along at a feverish pace. Michelle, Joe, and the other paramedics worked in a frenzy to keep up with the growing number of patients, handing out blankets, applying heat packs, and dressing wounds. But there was only so much they could do. Michelle focused on the job and went to work like a professional as she struggled to keep up. Then she heard the hysterical screams from a woman who had just been delivered to the shoreline. Michelle was the closest and rushed to her aid. The woman howled in agony and thrust the baby into Michelle's arms.

"My baby!! Please save my baby!"

Michelle took the bundle of blankets and parted the covers to examine the child. Cold—lifeless—milky-white eyes stared back at her. The tiny thing had turned blue and shriveled up in a most awful way from the frigid water. Michelle touched the infant's skin and knew the little girl had been under for far too long. She proceeded to rub the child's chest while the frantic mother howled as if the baby had been ripped from her womb.

One of the firemen who had witnessed the scene intervened and ushered the woman into an ambulance, assuring her that her baby was in safe hands. Michelle continued to stand there, rubbing the child, staring into its milky-dead eyes, rocking the frozen bundle in her arms. Then the world stopped spinning. Michelle gazed into the pleading eyes of the baby she couldn't save. She placed her lips over the child's mouth and breathed into its frozen lungs. She was told later that Joe had to wrestle the dead infant from her grips. Michelle didn't remember any of it.

The doctors said she experienced a traumatic breakdown that afternoon. She was put on medical leave and started counseling after spending over a month in the hospital. St. Claire's specialized in psychiatry and mental illness. The treatment helped, but the daily visits from Joe helped Michelle even more. He had attempted to prepare her for the ugliness of the world, but she hadn't wanted to hear it. And the day of the flood had been a baptism by fire. They talked a lot over the following six months. And although she was never able to get the image out of her mind, she eventually managed to get a full night's sleep. Less than a year later, Michelle wanted to go back to work.

Joe wasn't the only one who doubted if that was a good idea, but Michelle was cleared by her psychiatrist and, much to everyone's surprise, appeared to have rebounded from her breakdown. She was allowed to come back, in a probationary capacity, and reassigned to work with her old partner. Joe was skeptical at first, but after a few weeks of seeing Michelle in action, even he had to admit she appeared ready. Michelle found a way to disconnect and turn off the emotion switch; she had bounced back from a place no one believed she would have returned.

Unfortunately, Michelle's ability to "turn it off" transcended into other aspects of her life. She became disconnected from her family and friends. And when it came to relationships, the most she was interested in were one-night stands. She wasn't about to get that close to anyone. Her shrink might have been concerned about such behavior, but by then, she had stopped seeing him.

She lived alone without any pets or even a house plant. She rarely spoke to her family, and if she ever felt the urge, she would stop at one of the bars on 202, pick up a random quarry worker, get her rocks off—hopeful-ly—and kick the guy out the next morning. It was acceptable for men to do, and it suited Michelle's needs just fine. Best of all, now she could pull a dead child from a tangled car wreck and not feel a thing. *Because you can't save them all—right?*

"What the hell is that?" Dr. Freedman screamed as the massive figure dropped from the trees in front of them.

Michelle reacted quickly, slamming the brakes and causing the ambulance to skid for about fifty feet before coming to a complete stop. The doctor was lifted from his seat and smacked his head against the windshield. Michelle looked at him with her jaw hung open. *You're a doctor, for Christ's sake, and you never heard of a fucking seatbelt?* Freedman flopped back into his seat with fresh blood pouring from a gash in his forehead.

"My head. What are you doing?" He stared at her through a veil of red.

The thing in front of them rose to its feet and squared off. It was difficult to see through the cascade of rain and the slap of the wipers, but Michelle thought whatever it was looked a lot like a man. But no ordinary man, the guy was massive, with arms as big as cinder blocks. Also, the bastard was naked. His muscles and veins bulged and popped as if they might burst through his skin. Then Michelle noticed the grotesque abnormality of the guy's package swinging between his legs; it almost touched the ground.

"What the fuck?" She watched as the freak approached the vehicle. "Oh, no the fuck you don't," she said, punching the gas and turning the wheel to the right. The front tires of the ambulance bounced over the curb and skidded onto the sidewalk. Dr. Freedman was tossed like a salad as Michelle maneuvered the vehicle around the thing in the street. She had no idea what it was, but she wasn't about to let it anywhere near her, not with a dick the size of a baseball bat.

She got a better look at the creature as the ambulance lurched over the sidewalk and into the field. Although it initially looked like a man, it was clearly not. It was hairless and stared at Michelle with eyes as black as the devil's asshole. It shrieked as she drove away, revealing a mouth full of razor-sharp bad intentions. She pressed the gas harder and made a split-second decision to head for the fence bordering the high school football field.

The beast crouched low to squat, then pushed off the ground with its massive legs. It took to the air, flying over the ambulance and landing on the far side. It raised both of its hulking arms and smashed the passenger's door where Freedman sat, bringing the vehicle to a complete stop. It proceeded to shake and tear apart the sheet metal as if it were nothing more than the front page of the *Sunday Times*.

"You have to save me; I'm a doctor! I'm important!" Freedman turned to Michelle and pleaded.

She grimaced at him as the gorgon smashed the window and seized the self-righteous bastard by the throat. Freedman latched on to her arm as the beast attempted to extract him from the ambulance. She was yanked toward him and struggled to free herself from his clutches, but the doctor held on for dear life. Michelle braced her feet against the floor, reached into her jacket pocket with her free hand, and removed the .38 she had been issued the previous night. She aimed the pistol at the doctor and pulled the trigger. The bullet hit Freedman just below the cheek, which was enough to do the trick.

The man's eyes bulged outward, and then his jaw went slack. Blood leaked from the small wound, and he released his hold on her. The monster ripped him from his seat like a child plucking a dandelion from the front lawn. His feet flailed and kicked off one of his shoes, which landed on the seat next to Michelle, who punched the gas and took off through the field.

She checked the rearview mirror to find the beast had discontinued its pursuit for the moment and gone to work on the very important doctor. She wondered what the creature intended to do with the giant shaft between its legs. *Better him than me.* Michelle picked up Dr. Freedman's discarded shoe and tossed it out the broken window, then pointed the ambulance toward the school and floored it. The paramedic replaced the gun in her jacket pocket and smashed through the fence.

The men in the yellow rainslickers stationed in the back parking lot saw the vehicle approaching. Michelle slammed on the brakes and turned the wheel, bringing the ambulance to a screeching spin-out, stopping at the gym door. Bob Jones and Brandon Canfield rushed to her aid and immediately noticed the damage to the vehicle.

"Jesus, what happened?" Bob yelled.

"Something got Dr. Freedman. I tried to save him, but there was nothing I could do." Michelle did her best to look distraught and even managed to shed a few tears, but she wasn't sure if the act had been convincing enough. She had turned that switch off a long time ago. "The medicine and supplies are in the back," she told the firemen as she pretended to give a flying fuck about the man she had just shot in the face.

Deputy David Rainey oversaw the operation at the elementary school, making sure all the children were loaded safely onto the buses and the building was clear. He assisted his kid sister, Kelly, and her best friend, Caroline, and assured them everything would be all right, that he would meet them at the high school. The evacuation had been a success, except for the three missing children who left the school during the unplanned fire drill. Sheriff Primrose and Lois Fischer set out after them, but the kids couldn't have picked a worse time to play hooky. With any luck, they would survive long enough to get their fannies tanned by their parents. The streets of Garrett Grove weren't safe for anyone, especially three children.

David did a final sweep of the school to make sure no other students had slipped through the cracks. He checked the classrooms and principal's office on the first floor; all were clear, which left only the basement. David took the stairs and proceeded to check the boys' bathroom. "Hello," he called into the empty lavatory, receiving no reply. He made his way back into the hallway and was greeted by the sound laughter. "Hello," he called again.

There were footsteps, soft and furtive, coming from the girls' room. It was followed by another burst of laughter. *Dear God. We missed one.*

He entered the bathroom expecting to find the child standing there … but stopped short. The place was empty; there wasn't anyone inside.

"He-he." The voice floated from the back of the room.

"Hello," he called. "We need to get you out of here." David took a step forward, then froze when the strange voice answered him.

Hello …

It wasn't the voice of a little girl; it was hoarse, distorted, as if the owner had spoken through a mouthful of dirt. Then it spoke again.

Hello, David … did you miss me?

Searing pain erupted behind the deputy's temples and in the center of his head. It was the same voice from the other night. The one he had heard at the morgue.

Don't move, David.

He tried to run, but his muscles wouldn't respond. His legs felt cemented in place, his arms frozen at his sides, and his head screamed like it had been placed in a vise with the torque bar being tightened. Tears streamed from his eyes as he fought to pull himself from the overwhelming compulsion to remain right where he was. Then the door to the back stall swung open, followed by the sound of wetness slapping against the floor. A hand reached out and revealed itself. Dark, moldy skin hung from the twisted bones; deep red sores ate into the flesh like an acid.

Slosh ... Slosh ... Slosh

The thing that emerged from the stall looked like it had been underwater for a very long time and something had been taking bites out of its hide for even longer. Most of its skin had turned black, making it difficult to see the leeches that crawled across the creature's face and eyes. Still, David saw them.

He no longer felt his legs and had no idea he had stopped resisting the pervasive invasion within his head. The deputy stared slack-jawed at the abomination, rocking back and forth on his heels as the beast penetrated his brain and ransacked the shelves. It felt like being raped, a violation of his memories and emotions. The presence ravaged his psyche, and David's stomach tightened, then he vomited on the floor.

Oh, David ... this will do nicely.

The voice originated from deep within his skull, and then ... it released him.

Deputy Rainey woke to find himself in the girls' bathroom, standing over a puddle of vomit. He was alone; the creature that had been there only a moment ago was gone. *But how?* He didn't wait for a reply and spun on his heels out of the bathroom, up the stairs, and toward the front doors. He ran straight to his cruiser and jumped in. Somehow, he had been spared ... a second time. He damn sure wasn't going to wait around and offer it a third.

His ears rang, and his stomach lurched from the acrid taste in his mouth. David could still hear the awful presence tearing through his brain; he had never felt so violated. Putting the cruiser in drive and pressing his foot on the gas, he sped off toward the high school. He was overcome by an urgency to see his kid sister, a compulsion he was unable to describe and one he couldn't resist.

258

CHAPTER 73

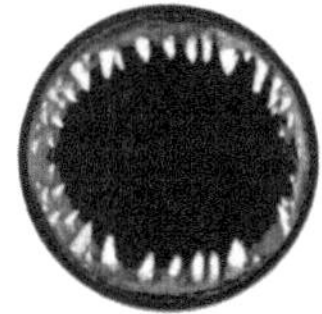

Beau Jenkins rolled his eyes at Drew Halberg, shrugged his shoulders, and raised his hand, indicating the number five. The siren had rung nonstop for the past twenty minutes, which had to be long enough. They would give it another five and then head to the high school. Neither man wanted to miss their chance to get inside; Chief Jones would soon be locking the doors for the night. Drew set the timer to five minutes, its longest duration, and slid in behind the wheel of the remaining pump truck. Beau Jenkins joined him, hopping into the passenger's seat.

By the time they reached the Turnpike, the sky was as dark as a solar eclipse. The storm was a full-on barn burner, and Beau was hit with the realization that he and the kid had waited too long. The main drag of Garrett Grove looked like a war zone. From their position, Beau could see at least two houses engulfed in flames and a tangle of burning vehicles littering the road. Drew swerved wide around an overturned Volkswagen Beetle and slowed to look at a truck that had crashed into the front window of the Plains Pharmacy. The vehicle was smoldering, and it looked like people were still stuck inside.

"Sweet Jesus," Beau said as Drew pulled the truck to the side of the road. The retired officer leaned his head out the window to get a better look, then motioned to the boy.

"Don't stop the truck, kid!" he shouted.

"But—there's people," Drew cried.

Beau watched in horror, feeling his own blood turn to ice in his veins. He suppressed the urge to scream and could only stare in silence as the creatures rushed toward the disabled truck. There were five of them, each one more hideous than the next. Their malicious intent was evident from the violent flailing of their bodies as they descended upon the vehicle's occupants. With ape-like strength, they smashed the windows of the truck and extracted the man with ease. He fought to get away, kicking and throwing his fists at his attackers, but there were too many of them. The beasts seized him; as if engaged in some barbaric game of tug-of-war, they tried to tear the man in multiple directions. His right arm separated at the shoulder; the attacker took off with his prize in hand, tearing into the torn flesh like a short rib. Beau could see the man was screaming but couldn't hear him over the rain and sirens. The other assailants swarmed him and wrestled the man to the ground, then they turned on the woman in the passenger's seat and began to tear into her as well.

"I said don't stop the fucking truck, kid!" Beau screamed, sure he was about to vomit or pass out.

Drew didn't need to be told twice and pressed his foot on the gas.

Beau didn't know he had drawn his revolver and sat there with it trembling in his hand.

"What was that?" Drew asked. "We should have helped those people."

Beau focused on the road in front of them. "It was too late, kid." He rolled down his window the rest of the way as they approached another car stopped in the middle of the street. There was something on top of the vehicle, slamming its mitts against the roof, clawing and scratching to get inside. Beau looked closer at the scene and noticed there were still people in this car as well. The faces of three children stared back at him from their position in the backseat.

"You can slow down now," Beau said, leaning out the window. He aimed his .38 and fired. The round hit the creature in the chest, which only seemed to piss it off. The thing on the roof of the car looked like every picture Beau had seen of Bigfoot, only smaller. It was covered in long, matted hair that hung from its limbs in tangled clumps. He fired a second round and hit the beast in the jaw, drawing its full attention. The mini-Bigfoot shrieked, jumped off the roof of the car, and ran toward the truck at top speed.

Beau fired off two quick rounds, missing the beast completely. It was too fast, and it was almost on them. The creature took a giant stride in their direction; Beau focused his sights on the area in front of it and squeezed the trigger. The round penetrated the thing's skull just above its left eye. The Yeti's legs gave out, and it fell to the pavement less than three feet from the truck. Beau jumped out and fired another round into the back of the creature's head, just to be safe. He reloaded as fast as his fingers would move and ran to the disabled vehicle.

"Oh, sank Gott, Herr Jenkins! You saved us!" Günter Bentley exited the car with his wife, Hazel, and his three children.

Drew opened the back door and motioned for the family to pile in. Günter's three little girls looked to their father to make sure it was safe to enter the stranger's vehicle. He assured them it was. "Ja, children, move along. Deez are mine friendz." He shooed the girls and his wife, Hazel, into the backseat.

"You're in the front with us, Günter," Beau told him and waited for the man to climb in. Günter jumped up and checked the backseat to make sure his family was safe and sound.

"All set den, sehr gut, ya sehr gut."

Beau grabbed the door handle and lifted his foot into the cab. Before he could pull himself into the vehicle, he felt it wrap around his leg. He clutched at the handle and seat as it grabbed him from behind and yanked him off balance. Looking up at Drew, he opened his mouth to scream but was ripped into the street. He came down hard on the pavement and nearly blacked out from the impact. The wind rushed from his lungs in one crushing blow as the unseen force clamped down even tighter.

"Get them out of here!" he called back to Drew as the beast dragged him away and he disappeared in the rain.

Drew stared in disbelief; it had happened so fast.

Günter reached over and slammed the door shut. "I sink ve better do as he saiz, ya."

The young fireman hit the gas and took off down the Turnpike at breakneck speed. The truck handled well in the rain but still fishtailed at first.

Günter turned to his family again. "Ya, I sink ve vill be vearing are seatbelts den, quickly, children."

The Bentley brood listened to their father, and all fastened their seatbelts, including Hazel. Drew looked in the rearview mirror for any movement in the street but didn't see a thing. He had no idea what happened to Deputy Jenkins, but the man had gone out a hero. He had saved Günter's family, and that was a noble way to spend the last day of your retirement—also a rather dignified way to die.

Cars, trucks, and vans continued to arrive at the high school as the people of town realized the urgency of the situation. One of the vehicles had been chased by something that looked like it belonged on a platter at Red Lobster. Then Michelle Marks tore across the football field and smashed through the back fence. After coming to a screeching halt at the gym doors, something gigantic, naked, and clearly male chased after her, dragging the body of Dr. Freedman in its grip—the creature had resumed its pursuit. Bob's men were ready and dispatched the abnormality before it ever breached the parking lot. The freakishly endowed creature and Dr. Freedman now lay somewhere near the visitors' thirty-yard line.

The steady flow of vehicles trickled down to almost none, but Bob still held out hope. He wanted to give the citizens and his men every opportunity to get back before he locked the place up tight. Drew Halberg and Deputy Jenkins were working the siren at the station, others were canvassing the town in the trucks, and Carl, along with several of his deputies, hadn't returned either.

He looked up as a Plymouth Skylark took the turn into the parking lot way too fast and almost collided with a light pole before swerving and making its way to the back doors. The car came to a skidding halt, and a woman wearing a bright pink slicker stepped out into the rain. Bob rushed to assist her and offered his hand.

"Right this way, miss," he said.

"Who're you calling miss, sailor?" Tyler Harrison looked out from under the brim of his Day-Glo rain slicker. He smiled at the chief, then batted his eyes.

Bob released his hand and stared with his jaw slack.

"Why don'tcha take a picture; it'll last longer," Tyler said, then hurried into the warmth of the gym, where he was directed to the basement.

Bob shook his head, looked at Brandon Canfield, and shrugged his shoulders. He grabbed his radio again, praying this time he would get an answer.

"Jones to Primrose. Answer your radio, Carl."

But there was still no reply.

Howard Bell didn't listen to the warning he received from Ed Koloski. *Who the hell does that guy think he is anyway? Coming in with his gang of hoodlums, looting the place, waving around fake documents.* The bastards had ransacked the hardware store like a bunch of mobsters. As far as Howard Bell was concerned, the only emergency in town was the fire department had appointed themselves the secret police. No way in hell he was about to close his business at the recommendation of a couple thugs. He didn't care what the document said, even if it did state he would be reimbursed.

It didn't help that Howard wasn't in the best frame of mind when the men showed up this morning. Lately, he and his wife, Kim, had been fighting even more than usual, and he had a good idea she was screwing around behind his back. He didn't know with who and had no idea how to deal with it. They got married right after high school, much to Howard's surprise. Kim was a fox, way out of his league. Still, she had chosen him, with all his faults and insecurities, of which he had a boxcar full—insecure about his appearance, his weight, the size of his dick, you name it. In truth, the only thing different about Howard Bell was his debilitating insecurity issue. Kim hadn't been cheating, but she was sick and tired of being accused of it.

Monday morning, after Howard left for work, Kim had packed a suitcase full of clothes, loaded their two-year old son in the car, and headed to her parents' place in Nashua, New Hampshire. Howard came home to a note, an empty house, and proceeded to lose his shit. Figuring he'd been right all along, he drank himself sick and then started hitting the valium. When Kim didn't return home on Tuesday, Howard considered taking the whole bottle of the little yellow tablets. After getting no answer at her parents' house, he knew she wasn't coming back. And the phones had stopped working. Then Ed Koloski and the sheriff's gestapo showed up and damn near cleaned the place out.

Now he was expected to close shop and spend the night in the basement of the high school. What if Kim changed her mind and came home? What if the phones started working? There were too many variables. But the real reason why Howard Bell didn't want to go was because he had been ordered. Howard didn't like being ordered around—not one bit.

Soon after the men left, the fire whistle blew. Apparently, they were serious about getting everyone in the shelter. Then the rain started, which didn't help Howard's disposition. Rainy days always got him down, and when Howard got down, he got dark … and not just a little. A psychiatrist might have diagnosed his manic depression and prescribed a medication that helped, rather than the valium, which only made things worse.

Howard watched the rain hammer the parking lot from his storefront window. The sky was as grey as his mood, and it occurred to him in a moment of clarity, he had driven Kim away. But thoughts of such were pushed to the side when the first beast appeared. It ran in front of the store, chasing a Volkswagen Beetle up Jackson Ave. The thing looked primitive and wore a mechanic's uniform. Howard tried to tell himself he imagined the strange sight but was unable to when a second one showed up in the lot. This creature could almost have passed for human if it weren't for the face, which looked warped and deformed, as if it had melted.

He stared at the nightmare, unable to pretend it wasn't real. Then several more abominations found their way into the lot. They maneuvered on all fours and were fast as hell. Howard locked the deadbolt, drawing the attention of the primates in the process, causing them to descend upon the building like a plague. They tore at the windows and doors in a frenzied heat to get at the man inside. He retreated to the back of the store and then into the basement. The place was built well, but it wasn't a fortress, not by a long shot. The atrocities quickly found their way inside and proceeded to rip the store apart. Howard shrank to the furthest reaches of the cellar as chaos ensued overhead.

He told himself it was all his fault; he had driven Kim away with his constant accusations and this was what he deserved. He listened as the sound of destruction drew nearer and knew the freaks had found the door to the basement. It was the end of the world; he was sure of that. And with Kim gone, there was no sense in going on anyway. Howard knew that as he searched through his stock of supplies on the back shelf. He removed the bottle of Quaker State anti-freeze and cracked it open. The deafening smash as the beasts tore the basement door from its hinges almost caused him to drop the container. He raised the bottle to his lips and swallowed as much of the vile contents that his body would allow. Howard Bell died before the first creature made it off the staircase. They say suicide is the coward's way out, but whoever said that had no idea how much courage it took him to swallow that quart of anti-freeze. Some might even say that it took a hell of a lot of guts.

Howard Bell wasn't the only resident of Garrett Grove who decided to end their own life that day. Marcie and Gottfried Eichmann heard the alarm and took the warning seriously. Baby Lavern was still nursing, and Marcie had just run a warm bath for both her and the child. Then the whistle went off. Gottfried immediately took to gathering everything he thought they might need for the baby, throwing diapers and ointments into bags, and cans of formula in case Marcie went through a dry spell. Then he proceeded to load everything into the car.

Marcie stood at the front door watching her husband load the trunk when the storm hit. It came down fast and sudden, soaking Gottfried in seconds. It was then that Marcie noticed the woman lumbering up the sidewalk as if she were drunk, with her arms hung slack at her sides. Something was very wrong with the woman, her mindless shuffle, the intoxicated sway of her body, not to mention she appeared unfazed by the storm.

Gottfried spotted her and approached to see if she was all right. But it was apparent she was not. He walked toward her with his arms held out as she turned and entered the driveway. The woman lunged at him with the speed and accuracy of a viper. Her mouth clamped down on the side of Gottfried's neck, and in a hot flash, a kiwi-size section of his flesh was torn away. He tried to scream, but the shock gripped him before he could react. A rivulet of crimson pulsed outward from where his carotid artery had been breached, soaking both he and the woman, running down the driveway and into the street. He fell to the pavement and bled out while Marcie watched from the front door, clutching baby Lavern to her breast.

Marcie screamed as Gottfried's leg twitched for the last time, then the attacker turned toward her and the baby. A section of the woman's face was missing; thick white worms crawled within the gaping wound. Marcie froze at the front door, staring at Gottfried's body where it lay in the driveway and the impossible features of the monster that had killed him. Her world heaved and spun out of control, and something inside her popped like an overloaded circuit breaker. Before she could move from her position, three more figures appeared on the far side of the property.

Marcie slammed the door and attempted to lock it but was unable to execute the action with Lavern stuck to her breast. *Dear God, they're going to eat my baby!* The thought resonated in her head and tipped Marcie the rest of the way over the edge. She had seen the movies about the living dead and wasn't about to let that happen to her or her baby. She ran up the stairs, into the bathroom, and locked the door behind her. The floor shook beneath her as the first intruder entered the house. Marcie stared at the tubful of bathwater, nice and warm, soothing, and relaxing. She had just drawn it for her and Lavern and couldn't think of a nicer place. She lowered the baby into the tub, pushed her under the water, and started to sing.

"Hush little baby, don't say a word."

It took less than a minute for the child to stop struggling; by then, there was little that remained of Marcie. She threw open the top drawer of the vanity and removed Gottfried's straight razor. She slid the cold steel across her throat with enough force to not only sever the vein but her windpipe as well. It was unsure whether Marcie bled to death or suffocated. At least she hadn't been eaten … not until the beasts found her lifeless body on the bathroom floor.

Sven Peterson watched the creatures tear at the cedar panels on the side of his house. His wife and two boys retreated to the back bedroom as the place was dismantled board by board. He first saw the creatures enter his neighbor's yard and attack several children playing with slingshots. Sven couldn't be sure if the kids had gotten away, as they ran to the far side of the property. By then, there were more of the strange attackers. Sven got a good look at them, thinking they almost resembled gargoyles as they ripped the plywood from his house. Soon they would be inside, and it would be all over for the Peterson clan. Sven had always been a practical man, didn't believe in ghosts, UFOs, or even Bigfoot, and had no way of knowing exactly how he might react in a situation like that. If Sven had been asked on Tuesday if he was the type of guy who would use a shotgun on his entire family and then turn it on himself, he would have said *Absolutely not!* But on Tuesday, he never imagined he would be around to witness the end of the world.

Angelo and Donna Franco heard the warning signal and took the message seriously. After the week they had had on Poplar Ave. with the house fire and the disappearance of several of their neighbors, they weren't about to take chances. The whistle sounded, and then a fire truck drove by, delivering its message. So, Angelo and Donna did what any self-respecting Italian couple would do ... they got their asses to church! Which appeared to be a popular decision. They arrived at Our Lady of the Mountain to find the parking lot more than half full, which was unheard of for a Wednesday afternoon. The couple exited the car and hurried through the rain toward the entrance just as the front doors burst open. Two men carrying hunting rifles greeted them with hearty smiles.

"Welcome, friends," one man said. "Glad you could make it."

"Hurry on now. Don't want to stand there too long," the other man told them, then shouted over his shoulder. "Look alive! We got company!" He dropped to his knee and raised the rifle level with his eye. Angelo and Donna were rushed into the church by the first man, who then turned and pumped a round into his shotgun.

Donna jumped into her husband's arms when the first shot was fired. It was followed by a second and then a third as the men took action. The couple stood in the center of the aisle clutching each other in shock. They had come to the church to find solace in faith during a time of crisis; what they found was something different. Suddenly, a man they knew very well charged toward them. Father Kieran had performed the ceremony at their wedding eighteen months ago. The Francos knew him to be a compassionate, understanding man who was old-fashioned like every other Catholic priest. They liked him, felt comfortable in his church, and had made it their church as well.

Father Kieran barreled toward them with the small caliber pistol raised above his head. "Stand back. The evil ones are upon us," he shouted as he passed the couple and ran out the front door. Several parishioners followed him. The sound of gunfire stifled the blare of the sirens and pouring rain. Donna and Angelo stared at each other, unsure if they should give thanks or run for their lives.

Carl maneuvered the cruiser through the Village. He'd been concerned the cloud cover of the storm would provide enough darkness for the creatures to wage an attack but never imagined the destruction that could take place in such a short time. Lois stared out the window in silence, tears streaming down her cheeks as she directed him to Janis's house. They arrived a moment later, and Carl brought the cruiser to a screeching halt in the driveway.

The place looked dark and empty, but it was impossible to tell in the storm. "Stay here!" He grabbed her purse, removed the handgun, and thrust it into her hand. "For Christ's sake, hold on to this. You're going to need it!"

Lois stared at him through a river of tears. Carl wasn't even sure she had heard him, but there was no time to repeat himself. He had waited too long to start the evacuation and the relocation of patients into the center's basement. Every move he had made had only been reactionary, ineffective, and counterproductive. How many deaths was he responsible for? How many men had he lost by making the wrong call? He was in over his head and had no idea how to bail himself out. He had even missed the chance to send for help.

Lightning flashed blue overhead as he ran to the house. Thunder immediately followed, causing Carl to jump as he climbed the steps. *Please don't let the power go out.* He tried the handle, only to find it locked, then backed away and kicked without knocking. The door flew inward, and Carl rushed into the house with his firearm raised. A moment later, he exited and jumped in the cruiser.

"That's a good sign." He nodded to Lois. "If they were here, they're probably already at the high school." He threw the car in reverse and backed out of the driveway just as the windows of the house across the street exploded outward. The concussion shook the cruiser, and a wall of flames billowed across the lawn and rushed toward them. Carl grabbed Lois, forced her down, and lay on top of her. She screamed as shards of glass and pieces of debris landed on the hood of the vehicle.

For Christ's sake. I'm going to lose the entire town.

"Where does the other girl live?" he shouted and drove away from the destruction.

Lois pointed forward; her hand shook with a spastic tremble.

"We're gonna find them," he said. "But we need to stay focused. I know you're scared, just stay with me, Lois."

Lois stared down at the gun in her lap, then looked back at him. "Wendy lives two blocks up on Winding Way." She continued to point ahead as they left the carnage behind them.

"You there, Bob?" Carl shouted into the mic. He took the turn onto Winding Way and was jolted by the blare of a horn. The pickup truck screamed toward them, taking up both lanes of the road. Carl dropped the mic and pulled the wheel hard to the left. Every muscle in his body tensed, anticipating the impact. The cruiser's tires bit into the pavement and squealed, sending the vehicle and its passengers over the curb and through a hedgerow. Carl regained control and steered back onto the roadway as the pickup continued without stopping. *Jesus Christ!* It had been too close. He looked over at Lois, who gripped the dashboard with both hands. All the color had drained from her face. *Too fucking close!* He gripped the wheel and hyper-focused on the road in front of them.

"Carl, thank God. Where are you?" Bob's voice boomed through the speaker.

"We're still trying to locate the kids. Are they there yet? They might be with the girl's aunt, Lynn Donovan."

There was a pause that felt like it lasted a year before Bob answered. "The Donovan woman showed up about fifteen minutes ago looking for her niece. But no sign of the kids yet."

"Roger that," Carl replied. "I'll be in touch as soon as we find them." He knew exactly what Bob was thinking: they couldn't keep the school open much longer. Soon, they would have to bolt and chain the doors shut. But neither man spoke a word about what was on their minds.

"Copy that, Carl. We'll leave the lights on for ya."

CHAPTER 74

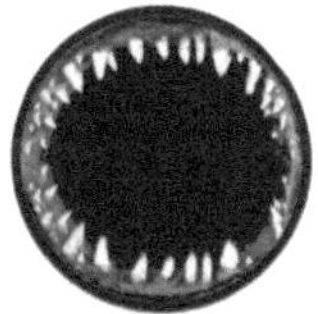

Don and Stephanie sat with Gail at the entrance of the cave eating a late lunch and watching the dark clouds gather in the west. There were periods of awkward silence and moments where they caught themselves staring at each other. They had crossed a major line without giving it a second thought. Don couldn't believe he had acted so impulsively and was sure Stephanie felt the same. Still, despite the guilt, he didn't regret what had happened. It had been incredible, erotic, and confusing as hell. After lunch was finished, they acted like nothing happened and went back to work.

The back of the second chamber was where the final three cave paintings were located. Don and the women rearranged the work lights to illuminate the far-right corner, revealing the image that had been painted over four hundred years ago. It was a depiction of a ritual involving several Lenape children. They were adorned in elaborate clothes and jewelry, and the elders of the tribe looked as if they were praying to them. There was nothing dark or ominous about this painting, no black eyes or jagged teeth like there were in the others. This mural was a juxtaposition of the ones they had previously examined.

"Did they worship their kids?" Don asked.

"No more than we do ours," Stephanie answered. "There were certain rituals intended only for children, but their interactions weren't that different."

Don turned his flashlight on and examined the children. Each wore an elaborate medallion around their necks, a large emblem of an ornate sunburst nearly as big as their chests. Don had a good idea what the necklaces were made of—magnetite—the same as the weapons and the cave itself.

Gail clicked off a series of shots, running another roll of film dry. She reached into her bag to replace it and rummaged around for a few seconds. "I have to head to my Jeep and grab some more film. I'll be right back." She made her way toward the front of the cave, and Don and Stephanie found themselves alone once again.

They stared at each other for a full minute without talking. Finally, Don broke the silence. "You're probably thinking I'm an asshole."

Stephanie burst out laughing. "And you must think I'm the biggest slut going. You're married, for Christ's sake, and I just dropped my pants like some love-sick teenager on prom night." She turned away, shaking her head.

"Don't be so hard on yourself." He smiled. "I'm kinda irresistible."

"Well, Mr. Irresistible, let's try to move on from this. It doesn't take a collective unconscious to know this doesn't end well. Either way, someone gets hurt. I don't want to be responsible for that, and I don't need to go through it myself. Not again."

Don stared off into the farthest reaches of the cave, where the small opening disappeared into nothingness. "I understand," he said.

An uncomfortable silence fell over them, accompanied by an icy chill racing in from the cavern's entrance. The moment was shattered by a loud clap of thunder that resonated off the lodestone walls. They jumped at the sudden sound, then moved to the front of the cave to check the coming storm.

"I hope Gail hurries back, or she's gonna get drenched," Don said and poked his head outside. The town's whistle sounded a moment later, growing in volume as it echoed throughout the quarry. Don waited for the rise and fall of its pitch, but the whistle continued to belch out an endless cry. "That can't be right," he said. "That's the air raid signal."

"You mean the duck and cover kind?" Stephanie raised her brows in question.

"Yeah, that kind. The siren must be broken."

Outside, the rain started to fall against the dusty hardpan. Don looked toward the parking lot to watch Gail retrieve her bag and start running up the slope of the hill toward the cave. There was another quick flash of lightning, then the skies exploded, dumping rain in a fat torrential downpour. They backed away from the entrance as a cascade of water sheeted off the cliff in front of them. A horrible shriek sliced through the din of the storm, high-pitched and ear-shattering like the wail of a great cat caught in a trap. Stephanie turned to Don, wide-eyed and terrified. The cry was followed by another, even more mournful than the first.

"Probably a mountain lion!" he shouted to be heard.

Then he saw it.

At first, he thought the rain had loosened the rock on the western ridge, but as he looked closer, he realized it wasn't rock or mud or anything like that. Something was making its way down the rockface on the opposite side of the quarry. It was an animal of some type, clinging to the cliff. But it was moving too fast. Then he noticed the second one and then a third descending the rock. Soon, there were a dozen of the things rushing toward the canyon floor.

The air in his lungs sizzled like molten metal as he finally exhaled, unaware he had been holding his breath. Don gripped the wall next to him as the tremble started in his legs and worked its way throughout his body. It happened so fast. Terror spiked with uncertainty running through his veins as he watched the impossible scene unfold. *What in the name of God?*

From where Don stood, they looked like spiders—huge fucking spiders! The damn things were almost the size of a grown man. Even at a distance with the rain, he could see the creatures had nearly as many legs as spiders and were covered with dark brown hair, everywhere but on their heads, which was reddish orange.

"What the fuck?" Stephanie cried and hid behind Don.

The creatures had made their way to the ground and took off in several directions, scampering across the hardpack to where Buzzy and Mark had set off to relocate the explosives.

At first, Don thought the red part of the strange arachnid's body was the head, but now he could see them clearer. It was a stinger, and they weren't exactly spiders. The monstrosities that descended the quarry walls looked more like scorpions with deadly red stingers at the end of their tails. "Jesus Christ!" Don hissed as he watched the beasts make their way toward the trailers. His men had no idea what was headed their way.

Then something else emerged on the canyon floor that wasn't a spider or a scorpion. It was a man, and something was terribly wrong with him. His head hung limp and lolled from side to side as he shuffled through the wet dirt on a left foot that appeared to be broken at the ankle. The injury didn't impede the man's speed in the slightest; he ran straight toward the trailers with his foot flopping behind him.

Gail, who had been preoccupied with her equipment and the rain, ascended the rise and finally spotted the creatures. She screamed, dropped her bag, and bolted toward Don, who stood at the entrance, waiting to assist her. He hung out of the cave as much as he dared but took a step backward when another cry echoed from the direction of the trailers. It was high-pitched, intense, and agonizing, sounding like someone was being burned alive.

"Help me!" Gail screamed. She ran the last few steps to the entrance, reached out, and latched on to Don's hand.

He grabbed her and started to pull her inside, then froze when the front of her shirt exploded, basting him in a wash of crimson. The giant pincer drove itself into her back and penetrated the photographer's torso. A look of disbelief stole across her face as the red ball pushed its way through her skin, skewering her like a beef kebob. She grabbed at the impaling object as the creature lifted her with its monstrous tail and held her up for Don and Stephanie to see.

At only a few feet away, Don was able to get his first good look at the creature. There were characteristics that were scorpion, like the tail and the pincer, but there were some spider-like qualities to it as well. Thick black hair covered the creature's entire body, which had to be over five feet long. It had at least eight legs, as far as Don could tell, but that was where the arachnid similarities ended. Don stared at the impossible with a heart-stopping scream stuck in his throat.

Where the monster's head should have been sat the face of a human woman ... and there was something familiar about it. Don wasn't sure who had been the owner of the face, but he recognized the look in its eyes immediately. They were horrible, and piercing, and pitch-black.

Blood poured from Gail's mouth and cascaded from the massive opening in her chest; still, she continued to fight against the beast, kicking and flailing and beating against its giant pincer. The monster backed away from the entrance with the woman suspended from its deadly mandible and howled. The repulsive sound of its voice churned Don's stomach. He wanted to run, but his entire body had gone numb. He stood transfixed, staring at a dozen rows of God-awful razor-sharp teeth. The very same as the ones depicted in the murals.

He moved to the side to shield Stephanie from the creature, only to find she wasn't there. She had retreated to the back of the cave; he thought he should probably do the same. But he could only stand there, watching. Gail stopped fighting a few seconds later; her body went slack as the life dripped out of her. The scorpion-creature shook her one last time, then tossed her body away like a scrap of paper.

The great freak opened its human mouth and howled again, allowing a tendril of dark smoke to lift from its maw. Black eyes stared down at Don and began to smolder as if something inside them was burning. The thick cloud poured forth and accumulated around the creature's hideous head in a swirling mass. Don stood there, hypnotized by the concentric motion of the cloud, until a thunderous crash from the direction of the trailers broke his trance. He backed away, but the beast held its ground, with the growing cloud picking up momentum and churning before him.

Don felt the air disrupted near his head as something whistled past him. The beast bellowed with a thunderous squeal that penetrated deep into the cave. It reared up on its hind legs and came down hard, twisting and writhing like an ant under a magnifying glass. The whistle of a second object sailed past his head a moment later, and the creature screamed as if it were about to erupt. It curled up like a giant pill bug and rolled down the slope of the hill, where it came to rest and stopped moving.

Don spun on his heels to see Stephanie standing behind him. She held one of the wooden tubes in her right hand and several lodestone musket balls in the other. Her breath was ragged and exaggerated; tears coursed down her cheeks.

"Get your ass out of the way before you get yourself killed!" she screamed and loaded another musket ball into the tube.

Chapter 75

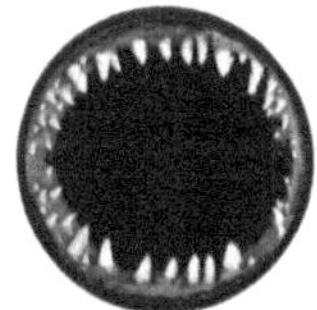

Troy and the girls huddled together in the tight confines of the makeshift cage. To flee their pursuers, he had led them through the concealed opening that originated in the graveyard room to the narrow hallway where the inner workings and mechanisms that controlled Scream in the Dark ran through the center of the garage. With nowhere left to run, they had made their way in the dark, past the rat room and the spider palace, only to come to a dead end in the confines of the cage. Troy prayed it was hidden enough but knew the only thing between them and the creatures was a thin layer of cardboard.

He pulled the girls close and explained his plan but couldn't be sure they had even heard him over the sirens and the pouring rain. Sliding his foot forward, he found what he was looking for and prayed the cord was still plugged in. He rested the tip of his sneaker on the plastic switch, dug into his coat pocket, and removed the item. The ghouls were closer now. Their grunts and barks bounced against the walls of the maze, making it impossible to pinpoint their exact location. Troy was almost certain they were now in the rat room, following the path of least resistance, which he had been counting on.

The wheel that controlled the Day-Glo spiders began to spin at a feverish pace as the fiends ripped the hanging arachnids from the ceiling. The diversion of fishing line and plastic decorations lasted about two seconds, and the creatures pounced into the space in front of them. The rancid stench of sour milk and wet dog filled the confining area, causing Troy to gag. He held his breath and fought the urge to vomit. But they were so close, inches away on the other side of the makeshift cage, standing in the exact spot where Wendy had kissed him. The overpowering stink of the beasts was oppressive and awoke Troy to a horrible possibility. If he could smell them, then could they smell him and the girls as well?

An ear-splitting shriek erupted in front of them, and Troy knew their hiding place had been discovered. It was now or never. He pressed his foot down on the small plastic button taped to the floor. The strobe light came to life, filling the room with a white-hot pulse, illuminating the creatures before them. The boom box exploded, blaring its soundtrack of prerecorded screams, adding to the confusion of the moment. Troy, Wendy, and Janis found themselves face-to-face with the repulsive creatures just as the Tobin boys had ambushed the children Saturday night. The searing light had the exact effect Troy had hoped for. The demons screamed and shielded their eyes, howling and writhing as the pulse hammered at them like a branding iron.

Troy released the magnet he held in the pouch of his wrist rocket, sending the projectile point-blank into the first creature's chest. The monster hissed and jumped back in the confines of the small area. Troy loaded another round into the pouch as Wendy and Janis released their weapons of destruction. It was impossible to miss from the short distance, and the sound that came out of the creatures when the projectiles made contact was ghastly. The children loaded their weapons and released their arsenal on the beasts, who twisted and screamed and fell to the floor tweaking like a couple of trout.

Troy urged the girls back the way they had come through the tight passage, leaving the creatures behind. They exited into the storm to find the fire whistle no longer ringing and no creatures in sight.

"Quick!" he yelled. "Back into the house!"

Both girls wore similar expressions; half-crazed and wild-eyed, they stared back at him. He wondered if he looked the same as he led them across the backyard, into the house, and slammed the door behind them.

"That was amazing!" Wendy shouted, grabbing him and kissing him on the cheek.

"You saved us," Janis cried and planted one on his other.

The celebration was short-lived when something hard and heavy slammed against the back door. The children jumped and looked up to see the horrendous face. The creature that stood before them was repulsive. It stared through the eye-level window set into the door and began to sway to the left and right as if moving to a tune only it could hear. It looked slow and deformed, as if something had gone wrong in the mutation process. Troy watched the distorted head bob about like it belonged to a drunk or a toddler; he assessed that the threat was minimal.

Then the freak reared back and opened its mouth, revealing a lethal set of fangs. It screamed at the children as both sides of its neck flared like a cobra ready to strike. Horrible black eyes pierced Troy like an arrow, now making the creature look as dangerous as a switchblade.

It butted its head against the glass, sending shards flying in every direction. It took out a sizable section of wood with its single blow and nearly gained access. Wendy scooped up a handful of magnets from the drawing table and deposited them into her pockets. She turned to join Troy and

Janis, who were already headed for the stairs, when the back door exploded inward. The cobra-looking horror stepped into the rec room, dripping puddles onto the tile floor.

It was on them before anyone had a chance to load their weapons. Swift and accurate, it approached the children where they stood frozen in place. It took an exaggerated step and lunged at Wendy. The beast's foot slipped in one of the large puddles of rainwater, and suddenly it was airborne, losing its balance and coming down hard on its back. The creature's massive head slapped against the tile floor with a resonating thud.

Troy didn't hesitate and forced Wendy and Janis up the stairs toward the front door. He was about to tell them to head outside when they rounded the landing and headed to the second floor. His heart stopped. There were no exits on that level of the house; they would be trapped. The magnets weren't exactly a super weapon; they took too long to reload and too many shots to take down the creatures. They would soon find themselves outnumbered and out of magnets.

The beast that had fallen let out another mournful shriek and regained its footing. Troy noticed movement out of the corner of his eye but didn't dare look back. Panic flooded his brain, making it impossible to focus on any constructive thought. He ascended the stairs in pursuit of the girls and was nearing the first landing when the front door flew open as if it had been hit with a battering ram. Splinters of the jamb sailed past his head, and the door almost smashed into him.

Sheriff Primrose rushed into the house with a rifle pointed in front of him. There was just enough time for Troy to duck before the sheriff started firing. The concussion of the weapon was deafening as each shot ripped through the stairwell like a wrecking ball. Troy was sure he had been hit. He closed his eyes and hugged the carpet as the sheriff fired round after round.

Carl and Lois turned onto Pine Street and saw the children run from the garage to the back door. A small pack of the strange brutes spotted the kids as well and took off after them.

"Oh, Carl, hurry!" Lois screamed.

After finding both girls' houses empty, they'd sped to the Fischer residence with the urgency of a four-alarm fire. Carl slammed the brakes and leapt out of the vehicle before it came to a complete stop. He ascended the front steps and took a running jump at the door, kicking it in mid-air. The flimsy wooden structure flew inward, and Carl found himself facing Troy with several of the crazed beasts hot on the boy's tail. The child ducked just as Carl aimed the Marlin and fired at the first attacker.

The seven-round, reloadable 30-30 was deadly accurate and Carl's weapon of choice. But the thing was close enough behind the child to be on top of him. It stretched out a hulking arm and lunged for Troy; its mangled fingers reached for the boy as the gun thundered. The bullet connected with its mark, taking out a massive portion of the monster's head; it fell backward into the rec room, where it ceased to move. But more followed and rushed through the back door. Carl fired on the horde, making the most with each shot, taking the time to aim for the heads. But their breach was too fast; they flooded into the house in a swarm and zeroed in on them.

"Everyone, outside now!" he screamed to the girls at the top of the stairs, and lifted Troy off the floor. They followed him and met Lois on the front lawn. Carl turned, fired off his last round, and reloaded. His fingers flew in a dizzying blur as the group tore across the lawn toward the squad car. Lois urged them into the backseat, then entered the vehicle herself. A second later, Carl pounced behind the wheel, threw the car in reverse, and screamed out of the driveway. He took a hard right, and the Fischer residence faded from view. The vile ghouls poured out the front door like a plague. More of the beasts gathered on the front lawn like a demonic band of trick-or-treaters.

Lois turned to the three children in the backseat and opened her mouth to speak. She reached out and took Troy by the hand as the tears flooded onto her cheeks.

Chapter 76

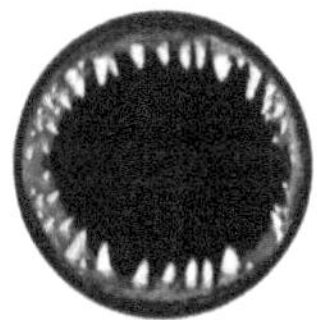

Chris Fredericks took the lead position of the bucket brigade at the top of the stairs. He handed weapons and supplies to Phil Reardon, who passed them along to Derek Fisk, who in turn delivered the cache to Dee Riker at the bottom of the stairs. A severe flash of lightning lit up the entire lobby of the medical center as if someone had thrown a flash bang through the front window. Chris thrust the weapons into Phil's hands at a faster pace but froze when a shriek sliced the air like a machete. It was followed by a second that sounded closer than the first.

"Don't take too long with that!" Deputy Lutchen called from the stairwell.

A second later, Chris heard the sound of chains being threaded through the front doors.

Chris watched the front lobby with growing concern. Shadows reflected off the glass, growing darker by the second. Underneath the sound of the rain and sirens, he was sure he heard something else, the guttural grunting of wild animals. Moments later, the front windows of the lobby exploded inward; a horde of bodies poured through the opening like a flood. Chris lowered his hand to his side and gripped the .38 he'd been issued, but the weapon never left the waistband of his jeans. He was knocked into the cart and blinded by the throng of bodies that fell on him. Some went right to biting and clawing, but a far worse sensation overtook Chris. It entered him like an electric current and tasted like a tin of copper pennies, ravaging what was useful and tossing the rest to the side like a piece of leftover meatloaf.

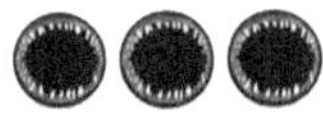

Derek Fisk was standing at the bottom of the stairwell when the creatures breached the building. He watched as they descended on Chris Fredericks, then attacked Phil Reardon. Derek spun about, colliding into Dee Riker, and shoved the boy backward into the basement. None of them had considered for a minute they'd be ambushed before they were safely locked inside the shelter. Steel cleats had been secured to the wall on either side of the door with four-inch lag bolts. The half-inch reinforced steel plates they were designed to support were tempered and strong enough to prevent even King Kong from getting inside. Provided they were set in place first.

Derek turned back to see Phil Reardon overcome by the swarm of creatures. Growing tendrils of dark smoke lifted into the air and swirled before the man's face. Phil's eyes rolled into the back of his skull and glossed to a black onyx, then he screamed. "Lock the door, now!"

The sight of the smoke disappearing into Phil's mouth was enough to break Derek from the spell. He slammed the door shut, leaving his friend behind on the stairs. He engaged the dead bolt and turned to Dee, who was there to help and slid the first plate into the steel cleats. The men moved fast and inserted the rest as the horde of demons made their way down the stairs. Several other firemen joined them at the door, stacking sandbags against it, and then stepped back.

They retreated to a barricade of filing cabinets set approximately thirty feet from the door. Weapons and boxes of ammunition were strategically placed at various vantage points on the makeshift stronghold. The gauntlet was where they would make their final stand should the monsters breach the fortification of the shelter door. If that happened, Derek didn't think it mattered how many weapons they had. *God help us if they do.*

They had a ton of firepower, but there were also a lot of patients and staff that would be useless once the fighting started. The firemen would perform well, but as Derek surveyed his forces, he realized there were less of them than he initially thought. Dee Riker dropped to one knee and held a shotgun trained at the basement door. The kid didn't so much as tremble. To Derek's left stood Greg, a large orderly who had fed breakfast to the patients on the second floor almost single-handedly. Greg adjusted the sight of his weapon, and it looked to Derek as if the guy knew what he was doing. Further down the line of defense were Fred Ramos, Kevin Grish, and Kurt Harrington, the fire inspector's nephew. All the men were avid hunters and comfortable handling firearms.

Behind them stood a second firing line of medical staff who had taken up arms, using several overturned carts for cover. Lee Chen, the lab tech, crouched next to Joe Santos from the first aid squad, but the most surprising of the volunteers was the center's own Dr. Halasz. Derek didn't know what to expect from any of them but was thankful for the extra guns pointed at the door.

Derek scanned the room, taking in the terrified looks on the faces staring back at him. The patients in their cots, the nurses attending to them, and the citizens who arrived seeking shelter—they had all heard the attack in the stairwell. Derek focused on a young girl with a bandage wrapped around her head; she had been involved in a traffic accident yesterday. An older man sat holding her hand, most likely the girl's father. Derek jumped and spun about as the first beast threw itself at the basement door. He watched the door with a laser focus; it appeared as if it was going to hold. The second concussion rattled it in its jamb, and Derek could have sworn the cleats had moved.

He turned to Dee and the rest of his men. "Remember, it has to be the head. Don't fire unless you can make the shot!"

He was met with a shared look of acknowledgement and held his breath as the third blow hammered against the door. Derek felt his legs go numb and almost ran from his position; he was certain the upper cleat on the right side had started to come loose from its anchor.

Garth Redman had been admitted on Monday night after experiencing severe chest pain. Dr. Halasz examined him, put him on blood thinners, and was happy to report that Garth had not had a heart attack. At the ripe old age of forty-seven and weighing in at a hefty two sixty, Garth was elated to hear the news. Now, as he lay in the back of the basement, about as far as anyone could get from the stairwell, he began to feel lightheaded. The pounding at the basement door sent a tremor racing through him with every thunderous beat. Garth started to hyperventilate, and sweat dripped from his brow. It ripped through him suddenly and with the strength of bazooka. Garth bit his tongue as his chest locked up tighter than the tin man's ass. He clutched the left side of his body and struggled to scream, but it was already too late. He fell back onto the cot, clamping down on his tongue hard enough to almost bite it in half.

The assault against the basement door ceased, and the room was still. A young nurse rushed to the aid of Garth Redman and checked for a pulse, but there was nothing. Nurse Burns looked about the room for Dr. Halasz and located him near the front door holding a pistol. She placed her hands to either side of her mouth and prepared to call out. The straining sound of metal twisting and breaking caused her to jump. She spun and faced the back of the room, where the noise had originated. It was followed by a buckling crash and several loud thuds as something massive fell against the concrete. Nurse Burns watched as the doors of the freight elevator started to spread apart. There was something in the shaft.

They parted only an inch at first, just the slightest movement. Then, the elevator doors spread a half inch more. Nurse Burns crouched behind the body of Garth Redman. She gripped the sheets of the bed with trembling hands and a hitch in her breath and watched. It happened too fast to even follow; the elevator doors mushroomed outward as the creature blasted from the shaft like a projectile. The putrid stench that followed was oppressive. It filled her sinuses like a plague.

Nurse Barnes gagged as the vile thing entered the basement, its skin looking like a cross between runny egg whites and cottage cheese. Pieces of the beast's flesh sloughed from its body and fell to the floor, discarded and forgotten. It wore what could have been a pair of jeans and flannel shirt, but it was impossible to tell since its runny epidermis had fused with its clothing. Before she could catch her breath, it was on top of her, wrapping its soupy hands around her head and lifting her off her feet. The putrefying flesh wrapped around her like a wet, rancid blanket, blinding her vision and stopping her air. She flailed in the behemoth's grip until it finally dropped her to the floor. It tilted its head back and released an enraged cry. A massive cloud of black spewed forth and descended upon the paralyzed nurse in a rush. It spilled into her and went to work, consuming her consciousness and devouring her fear.

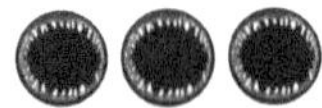

Derek was alerted by the sound of twisting metal and the crash of the freight elevator when the cables snapped. Earlier, the car had gotten stuck between the basement and the first floor, the circuit board blackened like a tin of Jiffy Pop. The men trapped inside were rescued, but there was no repairing it. Derek and the rest of the firemen figured the stalled elevator car would act as an impenetrable barrier and didn't give the shaft a second thought. The oversight was catastrophic.

The men stationed at the barricade could only watch as the horror unfolded. The elevator doors disappeared in a blur; a second later, the vile mutation bolted from the ravaged opening like a discharged bullet. The stench that followed was oppressive. Then it took her, grabbing and tossing the young nurse like a fitted sheet. As she lay on her back with the terror towering above her, the even more impossible happened. A plume of fog, almost black in color, poured out of the thing's mouth. It swirled for a moment, gathering and building in mass, then pounced on the girl. It surrounded her, entered her, then moved on to the others. The strange cloud attacked those in the neighboring beds, hopping from cot to cot in a storm. The rest of the patients and staff screamed and fought to get away from the dense mass, but it was everywhere.

A second flurry of movement thrust itself from the nonexistent elevator doors. Derek struggled to focus through the hysterical mass of fleeing bodies, expecting to find more of the dark substance. But what he saw looked nothing like the descending cloud. Hundreds, possibly thousands of birds, or what had once been birds, poured forth like the eighth deadly plague. Their bulbous bodies were larger than hawks and featherless with pink oily skin like newborn mice. The wings that propelled them upward were leathery and transparent, like bats with beaks tapering into sharp, defined points. Hideous chuffing, barking noises filled the basement, making them sound more like a pack of wild dogs than any murder of crows. The demon-flock circled overhead for a moment, then dive-bombed the unprotected patients in their cots.

Whatever was affecting the people of Garrett Grove had also affected the wildlife. The ravens—or possibly hawks—had been infected by the same thing that got Dr. Malcolm. The pterodactyl-like beasts dive-bombed the defenseless victims with pinpoint accuracy, tearing and impaling them with their talons and beaks, causing an ocean of red to flow throughout the entire basement.

The pandemonium and sensory overload were hypnotizing. Derek's head spun and his vision blurred as the swirling clouds of smoke and flying bodies increased in speed and momentum. He struggled to refocus, raised his shotgun, and fired at one of the demons as it banked toward him. It fell to the floor, twisting and convulsing; he stepped closer and pumped a second slug into it.

The onslaught from the open shaft was endless. Creatures resembling primates breached the shelter; others that looked reptilian joined the winged horde and ripped into the crowd like an army of chainsaws.

The firemen guarding the front entrance turned their attention to the back of the room and onto the flying militia. They fired into the dizzying flock, their bullets felling many of the creatures but missing even more. Behind them, the basement door imploded with the force of a detonation.

The steel slab, the plates, the cleats, and even the sandbags rocketed into the barricade of carts and cabinets, scattering the men like a handful of marbles. A degradation of atrocities stormed through the entrance and joined the slaughter.

The first beasts to push through the doorway were dropped by the firemen's defenses, but the magnitude of the attack was too great for so few guns. Kevin Grish landed on his back when the door collided with the barricade. A creature that looked like a cross between a tarantula and a Labrador raced toward him and pounced on his chest. The transfer was instantaneous—the freak ravaged Kevin like a chew toy.

Fred Ramos faired a little better than Kevin did, rising to his feet and firing several rounds into the mass of deformities. But he was silenced just as fast when one of the winged beasts swooped down on him from behind. Fred dropped his weapon as the ice water chill of spinal fluid leeched from his body. The strange bird had clipped the back of his neck with the front edge of its wing, slicing through the meat, the bone, and cartilage like a brisket. The man's head separated from his already crumpling torso and fell to the floor. Fred's lips continued to move, trying to deliver one final message, but his vocal cords were two feet away.

Kurt Harrington watched his friend's head roll across the floor, hypnotized from the shock. He never raised his gun to defend himself and slipped into a full catatonic state in two seconds. The swirling mass of black rushed in, took hold of the reins, and got the operation up and running again. Of course, Kurt was no longer able to participate.

Dr. Halasz and Joe Santos fired into the crowd of attackers at a frenzied pace. The doctor, who'd never shot a gun in his life, missed almost every target. Lee Chen also found it difficult to reload fast enough to keep up with the masses and was the first member of their group to be compromised. Joe was the next man to fall when he stepped up to fire at the thing that latched on to Lee. He emptied his revolver into the creature and proceeded to reload. However, none of his rounds had been head shots, and the beast was on him like a horny teenager. The doctor turned tail and ran, tossing his weapon in the process.

Susan Smith lay on a cot in the center of the basement, clinging to her father for dear life. She and her friends had encountered something the other night at the old sanitorium. Although none of them had seen it, one thing had been obvious: it was dangerous. If it hadn't been for Mick Petrie, she doubted if any of them would have made it off the mountain alive. Which might have been better in the long run. She buried her face into her father's chest and tried to block out the surrounding terror. Her head pounded from the concussion she'd received in yesterday's accident, and the madness around them made it worse. Her father pulled her closer as the man in the next cot choked on a vapor of suffocating smoke. A splattering of blood sprayed across the sheets, freckling his face with crimson. He wiped it away and attempted to shield his daughter. A young girl, no more than five or six, approached them with her arms outstretched. Susan didn't notice the child's eyes until it was too late. The girl latched on and bit into Susan's neck like a barracuda attacking a piece of squid. Susan screamed and beat at the monster to free herself but was unable. Her father stood up and latched on to the child's back with both hands but was thrown off balance by an unseen force. It picked him up and carried him away. Mr. Smith was gone before he hit the floor.

"Fall back!" Derek screamed as a primitive ghoul staggered toward his position. He blasted the beast in the face and navigated a retreat toward the center of the room. Dee and Greg rallied around him, leveling a path through the flying horde, making their way to the far wall. There were fewer screams to be heard, and the sound of gunfire was now minimal. The barking of the soaring pterodactyls and shrieking of the beasts was all that was left. Derek and his men reached the wall, slammed their backs against it, and sidestepped toward a set of steel doors.

Looking out across the scarlet river, surveying the total loss, Derek spotted two faces. The young nurses huddled together beneath one of the cots, their terrified eyes pleading for help. He continued along the wall to the set of doors and waved to the women, but they remained under the bed clutching one another. Derek gave them another exaggerated wave and opened the door behind him, urging them to follow. Finally, the nurses rose to their feet, hesitated for a moment, and ran. One of the winged devils spotted the two girls. It changed direction, banking in midair, and swooped down on the nurses, who were unaware of the threat. Derek saw it and reacted. He fired over the girls' heads and hit his mark. The mutant bird fell to the floor spewing a trail of oozing tar, then burst into a waft of tendrils that rose into the air and fused with the dense fog.

Derek ushered everyone into the utility room and slammed the door behind him. He went for the lock only to find there wasn't one. He quickly wedged the shotgun between the knob and the floor, pressed his back against the door, and planted his feet. He looked to the rest of his party. *Five ... only five!* The nurses were out of breath and terrified, Dee was frantic, and Greg faced the back wall trying to control himself. The large orderly had taken to rocking back and forth on his heels, as if moving to a tune only he could hear. Derek stared at the man for a moment and then returned his focus to the door behind him.

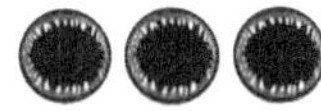

It started as an itch, one he was unable to scratch. Deep inside his head, with a pressure that made his eyes water. Greg thought he might vomit. He reloaded his 12-gauge as the pressure grew more intense and approached the threshold of pain. Shaking his head and biting down, he tried to deny the intrusion. Then it spoke.

Now, Greg ...

The penetrating voice was commanding, and Greg was powerless to resist. He spun about, raised the weapon, and pulled the trigger. The group watched as Dee took a round to the chest and fell to the floor. Derek had enough time to realize he was next and managed to latch on to the barrel of Greg's gun. The weapon exploded, leaving a three-inch hole in Derek's torso. He continued to hold on to the weapon for a moment before collapsing next to the body of his fallen comrade.

The nurses backed away from the man, crying and clutching one another. Greg approached the door, kicked Derek's shotgun from under the knob, and yanked it open. The world was eclipsed in a rush of black. The charging smoke rushed in, pinned the women to the wall, and devoured them.

CHAPTER 77

Deputy Ted Lutchen rushed his party up the staircase just as the first ghoul crashed through the front windows. Doris and Burt led the way, with Dawn, Ted, and Baxter on their heels, and Ed Koloski and Nurse Carole bringing up the rear. The group rounded the first landing and approached the door to the second floor. Then the screaming started.

Ted didn't need to see to know the building had been breached. He could envision the throng of attackers crashing through the front window and pouring into the basement. He could also tell from the lack of gunfire the men had been taken by surprise.

"Faster!" he screamed, urging them along.

In a blur, the second-floor door flew open. The assailants lunged forward and seized Doris and Burt. Baxter reacted and pounced on the figure closest to him; he grabbed it by the arm and pulled it away from Doris.

"Get it off me!" Will Tobin screamed, trying to shake the German Shepherd, but Baxter held fast.

Ted scrambled up the stairs and grabbed the dog by the collar. "Easy, boy." Baxter was reluctant to comply but calmed at the deputy's command.

Burt had run headfirst into Billy Tobin, and although the boy was still weak, the coroner was almost knocked off his feet. Alice stood behind them; the three had been on the second floor and ran for the shelter when they heard the crash.

"We didn't make it to the basement," Will explained. "We were waiting for the n—"

"There's no time. We got to keep moving." Ted pushed the group and its new members to the third floor just as the first shot echoed in the stairwell. Seconds later, the steady concussion of gun fire bounced off the walls, sounding like the beginning of World War III.

They reached the next landing, and Doris paused at the door before opening it, as if someone might be on the other side like the Tobins had been. She held her breath, turned the knob, and hurried onto the third floor with the rest of the group behind her. Koloski was the last man to leave the stairwell and stole a glimpse over the railing before leaving. They weren't being followed, but it sounded as if a massacre were taking place in the basement. The shrill of the screaming and the concussion of gunfire rattled the plaster from the walls, and the smell of gunpowder was detectable even from where he stood.

He left the stairwell to join his party and was met by a familiar face. Fellow fireman Grady Martin stood in the hallway next to a blonde candy striper—her name tag said: Hello, my name is Cyndi. Koloski approached Grady and handed him one of the guns he had slung over his shoulder. Then he dug into the duffle bag and distributed handguns to Will, Alice, and Billy. He held one out to the Cyndi with an i, who shook her head and declined.

"There're two ways off this floor," Doris said. "This stairwell and one at the end of the hall that leads to the roof."

"What about the elevator?" Ted asked.

Doris held out a set of keys. "I turned it off and stopped the car on this floor. We can operate it if we need to, but no one can use it to come up."

"Smart." Ted scanned the hallway to the left and right. "And the patients?"

"In three rooms near the nurses' station. Far end of the hall away from this stairwell. I figured it was the safest place."

"Good job," he said. "Please lead on."

They followed Doris around the corner and down a long hallway that dead-ended near a nurses' station. Ted nodded, observing the layout. The counter itself would serve as the perfect vantage point. If the creatures found their way to the third floor, the only way they could attack was via a straight run down the hall toward them. With several shooters positioned behind the safety of the heavy counter and the rest of them hidden in the doorways, their forces were as strong as they could hope for. "This is where we make our stand," he told them. "Everybody, dig in."

The sound of gunfire was quieter now that the door to the stairwell was closed. Baxter relaxed a little bit but still clung to Dawn's side. Ted bent down eye level to the girl and lowered his voice. "I have an important job for you. Will you help watch over the patients with Carole and Cyndi?"

"Is that Drowsy?" Cyndi motioned to the doll in the child's hands, and Dawn's eyes lit up. "I had Drowsy when I was a little girl. I haven't seen her in years. Does she still talk?"

Dawn smiled and showed the girl her doll. Ted watched the exchange and let out a deep sigh. It had been hard enough to get the child to use the bathroom by herself. With Cyndi and Carole to watch over her, he could at least focus on the fight. The women brought Dawn into the room across from the station, and Baxter followed.

Ted turned to the others and surveyed the strength of the group. Burt and Doris both held large-caliber revolvers and appeared ready to use them. Doris looked a bit more prepared than the old coroner, but looks could be deceiving. Then there was Koloski and Martin; Ted had seen them both at the range on numerous occasions and didn't doubt their ability. Which left the Tobins, possibly the weak links in the chain of defense. But this was the lot he had drawn, and it would have to do. He prayed the vantage point of the nurses' station would allow them the edge they needed, but there was no way to know for sure. He listened as the sound of gunfire lessened and then stopped. Nothing ... not a scream or a single shot sounded out. A gripping chill settled in the back of his neck. Things had gone terribly wrong in the basement.

"All right, I want someone in each of the doorways and two with me behind the counter."

The nurses' station sat on the left side of the hallway across from the three rooms with the patients. The door to a janitorial closet sat next to the station on the same side of the hall. With his army of eight, Ted figured he would stagger his firepower at choke-off points in each doorway with a sniper team positioned at the counter. He was a good shot with a scope, and if he could get a decent rifleman with him behind the desk, they would have a formidable line of defense.

"Who's good with a rifle?" he asked.

He wasn't surprised when Koloski raised his hand, then Billy Tobin stepped up as well. Ted threw the kid a skeptical look, but Will spoke up.

"He is. I've seen him hit a dime from fifty feet with a 30-30."

"You up for it, kid?" Ted asked, but he could tell from the cold determination in Billy Tobin's stare that he didn't need to ask.

CHAPTER 78

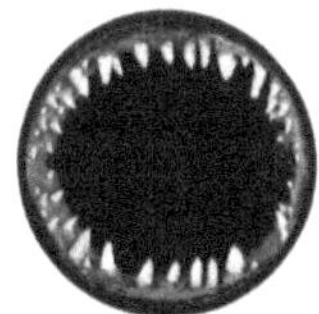

Jessica Marceau stood at the window of her new office overlooking the Turnpike. The town she grew up in now looked alien and unrecognizable. Abandoned vehicles and wrecks littered the two-lane street in front of the municipal building. A Volkswagen Beetle lay overturned near the entrance to the parking lot. Its front window had been smashed; a dark burgundy trail stretched out across the pavement like a carpet. Several of the businesses on the main drag were burning out of control, while others appeared to have been vandalized or looted. She watched as a station wagon careened past the building doing well over fifty in the twenty-five mile per hour speed zone. Four hideous ape-like creatures pursued it like a pack of bloodhounds. One of the strange vertebrates looked as if it were wearing a mechanic's uniform. "Grease monkey," Jessica said and cackled into the empty room. The sudden outburst even startled her, as she took to rocking in place, cradling herself in her arms.

She had been ordered to report to the shelter at the high school, but that felt like abandoning ship. How could she turn tail and hide while there were still people on the streets? She was the mayor, after all—newly appointed, of course. It looked like it would be the shortest term ever served. There were other things on the streets as well … horrible things. Some looked reptilian, others appeared to be from the primate family, and less than an hour ago, something had slithered across the front parking lot that could have crawled out of the Black Lagoon.

Jessica jumped back from the window as a shower of sparks exploded from one of the transformers across the street near the Lutheran church. "Oh my," she giggled. "That can't be good." The lights in the mayor's office didn't flicker or dim; they stopped working at once, leaving her standing in the dark. The last of the dim daylight was fading fast, and Jessica let out another burst of laughter, making her sound like she was raving mad. In truth, Jessica Marceau was well on her way.

Bob Jones watched from the side of the school as the brown Ford pickup banked hard into the parking lot with the massive creature hanging from the driver's side window. The operator of the vehicle had his foot pinned to the floor and missed running down John Sampson and Eric Collins by inches. Both firemen jumped out of the way at the last second as the truck and its unwelcomed passenger slammed into a light pole. A moment later, the entire shooting match went up in flames. The beast paid no attention to the fact that it was now on fire and continued to claw its way into the vehicle. Both the driver and assailant burned to death in less than a minute.

There were other vehicles that carried unwanted passengers, leading the creatures right to the high school. Bob and his men had been lucky so far and managed to put them down, but he knew their luck would eventually run out. Things were getting worse by the second, and it was looking like the round-up crew had done the best they could. However, far fewer citizens had shown up than even Bob anticipated. Either people hadn't taken the warning seriously or most of the town had already been massacred in their sleep. At least they got the kids out of the elementary and junior high schools. Bob figured whoever was still out there was taking things seriously now.

The pump truck entered the lot, driving past the still-burning pickup. It pulled up to where Bob stood, the doors opened, and Drew Halberg stepped out. Expecting to see Deputy Jenkins join him, the chief did a double take when the manager of the A&P exited the vehicle. Günter Bentley was followed by his entire family.

"Hello, Chief Jones," Günter greeted him. "Dis ist mine beautiful vife, Hazel. And deez are mine chilrun; dis ist Gretel, und dis ist Gisela, und dis ist mine little princess, Marilyn." The three toe-headed children stared up at Bob with their giant blue eyes.

The absence of Deputy Jenkins was obvious, and Bob didn't have to ask to know what had happened. He winced and shook his head. He had known the man almost as long as he had known Carl, and now he was gone. Bob could feel it in the air, pressing down against him and weighing on his shoulders. It was loss and pain, and no one was beyond its reach. Before this day was over, Bob knew that everyone in Garrett Grove would experience it on some level. He stood there and kept a watchful eye; time was running out ... for all of them.

Mike Turino enjoyed getting the chance to sit behind the wheel of the police cruiser. Although he had ridden in them before, this was his first time in the front seat. As a kid, Mike found himself in trouble a bit more often than other boys his age. Nothing serious, just some underage drinking and vandalism, and the one occasion when he got caught stealing from the Radio Shack. Which was the first time Deputy Jenkins had made him ride in the back of the cruiser.

When Mike turned eighteen, things got a bit more complicated. It started out simple enough, tossing back a few with his buddies, sharing a bottle on a Saturday afternoon at the lake, but in truth, there was nothing simple about it. A light switch had been turned on, and Mike found a sense of ease and comfort that only booze could bring. He was a likable drunk, a hit at the parties, and was even able to talk to girls without acting like a buffoon. He had suddenly found the missing ingredient of life, thanks to John Barleycorn. Simply put, Mike liked beer ... it made him a jolly good fellow.

Mike had known Brenda Pritchard since high school, but they had never talked much. That was until one night at the old sanatorium. The six-pack he downed on the walk up to the place was all the liquid bravado Mike needed to approach her. Brenda twirled her hair when he spoke, laughed at his jokes, and let him get to third base on one of the cots in the old hospital. And from there, it was game on. Mike asked Brenda to the drive-in the following Saturday, and she agreed. He packed a case of Michelob into his cooler, thinking if Brenda had a few drinks in her, it would be easier to get the rest of the way around the bases. Before the movie was half over, with only two six-packs down, she proved his theory correct. They had sloppy, drunken sex in the backseat.

Later, when they made their way back to Garrett Grove, Mike was what most people would call piss drunk. He succeeded in keeping the Buick on the road and managed to get them to the edge of town without hitting a tree. He slowed as he approached the Gables Bridge and gripped the wheel with determination. It was going well too; Mike even made it halfway across before the truck barreled at them from the other side. Then he panicked. To avoid swiping the straight job, Mike jerked the steering wheel a bit too hard to the right. The Buick collided with the guardrail, sending the passenger's side into a concrete pier. Brenda, who wasn't wearing her seatbelt but had been relaxed to sleep by the combination of alcohol and drunken sex, smacked her head against the window and rebounded like a ragdoll. Fortunate for her, the doctors said if she had been sober, she most likely would have suffered worse injuries than a few contusions and hematomas to her face. Mike walked away without a scratch.

Although Brenda's injuries were minimal, her father, Gerald Pritchard, Esq., was none too pleased. The King County prosecutor was determined to see Mike swing for jeopardizing the safety of his daughter and filed negligence charges against him. Mike went before the judge and was forced to pay five hundred dollars in restitution, Brenda's hospital bills, and was sentenced to serve thirty days.

Deputies Colbert and Jenkins drove Mike from the courthouse to the county jail. They both knew Mike from town and had witnessed how the boy's drinking escalated over the years. Still, he was a good guy, and they liked him—even though they had each thrown him in the drunk tank on various occasions. They sent him off to jail with three packs of smokes, a deck of cards, and fifty bucks. The deputies told him he was allowed to bring the cigarettes, even the cards, but he would have to hide the cash.

"How the hell am I supposed to sneak this in?" Mike asked.

"You know." Deputy Colbert tossed him a rubber glove. "In the old jail wallet." Both officers tried to stifle their laughter.

"You mean in my ass?!" Mike blurted with a look of indignation.

"Well, look at it this way," Jenkins said. "As long as you have the money, chances are nothing else will have to go up there." He razzed the guy, though people seldom got raped in county jail, that was more of a state prison thing.

"It's easy, kid," Colbert explained. "Rip one of the fingers off the glove and put the money in it. Then tie it good and tight, spit on it, and you know—up the ole pooper." The deputy struggled to keep a straight face while he explained the process. The officers had an even harder time when Mike went to work concealing the cash. By the look on the kid's face, it was more than a little uncomfortable. Even funnier was when they brought Mike into the jail to get processed.

"What do you have to declare as property?" the guard asked.

"Three packs of smokes and a deck of cards," Mike answered.

The guard scribbled onto his paperwork. "Any money?" he asked.

Mike froze as he felt the fold of bills quiver inside him.

"Money … what do you mean?" He started to panic and thought for sure he was busted.

The guard threw him a dirty look. "Do you have any money, kid? You're allowed to have up to fifty dollars."

Colbert and Jenkins erupted into a gale of laughter. Mike tightened his face and scowled at the deputies who had been fucking with him all along and had probably pulled this one countless times before.

The guard cracked a smile and laughed himself. "It's in your ass, isn't it? Yeah. It's in your ass." Apparently, the joke was an oldie but a goodie. Mike was just happy the deputies hadn't given him the fifty bucks in quarters.

Mike did his time in county, and Brenda even came to visit. She said she felt bad for what her father had done. She gave Mike an old-fashioned hand job in the visiting booth. In fact, her father's actions backfired terribly, and Mike's jailbird status affected the prosecutor's daughter better than a dozen oysters and a bottle of Black Fly.

Once the town fire whistle stopped ringing, Mike delivered his message for the last time and headed for the high school. That's when he saw the girl waving from the alley between the diner and the beauty parlor. He turned into the parking lot, and the girl ran to the cruiser.

"Thank God." She was drenched. "My asshole boyfriend was supposed to pick me up an hour ago."

"I know you." Mike recognized the girl from the A&P. "You're Claire, right?"

"What the f—" Claire looked as if she might jump out of the car. "You're no cop. You're that guy Mike." She grabbed the handle, then thought better about it.

"Easy, I'm helping the sheriff. You could have been killed out there."

"I hid in the alley for the past hour. What the fuck is going on? Man, you wouldn't believe the shit I've seen." Claire pulled a pack of waterlogged smokes from her coat. "I don't suppose you got a butt, dude?"

Mike handed her his pack, then turned on the heat and focused the vents on her.

"My hero," she said and lit up. "So ... this is cool. First time I ever rode in the front." Claire looked into the backseat, and Mike knew they had at least one thing in common.

"Want to feel something even cooler?" he asked with an evil grin on his face.

"Dude, if you whip out your dick, I swear to God—" She tensed up and slid further away from him.

"Relax, that's not what I mean." Mike turned on the cherries, hit the siren, and punched his foot to the floor. The cruiser took off like a pulsar as they made their way back into town. Claire cracked a wicked grin of her own as she braced herself in the passenger's seat. She was glad the guy hadn't whipped his dick out.

Father Kieran took a sentry position at the front entrance of the church, flanked by Dick Wilson, and the terribly scarred, Jim Reilly. The priest now brandished a S&W .357, gifted to him by a member of the flock. With the coroner's .25 safely tucked in the waistband of his slacks, he kept a watchful eye on the parking lot and surrounding area. Stationed at the entrance to the sacristy was Dick's nephew, Josh, Frank Palumbo (the owner of the Texaco station), and Fire Inspector, Bill Harrington. The only other entrance was an emergency exit near the organ, where Luke Evans, Julie's husband, a truck driver named Rick Edwards; and Angelo Franco, who had just arrived with his wife, Donna, stood watch. All of the parties were backed up by larger groups of men and women who had been assigned the tasks of reloading and weapon replacement.

The overhang at the front entrance prevented the heavy rains from assaulting the men and offered an excellent vantage point. So far, only a few of the demons had been brave enough to leave the darkness of the woods and venture near the church. Kieran and his men made quick work of them. The priest's presence fueled the morale of the men and women of the flock, inspiring a determination and sense of courage most never knew they possessed. Kieran turned to the man with the scars on his face. Jimmy stood fast with his rifle raised and at the ready, filling the priest with an overwhelming sense of pride.

"You are a warrior, James," Kieran told him. "A fitting name for such." He patted the man on the back.

"Don't worry, Father. Nothing is getting past me."

"God bless you, my son." Father Kieran then turned to the man on his left. "Brother Richard, the Lord is with you."

Dick Wilson returned a smile and focused his attention on the tree line at the edge of the lot, but the downpour made it nearly impossible to see. A sudden ripple of movement caught his attention as something emerged from the woods. "I think we have company, Father."

Kieran raised a set of binoculars and peered across the parking lot; two creatures lumbered out from between the trees and made their way into the open. They were slow and there was only a couple, but that didn't mean they were alone. He raised his hand to Dick. "Hold steady. Don't fire until I give the word."

The demons that entered the lot were abominations. They were bald, and their skin hung slack as if it was too big for their bodies. Their ears were pointed, and Kieran thought they resembled bats or some type of rodent. He could see the onyx black of their eyes, with the help of the binoculars, and how misshapen their features were. One beast turned to the other, and there was an evident exchange, as if they were communicating the plan of their attack. There was an intelligence at work, a malevolent one. Kieran knew the imps were waiting for him to make the first move. He scanned the woods, adjusting the focus of his binoculars, and saw the rest of them. An army of repulsive creatures hid behind the cover of the tree line.

"I see you," he said under his breath. "Brother Richard, gather more men to flank our position."

Dick retreated into the church and did as the Father asked. He returned with the recruits, who took their positions on either side of the men.

"No one fires till I give the word," Kieran said. "They are trying to wait us out, trying to test our defenses. They will learn, you cannot test the Lord. Hold fast, men."

Josh Wilson held point at the entrance of the sacristy, where he and his men could see across the side lawn all the way to the rectory. A tangle of trees on either side of the house provided enough cover for something to hide within, but there hadn't been any movement yet. He scanned the area and squinted to get a better look. There was motion. Slow and concealed, but he caught it just as something moved from the far corner of the building to the wooded area.

"You sneaky bastards," he hissed. The men to either side of him gripped their weapons and stared off in the same direction. There was something out there; they all saw it now. "What the hell are they waiting for?" Josh wondered what was happening at the other entrances and called to Allison Aigans, who stood behind him in the reloading party. He sent her to check on the other groups and report back.

It felt good for Allison to have something to do after losing her mind over the past few days. It was unlike Mick to disappear like he had. When she learned the Tobin boys were missing too, it all made sense. Billy Tobin had a way of talking people into doing things. She knew the boys had gone back to the sanatorium and sensed that something terrible had happened. She wanted to talk to someone about it, but things got very strange at school after that. More people went missing, and not just a few. Almost half of Allison's homeroom class didn't show up for school yesterday, including Susan and Debbie. So, she left school early and drove to King Lake to figure out her next move. It was where she and Mick had made love the first time. She remembered how it felt to hold him close as they lay in the sand beneath the stars. Just being there reminded her of him and made her feel as if he was still with her. But Allison knew he wasn't, and she knew something had happened to him. That was when she decided to head to the church.

She approached the men at the side entrance near the organ and asked if they had any information. Similar sightings of the creatures were reported, lurking just behind the tree line, waiting for the right moment. Allison shared the group's information with Father Kieran and reported back to Josh with explicit instructions for everyone to hold their fire until they got the word.

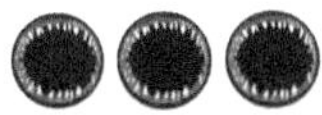

It was a waiting game, and Kieran had a good idea what the demons were up to. They were waiting for nightfall; that was when they would strike. And it was approaching fast. The evil one thought Kieran's forces would fold once the attack began. But the priest was clever and had a counter-maneuver in mind. Once tonight's victory was in hand, they would bring the war to the Devil's doorstep and slaughter Satan in his sleep.

CHAPTER 79

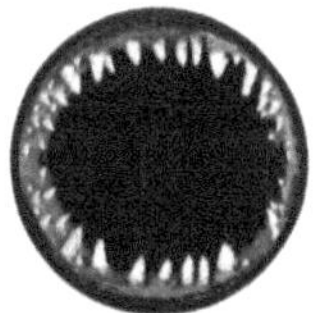

The third floor of the medical center went dark as several of the transformers in town overloaded. It took the emergency generator almost a full minute before it kicked on. The dim red glow of the auxiliary lighting cast long, deformed shadows across the faces of those standing outside the nurses' station. Ted and the members of his group stared at each other in the wash of twilight. All was silent, save the hammering of the rain against the windows. The gunfire had ceased, the cries from the basement had been quelled, and the strange disquiet that fell upon them was unsettling. Ted waited, listening for any sound other than the rain or wind. Finally, he turned to Koloski.

"Your man in the basement, Fisk, right?"

"Yeah, Derek Fisk," Koloski answered as Ted lifted the walkie-talkie to his lips.

"This is Deputy Lutchen to Fireman Fisk, come in, Derek." A crackle of static filtered through the speaker and echoed throughout the hallway.

"Deputy Lutchen to anyone in the basement. Come in, over." Ted waited for a response, but there was nothing. He thought it possible the concrete of the shelter might be preventing the signal from getting through but had a feeling it was worse than that. The looks on the faces staring back at him suggested they thought the same. Then the radio garbled, and a voice spoke through the speaker.

"Ted, it's Carl. What's the situation at the center?"

"We were ambushed, Sheriff. I can't get through to anyone in the basement. It sounded like a damn war down there." There was a long period of silence, and Ted was about to repeat the message when the sheriff replied.

"You're on the third floor, Ted?"

Ted looked at the anxious faces of Alice and Will Tobin and knew what they were thinking. Lois had left with the sheriff to pick up Troy. "Roger that, Sheriff. I'm on the third floor with the Tobin family, Nurse TenHove, Coroner Lively, Koloski, Martin, and several others."

"Roger that." Carl sounded relieved. "I need you to hold tight till I can get some backup over there. I have no idea how soon that might be. How are your defenses?"

"I think we have a tactical advantage, sir. I can set up a gauntlet and pick them off if they attack."

Burt grabbed the radio out of Ted's hand. "Carl, I figured out why the MRI machine killed it. It's a giant magnet, and this thing is made of some type of metallic alloy."

The radio crackled, and the sound of several people talking at once distorted the speaker. "All right!" the sheriff shouted and was followed by a moment of silence. "Yeah, I was just told the same thing about ten minutes ago by a group of fourth graders. But good job, Burt. Glad you're safe, and I hope that info helps us."

"I take it you found the kids?"

"That's a big 10-4—" There was a loud garble of static and the sound of a woman screaming, *"Look Out,"* then there was silence.

Ted grabbed the radio. "Sheriff, come in. Sheriff!"

There was no response.

"What happened?" Alice pleaded with him, but Ted didn't have any answers for her.

He tried to reach the sheriff again with the same result ... static. There was a tremendous thud as the floor shook beneath their feet, then the sound of shrieking filled the hallway. The beasts had found out where they were and had begun to ascend the stairs. Terror flashed from face to face, and time stood still ... for a moment. They had all anticipated this, and although they prayed it would not come to fruition, they sprang to action and took their assigned positions.

Ted, Billy, and Koloski retreated behind the nurses' station, while Grady Martin took point in the room closest to the adjacent hallway's intersection. Alice stood in the doorway of the janitorial closet between Martin and the station, and the rest of the group made their way to the rooms on the opposite side of the hall. Will on point, Doris in the center, and Burt in the last, nearest the exit to the roof. Patients occupied the three rooms, and Dawn, Carole, and Cyndi were tucked away in the last one behind Burt.

A high-pitched shriek ruptured the air; the group leveled their weapons in the direction from which it had come. They stared down the hallway, waiting for something to charge. Every one of them jumped when something large slammed against the stairwell door. The force on the opposite side proceeded to batter the steel and the surrounding frame with relentless abandon. The group gathered their munitions, checked their weapons, and prayed it would be enough.

A clowder of fists assaulted the door until it gave way under the strain and was ripped from its hinges. The bodies swarmed the hall and flooded toward them. Ted rested the 30-30 on the counter and focused his scope on the area where the two hallways intersected. He had a good vantage point with a perfect line of sight. Anything coming their way would have to pass his firing line. He wiped a drop of sweat from his nose and watched as the first shadow bounced off the far wall. Then a darting figure rounded the corner and screamed. Ted didn't even have time to fire as three other members of his team let loose on the beast. It dropped to the floor and ceased to move.

The dark glow of the emergency lights added to the tension as they waited for the next attacker to appear. The flailing shadows grew shorter as a mass of figures bounded around the corner and advanced on their position. The sound of eight different weapons firing simultaneously in the narrow hallway was deafening and intoxicating. Smoke filled the area as the group continued to fire and the bodies of the assailants piled up at the end of the hall.

The gauntlet was effective. Grady and Will were closest to the approaching horde, and the number of enemies was endless. Ted was now certain the men and women in the basement had been slaughtered. His attention was suddenly drawn to Will Tobin, who had stopped firing his weapon.

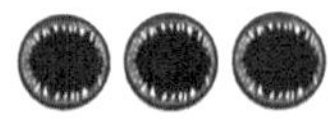

The pile of bodies littering the floor helped slow the progress of the creatures, but it didn't stop them. Will reloaded his rifle, slamming the last cartridge into the chamber, but the monsters were closer than ever. He raised the barrel and froze when one of the beasts lumbered in front of him. *No!* Will stared at the shirt the thing wore. It was a John Deere T-shirt covered in dirt and blood ... his blood froze in his veins. The creature was bald except for a few stubborn strands of hair that clung to its scalp, and its skin was a greyish green. Its head hung slack, and its features were deformed, but there was no denying. "Oh God, no," Will cried with the rifle trembling in his hands.

The creature that started out life as Eric Tobin lunged at the man in the doorway. It still wore the clothes it had on when the boy went missing Sunday afternoon. The John Deere shirt belonged to Will, but Eric was always borrowing it. Will lowered the rifle, backed up into the room, and his youngest child followed. The Eric-creature allowed its lower jaw to descend, revealing an impossible mouthful of teeth. It leapt at the man and tackled him to the floor.

"I'm sorry, son. Please forgive me," Will said as the thing lowered its horrible mouth to his neck. Will pulled the trigger of the .38 he had removed from his belt, and the back of Eric's head sprayed against the far wall. The body of the boy slumped into his father's arms. Will Tobin sat up and pulled Eric close. "Eric," the man cried. "What have they done to my boy?" Will had thought about turning the weapon on himself. But there was no way he could allow his own son to exist as an abomination. His face was deformed; his body was twisted. No father should have to see their child like that. The man sat on the floor holding his son, rocking back and forth as he had when Eric was a baby. "I'm so sorry," he repeated.

It was a burden Will Tobin wouldn't carry for long. Several small creatures scurried into the room and surrounded him. They moved much like spiders, and one appeared to have appendages growing from its abdomen. Their strange black eyes sized him up. Will raised the weapon and pointed it at the creature closest to him, but before he could fire, the beast opened its mouth and sprayed a hazy film. The filament latched onto his fingers, scaling his grip in place, making it impossible to pull the trigger.

As Will stared into the strange arachnid eyes, a second creature shuffled toward him and spread its jaws wide. There one second, gone the next.

Will's anguish and burdens disappeared in a splash of red as the ghoul pounced on his chest and went to work with its sharp, sharp, teeth.

Grady Martin took position in the room directly across from Will Tobin and had an unobstructed view when the creature backed the man into the room. Three smaller creeps entered shortly afterward, and Will never returned to his post. It didn't take a genius to figure out what had happened. Grady considered himself fortunate for choosing the shotgun over the hunting rifle and had also grabbed a .45 as a sidearm. Both weapons were easy to reload, and Grady had a jacket full of extra magazines and shotgun shells. He unloaded on the approaching horde. The sound of gunfire echoed off every surface, and the din of the battle was intoxicating. The ink-like blood that oozed from the attackers' bodies covered the walls and ceilings and ran like a river down the center of the floor.

The smell of gunpowder and gore made Grady delirious. Sweat dripped from his brow and landed at his feet. Smoke filled the hallway and swirled about his head as if it had a life of its own; it tasted like copper pennies. The nauseating funk had begun to tickle in the very back of his throat. Grady struggled to breathe and fought to stay focused. Then he felt it between his eyes and at the base of his skull. An itch ... impossible to scratch ... it gnawed at him like a rat chewing into his soft tissue. Then he heard it.

Grady...

He dropped the shotgun and froze in the doorway. Gunfire continued to erupt around him as the other members of the group fired blindly at their targets, unable to see due to the smoke. Grady listened to the voice as it gnawed deeper into his brain ... such a hungry little rat. A nibble here, a morsel there, until a sizable portion of the man had been devoured like a Triscuit.

Grady stepped into the line of fire but was somehow spared from being hit. He walked along the wall to where Alice Tobin stood. The woman's attention focused on the battle before her, she hadn't seen the man as he approached. She fired her last round and proceeded to reload the weapon. Sliding the last bullet into the cylinder, Alice looked up in time to see the .45 pointed at her temple.

Grady pulled the trigger, and the pistol discharged. The slug tore through the woman's head from point-blank range. Alice Tobin was dead before her body hit the floor—she had been one of the fortunate ones.

The four patients in the room where the body of Will Tobin lay had not been as fortunate. After the three spider-like beasts picked the man clean, they helped themselves to the sleeping patients. However, they weren't exactly sleeping, just unresponsive. All were hooked up to various life-support systems to keep their vital organs functioning. Three of the four were considered brain dead and didn't feel a thing when the arachnids began to nibble on them. But the patient in the furthest bed near the window had been in a coma.

It's said when you are in a coma, you are aware, you can hear people talking, touching your hand, even a change in temperature. But no one ever mentions what happens when a giant spider decides to turn you into a late-afternoon snack. The woman in the bed near the window could have enlightened the students at Johns Hopkins; she could have told them—you can feel it—you can feel every single excruciating nibble.

Doris watched the fireman raise his weapon and fire on Alice Tobin. Even through the dense cover of smoke, she could tell he was no longer himself. She followed the man in the sights of her revolver and pulled the trigger. The hollow click of the empty chamber resonated within her. Fumbling for the shells in her pocket, Doris sped through the task of reloading as Grady stepped over the woman's body and made his way toward the nurses' station. *Dear God, he's going to kill them.* She slammed the last round into the cylinder, raised the weapon, and fired. A large chunk of plaster wall vaporized behind him. She steadied her hand and focused on the area just above Grady's left ear and pressed on the trigger. The piercing sounds of breaking glass invaded the room behind her. Doris pivoted to see the beasts throw themselves through the window. They were on the beds in a frenzy, tearing into the patients.

Four hideous monstrosities had somehow scaled the exterior of the building and located their position. They scrambled over the window ledge and attacked the patients in the beds, not all of which were unresponsive. Doris watched the river of red spread out before her. One of the creatures threw itself at the wall and clung to it in a gravity-defying exhibition. It stared at Doris, licking its maw with a tongue that was much too long. It scurried toward the nurse, and she fired on it until she depleted her ammunition. It snapped its tongue in her direction, almost making contact, and that was all Doris needed to get her ass moving. She bolted into the hallway and headed to the farthest room. She prayed Burt wouldn't shoot her by mistake.

The horde advanced on Doris's position as she fled down the hall and darted through the doorway. She plowed into Burt, who was reloading his weapon. Doris frantically scanned the room to find Carole, Cyndi, and Dawn sitting on one of the beds. There was movement behind them ... shadows against the window. Doris saw the beasts just before they crashed through the glass.

"Look out!" she screamed.

CHAPTER 80

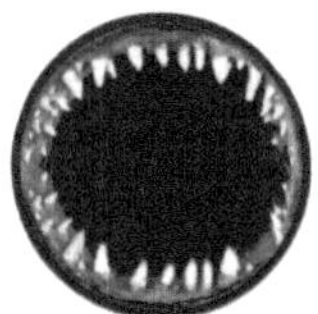

Carl sped away from the Fischer residence, leaving the house and carnage behind. He scanned the faces of his three young passengers in the rearview. Troy sat in the middle, between the girls, with tears streaming down his cheeks. The dark-haired girl occupied the passenger's side, her eyes vacant and her complexion a ghostly white. It had been too close of a call; only a matter of seconds and things would have turned out horribly different. Carl continued to check his passengers and noticed the blonde who sat directly behind him. The girl stared back at him, beaming with a huge smile on her face. Carl did a quick double take as their eyes met.

"Sheriff," she said, "you can kill them with magnets."

"What?" Carl's jaw dropped. "What did you say?"

"The Ojanox, you can kill them with magnets." She held up a wrist rocket and a handful of broken magnets. "That's why we left school. We needed to get weapons before it got dark."

Lois looked at Carl and then turned to Janis at the mention of the name.

"I'm sorry—" Carl squinted.

"Janis," she said.

"I'm sorry, Janis. But how do you know this, and what the hell is an Ojanox?"

"Those things out there, you can kill them with magnets, but they got to be really sharp," Janis continued. "My mom is an archeologist, and she's studying the cave at the quarry. She's known about the Ojanox for years."

Carl could see the girl's testimony had a soothing effect on the other children, who were now ready to chime in. Troy fidgeted in his seat, busting to speak up.

"How do you know they're called Ojanox?" Carl asked.

"That's what Mom called them," Troy said. "She told us the story, then they chased me through the graveyard on Monday. Wendy said they sounded like Ojanox because how they hid and tried to get me."

"What the hell is an Ojanox?" He turned to Lois and shrugged, wondering how three fourth graders had done a better job than his entire department. They'd figured out what was happening, given it a name, and made him look about as inept as all the three stooges put together.

"I told the kids a ghost story Saturday night at the party," Lois said. "It was a combination of something I wrote in college and a little improv. I made up the name years ago, Ojanox, mostly because I liked the way it looked on paper. Troy didn't care for it much." She looked at her son in the backseat, who crinkled his nose as if he smelled something rancid. "I'm sorry I didn't believe you the other day. You said something chased you; I thought it might be a dog or you were confused. I'm so sorry, kiddo."

"It's okay, Mom," Troy said.

"Oh, I get it." Carl nodded. "But how did you figure out the magnets?"

"My mother has pictures of what they found at Cahokia. And Troy said the cave up at the quarry had weapons just like it and they were all made of lodestone."

"What!?" He turned to Lois again. "What cave? How come I'm just hearing about this? Why didn't anyone at DuCain notify me?"

Lois shrugged and raised her hands. "I figured you knew."

The radio crackled before Carl could finish. *"Deputy Lutchen to anyone in the basement. Come in, over."* Carl held his breath and waited for someone to answer Ted's call. He knew the medical center's basement wasn't that secure and had wanted to get Lois and Troy to the high school instead. Still, her sister's family was there, and if something happened, and it sounded like it already might have, Lois would never forgive herself. Silence filled the cab as they waited for a reply.

Janis looked across the backseat to her friends and offered a toothy grin, which seemed to ease their apprehension. It was amazing what one look could do, and Janis had the ability to affect the world with her bright eyes and genuine smile. It helped comfort Wendy especially, who struggled to maintain her tough exterior; the little Italian girl relaxed a bit, then returned the gesture.

Janis was just happy to finally have friends who liked her for who she was. The first day of school, when she walked into the classroom, all the boys started acting goofy, just like the boys in her old school. But not Troy, he had smiled and said hello while the other kids were snickering and whispering to each other. Troy hadn't acted like a dork just because of her changing body.

She was self-conscious about the stupid things as it was and couldn't wear half her clothes anymore. Everything was either too tight or made her look ridiculous; at least that's what Janis thought. At first, she tried to hide them, telling her mom and aunt how much she hated being a girl.

They tried to console her and told Janis one day she would feel comfortable and maybe even like them. But she didn't think it likely. And the idea of the new school was terrifying. Especially after the way the boys in her old school acted. They all wanted to talk to her; they acted goofy and said the dumbest things. Now she would be walking into a new classroom with her new boobs, and everyone was going to see them. And she had been right. Miss Walsh introduced her, and all the boys snickered; even the girls gave her dirty looks. Janis had wanted to crawl into a hole and die.

Then at lunch, she noticed Troy and Wendy sitting by themselves, sharing their sandwiches, and acting like grown-ups. Janis didn't know if it was jealousy, but she thought it would be nice to have a friend like that. Someone to talk to and share her lunch with; someone who didn't act like a total dork. The girl seemed nice too, but that wasn't why she first approached them. She wanted to know the boy who was immune to the power of the boobies.

"Hi," she'd said. "Can I sit with you? Those boys are acting silly." And that was how it all started. Wendy and Troy welcomed her and treated her like one of them. It was obvious Troy was uncomfortable, but Janis thought that it was kind of cute. And he never stared at her boobs; in fact, he deliberately didn't look at them. So, she decided to mess with him and asked him why the other boys were treating her different. Wendy knew what she was up to and played along. It made Troy even more uncomfortable, and it looked like he was about to explode when he finally shouted, "It's because you have boobs!"

It was priceless. There was something about Troy that was refreshing, and he and Wendy made her feel like she was going to fit in after all. She had missed the chance to go to the Halloween party by less than a week and wished she had moved to town sooner. It probably wouldn't have made a difference, but she wondered ... If she did, maybe Troy would have kissed someone else instead of Wendy ... maybe.

Janis looked across the seat and smiled at her new friends. Both Wendy and Troy returned the gesture, which made her feel better than she had in a long time. They made her feel like she belonged in Garrett Grove.

Andrea Geary's head spun from the sensory overload coming at her from every direction. The shelter at the high school was a flurry of activity. The ocean of faces and the roar of a thousand different conversations was intoxicating, but it was a thankful respite. For the moment, thoughts of Joel and of her loss had been put to the side as she busied herself helping others. She handed out blankets, assisted children and the elderly, and answered as many questions as she possibly could—but most of which she was unable.

"Have you seen my boy?" a distraught woman asked.

"How long do we have to stay down here?" an older gentleman questioned.

"I can't find my mommy. Have you seen my mommy?" a frightened girl cried.

"Excuse me, but could you tell me where the bathroom is?" That was one question she could answer. The others were impossible to, and each one chiseled at her heart. She took it all in, all the faces, all of the pain, and all of the loss.

But every now and then, she would be offered a glimmer of hope and see an entire family lucky enough to have been reunited. Unfortunately, luck was in short supply and most of the families in Garrett Grove had not walked away intact. Andrea smiled at Günter Bentley from the A&P,

who sat with his wife and three golden-haired daughters. The girls looked as if they had stepped out of a nursery rhyme as they huddled in close to their father. Principal Grace had gathered no less than fifty children and occupied their interest with a story she was telling. Another cluster of children flocked around a woman and her pet beagle. The dog was in heaven from the attention the children gave it and at serious risk of overdosing on belly rubs.

Andrea handed out the last of the blankets and turned down the small hallway toward the ladies' room. She rounded the corner and stopped short; one of the firemen had a man in a bright paisley shirt backed up against the wall and was in the process of giving him a serious mouth-to-mouth session. The men separated when they noticed Andrea. The one against the wall pressed his lips and smirked, while the fireman attempted to act as if nothing had happened, like Andrea hadn't seen him with his tongue in the other guy's throat. She excused herself and proceeded to the ladies' room.

Andrea entered the bathroom to find Jill Boriello running her hands at the sink and staring into the mirror. The woman reacted to the deputy's uniform and introduced herself. "Can you tell me anything about what's going on out there?" the teacher asked.

"I don't know much, really." Andrea forced the same smile she'd been offering for the past two hours. "Right now, this is the safest place you could be."

"I went to my neighbor's house this morning," Jill said. "She was missing, and the place had been torn apart."

Andrea's upper lip began to tremble, and then the lump in her throat she had so far managed to swallow rose and nearly choked her. A half second later, the first tear leaked from the corner of her eye. "I'm sorry," she cried. "I lost someone today."

"I'm so sorry." Jill gasped. "That was horrible of me."

"No-no." Andrea brushed it off and attempted to control herself. "We've all lost someone. I know things are insane and you're scared. I'll tell you what I know."

Jill Boriello took the deputy's hand and listened to everything she had to say about the disappearances that plagued the town, starting with the death of Felix Castillo, up to the sheriff's decision to evacuate everyone into the shelters. Her reactions were a mixture of shock and awe and even understanding. Then she told the deputy how three of her own students had addressed the entire student body earlier today. Somehow, the kids knew what was going on, while the parents and teachers were in the dark. Then the boy and the two girls vanished during the fire drill, just before the world went to hell.

"Has there been any word on the missing children from my class?" Jill asked.

"I'm sorry." Andrea frowned. "Our radios don't work in the shelter, but I know the sheriff is looking. He'll find them."

"I pray that he does. I'll never forgive myself if something happens to them." Jill let out a muted cry. "You see, I'm the kindergarten teacher, and this morning, Troy asked if I even knew how to teach fourth grade. I guess I don't. I mean … I lost three kids on my first day."

Andrea took the teacher in her arms as she broke down and sobbed onto her shoulder. There was nothing she could say to take away her burden. There was so much sadness in the basement of the shelter you could feel it in the air. It was heavy; it had weight. Andrea herself had every right to cry and to mourn the loss of her coworkers and the man she loved. And Jill Boriello had every right to mourn the loss of her neighbor and the disappearance of her students. If you couldn't cry over missing children, then what could you cry over? The woman had every right to feel her pain, and who was Andrea to talk her out of it? She'd earned it; they all had.

The teacher jumped at the sound of someone throwing a firecracker just outside the bathroom door. Jill looked at the deputy with frantic eyes, searching for answers. But Andrea thought differently of the sound and rushed the woman into one of the bathroom stalls.

"Whatever you do." Andrea stared her in the eyes. "Stay down and don't come out." The deputy unholstered her weapon and closed the stall door, leaving the teacher inside.

Jill covered her ears as the roar of semi-automatic weapons fire cannoned from somewhere in the shelter. The woman began to cry as bullets rattled off the concrete ceiling and echoed in the old, moldy bathroom.

CHAPTER 81

The pump and ladder trucks pulled in behind one another. Tank Ferguson and Gabriel Ford had canvassed the town, delivered their message, and made it back safely. And they had each done one better in the process. The cabs and even the backs of the vehicles were loaded with passengers both men had picked up along the way. Nearly forty people in total clung to the ladders and side walls of the fire trucks and jumped off when they arrived at the back entrance of the school.

Bob Jones and Brandon Canfield assisted the soaking wet passengers to safety and directed them into the shelter. Then one of the yellow school buses pulled in behind the trucks. Bob thought they had all been parked in the back lot and had no idea someone had taken one out. The door opened, and a swarm of people exited and made their way to the gym. The group shuffled along at a snail's pace, using their canes and walkers to assist themselves along.

Botany Village, the senior house! Bob realized they had forgotten about the place. He cursed himself as he made his way to the bus. *How could I be so stupid?* He leaned to look inside and found a smiling Anthony Leone staring back at him.

After delivering a busload of screaming first graders, Anthony had second thoughts about spending the night in the shelter. In fact, he had more than just second thoughts and had taken the school bus with every intention of riding it out on his own. That was until he passed Botany Village and saw the frightened faces staring at him from the windows. They had forgotten about the place; no one had been sent to take care of the town's senior population. There was no way they could make it to the shelter on their own.

So, Anthony pulled into the lot, went from door to door, and loaded everyone on the bus. He had driven by thinking only of himself and was caught completely off guard when the altruistic inspiration overcame him. It was as if his own heart had grown—three sizes like the Grinch himself. The crowd from Botany were so grateful they had broken into a few verses of "For He's a Jolly Good Fellow." Who would have thought Anthony Leone a jolly good fellow? Certainly not Bob, or Anthony, for that matter.

Bob was about to say something, couldn't find the exact words, and gave Anthony a thumbs-up like he was Fonzie. The sound of screeching tires alerted him to the police cruiser as it pulled in. He half expected to see Carl; instead, Deputy Rainey exited the vehicle and proceeded straight to the trunk. The man removed several rifles and a large bag, then made his way across the pavement toward the front doors.

"Deputy Rainey, what's it looking like out there? Did you see the sheriff or any of my men in the cruisers?"

Rainey kept his head down and stared at the pavement to keep the rain from hitting him in the face. "It's not good; the town looks like a war zone. I stayed behind at the school to make sure everyone got out, then did a quick once-over down the Turnpike. No sign of the sheriff or your men.

Those things are everywhere; we need to lock this place up right away." Rainey stepped into the gym and out of the rain, then proceeded to make his way to the shelter.

"Deputy," Bob called to him. "Shouldn't we wait for the sheriff? I've still got men out there!"

Rainey spun around like a water moccasin. His face was white as death, and he looked as if he had seen the devil himself. "If the sheriff isn't here in five minutes, it's because he's already dead. The same thing goes for your men." Water dripped from the deputy's clothes and the arsenal he carried with him. "If we're going to keep these people alive, we need to lock the doors before it's too late."

"Understood," Bob replied, and stepped back as the deputy turned and headed across the wooden floor toward the basement. The deputy had seen something terrible out there. Bob didn't want to imagine what might happen if even one of those horrors found their way into the basement. Rainey was right; they couldn't wait much longer; it was getting darker by the second. Bob picked up his radio and made one last try. After that ...

Deputy David Rainey walked across the gym floor toward the entrance of the shelter, paying no attention to the trail of rainwater left in his wake. He toted two rifles slung over his shoulder and transferred the duffle bag from his right hand to his left. He had loaded it with as much ammo as he could fit. The M1 Carbine had been his father's in WWII. The old man had mailed the Garand back home piece by piece once the war had ended, and Uncle Sam had been none the wiser. It was a reliable weapon and a favorite among servicemen for years. David had fired it only a few times, since you couldn't just take a semi-automatic weapon up to Garrett Mountain. But the sheriff had allowed it at the range from time to time, mostly because he wanted to fire it himself. It was an impressive firearm with lethal stopping power. David had been compelled to stop by his house and transfer the gun to the trunk of his cruiser. But for some reason, he had no memory of ever doing so.

He rubbed his temples, trying to soothe the dull thud that had settled between his eyes and the sides of his head. It was an annoying ache, constant and grating, and one he couldn't shake. David approached the door to the stairwell and stepped inside. He gazed down the long set of steps, remembering he had been there just earlier today. It felt longer than that, and even longer since he had gotten any sleep. More than anything, David Rainey just wanted to close his eyes, needed to, but there was no time. There was work to be done.

David stepped onto the landing, engaged the deadbolt, and descended the steps toward the shelter. Closing the basement door behind him, David placed the duffle bag on the floor and looked out across the room. *Dear God! There's so many of them. How did they all get here? And how long before they realize I've discovered their nest?* He moved slow and deliberate, removing the weapons from his shoulder. He placed the M1 to the side and wedged the other rifle between the doorknob and the floor.

"Carl, this is Bob, come in." The radio remained silent, not even the static audible over the thundering drive of the rain. "Bob Jones to Sheriff Primrose, come in."

He waited and then tried to reach the other men. Glenn Gillick and Mike Turino were in patrol cruisers delivering the evacuation message. Neither man answered. Bob's stomach twisted as he waited for a reply from any of them. Something had happened; he was sure of it. A cross between what the deputy said and the feeling in his gut told him neither Carl nor his men were coming. There was nothing left to do but chain the doors. The lives of every person in the basement depended on it.

"Carl, I don't know if you can hear me, but I'm locking the doors. If you're out there I hope you're somewhere safe. Jesus Christ, Carl, answer me!" Bob tightened his fist against the radio and prayed.

"If anyone can hear me, God be with you." Bob waited for Brandon to enter the building and closed the doors behind him. The men laced the large chain through the handles and padlocked it shut. The gravity of the moment hung in the air like a dead man at the end of a noose. Neither said a word as they made their way to the entrance of the shelter on the opposite side of the gym.

The first gunshot sounded more like a firecracker than a bullet. The second and third happened in rapid succession, causing Bob to freeze in mid-step. *Was that a gunshot? Why on Earth would someone be shooting a weapon?* The singular bursts were followed by the sound of semi-automatic weapon fire. Bob bolted across the wood floor like a cheetah. *Dear God!* There were women and senior citizens down there, and there were so many children!

The gathered horde still hadn't noticed him, but soon they would. David worked fast, unzipping the duffle bag and loading as many extra magazines as possible into his pockets and waistband. He replaced his .38 with a .40 and added several extra magazines to his belt as well. There was no way he could take out all of them, but he had to try while he still had the element of surprise. David positioned himself in a shallow nook beside the door, which offered a clear view of the entire basement. He raised the M1 eye level, sighted the first beast, and placed his finger on the trigger.

Peanuts lay on her back with her paws in the air as the children took turns rubbing her belly. Lynn Donovan did her best to entertain the kids from Janis's elementary school and keep their minds occupied, but Peanuts stole the show. The pup let out a noise from the back of her throat that sounded like she was moaning, and her eyes rolled back in her head.

Lynn had arrived at the high school to find Janis and her two friends had gone missing during the fire drill. She was ready to go back out and look for them but had been stopped by the fire chief, who said no one could leave the school. Lynn herself had been pursued by something monstrous on her way to the shelter. It looked part sea creature and part man but behaved like nothing she had seen in her life. She thought if this was an acid flashback, it was the worst trip ever.

"Is this your dog?" Lynn looked up at the man who spoke. He had dark hair, appeared close to her age, and wore a shirt with a FD insignia on it.

"This is Peanuts," the young girl rubbing the pup's belly replied.

Lynn got up from the floor and extended her hand. "Hi, I'm Lynn Donovan."

"Nice to meet you. Drew Halberg with the fire department. Just making my rounds, seeing if everyone is all right."

"Do all firemen carry guns?" she asked, noticing the weapon on his hip.

"Well, it's just a precautionary measure."

"I hope you don't expect to have to use it down here."

"You know what they say," he told her. "Better to have one and not need it than the other way around."

"Like a condom," Lynn laughed.

Drew's face turned red at the remark. "Yeah, something like that."

Now that Lynn was on her feet, she was better able to see and noticed just how many men in the basement were armed. Firemen with shotguns mulled around as if they were on patrol; some carried weapons on their hips. There were several other men in the crowd who had taken up arms as well.

"I feel safer already," she said, her attention drawn to the deputy who had just entered the shelter and closed the door behind him. Drew continued to talk, but Lynn focused on the young officer as he placed a bag on the floor and then wedged one of his weapons against the door. There was something off about the way the guy was acting, scanning the room with his wild eyes and then proceeding to load ammunition into his pockets. He looked as if he were terrified—as if he were preparing for something.

"I haven't seen you around. Are you new in town?" Drew asked.

Lynn hadn't heard a word he said. "I'm sorry, but do you know that guy over there?"

Drew Halberg turned to the door and began to walk toward the man who had backed up against the wall. "Deputy Rainey," Drew called. "What the heck are you doing over there?"

Lynn watched the color drain from the deputy's face when the fireman called to him. Panic and fear flooded his features, and suddenly, Lynn knew what the deputy intended to do. She opened her mouth to yell as the man stepped out from the nook and raised his weapon. But time was either moving too fast or it had stopped completely, and Lynn was unable to speak. Then the deputy fired.

Lynn jumped as something wet splashed across her face and into her open mouth. She looked down and saw the red splattered across her shirt. The fireman standing in front of her swayed for a moment and then fell to his side on the concrete. Lynn stood in shock, not sure what was happening.

"Drew," she called out.

The deputy fired again, and Lynn knew exactly what was going on. One of the men patrolling the basement screamed and fell onto his back as the deputy's bullet caught him in the chest. The sound of a third bullet echoed off the ceiling like an avalanche. Then the deputy unloaded his weapon at a feverish pace, sweeping the barrel of his gun from left to right, into the crowd. Lynn darted around and threw herself at the group of children. She pushed them to the floor, attempting to shield everyone as they wiggled and squirmed from the concussion of each explosion.

Gunfire ripped through the shelter like cherry bombs in a toilet. Another man was thrown backward as the deputy's bullets tore into him. Chips of concrete flew into the air as weapon fire ricocheted off every surface. Screams and cries of terror lifted from the trapped citizens, who scrambled to flee from the attack but had nowhere to run. Men, women, and even children were caught in the crosshairs of Deputy Rainey's weapon and slaughtered in a bath of crimson.

Lynn struggled to protect the children but was losing her grip to gather them together. "No!" screamed the girl who had been rubbing the dog's belly. She jumped to her feet and ran from the man with the gun. Lynn watched as the deputy turned his weapon on the child and drew down on her. *God no!* Lynn rose to her feet and took off after her. The girl hadn't gotten far, and Lynn snatched her up and cradled her like a bag of groceries. She shielded the child and attempted to crouch as low as she could.

The explosion from the deputy's weapon was more jarring than the bullet that entered her back. It felt no worse than getting hit with a snowball; cold at first, then her legs gave out from under her. Lynn dropped the child and fell to the floor. She tried to reach for the little girl, who simply stood there. "Get down," she managed. But she was already too late. A pinprick of red appeared on the front of the girl's dress. It grew to the size of a quarter and then to that of a grapefruit. The child fell on her back and was quiet.

Lynn was aware of movement, a great deal of it, and the fading resonance of sound. Children and adults running in every direction, bodies falling, and surfaces painted red. The rapid fire had been replaced by the methodical blast of single shots, and then there was another sound. Growling and barking followed by a horrible whimper and the echo of the gun. Lynn raised her head enough to see the small body laying at the feet of the monster. "No, Peanuts," she cried. Lynn Donovan lowered her head and stopped breathing.

Deputy Rainey discarded the spent rifle and removed the pistol from his holster. He fired into the throng of deformities, making head shots when he could and avoiding their counterattacks. The creatures had infected far more of the town's population than either he or the sheriff anticipated. Men, women, and so many children had been compromised, taken over by the virus and turned into something unimaginable. Their deformed features and hideous bodies rose up and turned on him, but David was fast and laid waste to their suffering. The roar of the fight was so consuming he never noticed the constant itch deep within his skull, and the voice inside him sounded too much like his own to be anything else.

A group of children from the fourth-grade class had spent the after-noon gathered around Principal Grace, playing games and listening to stories. Kelly Rainey, Caroline Smith, and Scott Cole sat together, giddy, punch-drunk, and feeling more and more apprehensive as the minutes passed. Some of the children's parents made it to the shelter, but for everyone that did show up, there were at least two who had not. Kelly saw her brother, David, when he entered through the basement door. She perked up and left the group to approach him. He didn't notice her and went straight to checking his equipment and locking the door.

Then David stepped out and started shooting. Kelly jumped at the sound of the first explosion, her breath frozen in her chest and every hair on her body stood at attention. A man in the crowd screamed and then fell to the floor. Kelly wondered what the man had done. There had to be some reason why her brother would shoot him. David turned his gun on another person. Bullets sailed past Kelly's head as he fired into the crowd, connecting with one of the third graders from her school. And then he started shooting at the mothers, and the fathers, and even more of the children. *What's happening?* It was more than Kelly's ten-year-old mind could comprehend; she stood fast, unable to move as her brother gunned down her friends and classmates.

"Get down, Kelly!" Principal Grace screamed and ran towards her.

Kelly turned in time to see the bright splatch of crimson spread out across the front of Scott Cole's shirt. The boy fell backward onto the floor, causing the other children of the group to scream and take off running. David shot them in the back, picking them off one by one. A spray of bullets danced across the arms of Mrs. Smith, who attempted to shield her daughter from the attack. Both she and Caroline fell together amongst the other bodies.

Principal Grace dove at Kelly and tackled her to the floor. Kelly struggled to breathe as the weight of the principal bore down on her. Somewhere off to her right, she could hear a dog barking. She twisted and turned under the woman's weight and managed to slide out from underneath her. Principal Grace stared at Kelly without blinking as the bullets exploded around them. A thin line of blood trickled from a small hole in the woman's forehead. The little that was left of Kelly's resolve vanished like a wisp of smoke.

A shadow crossed her face as she sat with tears in her eyes. Kelly looked up into the barrel of the gun pointed at her head. It was her brother, only it wasn't David at all. The face she saw was contorted and twisted and unrecognizable.

David stared down at the small creature on the floor before him and pressed his finger to the trigger. Then one of the firemen rushed forward, grabbing at his weapon. The men wrestled and stumbled backward over the litter of bodies. David managed to throw the fireman aside and turned his weapon on him, firing several bullets into the man. He scanned the room for the target he had been focused on but was unable to locate it. He moved on to his next, emptied his weapon, and reloaded a fresh magazine.

Kelly had crawled back beneath the body of Principal Grace. She cried and covered her ears, struggling to block the sound of her brother's bullets. But the resonating sound of the weapon and the cries of her classmates would stay with Kelly the rest of her life.

Andrea opened the bathroom door and stepped into the roar of semi-automatic weapon fire. She crouched low as she made her way through the hall toward the shelter. The sound of women screaming and children crying was just audible over the deafening concussions. Someone was unloading the hammers of hell on the people of Garrett Grove. Andrea turned the corner with her weapon drawn and stopped in her tracks.

She watched David Rainey as he tossed an old semi-automatic rifle to the side and drew a pistol. *Christ, where did he get a weapon like that?* She scanned the tangled mass of bodies through the haze of red. David had to have fired at least five magazines on the crowd. So much blood, so many bodies, and far too many of them were children. It was impossible to tell who was living and who was dead amidst the gun smoke and crimson. She held her breath as her partner approached a woman and shot her in the head.

No!" Andrea broke cover and fired. Her first bullet went wide; she pulled the trigger again as she advanced. Rainey turned and raised his weapon in her direction, but Andrea rushed him and fired. "Drop it, David!"

The bullet hit David Rainey in the shoulder. The features of his face suddenly changed as he looked down at the wound and examined the blood with his fingers. He looked back at Andrea with a question on his lips and confusion in his eyes, but the moment of recognition vanished. David's face twisted into a snarl; he lifted his gun in Andrea's direction.

She felt the slug bite into her thigh and almost toppled over from the pain. Struggling to maintain her focus, she gritted her teeth and pulled the trigger. David fell backward as the bullet took him in the chest. He lay on the floor flailing and scrambling to get back on his feet.

Andrea closed the distance between them as fast as her injured leg would allow. She came up on the deputy and kicked his weapon to the side. Blood sprayed from his mouth; he looked up at her with fear and hatred in his eyes. Then in a flash, his features softened, and the glaze in his stare lifted.

"Andrea." He coughed. "You have to help me. They're everywhere."

She stood over him with her weapon drawn. "What are you talking about? Why, David?" The gun trembled in her hands as the tears fell from her cheeks and hit the red-stained floor.

"They're infected. I had to kill the monsters; I had to put them down. Just like I did for Kovach."

Andrea's breath stopped cold. Her eyes blurred as Rainey's words slipped between her ribs like a dagger and pierced her heart. *Just like I did for Kovach.* They continued to resonate on an endless loop. *Just like I did for Kovach.* The gun wavered in her hands; her throat tightened, and the tears flowed without resistance. The slow tremors in her arms ebbed throughout her entire body and raked deep within. The man she loved, dear sweet Joel, gunned down by one of their own. Killed by David Rainey in cold blood. Andrea forced herself to focus past the pain in her chest and allowed the throbbing in her leg to propel her anger even further. She aimed her weapon at the man who killed Joel Kovach and exhaled.

"You're the only monster I see," she hissed and pulled the trigger.

The presence had first invaded Deputy David Rainey's head Sunday night at the morgue as he stood over the reanimated body of Abe Gorman. It invaded him a second time that afternoon in the girl's bathroom at the elementary school, only this time, it left something behind. Just a suggestion, an itch the deputy felt compelled to scratch. It was impossible to ignore and too tempting to refuse. It played with David as if he were no more than an ant beneath a magnifying glass, ransacking his brain like a thief until it found exactly what it was looking for. It saw the semi-automatic weapon David owned and seized the opportunity. It was exactly what was needed to reduce the simple ones' numbers and render them defenseless. David had no recollection of stopping at the house, using his service revolver, and leaving his parents' bodies lying in the kitchen. He also didn't remember removing the weapons and blowing out the pilot light before leaving. When David entered the shelter at the high school, he believed he had finally stumbled upon the creature's nest and that he was looking at those who had already fallen to the beast. David would never remember raising his weapon on his own sister and nearly pulling the trigger.

It had ransacked his brain twice, but there would never be a third. David Rainey would never have to live with the knowledge of what he had done. He would never know the number of children he had slaughtered or parents he had gunned down in cold blood. And the last thing to invade David Rainey's brain was the .38 caliber slug fired by his coworker Andrea Geary.

CHAPTER 82

The men working at the quarry saw the abominations descend the cliff face, but no one was able to digest what they were seeing until it was too late. By then, the strange insect-like creatures were already upon them. Mark and Buzzy fled toward the trailers with a handful of the other rockhounds but were outmatched by the speed of the beasts. The stingers at the ends of their tails were not only sharp but dripped an ancient poison more lethal than any other known to man. It possessed the equivalent toxicity of the box jellyfish and the blue-ringed octopus combined. This particular brand of venom had disappeared when the dinosaurs went extinct—which was a good thing; otherwise, nothing else would have ever populated the blue planet.

The scorpion-human hybrids were joined by other creatures a bit more humanoid in appearance, although not entirely. The large, deformed zombies appeared to have maintained a better hold on their own DNA signature than the insects had. However, the flood of new information being transmitted to their mitochondria as well as their own DNA sent their bodies' cellular processors into overdrive. It was impossible to translate. In some cases, the rapid transfer altered the host to its original primitive state. But in most, the human body found the multiple genetic codes impossible to decipher, resulting in a transformation into myriad creatures.

It was a collector, a harvester, and had consumed information since the beginning of time. The simple ones were easily molded and made the perfect foot soldiers. They were malleable but far from impervious. They could only last so long with its seed inside them. But the young, the children were much stronger and could last a great deal longer. They were the only vessel powerful enough to contain its true essence.

It had divided into three, the original three, and had kept them safe. The one called Butchie was there to protect, but the flesh of the simple ones had grown weak. Even the original three were waning, and the time to replace them was soon.

It could have chosen any of the children from town, but after possessing the mind of Robert Boyle and tasting his friend in the graveyard, it craved the one called Troy. The child had made a game of creating fear, and that was a consciousness worth possessing. A controller of fear could possibly withstand the whole of its presence. Soon, it would have the child; it was just a matter of time.

Stephanie's father, Dr. Edgar Donovan, had studied the disappearance of civilizations for the greater part of his career. Countless depictions similar to those in the DuCain cavern had been found across the globe. From the Indus River Valley to the Olmecs, and even the Mayans, the correlation of recorded events was near identical. The die-off of biological life in each location always coincided with archeological findings that were beyond explanation. The possible causation of such led Dr. Donovan and his colleagues to dig deeper into more recent occurrences, specifically those taking place in the new world. There had been at least three between the years 1400 and 1600, the first being Cahokia, also known as America's forgotten city, located in modern-day Illinois. Cahokia was home to somewhere between 10,000 and 20,000 Native Americans who simply vanished overnight. Similar paintings and unidentifiable teeth were uncovered at the site. An animal skull had been found containing human molars that had been drilled and filled with gold. There had been the lost colony of Roanoke in 1587, where Donovan had worked the excavation himself. And then there was the disappearance of the Lenape Tribe in the eastern US, which occurred somewhere around 1600. All previous excavations showed a recorded history of each civilization's battle with an unstoppable force. One Donovan and his partners referred to as The Dark One.

Stephanie followed in her father's footsteps, studying at his side for years and then taking over the research after his death. Together, they postulated that the force responsible for countless disappearances, the Entity called The Dark One, had originated from antimatter. They also believed it to be cognizant. As a juxtaposition to matter, the Dark One was the antithesis of creation. Thinking in terms of matter as creation, the destructive force of antimatter wasn't that far of a stretch.

The battle between good and evil was recorded in every religion and in every culture. The monotheistic God didn't come about until somewhere around 5000 B.C. Evidence of this Entity had been around much longer than that. In fact, the Dark One appeared to be present since there were hands to record it. It was the original evil, the original sin. And Stephanie believed this Entity was the inspiration behind the story of the Devil himself. She also believed it was the originator of nearly every mythological creature story known to man, from the Kraken to the werewolf and even the vampire.

There were countless names for the Entity and far too much evidence to ignore. The signature teeth were found in each location, usually alongside weapons manufactured from magnetite. The only other information Stephanie Thompson was sure of was the Entity's preoccupation with children. She couldn't explain why, although she had a working theory.

A second beast stood at the entrance of the cave with blood dripping from its stinger. It approached the small opening and backed away howling as if it had been scalded. The onyx eyes surveyed the area for a breach in the defenses and found none. It reared back on its haunches, exposing a lamella-lined abdomen, and screamed; the humanish face at the end of the monster contorted as it stared at Stephanie. Again, she raised the ancient weapon in the direction of the abomination and threatened to unleash her arsenal. The display was effective, and the scorpion retreated into the quarry, then sped off toward the trailers in search of a more accessible meal.

Don stood behind her, half-concealed by a small outcropping, with his analytical mind performing calisthenics. *It's not possible.* He searched for logic and rational explanations and found none. Gail's blood was still wet on his brow. He held out his palms and stared at the exaggerated tremble of his hands. It radiated into his chest and threatened to overtake him. Everything Stephanie had said, all the insanity about lost civilizations and entities—it had all been true. But that was impossible. He opened his mouth to speak, but a dry croak was all that left his lips. Don reached out and grabbed the rock to steady himself as the world turned grey around him. Outside, the fire whistle stopped ringing, leaving only the shrieks of the creatures and the screams from the last of their victims.

Stephanie lowered the weapon and approached him. "Are you all right?" she asked.

Don shook his head. "I—I didn't—"

"Easy, you've got to breathe or you're going to pass out." She placed the musket balls and weapon on the rock in front of Don and took him by the shoulders. "Easy, in and out, like that."

He followed her lead and focused on his breathing. He was certain he would faint, and then the moment passed. After several seconds, he looked up at her and spoke. "I'm sorry I didn't believe you."

Stephanie offered a half-smile and wiped the tears from her face. She had been able to act and fend off their attacker but was struggling just as much as he was. She held up her hand and steadied herself. "It's impossible to believe. Not something I ever imagined witnessing in my own lifetime."

"You said this thing is responsible for the disappearance at Cahokia." Now the questions were flooding into Don's head at a faster pace than he could process and spit out. "Where has it been all this time? Why did it wait till now to show up?"

"I don't think it waited, exactly. I think maybe it was either trapped in here or hibernating in your cave."

Don swayed and clutched at the rock. "You're telling me I let this thing out?!"

"You wanted to make a name for yourself in the field of geology—congratulations."

It hit Don in a frenzy, the vandalism at the quarry, the missing explosives, the destruction of the bridge and the Sunset Pass. His heart beat faster as he realized the implications. "Jesus Christ! Just how intelligent is this thing? Is it capable of tactical thought?"

Stephanie pressed her lips together and tilted her head. "Well, how intelligent would something have to be to wipe out an entire civilization?"

Don knew the answer before he even asked. It was Combat 101. If you wanted to conquer your enemies, the first thing you needed to do was isolate them—destroy every escape route and leave them trapped. Then you could pick them off one by one. *For fuck's sake, Garrett Grove's cut off from the rest of the world.* And Lois and Troy were out there in the middle of it.

He had been so worried about himself, about his job, and hadn't stopped to think about his family. *What have I done?* But Don knew. He had been the same guy he had always been, only caring about Don, only focused on his own life, and the hell with everyone else. He prayed there was still time, that it wasn't already too late.

"We have to get back to town and warn everyone. They have no idea what they're up against."

"You wouldn't last five minutes out there." Stephanie walked to the tangle of bones in the center of the floor and removed the stone dagger from the remains. She tested the balance of the lodestone weapon and slid it behind her belt. "I know what you're thinking. I need to help my family too, but we're no good to them dead. And this cave is the only thing protecting us from being ripped apart. Our only chance of helping them is in the daylight. I'm sorry, but we have to wait till morning."

"We can't just sit here. We need to warn them."

Stephanie pointed to the opening, where several of the massive arachnids gathered at a distance. "I'd say from the sound of the sirens, they already know."

Don hated it but knew she was right. They would never make it even if they tried. The things outside hovered near the cave's entrance, never daring to step too close. They appeared to be more afraid of the cave itself than they were of the actual weapons, which had taken more than a few shots to be effective. He knew their only chance of survival was to wait inside the safety of the cavern, at least until morning. He prayed that daylight would offer the protection they needed to make it back to town. "So, how the hell do we stop these things?"

"Are you serious?" She turned toward him and shook her head as if he hadn't been paying attention. "This thing has been around forever. It's responsible for the disappearance of countless civilizations, hundreds of thousands of people—and that's just the ones we know about. You don't stop it; you can only get the fuck out of its way."

"Oh bullshit!" Don barked. "It's vulnerable to lodestone, to magnetism, that means it has a weakness and can be stopped. It must have a metallic signature in its makeup if magnetite affects it adversely. The Lenape figured out a way to trap it, and it would still be stuck in this cave if I hadn't come along and blown it up."

"I said maybe it was trapped. Or maybe it was just sleeping. The point is, nothing anyone has done in the past has been effective because it keeps coming back. I think it only goes away once the food source is depleted in its hunting grounds. Right now, it's found a home in Garrett Grove, and it's not going to stop until it's destroyed everything in its path." She stared at him, out of breath with tears streaming down her cheeks.

"So, what are you suggesting we do?"

"We wait till morning, then we go find our families and get out of town. I don't care if we have to walk over the mountain all the way to California."

"I thought this was the chance of a lifetime to study your father's work." Don wished he could take back the words as soon as they left his lips.

"I can't study it if I'm dead," Stephanie hissed. "I'm a scientist, not a statistic. You of all people should understand that."

Her words cut back at him like a broadsword, and he deserved that. "I'm sorry. I'm just not ready to write off the entire town. We can't even be sure how many of those things are out there. For all we know"—he pointed to the entrance—"that could be it. Somehow it got stuck in this cave, either trapped or hibernating. And if it was trapped, the Lenape figured out a way to lure it inside." The analytical gears and pistons were firing again, and he was able to think straight. "There are only a few skeletons in here, so the Lenape didn't lure an army of creatures in here; they lured the Entity itself. Whatever this thing really is, it was trapped inside this cave."

Don picked up one of the flashlights and started walking as he reasoned the impossible possibilities of the scenario. "Okay, if this thing is an Entity, like you said, then it has to have a main consciousness. A central intelligence hidden somewhere. When a country goes to war, the president doesn't join the troops on the frontline. Shit! You killed that thing with a handful of rocks. Why would it expose itself? If it were me, I would be holed up somewhere while I sent my peons out to do the dirty work." He turned on the light and directed it onto the far wall, revealing the mural of the children. He stared at it for a moment, thinking. *What about this place is so damn familiar? Where have I seen something like this before?* "In fact, if I was this thing, I would be hiding until the coast was clear before I showed my ass. I'd be worried someone might try to pull the same shit that the Lenape did."

Don made his way into the second chamber, inspecting each mural along the way. He turned to find Stephanie a step behind him, hanging on every word. "You know what I think?" he asked. "I think this thing isn't half as smart as you give it credit for. I mean, if it's as old as you say and as powerful as you tell me, then it's pretty goddamn stupid. I'll bet it's grown so cocky and sure of itself it had no idea what was happening when the

Lenape pulled the rug out from under it. I bet if we get a look at the rest of these murals, we'll find out just how stupid this thing is."

Don turned the light on Stephanie. The look on her face spoke volumes; it was the broken look of someone who had accepted their fate.

"The Lenape tribe in this area were slaughtered," she said. A sizzle of lightning flashed outside the cave, illuminating half her face as she spoke. "They were exterminated like a colony of ants."

CHAPTER 83

Janis looked across the backseat of the cruiser at her friends. She offered a toothy smile that helped ease their apprehension. Although she was soaked from running through the rain and falling onto the wet grass, her bubbling attitude hadn't dimmed a single watt. Her warmth was infectious like a plate of fresh chocolate chip cookies and radiated outward. Troy could feel it filling the backseat as if a space heater had been focused on them. Then a voice spoke over the sheriff's radio.

"Deputy Lutchen to anyone in the basement. Come in, over."

Troy sat between the girls and pulled them in close as the sheriff started speaking. "Do you think we're gonna get in trouble for pulling the fire alarm?" he asked.

Both Janis and Wendy laughed and elbowed him in the ribs. Apparently, neither thought there was anything to worry about. Their attention was drawn again when another voice crackled through the tiny speaker.

"Carl, I figured out why the MRI machine killed it. It's a giant magnet, and this thing is made of some type of metallic alloy."

Janis sat upright at the mention of the magnets and began to smack the back of the sheriff's seat. Wendy and Troy also chimed in shouting, "I told you; you see—you see." They were so excited that they had figured it out first, none of them could contain themselves.

"All right!" the sheriff shouted and turned to the back seat. "Would you mind keeping it down back there?"

The group of children settled down and sat upright. Troy had never been yelled at by the sheriff and had no idea he could shout so loud. Janis, however, started to snicker almost right away, which in turn got Wendy giggling. A second later, both girls were unable to control themselves. Troy relaxed a bit and joined them. Even his mother and the sheriff were infected by the laughter and offered smiles of their own.

"Yeah, I was just told the same thing about ten minutes ago by a group of fourth graders." Carl laughed and looked in the rearview mirror. "But good job, Burt. Glad you're safe, and I hope that info helps us."

"I take it you found the kids?" the voice asked.

"That's a big 10-4—"

It shot at them in a blur, screaming across the Turnpike from out of the side street. Dark and fast and on top of them in an instant. Lois grabbed the dashboard and screamed, "Look out!" Then the world was eclipsed.

It hit them with the force of a charging rhino, tossing everyone in the vehicle about as if they were nothing more than a little girl's dolls. It crashed into the driver's side rear quarter panel, and the back windshield imploded. Glass rained down on the children in a violent barrage. The sound of crumpling metal and breaking glass was all that anyone could hear. Suddenly, they were spinning out of control and around like a pinwheel for what felt like an eternity.

Janis had been trying to contain her laughter when the car was struck. She was thrown hard to the left, propelled toward the back passenger door.

Her head hit the glass with a sickening thud nearly as loud as the initial impact. The girl's smile disappeared, and her face went slack.

Janis's eyes rolled into the back of her head, and her body went limp. She collapsed into Troy's lap. Her blonde curls darkened as blood flowed from the wound and began to spread. It matted her hair, ran down her face, and soaked into Troy's jeans. He tried to focus on his friend, but a million impossible thoughts assaulted his senses as he struggled to comprehend what was happening.

The vehicle continued to spin out of control on the wet pavement until it finally came to a halt several seconds later. Troy looked down in horror at the sight of the indentation on the side of Janis's head. Every nerve in his body fired at the same time, and he had no idea what to do. He didn't know if he should touch her or not, if he should attempt to cover the wound to stop the bleeding or not dare try. With tears coursing down his cheeks, Troy looked up and screamed.

"MOM—HELP!"

Mike Turino pushed the cruiser to fifty-five miles per hour while Claire Rizvi cheered him on with cries of approval. Her cold, wet T-shirt clung to her like a second skin even though Mike had turned on the heater—and he dug the way she looked in it. The scenery flew past as they barreled down Garrett Grove's deserted streets like they had been granted a free pass.

Mike was so mesmerized by Claire's goods he didn't realize he had blown the stop sign until it was too late. He smashed into the back of the sheriff's vehicle without ever taking his foot off the gas. Mike and Claire were thrown at the windshield like a pair of crash test dummies.

Mike's chest was formally introduced to the steering wheel and caved inward. Claire's body continued travelling fifty-five miles an hour as she left the seat and hit the windshield. She was expelled from the vehicle, sailed over the sheriff's cruiser, and hit the Turnpike before coming to a rest some thirty feet away. By then, she was nothing more than a stubborn stain that would never come out. The sheriff's vehicle continued to spin for a half a minute before it finally stopped on the side of the road, ruined and inoperable. Rain pounded the wreckage, mixing with the gasoline that had begun to seep from the cracked tank of the cruiser.

Carl's vision swam and his head spun, but he retained enough awareness to understand they had been in an accident. He had hit his head on either the window or the steering wheel, and blood dripped from a small cut above his left eye. He turned to Lois, who had been wearing her seatbelt, but she was already on the move. A cry as piercing as a cattle bolt erupted from the backseat. Carl turned to look and was washed away by the sea of red. There was so much, and it was impossible to tell whose blood it was at first. Then he saw the little girl sprawled in Troy's lap. *Dear God!* His pulse flew off the rails as he unfastened his seatbelt and attempted to exit the vehicle. But his door refused to open as he pressed against it.

Lois had already exited the car and run into the street. Carl followed, sliding across the seat and out the passenger's side. He threw his hat on to shield himself from the rain and reached Lois as she opened the back door. Wendy stepped out of the backseat first, hysterical and convulsing; she was swept out of the way into Lois's arms. Carl rushed in next to Troy and nearly cried out. His gut twisted as he looked down at the child laying in her friend's lap. The head wound was massive and had been dented in close to an inch or more.

Troy held on to the girl, his body shaking, the tremors ripping through him in concussive waves. Blood soaked his clothes and ran between his fingers and underneath his nails. Janis lay motionless in his arms.

"I've got her, Troy," Carl said and slid his hands between the girl's head and Troy's legs. "Let me take her. Slide out of the car."

The boy didn't move, only sat there crying and in shock until Lois reached in and offered her hand. He took it, slid across the seat, and buried his face in her bosom next to Wendy, who had done the same.

Carl looked for something to cover the wound and spied the wet sweatshirt on the seat. Being as careful as possible, he wrapped it around her head, managed to get his arms around her, and eased Janis out of the vehicle. She was so light and frail and hung limp like a doll in his arms. As Carl stepped out of the car, he smelled it. There was no mistaking that smell, not for a guy who had seen as much napalm as Carl had. It was gasoline, thick and heavy and leaking from the cruiser's tank. He moved as fast as he dared, trying not to jar the child or cause her further injury.

He stepped from the cruiser into the pouring rain and surveyed the scene. The other vehicle had come to rest further down the road. Although it was impossible to tell the condition of the driver, it was obvious the passenger hadn't made it. There was no time to worry about that asshole anyway.

"Over here!" A shout came from across the street. Carl looked to find the owner of the voice standing in the parking lot near the main entrance of the municipal building.

"Follow me," he called to the others and started moving. They were out of options, and at least there were medical supplies in the building. But as Carl watched the sweatshirt turn a deep scarlet, he doubted if it would make any difference. Janis didn't so much as stir as he raced into the parking lot carrying her.

Jessica Marceau had witnessed the accident from her second-floor window. She met them at the side entrance to the sheriff's department. "The keys are in my right pocket!" Carl yelled out.

Jessica dug in and pulled them out in one quick motion. She ran up the steps, opened the door, and held it for the others. Carl rushed into the building just as the first cruiser caught fire and exploded. The gasoline had spread quickly, and a moment later, the second vehicle detonated. There was no need to check on the condition of the driver. Carl focused on the girl and made his way toward the back of the station, where several cots were set up.

He entered the room with Janis's condition looking more dire by the second and motioned for Lois to take the other children down the hall. They would only get in his way and there was nothing they could do to help. He lowered Janis onto the cot and heard the deadbolt engage as Jessica locked the door behind them. The mayor rushed in to join him with a first aid kit and a flashlight. She turned it on and searched for gauze, bandages, and whatever else she could find.

Carl removed the sweatshirt from Janis's head, revealing the injury. Jessica gasped and continued to lay out gauze for the sheriff to use. He examined the intrusive dent in the child's skull, then fumbled about to find a pulse. He searched every inch of her neck but was unable to find even the faintest sign of life. *Don't die on me, Janis,* he chanted to himself as he pressed into her flesh with his fingertips. Then—he felt it—so faint it was nothing more than a tremble. But it was something; it was still a pulse. She was still alive.

He eased the gauze over the wound. The first layer soaked through in seconds, but the next layer appeared to slow the flow of blood, at least a little. There wasn't much he could do. The child had a massive concussion and needed a doctor, but Chilton was a war zone. Jessica removed a large bandage and assisted Carl as he proceeded to wrap it around Janis's head.

He finished the wrap, which appeared to stop the flow of blood a bit more. Then Janis's eyes fluttered, and a faint moan escaped from between her lips.

"Where is your car?" he asked the mayor. The medical center was off-limits, but one of the doctors and a paramedic would be at the high school by now. If they could get Janis there, there was a chance they could save her.

"In the back lot," Jessica answered.

"Thank God." Carl rested Janis's head against the pillow, stood up, and grabbed his radio. "Bob, come in. It's Carl, come in, Bob."

There was a blast of static, and then a man spoke; his voice was unrecognizable. The strained sobs warbled through the small speaker. "H-he killed them, C-Carl. Jesus Christ, it's a bloodbath."

The sheriff and mayor stared at each other, unable to make any sense out of the chief's transmission. "What are you talking about, Bob? What's going on?"

There was a long pause before Bob returned. "Your deputy—Rainey. He went insane and killed them. It's awful—God, Carl, it's so fucking awful. He slaughtered them. Christ, Carl—the children!"

Carl hadn't known Bob Jones to register a visible emotion the entire time he had known him. He had seen the man pull bodies from house fires. The guy was a rock if there ever was one. But his words came over the radio too fast and distorted to comprehend. Carl struggled to grasp what the man was saying. "What are you talking about, Bob? You're not making sense."

"Rainey! Deputy Rainey went crazy and shot the place up. It's a massacre, Carl. Jesus Christ, he killed them."

It hit Carl like a derelict squad car. He wasn't sure how he knew, probably a feeling in his gut. But suddenly he understood what the chief was talking about. Deputy Rainey had walked into the shelter and fired on the civilians. Only it hadn't been David Rainey at all. It may have looked like him and had no doubt been wearing the deputy's skin. But whatever it was that had gone into that shelter wasn't Deputy Rainey. It was the thing that had gotten into his head. *Dear God, it never left!* It had used the deputy as a weapon against his own people. *Dear Lord, please save us.* Carl pinched the bridge of his nose and winced as he prayed to whoever might still be listening.

By the time Bob Jones and Brandon Canfield forced their way into the shelter, it was already too late. They were assaulted by the oppressive cloud of gun smoke and gagging stench of gore. A river of red ran from the twisted tangle of bodies strewn about the floor. The neglectful way in which their arms and torsos tangled and heaped was nothing either man was prepared to witness. Bob had seen how disfigured and unrecognizable a flame could render the human body. He also knew what a man looked like after he was eaten alive by a pack of wild boar. But what lay before him was worse than any of that. And he had sent everyone into the shelter himself.

Bob struggled to keep his head and tend to the injured, but the stench of bodily fluids was as thick as a landslide. Brandon had an even harder time keeping a grip on the contents of his stomach and ran back up the stairs to purge on the gym floor. He returned minutes later looking pale and beat down. They moved from one pile of corpses to the next, checking for pulses and trying to focus on one single body at a time. There were some moans, a few cries, and even the occasional screams, but they were scarce. A chilling hush blanketed the large room, snuffing out all other sounds. The lack of injuries was surprising; the lack of survivors was staggering.

The gravity weighed heavier with each step the men took toward the center of the room. A discarded semi-automatic rifle lay on the floor next to several spent magazines, all tossed about in a haphazard fashion. Bob averted his eyes, frantic to find a single soul he could help, but it was impossible not to focus on the carnage. Parents had used their own bodies as shields to protect their helpless children. The rifle's bullets had torn through the little ones regardless; flesh was no match for a .30 caliber fired at close range.

The chief stood beside another cluster of victims and knelt to check for pulses. He was met by the unblinking stare of a child hidden beneath a tangle of limbs. Bob rolled one of the bodies to the side, revealing the terrified little girl. He held out his hand, thankful he had found a survivor. "I've got you," he said. "It's all over."

The girl allowed the fireman to lift her from the heap and buried her face into the crook of his neck. He stepped away from the mess and carried her toward the hallway leading to the smaller rooms. Bob passed the women's bathroom and jumped back when the door flew open and the woman rushed at him.

Jill Boriello had hidden in the bathroom as instructed and didn't move. She had waited until the bullets stopped flying before even leaving the stall. "Oh, God!" she cried. "I'll take her." The teacher held out her hands and took the young girl. "I've got you, Kelly," she said, but Kelly hadn't heard a word she said.

"Stay here," Bob told her and turned to leave. "This might not be over yet."

Bob made his way back into the nightmare of the main area with a bit more clarity than he had previously. The act of helping one individual lifted him enough to keep going and inspired the idea there might be others. His hopes lifted even more when he saw the deputy in the center of the room. The woman had fallen to the floor and was struggling to get to her feet.

"Andrea," he shouted and approached her. "Are you all right?" The deputy lifted a hand, revealing the .38 in her grip. Bob stopped in his tracks and removed his own sidearm, concerned it had been Andrea who was responsible for all the death. But as she rose to her feet and holstered her weapon, the idea became less likely. The deputy limped a few steps and kicked at a body on the floor in front of her.

Bob made his way toward her but kept his weapon in hand. He reached Andrea and gasped. On the floor lay the body of Deputy Rainey. He had been shot several times in the chest and once in the forehead. An arsenal of ammunition decorated his utility belt. Bob knew—Rainey had been the shooter.

"Dear God," he hissed.

"He killed them." Andrea focused on the body with a blind intensity. It looked as if she were staring through the man.

Bob noticed the wound in her leg and offered a hand, but Andrea refused and pushed him away. The rigid steel glare in her eyes and the icy tone of her voice told Bob everything. He recalled hearing how Rainey had nearly killed Carl at the morgue, how the creature got inside his head and manipulated the deputy like a puppet. Bob knew it had happened again, or the creature had never left at all. The result was the same either way. Deputy Rainey was used as a weapon and had slaughtered almost everyone in the shelter. The look in Andrea's eyes told Bob even more. She had silenced the beast.

Several people emerged from one of the back rooms, led by Michelle Marks. The woman sent them straight to work, turning her own emotion switch off and focusing on the job at hand. She tended to the victims' wounds, helped them to their feet, and led them away from the massacre. The small group of survivors lumbered off like war prisoners still untrusting of their rescuers. Looks of shock, horror, and disbelief filled the faces of those who had been spared. Although no one had been spared at all, not really. Everyone had lost something—a child, a mother, their spouse.

There was one miracle that occurred in the basement of the high school. Günter Bentley and his entire family had managed to survive the massacre. A combination of where they had been sitting when the shooting started, the man's instructions to his family to lie as if they had already been shot, and dumb blind luck were to thank. They were the only family to survive intact. Not that many had been intact before the shooting started.

Of the ten men Bob had stationed in the basement, only two survived. Anthony Leone suffered a grazing wound to the temple, and Rich Marek had been unharmed. Both men aided in helping with the survivors alongside Bob, Brandon Canfield, and Michelle's tiny group.

Their numbers were few, and those who were left were in no shape to defend themselves. The groups were taken into one of the back rooms, where they huddled together in silence. Survivor's guilt and shock swept them up like a blanket. Bob whispered a few instructions to Michelle and then returned to the gym to check the doors and resecure their defenses. That's what he told her at least. In all honesty, he needed to step away for a moment. The thick smell of gore still ripe in the air was inescapable. He climbed the long staircase, a weight like no other imposed upon him, and he entered into the openness of the high school gym. He was relieved for a brief moment until Carl's voice flooded through the radio's speaker.

Then Bob lost it. It rushed at him at a thousand miles an hour. The face of every fallen child appeared in his mind like a Polaroid. Every pulse he had checked on, every blood-soaked body, like a snapshot on his brain. He saw the look in Andrea's eyes, the body of Deputy Rainey, the snarl on the face of Earl Hillman, and he saw Sally. Dear, sweet, perfect Sally. He saw her as she was when she had loved him years and years ago, and he saw her the day she arrived in town with her face bruised and shoulder dislocated. Then a different picture of his first love entered the chief's mind: an image of Sally face first under nine inches of loose dirt. Bob broke down and let his tears fall. He had been holding them for so long, but the dam had finally broken.

His breath hitched in his throat as he tried to tell Carl what happened. "H-he killed them, C-Carl. Jesus Christ, it's a bloodbath." Bob's tears hammered through him like the rain. A second later, the lights in the gym flickered and then went black.

The first transformer blew when a random bolt of lightning hit the pole across the street from the sheriff's department. Jessica Marceau witnessed the explosion as the overload cut power to the surrounding area and interrupted service in the Village. The unthinkable happened not long after when a Chevy truck driven by Denny Birch crashed into a second telephone pole on Mandeville. After having Dr. Freedman remove a Hula Popper from the side of his head, Denny had spent the morning nursing his pain the only way he knew how—with a fifth of Jack. By the time he realized the fire whistle wasn't broken and was on his way to the high school, Denny was sufficiently shit-faced. He hit the pole doing fifty-five miles an hour and cracked it in half like a wishbone. Denny was killed on impact—which was unfortunate. The loss of two transformers plus a mile of damaged high-tension line was devastating. The substation on Route 3 overloaded, and Garrett Grove went dark minutes before nightfall.

375

CHAPTER 84

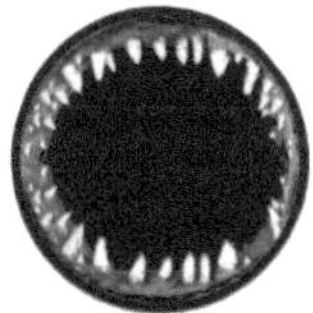

The three small creatures watched while their numbers advanced. They remained hidden, observing the entrances of the church, assessing not only the simple ones' strength but their weakness. The shared consciousness of the one coursed through them and was then relayed to the horde. They instructed and ordered the execution of the attack. The strange bodies once belonging to Robert Boyle, Erin Richards, and Ben Richards resembled nothing human in the least. Their distorted features, reptilian and sleek, were designed for speed and evasion. They watched through collective eyes from every possible angle. They listened as the simple ones gathered under the watch of their cunning leader and discussed their defenses.

The sentinel guarded over the three. It had been called Butchie, a being consumed by random chaos. Now it was a soldier, ruled by intention. But the vessel was strained and wouldn't last forever. The three were waning as well and would soon need to be discarded, replaced by new vessels, fresh skin to contain its essence. Then, when it finished with this colony, it could move on to the next. The map of humanity spread out in detail before it. Places called Warren, Parker Plains, and Millville were in the thoughts of the consumed. The simple ones had sealed their demise, populating the sphere on top of one another. Now nothing could stop it from spreading as it had always intended. One by one, colony to colony, city to city.

The three transmitted the plan to the soldiers surrounding the church. It directed them and ordered the attack. Then they retreated further into the woods and waited.

The lights in the church winced out, and their artificial illumination was replaced with the natural glow of a hundred or more candles set in every corner and all the pews. Lanterns were lit and flashlights were aimed into the dark as a bastion of beasts cascaded across the parking lot in a wave.

"Here they come!" Father Kieran shouted over the driving rain. Weapons were drawn and extra guns were positioned at the ready. The people of the parish reacted and worked together as if they had trained for years. "Steady," he called out to every man and woman. The horde made a rapid advance past the sixth row of parked vehicles and continued to the fifth.

"Steady now, steady!"

The legion of demons breached the fourth row of vehicles and approached the third. "Fire!" Kieran screamed and leveled his revolver into the writhing crowd. The night came alive with the thunder of gunfire blasting from every entrance of the church.

The beasts fell in rapid succession. As fast as they advanced, they were silenced. Kieran observed the men who flanked him, firing their weapons with zest, defending their church like Templar Knights. His heart swelled with pride, and he knew they would walk away victorious.

The assault on the sacristy entrance was much lighter than anticipated. Josh's men found it easy to fight off the small number of beasts advancing on their position. Josh fired into the darkness, then turned back to Allison and shouted his instructions. The girl turned and ran to Father Kieran's position to relay the information.

It felt good for Allison to stay busy. She hadn't been sure about coming to the church but had nowhere else to go. After the experience at the sanatorium, she knew whatever was out there was evil. And when Mick had gone missing, Allison had found herself alone. Now that she was here, helping Father Kieran and the others, she was certain she had done the right thing. She kept her head down, made her way to the front entrance, and delivered her message to one of the men, who passed it along to the father. A moment later, he turned back and shouted over the rattle of gunfire. Allison nodded, getting most of what he told her, then ran back to deliver the instructions to Josh.

She crouched again, staying low, and slid along the side wall of the church beneath the stained glass windows. She looked up at the portrait of Jesus and Mary Magdalene; it was the very image Father Kieran had been looking at earlier. The woman stood before the Lord, risking her own life to offer him a drink while his own disciples fled. She had never left his side and had been the first to see him resurrected. But for some reason, it was always Peter who was exalted. The man had denied Jesus and hid when he was crucified. But not Mary, she had remained faithful to the Lord. Allison felt proud to belong to a sisterhood of such devotion. She made the sign of the cross on her forehead and stopped to pray.

A dark shadow darted behind the window a second before the glass imploded. A polychromatic waterfall of art and color rained over Allison and onto the carpet. She shielded her eyes from the force of the shock, then the beasts were on her, grabbing her by the arms and throat. Allison was propelled upward and forced out the window into the night. She landed hard and was dragged across the lawn in a flurry. Her body jerked and bounced off the pavement as she was yanked into the parking lot and then carried off into the woods. Finally, the monster released her.

Allison lay on her back gasping for breath. Rain fell hard into her eyes, blurring her sight and obscuring the vision before her. It drew in closer and hovered over her, and then it spread its lips. The demon's teeth were pointed; its eyes were piercing and black. The creature's grey skin hung in loose tatters no longer fitting its small child-like body. Then it sneered at her and drew in even closer. The first waft of smoke lifted from its jaws and swirled before her in hypnotic waves.

"The Lord is my Shepherd," she said as dark tendrils gathered about. "I will fear no evil."

The beast made a strange gurgling sound that could have been laughter, but it was impossible to tell over the din of the rain. It pounced and entered Allison like a tidal wave; it extracted what it needed and ransacked all that was left.

Julie Evans and Amy Sterling huddled in the center of the church, away from the fighting taking place at all three entrances. Neither woman thought it was nearly far enough. What did a part-time waitress and a high school secretary know about guns and combat, anyway? They had met earlier today and confided in one another. Julie about her recent infidelity with Mr. Garish, the principal, and Amy about the possibility that Father Kieran was out of his holy-rolling mind. The way the congregation had swallowed the priest's dogma, hook, line, and sinker, was more than unsettling. Amy had arrived shortly after Allison and watched Father Kieran systematically recruit his followers one by one in a cult-like fashion. Allison had swallowed the bait like a proselyte. Amy watched the transformation take place in the high school girl and knew the priest was dangerous. And although Amy knew it was no longer safe to be outside, she believed she had made a grave mistake by coming to Our Lady of the Mountain.

"I don't know if I will be any good with a weapon, Father," Allison had told the priest, then turned to Amy and smiled. Only a few of the parishioners had gathered when the three spoke earlier.

"You may not need to take up arms today, my child," Father Kieran had told her in a calm but deliberate tone. "But before the war is over, the time will come when you must."

"You expect an ongoing battle?" Neither Allison nor Amy had anticipated a lasting confrontation.

"Fear not," he assured them. "We will be victorious this evening. But I believe you have information that will aid in our counterattack. You know where the evil resides."

"The sanatorium," Allison gasped.

"Yes. If we are to defeat the beast, we must slay it while it sleeps. For the light is the Lord's domain, and no evil can walk by day. That is when we will strike."

That's when every red light in Amy's head fired at once. "You want to fight this thing on its home turf?"

"Worry not, young Amy." His voice was cold and calculating like a used car salesman. "The Lord is with you and no harm shall pass."

Amy wanted to mention the countless souls who had put their lives in the hands of God only to die horrible deaths. The Bible was full of such stories. She wanted to offer an alternate option, one where they defended themselves until morning and then got the fuck out of Dodge. Instead, she kept her mouth shut, knowing there was no swaying the preacher; it was too late for that.

"When the sun rises tomorrow," Kieran continued, "we will descend upon the sanatorium and vanquish the beast while it sleeps."

Allison met the priest with a huge smile, and Amy had offered one as well. However, hers was only meant to appease and buy some time until she came up with a plan of her own. One that got her out of Garrett Grove and far from the congregation of kamikaze nutjobs.

Amy told Julie what she had witnessed this afternoon, and the secretary was on board, for the most part. Unfortunately, her husband, Luke, had already bought the priest's message and taken up arms at the side entrance of the church, which was going to complicate things. The women watched Allison Aigans run from station to station delivering messages for the priest and his men like a good little minion. The girl stopped at one of the stained glass windows to pray for a moment. The depiction of Jesus and Mary Magdalene was one of twelve individual scenes, six on either side of the church in every window. The Stations of the Cross were staples in all Catholic churches. The mastery of craftsmanship in all was breathtaking.

Before either woman could react, the window where Allison was standing shattered into a thousand shards of red, blue, and gold. Then they were upon her. The beasts bounded through the opening and snatched Allison up like a door prize at a tricky tray. Amy froze as the monsters carried Allison off into the night.

The Erin-creature crawled onto the girl's chest, opened its mouth, and allowed the ether to slip out like a shadow. It swirled and grew in intensity, then penetrated the terrified child. Everything that had been Allison was consumed and categorized in a heartbeat. It knew everything the priest intended to do and how to defend against him. The information was simultaneously shared with the others, the one that had been called Ben and the one called Robert. The three communicated as one and transmitted the information to the hive. They accessed the collected memories and drew upon a vision of the one called Troy, the boy, the creator of fear. Fully understanding and able to now think in the simple ones' own language, it spoke to the soldiers. *If they want a fight, then they will get one. Let them come … and let them scream in the dark.*

CHAPTER 85

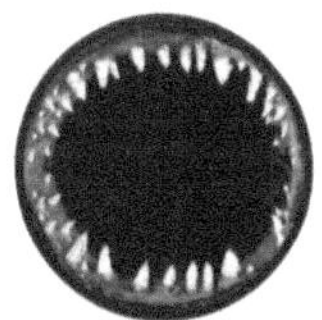

Burt slid the last cartridge into his weapon and was almost knocked to the floor when Doris TenHove rounded the corner and barreled into him. Realizing her position in the hall had been compromised by the fast-approaching horde, he craned his head from the doorway to get a better look. Although much was obscured by the thick cloud of smoke and the encroaching swarm, Burt looked up in time to see Grady Martin rush the nurses' station and raise his weapon. The fireman ambushed the area where Ted, Billy, and Ed Koloski were stationed, and fired. His bullet hit Koloski in the chest and leveled the man like a bag of Portland cement. Burt pulled the hammer back on his own gun and prepared to fire when Doris screamed from behind him. The room erupted with the sound of broken glass and the cries from the other women. He spun in time to see Doris take the first shot.

At least three of the horrible devils crashed through the window on the far side of the room. Nurse Carole and Cyndi, the candy striper, stood closest to the carnage and were taken by surprise. Doris's bullet hit one of the demons in the shoulder as it seized Carole and snapped her out of the building like a rubber band. Cyndi dodged the second beast's advances and evaded its grasp by inches. The girl rushed toward Burt with Dawn and Baxter at her side, ducking as the coroner and head nurse unloaded their weapons on the mob.

But there were more of them, forcing their bodies through the broken window and pouncing on the patients in the beds. Burt fired as Doris reloaded, but there was too much happening at once; it was impossible to register. The dog barked, and the beasts advanced, and Burt didn't know whether his bullets were even hitting their marks. He felt himself pulled backward and almost tripped over his own feet. The unseen force yanked him out of the room and into the hallway. He found himself in the stairwell leading to the roof and looked up to see Doris and the rest of the group already on the move. The door slammed behind him. Scanning the group, he counted their numbers. Burt's legs stopped working as the realization gripped him; they had already lost half of their party.

The stairwell leading to the roof was narrower than the others in the building. An initial set of risers approached the first landing, turned left, and were followed by an additional set that led to the roof's entrance. Ted followed his group and called to them as he reached the halfway point. "This is where we make our stand!" he yelled and turned his weapon in the direction they had come.

Billy Tobin was dazed beyond tears and grappling with the loss of both parents. Ted sized him up and watched the boy sway on his feet as if in a trance. He doubted if Billy would be of much use in the fight, but with only four shooters left, Ted prayed for the opposite. They needed to focus two of their weapons on the third-floor door below them and two at the door to the roof. If the creatures had been able to scale the building and ambush them through the windows, it was a sure bet they had also found their way onto the roof. Their only chance was to hold up in the stairwell and pick off the attackers as they advanced. At least they stood the chance of dropping enough bodies at the entrances and creating a barricade of the dead.

Ted had had just enough time to grab the ammo bag before Grady Martin and the rest of the horde descended upon the nurses' station. He reloaded the 30-30 and checked the 12 gauge slung over his shoulder. "Okay, Burt. You're with me." He motioned for the coroner to join him and help protect the third-floor entrance. Which left Doris and Billy to cover the door to the roof. They would make a strong team, provided the boy hadn't already lost it. The group moved into position, flanking Cyndi, Dawn, and Baxter on the landing.

Here goes nothing. Ted jumped when a slender hand appeared in front of him.

"Give me a gun," Cyndi said and looked him in the eye.

Ted removed the .38 from his hip and handed it to her. He figured she couldn't possibly do any worse than Burt and was glad she stepped up. He replaced his sidearm with a Colt Python he removed from the bag, then set the remainder of the ammo on the landing. There wasn't much of it, and it would only last so long.

The first battalion reached the lower door and threw themselves at it like a meteor crashing into the Yucatan. Cyndi jumped but kept her weapon aimed at the door. Ted noticed and knew he had done the right thing by arming the young candy striper.

A low growl escaped from deep within Baxter's throat. The Shepherd focused on the door, his hackles standing on the back of his neck and every muscle in his body poised to pounce. Dawn extended her hand and stroked the animal, which appeared to relax him a bit. But his guard was raised when something crashed into the door a second time, causing the dog to snarl. Ted looked to the members of his party and nodded; this was it, the point of no return. He turned back as the first monstrosity broke through the door and entered the stairwell.

It attempted to climb the stairs, and Ted dropped it with his first shot. It landed face first in the doorway, creating the beginning of the barricade he prayed would impede the others. A second creature, smaller and faster than the first, scurried into the stairwell over the body. Ted fired again, missing the creature's head and hitting it in the back. Burt was unlucky with his shot as well and missed the vital areas. It darted up the stairs at Ted, who was unable to track it in his sights and stood closest to the open door. Then it lunged at the deputy, lifting from the risers and hurling itself into the air. The concussion as the beast's head exploded was deafening, and Ted was bathed in foul brain matter. He looked up into the barrel of Billy Tobin's shotgun; smoke lifted from the end. The boy had leaned over the railing and fired on the aberration at the last possible moment.

Ted turned and shot, dropping another body on top of the first, adding to the barrier. He reloaded while Burt focused his weapon on the face of a man who looked as if he might have been dead for well over a month. The necrotic features twisted and warped in a repulsive spatter of black, then the beast fell as well. Ted slammed the last round into the chamber and raised his weapon just as the door to the roof buckled in its frame.

Baxter stared at the door, lowered his front haunches, and bared his teeth in a snarl. The battering filled the narrow hallway with the dull echo of flesh connecting with steel. The force of the blows made quick work of their minimal defenses. The door flew inward, the hinges ripped from the jamb. The disfigured being that entered the doorway was an abomination to life itself. They all stared up at the horrible deformity that had once worked for the coroner's office. Burt gasped and stepped backward. Although the man's face and body had been altered, he was recognizable. Tony wore the same clothes he had on the last time Burt had seen him. His medical whites were now soiled a putrid black from the dark substance that oozed from his eyes and mouth. The man had been ranting about vampires before he fled from the lab Monday night, which wasn't far from the truth. What had happened to him was right out of a horror movie.

Burt was unable to move or draw his weapon as he stared at the man he had known. Doris was quicker to react and fired at the lab tech, her bullet striking Tony in the shoulder. Then like an uncoiled spring, Baxter pounced and launched himself at the beast. The Shepherd broke from the child's grip and seized the monster by the neck, knocking it backward to the floor. The creature and dog twisted and tumbled out the door, into the night. Dawn reacted and bolted past Billy and Doris up the stairs and after her dog.

"Dawn, no!" Doris screamed. She chased after the child with Billy Tobin hot on her heels. Together, they ascended the stairs, exited onto the roof, and were swallowed by the night.

Carl stood in the darkness of his father's old office with the radio in his blood-stained hands. The room tipped and swayed as he attempted to digest the news he had just received. It had never left Rainey's head, or it had found its way back inside. Either way, the result was the same. The deputy had gone ballistic and mowed down nearly every living soul in the high school basement. There were survivors, but their numbers were few. Andrea Geary had made it, along with two teachers from the elementary school, an administrator from the high school, and several others. Bob and Michelle Marks were in the process of isolating the injured and the lucky into one of the smaller rooms in the basement. The woman was the only known survivor with medical training and Janis's only hope. There wasn't much time, and Carl doubted if any of the doctors at the center were even left. He could load his party into the mayor's car and make a break for it. At least he had to try.

He steadied himself, stepped behind his father's desk, and looked out the window into the parking lot. Carl jumped back. An army of demons gathered behind the building. Their masses huddled together almost on top of one another. He attempted to count their numbers but was unable. The creatures looked ready to launch their attack, as if they were waiting for the order to strike. Carl's heart skipped as it tried to keep up with his racing mind. There was no chance they could make it to the high school, let alone ten steps out the back door. They were trapped. Then one of the figures advanced toward the building and revealed itself. Carl recognized the uniform despite the shape it was in. Deputy Gary Forsyth, or what was left of him, stepped up to lead the attack, his body ravaged and disfigured. He looked like a demonic pincushion or some type of hybrid porcupine. Spikes grew from his face and chest, piercing his skin and shredding his clothes.

Carl ran from the window and out of the office. There was only one place in the building where they might stand a chance. He charged into the room where Lois and the two children were and shouted, "We need to move … now!"

Lois looked up, confused at first but immediately registered the urgency in his direction. She gathered Troy and Wendy at her side and rushed them out the door. Carl darted to the cot and threw his keys to the mayor. He laced his arms underneath Janis and lifted her as gently as he could. "I need someone to grab the mattress and first aid kit and follow me."

He led the group down the stairs with the child in his arms. Lois and Troy managed to grab the cot and followed with Wendy carting the medical supplies behind. Carl hurried them past two jail cells no bigger than three by nine and continued to the far end of the hallway. He stopped at a large steel door with a massive lock located in the dead center.

"It's the big square one!" he shouted to Jessica as she fumbled with the keys. She found the right one and inserted it into the hole. The clunking sound of heavy steel echoed down the hallway as Jessica opened the door. She pulled the handle, revealing the station's armory. Bare racks stood where weapons and ammunitions had been stored. The small room was empty except for a wooden bench and a few boxes of shells.

The mayor closed and locked the door behind them as the sound of breaking glass and splintering wood lifted from the station's back entrance. The beasts had found their way inside and begun their attack. A second later, the armory door shook as something threw itself at it. The noise was deafening. Carl's party backed away as if the extra foot might save them. Again, the sound of a battering ram slammed against the steel door, but this time it didn't move. The door held fast, at least for the moment. Carl prayed it would continue to do so. He looked down at Janis's limp body in his arms, wishing there was something he could do, but there was nothing. They weren't going anywhere.

With their defenses split, there was no way the remaining members could defend the stairwell. Ted fired into the growing mass of bodies, turned, and forced the others upward. Burt and Cyndi followed his lead and exited onto the roof. They stumbled out into the rain to find Baxter and the creature engaged in a deathmatch. The dog had the beast by the throat and tore into the man who had gone by the name of Tony, pulling him off his feet and dominating. The creature struggled to latch on to the dog but was no match for the brutality of the great Shepherd. Billy and Doris stood guard in front of Dawn with their weapons raised in either direction. They scanned the top of the building, searching for any sign of movement, but it was impossible to tell in the darkness. Baxter shook the beast with a violent tug, and the man's neck snapped loud enough to be heard over the rain. The dog released its hold and backed away as Billy rushed in and fired a shotgun round into Tony's brain.

Shadows darted at the edges of their vision. Then, one by one, they appeared; creatures of varying size and deformity moved in on them from every direction. They emerged from the stairwell and invaded on all sides. Ted huddled his party into a tight circle with their backs to one another. They raised their weapons at the approaching horde but knew it was senseless. Even Baxter shrank away from the ever-tightening circle of beasts. He drew in close to Dawn's side as she wrapped her arms around his leg.

All that was left of their party, Ted, Billy, Doris, Burt, and Cyndi, backed against one another with Dawn and Baxter wedged between them. They aimed their weapons outward at a throng of uncountable bodies. Over a hundred, by Ted's estimation. Not enough bullets to put down half. The creatures took another step forward, then stopped, as if taunting their prey.

Ted wondered if the others were thinking the same as he. *Is it really a sin? Surely under the circumstances...* He checked the cylinder of the Colt; four bullets left. More than enough to do the trick when pressed against the temple. He looked down at Dawn, her golden locks plastered to the side of her head from the rain, and knew he could never pull the trigger.

A fiery bolt shattered from the sky, striking somewhere in the parking lot. The blinding blue that flashed before them made it impossible to see, and it was almost a minute before their eyes were able to focus. Ted sprang to action, ready to fire on the creatures, who would no doubt capitalize on the opportunity. He pointed his pistol into the black, but there was nothing. He spun around, surveying the rooftop and the entrance to the stairwell, but all was empty. They were gone. The creatures had retreated into the storm and spared them.

He didn't hesitate and didn't need to figure it out. "Follow me!' he shouted and led his party back into the building and out of the rain.

Bob and Brandon checked the integrity of the gym doors, then locked and bolted the entrance to the shelter behind them. They entered the basement and stared across the ocean of wool blankets that had been laid over the corpses, each one conforming to the figure that lay beneath it. So many dead, and it had happened so fast. The men walked down the hallway and into the small room where the survivors were gathered. The eyes that stared back at them were so far gone, they were no longer able to cry. The shattered gazes of the shell shocked and despondent looked to the men for answers, but there were none to be found.

Kelly Rainey stared at the floor while Jill Boriello cradled the girl in her arms. Andrea Geary cleaned her service revolver for probably the tenth time in the past hour. Tyler Harrison and Rich Novack had come to the realization that life was too short to hide in a closet and sat together holding hands and comforting one another in hushed, deliberate tones. Günter Bentley, perhaps the luckiest man in town, kept his family close and continued to kiss his wife and daughters on their foreheads as if they might disappear any moment. Anthony Leone kept his wits intact for the most part and assisted Michelle Marks, who appeared unfazed and in her element. Bob noticed the resilience of the woman and could have sworn she had been smiling when he entered the room. The chief took a seat near the door and motioned for Brandon to do the same. The only thing left for any of them to do was wait until morning—that and pray.

The ramming against the armory door persisted, but the reinforced steel remained intact. As the night drew on and the hours passed, the creatures' attempts to gain access diminished some but never ceased. Carl stayed alert, with his weapon drawn and his back against the wall. He looked at Lois and the children, who had all passed out from exhaustion, then he turned to the mayor, who stood watch at Janis's bedside.

She whispered so not to be heard by the others. "I think we're losing her. She's lost so much blood."

Carl nodded; he had been thinking the same thing. "I can't risk moving her till morning. If just one of those things—" His voice cracked, and it took him a moment to recover. "I wish I could."

His hands were tied, and his options were nil. If they left now, they would be overcome in seconds. Their only chance was to wait it out and try to leave in the morning. He prayed Janis would make it until then.

"No, you're right." Jessica nodded and studied the deep circles etched beneath his eyes. "How long has it been since you slept?"

"I'm not sure," he said and pinched the bridge of his nose.

"Give me that," she told him and motioned to his pistol. "I'll watch the door, and you get some sleep."

"No, I'm fine," he said, struggling not to yawn. But he was so tired, and the door had held so far. Finally, he handed over the weapon and leaned back against the wall. "Thank you. Maybe just a few minutes."

Carl fought the urge for several seconds, then closed his eyes and fell asleep. Jessica guarded the door and listened to the sounds of the creatures as they tore through the basement of the sheriff's department. But the lock held, and for the moment, they were safe. Janis's eyelids fluttered at times throughout the night, and at one point, she cried out, but her words were mumbled and impossible to understand. Although Jessica could have sworn she heard one word clearly; she was sure the girl had said Chewbacca.

CHAPTER 86

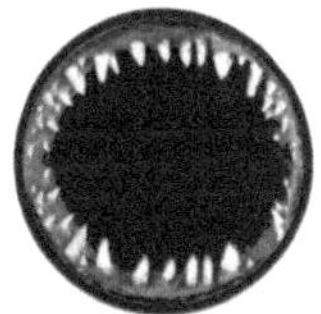

Night came early to the canyon and the area once known as Lonesome Mountain. It crept in under the guise of the storm and took root like a malignancy. The generator had long since run out of fuel, and the only light to penetrate the dense murk of the cave came from the flashlights and several battery-powered lanterns. Don and Stephanie retreated to the furthest reaches of the second chamber, far from the cavern opening, and occupied themselves by studying the remainder of the murals—which was difficult with the limited illumination.

The paintings appeared to follow a linear storyline. They stood before the fifth one in sequence on the far side of the chamber. Don stepped closer and raised his light, revealing a depiction of the same children who had been in the previous painting. They were the focal point of this one, with each child laid out on what looked like three individual altars. And although Don wasn't positive where the scene had taken place, he had a good idea. The children were depicted very human, without the dark eyes or animal-like teeth. They were featured against the dark background of the lodestone; no additional colors had been added to the scenery to illustrate stars or a moon as the Lenape did in the other murals. However, at the very center of the piece, a darker color had been added. A black circular hole spread out between the children. Their altars, which Don thought looked sacrificial, were placed at equal distances around what could only be a pit or a chasm.

The children each wore an elaborate medallion around their necks. He turned the light toward Stephanie, who studied the wall with unblinking intensity, then returned his stare as well. The initial murals in the front of the cave appeared to be autonomous and almost a statement of facts. But the ones in the larger chamber were clearly a succession of a storyboard, a chronological telling of events the Lenape felt compelled to record. This one, the eleventh they had seen, adorned the right wall as the cave dipped and funneled toward the small opening in the back. With ten feet between them and the mouth of the shaft, there was enough room for one final mural. *Lucky number twelve*, Don thought as he slipped past Stephanie and moved to examine it.

He turned his light to the wall, and Stephanie joined him, both anticipating what the final mural in the series might be. Don looked closer and furrowed his brow. He scanned the small alcove with his flashlight, aiming the beam to the right and then left. The wall was stark and barren except for one swatch of color in the lower left corner. A short whiteish smear had been drug across the base of the wall and then terminated, as if the artist had been silenced while making his first brushstroke. And that was all there was of the final mural.

"That's a bit anti-climactic," he said, continuing to search the rock in a futile attempt to find a message that wasn't there.

Stephanie approached the wall, extended her hand, and touched the small swatch of paint. A wash of emotion filled her face, confusion being the dominant, but there was something else. Maybe frustration or realization, and Don was unable to tell which it might be. He himself was ticked-off to have come all this way and found a single line of paint. It would have been more gratifying had they found nothing at all. But Stephanie was still intrigued and remained silent as she studied the brushstroke as if it might still be wet.

"Well, I guess we know what happened to the artist. Got killed before they could finish."

"I guess," Stephanie replied, her thoughts elsewhere. She had turned toward the small opening that led away from the second chamber. The darkness that lay beyond called out to both of them. "You know ... Now we have to go back there."

Don shook his head. "I knew you were going to say that. And you know my answer."

"We'll never get another chance," she pleaded. "We might not survive the night. So just tell me what to do, and we'll be as careful as we can."

Don was curious himself, more than a little. But it was dangerous as hell, even if they took every precaution. He couldn't actually stop her from going back there if she was dead set. And from the look in her eye, he could tell she was. He looked toward the entrance of the cave, where the scorpion-like creatures paced about, then turned back to the small opening. To step outside was suicide; to venture into the darkness and explore what was back there would probably result in the same. Still ... he had to admit he was curious. And the only way to make sure she didn't go in there and get herself killed was if he went first. Even then, there was a good chance they would never come out. He was about to speak, then noticed the smile crease her lips and the spark that had ignited in her stare.

"Why are you smiling? I didn't say anything."

"Because you're going to. I promise I'll follow your lead, and we'll be careful every step of the way."

"I'm going to regret this."

"Thank you!" Stephanie jumped once and then grabbed his face with both hands and kissed him. It lasted only for a flash, but the exchange was electric as her lips parted and she bit him gently.

Don pulled back slowly and looked at the floor. He remembered the fight he and Lois had had in the garage the other day and wondered where she and Troy might be. It didn't feel as if they were gone, but he wasn't sure he would know if they were. He had been distant and self-absorbed for a long time. Don didn't know if there was still a chance for him to do right by either of them, but he knew he had to make it out of this cave alive. He and Stephanie had to survive the night and make it to their families.

She released her grip on his face and nodded. "Sorry," she said. "Friends?"

"Friends," he agreed. "But I'm still going to regret this."

After donning the necessary safety equipment and checking it for the third or fourth time, Don secured the anchor line to a fixed point in the second chamber and tethered Stephanie's harness to his own. He approached the small opening and directed his light downward. The blanketing darkness stretched out before him without depth or restraint. It felt endless, cold, and damp against his skin, yet electric as well. Don pointed his primary light down, relieved to find the rock floor. He had been most worried about an abrupt drop-off just on the other side of the opening. He exhaled, relieved somewhat but nowhere near relaxed. He cast the beam as far as it would extend and followed the floor ... flat ... solid ... and presumably safe. To the left and the right, the beam penetrated only so far before it was swallowed by the suffocating density of terminal darkness. Then he turned the beam upward. The ceiling above them formed a cylinder that extended like a chimney for what could have been miles. The great tube that towered above them looked like a funnel—a giant funnel of magnetite.

"That explains why compasses never work on Garrett Mountain," he said.

"It's amazing." She leaned in to see for herself. "The Lenape were drawn here. They believed the mountain held magical healing powers. Maybe they were right."

Don stepped from the threshold into the chamber with Stephanie following in his exact footsteps as instructed. The noticeable drop in temperature was immediate, causing their breath to condensate in plumes. Somewhere, water dripped in the distance; the resonating echoes bounced about the chamber, making it impossible to pinpoint the exact location of the source. Don wasn't sure but believed not far from where they stood was a sizable body of water. He pressed on, taking one calculated step at a time, with Stephanie in his wake.

Twelve murals. Actually, eleven murals and one brushstroke, but Don was sure there were meant to be twelve. It bugged him that the final reveal was a bust, but not as much as the certainty that he had seen it all somewhere before. It had been on the tip of his brain since they first began examining the storyboard of designs. Six on one side of the chamber and six on the other. The history of the Lenape tribe, just waiting for someone to come along and find it. From the battle against the dark-eyed beasts to the depiction of the children laid upon their stone slabs. All of it sealed tight within the mountain, behind tons and tons of rock. The thought bounced around his head for a moment. *A ton of rock. A ton of rock!*

"*That's* it!" He stopped short, raising his voice, causing Stephanie to jump.

"Jesus Christ, you scared the hell out of me. What's it?"

"A ton of rock. I don't know why I didn't think of it before; it's so damn obvious."

"Slow down, cowboy. I'm not following you."

"The murals." He bounced on his feet as he explained, excited to have finally made the connection. "They're the Stations of the Cross, just like on the windows of the Catholic church. I've been trying to figure out what the paintings reminded me of, and that's it." Don grinned as he raced to explain it all to her. "You see, Our Lady of the Mountain has twelve stained glass windows that show in succession the Passion of Jesus Christ. The story of his crucifixion and resurrection. The painting of the children helped me finally put it together. They were laid out on slabs, and their story was sealed tight in this cavern, behind a ton of rock. Just like the story of Jesus. He was placed in the tomb, and on the third day—well, you know the story."

"Yeah." She grinned back. "Of course I know. It's the basis of Christianity, the story of their salvation from sin—and, of course … death."

"Maybe this is the Lenape's same story. I mean, it's unlikely this tribe had been exposed to Christianity, but if what you say about collective unconscious holds water, it's a possibility."

"It's more than possible." Now she was beaming. "I'd say it's very likely, and now I've really got to see what's back here."

Don nodded his head in agreement, turned around, and redirected his light. He walked further into the darkness, taking one careful step at a time. His heart thrummed from the connection he had made, and the warm sense of satisfaction shielded him from the chill of the cavern. The flashlight bounced across the floor, then revealed a dark object at the end of its beam.

"What's that?" Don asked and led them closer to the shadow.

The sound of water dripping into a larger pool was louder and now closer to where they tread. He squinted to focus better and proceeded forward toward the strange dark mass. Shadows spread out to the left and right as the light danced upon the formation. Don walked up to it and shined his light down onto the structure.

"My God," he gasped.

Stephanie approached from the side and added the beam of her own light. They looked down at the ancient altar before them. It sat about four feet off the floor, supported by a pedestal at the head and the foot, all constructed from lodestone. On the dusty surface of the slab lay the skeleton of a child. The remains were no more than three feet in length, intact, and covered with jewelry. Ornate bracelets and rings adorned the child's fingers and wrists. All pieces had been fabricated from magnetite and interlaced with gold chains and links. The precious alloy reflected at them in the flashlight's beam and danced across their faces. Neither spoke as they examined the four-hundred-year-old skeleton.

The large amulet that had been placed around the child's neck now rested on the bones of the ribcage. The intricate design etched out of the lodestone was breathtaking. A sunburst originating from a concentric sphere spread out into individual rays that tapered off in waves. Gold had been incorporated into the piece as well. It looked as if it had fused with the rock at places in the center of the disc and alternating sections of the rays. In addition, the entire chain of the medallion was fabricated entirely out of gold. Stephanie reached out to touch the item, which was twice the size of her hand. She rubbed her fingers across its surface and then slid them underneath the medallion and lifted it to check the weight. She replaced it, then directed her light at the skull and leaned in. The lower jaw hung open, allowing Stephanie a clear look inside the child's mouth.

"What do you make of it?" Don asked.

"All human. No sign of anything different. This was just a normal child. No alterations to the skeletal or dental remains that I can see."

"Seriously?" Don examined the skull as well. He wasn't sure, but he felt as if his eyes had adjusted to the absolute darkness of the antechamber in the short time they'd been there. Lighter shadows danced against the dark, giving the room the appearance of artificial illumination, as if a light had been turned on and then increased in small increments. He dismissed the idea, knowing he was fooling himself; it just wasn't possible. He scanned the remainder of the cavern, checking three sixty, expecting his eyes to revert to night blind.

"Son of a bitch!" Don hissed, realizing he could see much more of the cave than he could before. He turned his light to the cavern floor in front of them; it extended for approximately ten feet and then disappeared as if it were swallowed up. Sweat beaded on his forehead despite the icy chill that gripped his heart like a glacier. Don had sensed it when he entered the cave but didn't realize how close they had come. The drop-off lay less than ten steps in front of them.

"Jesus Christ." He removed a tether of line and snaked it around the pedestal of the altar, then tied it off and fastened the other end to their safety line.

"What's going on?" she asked.

"Whatever you do, don't move. There's a drop in front of us, and I've got a feeling it's one deep son of a bitch." Don inched forward with his light aimed in front of him. He made his way to the edge of the drop, stopped two feet from the precipice, and cast the beam of light across the pit to the other side. A large circular well occupied the center of the cavern, and Don was able to make out much of the detail. It was about thirty feet across, symmetrical for the most part, and, just as he imagined, deep as hell.

A thick plume of condensation escaped his lips as he stared across the abyss in amazement. Now he was positive it was getting lighter in the cavern. He focused on the walls and shadows he hadn't been able to see before. In the distance, on the far side of the chasm, stood another mass of rock that looked exactly like an altar. He shifted his light to the right and came upon a third that was also identical. Don scanned the full circumference of the pit in search of another, but there were none. *Three altars for the three children.*

Finally, Don aimed the flashlight into the massive well. The beam was reflected at him in glints and shimmers and took him by surprise. Tiny particles of mica or possibly pyrite caught the illumination of the artificial light and flickered in the dimness like the tip of a sparkler. Don gasped and squinted, allowing his beam to dip further into the pit. He leaned over as much as he dared, curious how far down he would be able to see, and gasped.

The vison before him defied possibility. Don looked down into the well further than a five-hundred-watt bulb was even able to reveal; he stared into the pit, over a hundred feet down, by his estimation, all the way to the bottom. He saw the pool below, reflected in it the glow of his own flashlight, dancing like a million mirrors on a disco ball. The water itself was a milky white and appeared to almost absorb the light before bouncing it back, as if it were dense with a skin-like surface layer.

Then it changed. It looked like it had started to move. Ripples formed in the water below as if something were swimming within. Left to right for a moment, darting back and forth. And then—it began to swirl. Suddenly the pool stopped reflecting the light, the prismatic appearance of mirrors vanished, and the water itself began to glow like a bulb had been turned on deep below the surface. The milky-white color took on an opalesque quality and moved as if it were alive. He tried to call to Stephanie, but all that left his lips was a dry croak. He knew he should step away from the edge and retreat, but as the light grew brighter and the strange sensation of growing heat washed over him, Don was unable to move; he could only watch.

It wasn't anything like artificial light, stark and assaulting. This was warm and glowing and natural, like the sun. It continued to increase in intensity and soon filled the entire cavern, dispelling every shadow, revealing every surface of every corner in the entire cave. The walls of the pit were perfectly smooth, as if they had been eroded by rivers of time. The terrain along the perimeter was about twenty feet wide and formed a walkway that led from one altar to the next.

Now Don could see the skeletal remains on the other slabs, even from his distance forty feet away.

"What the hell is happening?" Stephanie called out from behind him. Her voice wavered and sounded on the verge of shrill.

"I—I have no idea."

"It's warm," she shouted. "And look on the other side."

Don didn't reply; his attention was drawn to the massive funnel of rock that towered above him. The scope of its dimensions was visible due to the addition of the new light source, and he had to force himself to breathe. Lost in the depth of it, Don felt smaller than he ever had, like a speck on the pistil of a flower, possibly a dust mite on the surface of the moon. It was unlike any natural formation he had ever seen or any that had been recorded. The geometric perfection that twisted above could in no way be mistaken for accidental. At the mid-point of the cavern's ceiling, an opening centered directly over the pit. It spiraled upward in an almost snail-shell pattern, but not exactly. Don thought it resembled more of a helix and was reminded of a three-dimensional image he had seen of the Milky Way. He tried to imagine the slow movement of a glacier or the steady flow of eons of water creating what lay before him but was unable to. It was too perfect, too precise, too calculated. Don thought Fibonacci would have really lost his mind had he found this.

"It's amazing," Stephanie said.

"It's more than that," he answered. "It's the geological find of the century." He turned back to her with his eyes wide and mouth agape, then smiled. He felt like a four-year-old boy on Christmas morning.

"You see that? You didn't have to go to California to make a name for yourself. It was right here, waiting for you all along."

He stared at her, noticing the sweat beading on her forehead. The cave was much warmer than when they walked in, and the light, although not overpowering in intensity and glare, revealed everything in a clarity and detail he thought he had never known. Even from where he stood, he saw the tiniest flecks of grey against the pale blue of Stephanie's eyes. He was sure he hadn't noticed them before. The pores of her skin, symmetrical and perfect, and even the faintest touch of grey in the few strands that had started to sneak into her blonde hair. He saw it all in the bath of clarity that washed up from the chasm.

Feeling more confident about their safety now that the cave was illuminated, Don motioned for Stephanie to join him near the edge. She left the side of the altar, approached him, and looked over into the pit at the strange light within.

"What do you make of it?"

"No idea." He hesitated for a moment. "Bioluminescence, possibly, but like none that we know of. Its—" The words to describe it fell short and were hard to form. "I could study this the rest of my life."

They exchanged a look but didn't speak on it, although both had been thinking the same thing. Life was a funny word to use under the circumstances. It was an uncertainty, to say the least, and not to be used lightly.

Finally, Stephanie nodded to him. "That makes two of us." Then she looked out across the pit to the other side. "I'd really like to get a look at the other altars. Do you think it would be safe for us to try?"

Don thought it was, and together, they made their way from altar to altar, examining and comparing the remains. All the skeletons had been children, and all wore identical medallions around their necks. They discovered no sign of alteration in the skeletal remains. The structure of the skulls, the jawbones, and even the teeth were all perfectly human. Which was unsettling and left questions rather than answers. Then, as if on cue, the strange illumination began to fade. It was a slow disappearance, which allowed enough time for them to navigate their way back to the small opening to the main chamber.

Outside, the rain continued to fall, the monstrous beings darted about the hardpan floor, and at some point, the electricity to the trailers and the lights in the parking lot had been cut. A mixture of excitement and awkwardness was felt by both Don and Stephanie but was spoken of only in brief intervals. They settled in with their backs against the wall of the cave in an attempt to escape the stress and confusion. Sometime during the night, despite the din of insanity that raced through both their heads, they managed to fall asleep. And although it defiantly fought to hold on, Wednesday night released its grip on Garrett Grove and acquiesced to Thursday morning. For better or worse.

Many of its numbers had been sacrificed. But the assault at the medical center and church had been necessary. The bodies of the simple ones were weak—its essence burned through them like an inferno. The need to replace their ravaged husks had always been the problem. But for every soldier it lost, two had been added, and the threat to its army had been neutralized. It learned of the priest's intentions with the acquisition of the one called Allison. The information she held was the key element, so it discontinued the attack and called its army back. Kieran was a clever one, and could have become a problem, but now it knew. The three, the carriers, were relocated while the others waited. It planted a vital seed of itself intended for the priest and his army, and then it, too, waited. It was good at waiting—it had waited for a long, long time.

To be concluded ...

The Ojanox Book IV: Lonesome Mountain

Coming 10/1/2024

Thank you for reading!
Please consider leaving a rating/review on Goodreads and Amazon.

Continue reading The Ojanox Book IV: Lonesome Mountain

Download an excerpt from the conclusion of the Ojanox Series
Book IV: Lonesome Mountain

THE OJANOX SERIES: BOOKS 1 - 4

The Ojanox Series is now available at Amazon and Barnes & Noble.

ACKNOWLEDGEMENTS

If you ever find yourself in the town of Pompton Plains, New Jersey, and drive to the very top of Mountain Avenue, you will reach Mountainside Park, but you won't find an old road extension or an abandoned sanatorium. However, the inspiration for the old hospital comes from a place called the Overbrook, which wasn't all that far away. Neither is the real Garrett Mountain, for that matter. I took great liberties when writing this book, even changing the location to upstate New York, but many of the features are similar to the town I grew up in: Chilton medical center, the graveyard behind the Lutheran Church, even the hardware store at the corner of Jackson Ave. I just changed things a little to fit the story.

It's been four years since I first started writing this book, and there are many who helped bring this monster to life. Whether their assistance was inspirational, fact-checking, information gathering, or emotional support, I couldn't have done this without them. There are topics I touched on in *The Ojanox* that required the input of professionals and tons of research. When it comes to toxicology, lab work, virology, and bacteriology, I did my best to stick to the facts. When I got it wrong—when faced with serving the story or the hard medical facts, I chose the story. So that's on me.

First, I would like to thank Wendy Nastasi and my sister, Dawn Chiossi (Danielle), for a lifetime of inspiration, support, and for listening to me talk about nothing other than this damn book for the past three years. I would also like to thank them for lending their namesakes to this story, with written consent, of course.

There are several friends who read early versions of this book whose help was instrumental. Nick Gomes and Ed Koloski helped provide feedback and were my sounding board from the very start, back in the halfway house days. Greg Gillick and Mike Turrigiano have always had my back and were there to listen to my very first attempts at horror writing. And of course, Jack Wells. Jack has been my constant go-to guy with this project for years. He read it before the first rewrite, and he still came back for more. Now that's a true friend. In truth, *The Ojanox* wouldn't be half the book it is today without Jack's knowledge, skill, and literary prowess.

My editor, Lisa Lee Tone, took every page of this manuscript and made it better with her diligent attention to detail. I'm fortunate to have Lisa in my corner to call me out when I stray from the path, and I'm thankful she was always there to rope me back in.

I'd like to thank Ben Eads for his original developmental edits on *Scream in the Dark* and for the rigorous Jedi training and instruction. (Insert Yoda voice) Because of you, a better writer, I am.

Christy Aldridge has been so much more than a cover artist, or an illustrator, or even a contributor—she has been a partner, in every sense of the word. Without Christy's hard work and dedication, this project wouldn't be half of what it is today. For the past year or more, we have been joined at the hip. She took my vision and brought it to life. Thank you, Christy, I couldn't have done this without you. Now we need to start a new project.

Thank you, Don Noble and Jeff DeSantis for contributing your amazing illustrations and talents to this project.

Many thanks to my Alpha team and proofreaders for their time, input, and suggestions: Donna Latham, Heather Ann Larson, Jae Mazer, Kerrie Roylance, Bryan Moyer, Kristen Lynch, Susan Isenberg, John O'regan, Christina Marie, and Maryanne Pacheco Chappell.

And a huge thank you to Kira (Eagle Eyes) Seamon, for tirelessly hunting through these manuscripts, making sure that all the finishing touches were properly in place. It's the little things that make the difference, and had it been up to me, far too many little things would have slipped through the cracks. Thank you, Kira for squashing all those pesky little things into oblivion.

For all my friends who follow me on social media, for all the reviewers, bloggers, influencers who support the indie horror community, thank you. Also, thank you Tiffany Koplin, RJ Roles, and all the admins at the Books of Horror Facebook group for everything you do.

My life would have been very different if it hadn't been for my fourth-grade teacher, Mrs. Genevieve Smith, whose tutelage, undying devotion, and wealth of limitless stories molded not only myself but an entire generation. I especially would like to thank you for bringing my homework to the hospital when I broke my leg.

Thank you, Kelly Rainey, and all the fourth-grade classes of Pompton Plains school.

Anthony Lorraine helped by sharing with me his experiences in Vietnam. Without Anthony, the character of Carl Primrose would have been much different, as well as my knowledge of that moment in history. Sadly,

I learned of Anthony's passing when I was still in the halfway house. He was a good friend during a dark moment in my life. I miss you, Tony.

Thank you to my family and friends who helped contribute to the inspiration of this story through a lifetime of experiences, which I in turn felt compelled to fictionalize. And finally, for my mom, who told me my first ghost story, took me trick-or-treating, and allowed me to have a Halloween party at the house when I was ten years old. And for my dad, who let me build a haunted house and still reminds me periodically that I painted his garage walls black.

And thank you to the readers and horror fans who love this genre as much as I do. Thank you for taking this journey with me and thank you for allowing me to share this story with you. I hope you enjoyed it half as much as I enjoyed writing it.

Daemon Manx

ABOUT THE AUTHOR

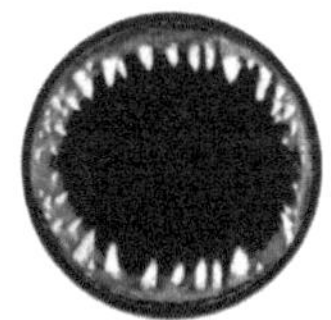

Daemon Manx is an American author with a backstory. He is a recovering addict who spent nearly a decade in the prison system where he focused on recovery and learned to perfect his horror writing craft. He has been featured in magazines in both the U.S., the U.K, and Germany. In 2021 he received a HAG award for his story *The Dead Girl* and was nominated for a Splatterpunk award that same year.

He was a bonus round winner on the gameshow *Wheel of Fortune* in 1999 and is infamously known for a motor vehicle accident he was responsible for, involving President Ronald Reagan's limousine.

After struggling with addiction and incarceration, Daemon now has over eleven years clean and sober. He uses his story to illustrate the positive outcome of sobriety and offer a glimpse at what life can be like when one receives a second chance.

He lives with his sister, author Danielle Manx and their narcoleptic cat, Sydney, where they patiently prepare for the apocalypse. There is a good chance they will run out of coffee far too soon.